The

Gardener

IVAN ARTHUR

ISBN: 978-1-089-50446-7

DEDICATION

Thanks to Sheila for her help, Aimee and Ivan love to you always and those who have helped me have insight.

CONTENTS

Chapter One: The Publisher

Mark Finch sat at his oak desk in his well-furnished and ample sized office at the publishers Finch and Faber, near to Russell Square and the London University School of Oriental Studies. In front of him was a manuscript, it was the first draft of a crime novel written by an unknown author, Jonathan Hope. He had asked the author to send him further chapters of the novel after reading the attachment to an e-mail Jonathan Hope had sent to him seeking publication of his work of fiction. He got up from his chair, poured himself a malt whisky, crossed over to the office sofa and sat down, then after making himself comfortable, he began to read the story for the second time.

The Gardener: by Jonathan Hope

ONE

When P.C. Rose came to his senses, his eyes and mouth were covered by tape and his wrists and ankles were bound to the arms and legs of the chair he sat on. The back of his tunic stuck to his body due to perspiration and beads of sweat lodged on his eyebrows. His head felt as if it had an axe lodged in it and he felt sick, in order to breathe he sucked air into his lungs through his nose. He could smell his own fear. He strained his hearing to try and orientate himself in this world of darkness. He listened for sounds or tried to sense smells that would give him some idea of his location. Then he heard the squeak of rubber moving towards him, the rustle of clothing and an intake of breath;

"My father told me that to be a policeman you needed to have a pointed head, so that the helmet wouldn't fall off. I know that is no longer true but whatever you are thinking in that sharp head of yours, I want you to know that you cannot escape the natural justice that awaits you. I saw your picture in the paper and on the news, you said, and I quote, 'Ecological warriors are just anarchists out for a good time and if they are stupid enough to bury themselves in the ground, well then, let's bury them alive. If they want to cling to the trees then maybe we should help them to swing from them.'"

Rose tried to speak, he shook his head from side to side, and then he heard the sound of metal scraping against metal. He flinched when the voice spoke again as it was close to him, to his right. He could smell rubber and wood preservative.

"I on the other hand love all of God's creations, except, and this is unfortunate for you, human beings. We have fallen from grace; we are the play things of the gods, thrown out of the Garden of Eden by our carnal knowledge. Nature is cruel; if deformed animals are born, they are allowed to die; when trees are diseased the rotten wood must be cut out, root and branch, to save the forest. You my friend are a rotten bit of wood."

The unknown man grabbed the right hand of P.C. Rose in a vice like grip. He struggled to keep the fingers of his hand grasping the arm of his chair, but his little finger was pried free. Suddenly razor sharp blades sliced through the flesh of his finger from top to bottom. He screamed in pain as the bone in his finger crunched. He felt a rush of blood, a whooshing in his ears and then blackness as he fell into the arms of darkness.

TWO

Detective Inspector Bob Kane opened his eyes slowly. The sun streamed through a gap in the window blinds and onto the bed where he lay. He realised that he was not alone. His mouth was dry and his head heavy. He tried to remember what had happened last night after they discovered the body of the P.C.? It didn't matter how many bodies he saw, if it was one of their own, it was different. What he saw was a fellow officer, who had lost toes and fingers and then had his throat slit, only to be discarded on a waste tip like so much garden rubbish. Last night he needed a drink, and as it seems, he needed company. One drink was obviously not enough, and whatever transpired led him to this bed and this lover.

Sophie pretended to be asleep when she felt Bob Kane move in the bed. She tried to put together the pieces of what had happened last night. She remembered that she had been shocked and frightened by what she saw, she threw up, and Inspector Kane was very kind. She went with the other officers to the Rose and Crown for a drink to forget and ease her anxiety that it could happen to her. She knew she was desperate for someone to hold her. She drank too much and he offered her a lift home. Oh God! She kissed him on the doorstep, she asked him in, and she seduced him.

Bob Kane wanted to feel, it was as simple as that. Over the years his job had made him feel frozen inside and disconnected from normal human beings. He was sick and weary of the cruelty that humans do to each other and in that moment by the dumpster he did not wish to be alone with the demons that haunted him. She made him feel. He raised the duvet slightly to look at the warm, soft naked curves of the woman who appeared asleep beside him, still breathing gently. She was younger than him, slightly plump, and very comfortable to rest on as he began to recall the tenderness they had shared in the night. She fell asleep with her head resting on his chest and his arms holding her. They had been able to lose themselves in the heat of their desire, skin-to-skin. Merged in each other's body, for a brief moment, they did not feel alone in this empty universe.

Kane, did not want to wake her, instead he placed a light kiss on her shoulder. Leaving her to enjoy the sleep of the innocent for a while longer, he eased himself out from under the duvet and slowly stood up. The paper trail of his socks, underpants, trousers and shirt, led him from her bedroom to the lounge. His jacket and shoes were next to her uniform, crumpled in a pile on the floor next to the sofa, her black stockings draped over them. Things for her were bad enough thought Kane. This was her first month in uniform, to see what she saw, and then end up in bed with a senior officer, was not the best start. Her mother should never find out about him. She did look lovely getting out of her uniform the night before, in a drunken striptease. He found some notepaper by the telephone and wrote, 'THANKYOU', in large letters on it, then placed it on top of her stockings. He held out no hopes of doing this again. He slowly and quietly opened the front door, stepped out into the morning sunshine and closed the front door firmly behind him.

THREE

The lads playing football in the street, making a lot of noise and swearing, didn't see the figure in the hooded coat watching them from a distance. They danced in and out of the parked cars in the failing light, hitting a car here, bending a car aerial there and cutting envy lines with coins in the shiny surfaces of the cars as they passed. Each time they came to a newly planted sapling rooted in the pavement one of them would take the slender branch in their hands and snap it. A lady unloading her plastic bags of shopping from the boot of her car shouted at the nearest youth;

"Please leave those trees alone. Do you have to do that?"

"Shut your face you stupid old bag!" said the boy nearest to her and swung his foot at her bag of shopping as he ran past. Her shopping spewed out of her bag onto the pavement. Another one of the group stopped and picked up a carton of milk, threw it in the air and kicked it, seeing it explode against the nearest wall. When they got to the end of the street they stopped to congratulate each other, they started singing, "We are the champions, we are the champions!" and then they shouted; "You'll get your fucking head kicked in!" When the tall lad with the red logo on the chest of his hoodie stopped chanting and looked around he suddenly looked worried.

"Where's Pete, where the fuck has Pete gone?" In the distance he caught a glimpse of a white Ford van driving around the corner at the end of the road and driving off at speed down 'Redemption Way'.

Jeff the postman was on his normal delivery round and when he turned the corner into Wildwood Way an unusual site confronted him. He immediately dropped the letters and a package meant for Mrs Lilac at number 22 onto the ground. What he saw was a young man wrapped in barbed wire, tied to a stake which was driven into the ground of the green verge between the path and the road. He was propped up with his arms above his head and with both his hands secured to the wooden stake by a nail through each palm. His head was covered by a black plastic bag; blood drenched his tee-shirt. Jeff took out his mobile phone and with shaking fingers dialled 999.

FOUR

"Have you met Sophie before? She seemed a bit on edge. You haven't given her one of your withering dressing downs for something she's done on the job, she's only been doing it for a few weeks?"

Detective Sergeant Sheila Tennyson, the scene of crime officer, and a long term colleague of Inspector Kane, knew how intimidating he could be to young officers.

"I don't expect any favours Bob but I would like my daughter to last a bit longer in the force, it took me long enough to get her to give it a go."

"Well yes I do Sheila; we met the other day when we found the body of PC Rose, nasty business."

Inspector Kane turned to face Police Constable Sophie Tennyson;

"Hello Constable, we seem to have another victim of our killer. No message for us like the last time. Please tell me if you're not happy with this, you don't have to deal with it today if you don't feel ready."

"No Sir, I am ok, I had some good support after that, real kindness and understanding from colleagues, one person in particular, and I am ready to find this murderer Sir. Tell me what do you want me to do?"

"Secure the perimeter and keep people outside the tape. Stop nosey onlookers and reporters getting too close, it's good to see you on duty constable."

P.C. Sophie Tennyson walked purposely towards the gathering onlookers, hoping that her mother did not see the red blush spreading on the skin of her neck, working its way up from her collar to her cheek.

Watching her daughter walking away from them Sheila commented;

"Lovely girl Bob, she will make some lucky man very happy someday, but it is tough in this job to meet the right person. I told her to steer clear of anyone in the force. A disaster waiting to happen, look at you and me Bob, train wrecks. Still bitter and twisted. Anyway, back to work. He's been dead about eight hours, a witness saw a white van in the road when walking his dog, a Ford he thinks, no number plates though. Forensics will send the full report on the body."

Bob Kane had seen most things in his years on the force, and one thing he did suspect of this killing was that the killer wanted to send a message. The killer had a purpose, and he would bet that they would kill again.

"This will not be the last Sheila, I am pretty certain."

Chapter Two: Sowing the seed.

Mark put the manuscript down on the cushion of the sofa, went over to the drinks tray, picked up the crystal glass decanter and poured himself another whisky. He contemplated whether this crime novel had what it took to sell at the bookstands in the airports of the world. Could this unknown author's novel become an Amazon best seller? Could 'The Gardener' be the start of a series of novels featuring the world weary Inspector Kane? Having dipped into this author's submission he was of the opinion that it was not particularly well written. However Mark knew that with some help from one of his crime fiction editors he was almost certain that they could knock this draft into shape. If he chose to, Mark was confident that he could turn this simple crime novel into a goldmine. This budding author would sign any deal he offered for a reasonable advance just to get his work published and therefore he, the publisher, would get the larger slice of the cake when the money from sales and other spin offs began to flow in.

Earlier that afternoon he had met with the author whom he had invited to his office to discuss this novel. The meeting did not last long. He made it clear to the author that he was not impressed by his work, was not interested in publishing his book, and therefore he would not be taking this submission any further.

"Unfortunately, Jonathan, yours is like many other crime novels I have been sent written by first time authors. It has within it a good idea, but it is not professional enough, or original enough to make me want to spend my money on it. So thanks for the offer but no thanks. I suggest you get an agent, if you can, and see what they can do for you."

Mark approached these initial negotiations with an author like a game of cricket. He was a fast bowler in his school team and liked to scare the opposition batsman by being aggressive from the first ball he delivered. In the summer with the sun behind his back, shining into the batsman's eyes, he usually bowled a bouncer aimed at their head. Being aggressive with his opening remarks towards this author was simply a test. He wanted to discover how resilient this writer, Jonathan Hope, was and how he would react. He could respond to his challenge by being equally aggressive. In cricketing terms, he could go on his front foot, walk down the wicket towards him and take a verbal swing of the bat at his head. Alternatively he could be the sort of player that reacts to this sort of provocation by appealing to a non-existent umpire about how unfair Mark was, throwing his bat down on the ground and leaving the pitch. Mark was testing Jonathan's mettle to see how compliant and open to manipulation he might be before putting any deal on the table.

While Mark was delivering this verdict on his work the author, Jonathan Hope looked intently at him. The colour drained from his cheeks as his face turned white. He clenched his jaw to stop himself shouting at the publisher, and his bottom lip started to quiver as he struggled to contain his anger. Although he remained silent, inside his head storms were raging, and the tension in his stomach made him feel sick. For a moment he imagined leaping across the desk in front of him and grabbing this jumped up, self-important literary businessman by the throat and squeezing every pompous breath out of his body. Free from the risk of prosecution, this would be the course of action he would have chosen, but with a sickening familiarity, he swallowed his rage which in turn quickly transformed into sadness, a tension in the pit of his stomach, and a vicelike tightness in his chest. If he lost control and let his anger get the better of him in this situation it could mean the loss of hope for a different future for him and his young family. He struggled with his emotions trying not to burst into tears. The night before, even though he did not believe in such things, he prayed in the darkness of his bedroom, that for once in his life someone would recognise his creative talent.

Behind his frozen stare fixed on Mark's face Jonathan struggled to remind himself that tis man was talking to an experienced teacher who had dealt with the behaviour of many difficult students in his career. He desperately needed the opportunity this man could offer, but what price did he put on losing his dignity? He gathered himself together, raised himself up in his seat and managed to speak;

"Do you get some sadistic pleasure by bringing people like me here just to humiliate them? I have taught English to students of all abilities and I wouldn't treat my students like this. I'm not totally stupid, I may be new at writing crime fiction but I'm not totally new at writing. I teach the bloody thing."

Mark seemed to ignore what he said and offered him a glass of water from the carafe on the desk in front of him, Mark replied;

"That might be true Mr Hope, I mean no offence, but perhaps teaching is the place for you. Teachers teach while others 'do', isn't that what they say? Do you play golf? No, well give it a try. If you are standing over a three foot putt to win money and fame and you miss it, it's no good telling yourself, I should have practiced more! It's too late the chance has gone. I live in the real world of publishing, there are a few winners but many more losers, and I must be brutally honest with you. If you want to succeed in my world you have to shake things up a bit, think outside the box, and find your own voice. I don't know if you watch T.V. but my wife loves that Saturday talent show, it's her secret pleasure. Think of this meeting as if you were auditioning for a place on that talent show on T.V. and I am like that judge who sits on the end of the row, what's his name?"

"Do you mean Simon Cowell?" The author answered not knowing where this persons self-satisfying sermon was leading.

Mark continued speaking.

"Look Mr Hope, you may not thank me now, but I am being cruel to be kind about your chances of being a writer. I am afraid, at this moment in time and having read what I have read, I have to say don't give up your day job just yet."

Jonathan Hope was a man in his mid to late thirties, attractive, studious looking, with greying hair, glasses and a beard. At first glance Mark thought he reminded him of one of his old private school teachers, but without the accent that established him as an ex public school boy. He was dressed in a worn green cord jacket and Levi's, with brown brogue shoes, that were well polished. He looked down at the floor while Mark spoke, and Mark thought he seemed accepting of what he had said. He looked a little off colour and his hands were shaking but he didn't remonstrate, or throw his glass of water at Mark. He half expected him to thank him for his opinion, rather like the ritual of a public school boy thanking his form teacher, after being given six of the best with a cane, across his buttocks.

Jonathan was controlling his temper as best he could. He glared at Mark and started speaking, trying to control the slight tremor in his voice.

"I don't like that kind of talent show; it's very rare that anyone who wins has a career that lasts. It's about celebrity. For me it's a hollow crown. From what I've seen it's as much for the egos of the judges as it is for the contestants. I don't know what game you might be playing but this is a fiasco. If you are an example of those who inhabit the world of publishing then God help us. I don't like you, your world and as far as I am concerned you are welcome to it. I have nothing left to say. I'm going!"

After he finished talking Jonathan got up out of his chair, grabbed his manuscript from the desk top and left the office without looking back. Despite his leaving remarks to Mark Finch he left the publishers office emotionally wounded by the publisher's harsh words of rejection. When he had been beaten with a cane on his hand at school for breaking a window the visible stripe marks it left eventually faded but Jonathan could not estimate how long the psychological hurt he had suffered at the hands of this narcissist would take to heal.

As he left the inner sanctum of the publisher's office he passed Mark's secretary Jodie who sat at her desk in the reception area of the office. Jodie watched him walk past her and she was certain she saw him use a handkerchief to mop a tear from his eyes, but to hide this from her he pretended to blow his nose. He avoided her gaze as he passed her on the way to the stairs but she was convinced she heard him mutter to himself; "Tory twit." or it could have been, "What a shit." before running down the stairs to the exit.

Jonathan could not leave the office of Finch and Faber quickly enough; all he wanted to do now was to get home. He tried to tell himself that this man was just one of a number of publishers and it was only his opinion of his work; however he could not help but wonder if his dream of getting a book deal was worth the humiliation he felt at that moment? Of course he knew that there were more important things in life than having a book published, but even so, someone needed to knock this man down to size and pull him off his high horse. He still regretted not hitting him, because hopefully the shock of his punch would somehow jolt this idiot of a publisher out of his smug sense of superiority. When Jonathan exited the office building and stood in the street to try to get his composure back it started to shower with rain and so as he looked up at the dark cloud in the sky he turned up his jacket collar, and then strode off in the direction of the Russell Square tube station.

In the first floor office of the publishers Mark had had enough for one day, he looked at the clock, and it was 4.45pm. On his desk laid an A4 size brown envelope that arrived in the post that morning. It contained pictures of him taken without his knowledge, by some stalker, and a typed message printed in large black letters on plain yellow paper. He picked it up; put it in his desk drawer, locked the drawer with a key and put the key in his trouser pocket. He would worry about the contents of the envelope tomorrow; right now he had other things on his mind. If he left now he would get the early train home. He picked up his blue Burberry raincoat, exited his office, said goodnight to his secretary Jodie in passing, and went down the stairs out into the street, on his way to the Russell Square tube station. He had waited long enough to avoid bumping into the latest irate angry author who might want to confront him in the street.

While standing amongst the crush of people at the edge of the tube station platform waiting for his train, Mark had second thoughts about Jonathan Hope and his novel. What he said to the author was really his opening gambit and he never understood why authors were so highly strung, so precious about their work and yet in the case of Mr Hope, throws it away? Mark saw this as a golden opportunity to get the best deal he could from this author. There and then, he decided to resurrect 'The Gardener', and save the story and Jonathan Hope from oblivion. Initially he would offer him a 'vanity contract' in which the author contributes money towards the cost of publication. He would get Jodie to complete the paperwork the next day.

Mark's journey to the platform had not been without incident. He should not have attempted to pick up the folder. He should not have annoyed the dog. He was desperate to get on the train and escape to his home in the country. Due to a problem down the line his connection had been delayed and the next train was a 'through' train. The platform kept filling up with more passengers all waiting for the next train to Leicester Square and beyond. He had stopped limping now, but it felt as if his right ankle was probably swollen because it was throbbing with pain. He could feel stickiness in his right shoe where blood had seeped into his sock. He felt hot and clammy and the material of his shirt was sticking to his back. He knew he needed to take off his raincoat but he hadn't got the energy to do so. Maybe he was delirious, but now he had changed his mind about the book, he would tell Jodie to contact Mr Hope tomorrow, about his second chance. Thoughts were jumbled in his mind like clothes in a tumble drier. What actor would be best for the Inspector? What advance would he give? Jodie could visit the set with him? Jonathan Hope would be so grateful. He would make money out of this crime novel after all.

He tried to ignore the pain in his foot and forget the problems of the day. He tried to focus on the fact that he would soon be on his way home; on the train he could sit down and relax. He would text Mary to tell her he was coming home earlier than usual and get her to meet him at Marden station. If his foot got any worse she would have to take him straight to accident and emergency. Then he had a faint recollection that today was in some way special, surely Jodie would have reminded him if it was and he had to buy a present but in his delirium, like a feather floating on the hot breeze in the tunnel, try as he might, he could not hold on to that thought.

At that moment he heard the sound of the tube train come whistling into the station at speed, Mark leant forward to try, as the train whizzed past, to get an idea of how full the carriages were. He felt queasy and was desperate to sit down on board the next train. It was then out of nowhere he felt a strong push in his back from someone or something behind him. He lost his balance and toppled forward straight into the path of the oncoming train.

The next day the papers were to report that his head was found some time later, approximately one hundred yards further up the track in the tunnel.

Chapter Three: Jodie

Jodie watched as Mark left the office dressed in his raincoat. He seemed preoccupied with his thoughts as he often was after seeing a potential author, and it was obvious to her that he was in a hurry to leave. She did not feel upset that he only briefly acknowledged her with a half-hearted smile and a nod of his head. She loved that Burberry raincoat and always felt he looked good in it. One afternoon when they were drinking white wine and eating chocolates in bed he told her he bought it because of a Leonard Cohen song. For her it was a famous coat for another reason, it was associated with a special memory of them lying on top of it in a secluded part of the park on Primrose Hill, making love. From their vantage point they overlooked the fairy lights of the city at dusk, as the summer sun went down. Their liaison was naughty, risky, impulsive and exciting and when she climaxed she felt as if a fireworks display had gone off in her head. Mark surprised her with a picnic in the park to celebrate their one year anniversary. The menu consisted of Champagne, strawberries, smoked salmon, fresh French bread and cheese. For pudding he had bought little pink, yellow and green meringues with her favourite fillings, all from her favourite patisserie. It was a magical memory and one she treasured.

When the affair began she knew he was older, married with children, but he had something different, a confidence and sophistication that younger men she had dated and the few she had slept with, did not seem to possess. Their liaison had to be kept a secret as he was an acquaintance of her fathers and it was through her father's recommendation that she got the job as his secretary/come P.A. in Mark's publishing firm. Jodie adored her father and had done so since she was a little girl. In her imagination, her father was like the knight who rode off on his horse from the castle of his home every day on a heroic adventure, and more often than not returned with some wonderful treasure in the form of presents for the family, but especially her. Her mother made sure that when he arrived home she was bathed and dressed in her bedclothes ready to greet him as he walked through the front door. She often watched out of the upstairs window of her house as his car turned off the main road into their drive. He made a habit of flicking the cars headlights on and off to say hello to her as he came to a stop outside the house.

Jodie felt a similar excitement at work waiting for Mark to run up the stairs to the office in the morning. She made sure that she was presentable for him and had the coffee on the percolator ready for his first cup of the day. When she started working at the office he made it clear to her that he could not function well until he'd had his first hit of caffeine which helped him face his inevitable list of e-mails. Her attraction for him had grown slowly over the three years she had worked closely with him. She felt that she had been given responsibility for formulating letters, dealing with client contracts much sooner than she expected. He trusted her to buy his sandwiches for lunch, get birthday cards for his loved ones when he did not have the time, and even go shopping with him to choose his wife's presents. He told her that her opinion really helped him make the right choice of things, particularly for his wife as when it came to clothes and underwear as Jodie was about the same size as her. One weekend, when he was going to stay in town with his wife and take her to see a musical, he wanted to buy her something sexy to wear, as a gift for her and a naughty treat for him. Jodie introduced him to the range of Victoria Secrets underwear. She remembered his initial embarrassment when she took him into their black fronted shop in New Bond Street.

With the extra responsibility at work came more money, more socialising, business lunches, work meetings at which she organised the catering, as well as visits to up market fine dining restaurants. With this increased frequency of interaction between them developed a greater familiarity. Nothing romantic or improper had happened during this time until last year's office party. Every year the publishers held a party for clients and business acquaintances. Mark's wife got very inebriated on vodka martinis and Champagne. Mark was socialising with clients and their partners in the boardroom while Jodie had the task of looking after his wife at the drinks table. His wife sipped her martini and studied Jodie intently over the rim of her glass. It was as if she was taking some kind of measurement. The expression on her face suggested to Jodie a mixture of admiration tinged with sadness in her eyes, while she swayed gently from side to side.

"My darling, can you hear that music playing, or is it the alcohol messing with my hearing?"

"Err... Yes I think it is Mrs Finch, it is from Mark's iPhone and the iPod in the other room." Jodie answered.

"I thought I heard one of my favourite songs, 'Wait', from my favourite medical drama. He bought me the boxed set for my birthday; I watch it when I am on my own, which is a lot these days."

Mrs Finch started to hum a tune quietly and then started to sing a fragment of a lyric,

'If you wait too long, he will be gone', I put together a mix of songs for us when we went on holiday, as something to listen to by the pool. Some songs get into your head and they just go round and round. Does that happen to you?"

"Yes, it does, and I suppose it does to most people. Mrs Finch, Mark, I mean Mr Finch told me you like musicals is that right?"

"Yes I do, how nice of you to remember. It's O.K. for you to call me Mary; all that 'Mrs' stuff makes me seem so old." Mary took another sip of her martini.

"I think I need to freshen this up, be a darling and pass me the gin will you."

Jodie picked up the nearest green bottle of gin, "Of course, here, Tanqueray No 10 is that O.K.?"

"Absolutely lovely, top me up." Mary held her glass out towards Jodie, so that she could pour the gin into it.

"Say when!" Jodie began to pour the liquid into her glass waiting for Mary to stop her.

"I should have said 'when' a while ago, but I suppose I don't know when to stop." Mary gave a wry laugh. "Cheers!"

Mary raised her glass towards Jodie and took another swig of her drink. Jodie continued the conversation,

"Sorry if I offended you but I didn't want to appear too familiar, as you are my boss's wife." Jodie explained.

"No that's fine, yes I do love musicals, old and new, most of them do something to me, things like West side Story, My Fair Lady, Sweet Charity, Sweeney Todd, even Mamma Mia. That song the mother sings in the film on top of the hill near the church with the James Bond actor makes me cry so much. You know, 'The winner takes it all, the loser standing small', so sad, so sad. Do you know it?"

"That was Meryl Streep, I think."

Jodie wanted to tell her bosses wife to slow down on her consumption of gin and start drinking water but didn't know how to do this without offending her.

"You are looking so beautiful tonight, you know you do, of course you do", Mary said.

"Thankyou that's very kind of you." Jodie was not sure where this conversation might lead.

"You look a bit like her you know, a younger version of her, lovely bone structure."

Mary leaned a little too far away from the chair she was holding on to and staggered forward, but managed to grab hold of the table to steady her stance.

"I felt like you once, happy inside my skin. I do what I can now, to stay in shape… I'm still you inside, you know. It seems to have gone tits up recently and I don't mean that I've had a 'boob' job. Excuse my French. Sorry, I shouldn't have come".

Tears welled up in her eyes.

"We were like two flames, once you know, couldn't keep our hands of each other, we were so hot together we sizzled. We used to sing this old song that my mother knew; we sang it in the car when we travelled. That male English film star with big eyebrows, married to Joan Collins."

She started to sing, and move her glass from side to side in time with the song.

"I'll never let you go, why because, I love you, you'll never let me go, why because you love me. We did you know, love each other, we did! God! How simple it all seemed then. Not so now."

Tears began to flow from the corner of her eyes. She took a gulp of her drink with the tracks of her tears lining her cheeks. At that moment the music selection Jodie had programmed earlier changed to 'The Best of

21

Motown" compilation.

"Oh shit, do you hear that? 'Tears of a Clown', bloody Smokey Robinson."

Mary took another gulp of her drink. Jodie was not sure what to say or do.

"He does love you; he talks so fondly of you and your children." Jodie tried to reassure her.

"Thankyou darling, that's sweet of you but I feel that things are slipping away…you know, my young beautiful woman, that you are, so like me in many ways. I feel that sometimes now, when he looks at me, actually, really looks at me I remember those feelings, but most of the time …I feel he is not in love with me but in love with all this, his work, his money, and not in love with his wife."

"Mrs Finch, Mary, you are still a really attractive woman, please don't…"

Before Jodie finished her sentence Mary slumped down into the chair beside her, and as far as Jodie could make out seemed to lose consciousness. Jodie felt that she had to find Mark quickly and let him know that his wife needed his attention. In her own mind her thoughts were confused, her mind was racing, battling with a rollercoaster of possibilities and feelings. She liked this woman, and felt sorry for her but what if things got so bad that she left Mark. The possibility of a future intimate relationship with him became a reality. She wanted their relationship to blossom. If it did she didn't want it to be constantly lived in the shadows. This conversation with his wife had given her hope. No matter how wrong it might be to have these thoughts or how disapproving her parents were bound to be, she felt a flutter in her tummy as if her desire had suddenly been given wings. She tried to be honest with herself, put her feelings in perspective but she adored Mark. She wanted him, but being honest with herself she never thought he would leave his wife and children. Now hearing Mary talk, perhaps his wife might leave him and sue for a divorce if she became so unhappy. Would Mark give up half his business for her? Would he risk his hard won fortune for love?. She went looking for Mark and found him in the semi dark of his office sitting on the sofa.

"Sorry to interrupt, I came to find you, your wife is a bit worse for wear, in the other room; you may need to look after her."

"Oh really, oh shit, I'm sorry if she's a bit out of order. I've just had some not so good news myself."

Jodie sat down on the sofa beside him. Mark bent forward, his head in his hands.

"One of the guys I play golf with in Marden has been taken into hospital; he may have had a heart attack on the golf course today, one of the other guys texted me."

Jodie put her hand on his, and put her arm on his shoulder to comfort him.

"Is he O.K. now?"

"He's in hospital in Maidstone and they are doing tests. Something like this makes life seem so fragile, I played with him last week and he was fine. He had his 'cholesterol special' for breakfast as per usual, before we went out; he seemed such a fit man for his age. I guess we all take life so much for granted. We come in to this world alone and we leave it the same way. Why put off till tomorrow what you can do today, you never know what the fuck's round the corner. It's too scary to think about. Jodie, sometimes I wake up in the middle of the night in a sweat, and I think that one day I won't wake up. I'll soon be getting to the point where I don't have as much time left in front of me as I do behind. It's a tipping point, a watershed. Age creeps up on you while you are looking the other way, doing what you are doing."

"What is it you told me your mates said? 'You're only as old as you feel or the last woman you've felt! Things are changing all the time."

Jodie hoped to lighten Mark's mood, but as soon as the words came out of her mouth she knew they were in poor taste.

Mark looked Jodie in the eyes and held her hand in his,

"Listen live your life while you can. I'm sorry to burden you with this crap. I just felt it's the surprise of it all, and I've had a few too many drinks"

"No, no, it's ok," Jodie tried to reassure him.

He looked so sad and alone and without thinking she gently pulled his head to the pillow of her bosom, to hold him and comfort him, and gently began stroking his hair. She felt so maternal, as if she was comforting a child in pain as she began to rock backwards and forwards. Mark seemed to relax and nestled into her. Then she noticed something different and more intimate happening. She felt his hand began to move slowly up her thigh under her skirt and she felt warm, gentle kisses on her bosom, where it was exposed by the cleavage of her low cut top. Her thoughts and feelings were confused as her body responded to his touch. It seemed to be saying one thing and her mind another. For a moment she stayed still, as if she was staring at an imaginary traffic light in her mind that was showing amber, but could change to red or green at any moment. Had he read her thoughts? Had he guessed that she wanted him? This was her moment. Jodie lifted his cheek off her breast and kissed him full on the lips. She pushed him onto his back on the sofa, slid her skirt up over her thighs exposing the tops of her stockings, and sat astride him. The light in her head had changed from amber to green. There was no going back now.

When appetites were satisfied, composure regained, and heartrates had returned to normal, Jodie left the office through the door to the reception area, while Mark left by the door to the conference room. Their affair had begun. From that moment she felt a liberated woman, and for a while, a long while, they could not keep their hands off each other. When they were alone in the office they used to joke that most stable flat surfaces in the place had an imprinted memory of their sexual adventures and bear witness to their passion. Whenever she watched C.S.I. on the T.V. she hated to think what their blue lamp would discover if it was passed over the furniture, and carpets of the office. They were on fire, they set each other alight like a match to a candle, and Jodie prayed that the flame would not be extinguished by anything or anyone. She vowed to herself that she would not let that happen at any cost. She would make sure she pleased him, keep him interested, be sexually available, be adventurous, and do what he liked. She wanted to devour him, to make him hers. Her appetite for sex was insatiable. She bought underwear from Victoria Secrets, suspenders, perfume, and makeup. With her smooth skin and toned body from her exercise classes she always excited him. He adored her naked back and neck, which he loved to kiss, sending shivers down her spine.

They would spend afternoons in London hotel rooms, making sure to avoid places he had been with his wife. Often Mark and Jodie could combine business lunches with a pudding of carnal pleasure. A couple of times Jodie accompanied him to book launches in New York and Berlin where she made sure they were in adjoining hotel rooms. All was fine, clear skies and plain sailing in their liaisons until approximately three months ago. Something changed in the way Jodie was feeling. It started when she was feeding the ducks in St James Park, walking by the lake. She suddenly felt a new and strange attraction to mothers with babies, and young children, as they pushed their strollers, and sat and ate their picnics, or licked their ice cream. She had this physical urge grow inside her that made her want to cuddle babies, smell them, and hold them close to her chest. Jodie knew something was emotionally wrong when she became disappointed that her period continued to start like clockwork each month. She toyed with the idea of accidentally but secretly on purpose, forgetting to take her contraceptive pill. She sat on park benches in the hope that they would sit down beside her and a toddler would smile at her and perhaps she could talk to them about their toys, or the ducks or swans that sat by the water's edge. She had strange dreams of finding a baby in a basket floating down a stream. Once she had a nightmare in which Mark served her a tiny baby on toast for breakfast. One lunch time, before she bought the usual coffee and sandwiches for the office, she found herself in Mothercare, looking at maternity dresses, and actually tried on one she liked. In the changing room she looked at her body in the mirror and imagined what it would look like if her breasts were engorged with milk and her tummy was swollen. Then it happened. At the height of their passionate lovemaking, as Mark could contain himself no longer and lost control, she made a wish. She wished for a miracle. This time, overcoming all obstacles, he would impregnate her. Their child would cement this relationship forever and tie Mark to Jodie for life.

Then one day she felt compelled to do what she thought was a strange thing. On the afternoon of one of their hot and steamy, very physical sessions of sex in an executive room of the Holiday Inn Mayfair, she excused herself from the bed as Mark eased himself off her body, and went into the bathroom. She had made a plan. She took one of the small complementary shower gel bottles and emptied it out into the sink, rinsed it out, and while she sat on the loo seat, tensed her muscles, and squeezed out some of Mark's ejaculation into the bottle and put it into her wash bag. When she arrived home she hid it in the freezer inside the box of Walls Cornetto's, her current favourite ice cream. She labelled the bottle D and D with a marker pen. The first initial 'D' was for Daniel after one of her favourite novelists, and the second, 'D' for David her father's name. She chose one name for a girl and one for a boy.

This secret act had a profound effect on Jodie. Now she felt she owned a part of Mark that could not be taken away from her. Her plan was not without flaws. She hadn't researched the process of artificial insemination in any detail. She wasn't thinking logically or rationally but she didn't care. She reassured herself that whatever happened in the future, now there might be the remotest possibility of her having what Mark and his wife had, their own baby.

From that moment something changed within Jodie. Her mind started to play cruel games with her. Her anxious thoughts would not leave her alone; she would be doing something, for example, talking to someone on the phone where she was meant to ask questions about something for work but because she felt tired or distracted, she lacked the courage and commitment to follow things through. It was as if the clients were more intimidating than usual and she was frightened to get something wrong and so she put the phone down. She began double checking her e-mails to clients and agents to make sure the wording was perfectly correct and not open to interpretation or misunderstanding. Mark lost his temper with her on a couple of occasions because things had not been completed in time. This made her feel more like a failure, and a person who lacked the courage and conviction to be Mark's chosen one. At other times she would find herself ruminating about risky situations she put herself in with Mark in the past or future and the impact these actions could have on her and others if they came to light.

This phase of anxiety coincided with a growing fear that she was being followed whenever she left the office, as well as on her journey to work. She started feeling guilty about giving in to her sexual appetite and satisfying herself in the secret sex fuelled encounters with Mark. No good could come of it; she could only bring shame upon her family, his wife and children, and in the process hurt those she loved who deserved none of it. Sometimes, lying naked on a hotel bed next to Mark, after they had made love and he was dozing, she felt a hatred for herself and what she had become. She was no longer the little girl that her Dad used to pick up and throw into the air or give piggybacks to. No matter how hard she tried she knew she could not rewrite history or turn back time and her guilt was something she had to live with. Her actions, her desire and his weakness, had created a stain on her personality that could contaminate whatever she did in the future, unless she could make it right. She had to find a way to give purpose to the things she had done.

No matter how much Jodie tried to put the thought out of her mind, Jodie still wished, against all odds, that Mark's love, desire and affection for her would eventually result in him separating from his wife and marrying her. She had thought about the type of dress she wanted, the location of the marriage, and the honeymoon destination. So far, Mark was the only man she had known in her life that could compete with her father in terms of her love and admiration. Mark was destined to be the father of her children.

After one particular afternoon of carnal pleasure Jodie finished drying herself with the hotel towels, rubbed lavender smelling lotion over her body, put on her bathrobe and walked back into the bedroom. Mark was sitting up in bed drinking a glass of whisky and watching the news on the television.

"Sweet heart please can you please switch off the T.V. and talk to me for a minute?"

Jodie climbed onto the bed and sat looking at him waiting for some sign that he may be willing to talk about their relationship, things that she had said in the past, things that were on her mind.

"Jodie my darling what do you want me to say that I have not said before. When we are together, you are my world. I love you, I need you, and I want you. You are my right hand. I would be lost without you, but please don't ask the impossible. You know, I will not leave my wife or my children. I have not worked all this time just to give it up and hand her half of my income on a plate. That sounds terrible, I don't mean that, but for Christ's sake, I love her as well, and I will not do that to her, it will fuck up her nice little world. Come on sweet; let's be happy with what we have, please. You know my kids are just about to go to University, they are coming home for the holidays from school for the summer, and I have to spend time with them. We've got a villa booked in France; you booked it for us for Christ's sake. I see you more than I do them, so please give me a break. You are special, this is special, what more can I say?"

"It's not what you can say to me it is what you can do. Leave her, be with me. You must know that every time you go away you take a piece of me with you. You know you make me whole, please!"

Jodie fought back her tears as she did not want to be the pathetic girlfriend that cries, or pleads. She knew that with Mark it was like tears falling on granite, she needed to be the woman who was angry, hurt, and frustrated, a warrior not a wimp.

In that moment and in a number of similar ones that followed, nothing changed in Mark. He told her on several occasions,

"Jodie darling, please don't wait for me to change my mind because mine is not the changing kind."

On his birthday she gave him a card and in it she wrote,

"Is this the way our love will be, lived in the shadows secretly. I hoped that one day it would see the sun."

None of her words made a difference to Mark and she came to accept a painful truth, that the beds and hotel rooms they made love in would stay silent forever. Unless her secret was discovered, unless she told someone, no one would know the love they shared and that she wanted to have Mark to herself. She was not happy skulking around in hotel rooms anymore, being careful what she said to her father and mother. This was not the way true love should be lived. She knew that she was partly to blame for seducing him in the first place, but surely now she was more to him than a mistress, a 'bit on the side'. In the beginning she was flattered by him and excited by how 'naughty' she was being. This was the first time in her fledgling love life that she felt adored and desired by a real man, someone of substance. She was not prepared for the depth of emotion that tugged at her heart strings. If the pain she felt in her chest now could be given a voice, it would remind her that although she loved him well, and the memory of his touch would never leave her, the night times spent crying and alone in the solitary darkness of her bedroom, told her how lonely this infatuation made her feel. It also emphasised how pathetic she was to hold on to a childlike hope that he would make her his chosen one and not his wife. She continued to have sex with Mark, but for her it was no longer making love. Sometimes in the midst of their lovemaking when she was not absorbed in the physical pleasure, she felt as if her mind became separated from her body and was like a camera floating above them watching their writhing bodies from a distance. Mark was an accomplished lover and she could not stop her body responding to his ministrations. Jodie still felt an obligation to reciprocate in kind as she didn't want him to become suspicious of any change in her, or sacrifice the precious time she spent alone with him. She knew she had to formulate a plan of action. She had a well-paid job and no matter how much pain she was in she had no intention of giving him an easy way out, letting his wife have the satisfaction of preserving the illusion of their marriage and keeping him all to herself. Neither would she resign, leave her job and sacrifice all she had worked for.

Chapter Four: Mary

On the day before her wedding anniversary Mary Finch sat on her comfortable couch in the large lounge of her home, a converted Oast house in the countryside near Marden in Kent Her husband, Mark had telephoned her the previous afternoon to apologise . He had forgotten to tell her of a late business meeting at a hotel in the City that evening and so he would be staying in town. She had a large glass of dry sherry in her right hand and on a plate in front of her, resting on her aged oak coffee table, was a half-eaten brie and cranberry sandwich. She was daydreaming, staring out through her glass patio doors, over the decking and the patio furniture, into the rear garden where Steven the gardener was mowing the lawn near the plum trees. In her thoughts she pictured herself as a ripe plum ready to be plucked from one of the overburdened trees at the bottom of her garden. She felt in the full flower of her womanhood, in her prime and ripe for harvesting, but her husband, the one person she wanted to take notice of this and pluck her from the tree, seemed to have lost his appetite for her. He left her high and dry, withering on the branch making her increasingly convinced that he had found other fruit to pick. She consoled herself in the knowledge that her gardener appreciated her and was happy to taste the succulent fruit she produced. As she watched him push the mower up and down the lawn, forming regimented lines in the grass she felt so alone. In her life she had been many things, from an excited child, a middle of the road student, a teenage showjumper, a lover, wife, and then a mother. Now, in this moment of contemplation, she was not certain who or what she was. She felt like a woman lost in the middle of life and she hated this gnawing feeling inside her that she had lost herself and was no longer a person in her own right.

When she was young she first dreamt of becoming a dancer like Ginger Rodgers, but this was too lowbrow for her mother, and so for a short time she was sent to ballet lessons. In her heart she wanted to tap dance and spring around the floor like Ginger and Fred in the old black and white films she watched on T.V. This dream passed and as she got older she fell in love with horses. When she saw Elizabeth Taylor in the film 'National Velvet', she knew she wanted to become a show jumper or a jockey. It had crossed her mind that perhaps, she could be the first tap dancing jockey, but that was not to be. When she watched Disney cartoons as a child she loved Cinderella, and remembered being terrified by the witch in Snow White. She loved children's' books where girls had adventures and were equally as brave and clever as the boys in the stories. Then later still she was overtaken by the idea of a new adventure, romance, and fell in love with the idea of falling in love and getting married. One day she would find her Prince Charming, and, as it happened in all the romantic comedies she adored as a child, they would find each other and live happily ever after. 'Love's true kiss ' when it happened, would awaken the princess inside her and as if by magic, destiny, or serendipity ,a prince would find her and that would be that, Kismet.

However, now with hindsight, her own romantic fairy-tale, as it unfolded in reality was less like Cinderella and more the Frog Prince. In Mark she met a frog in the guise of a prince. It had taken Mary some time to understand that the man she'd eventually married was more in love with the idea of romance and family, than the reality.
Mary first met Mark on a train. One evening, returning on the train from her place of work in London she thought she had lost her 'Coach' purse which had fallen out of her handbag. very courteous attractive young man, who seemed slightly older than her, found it on the floor of the carriage near her seat and handed it back to her. In doing so he took the opportunity to gently brush her hand with his fingertips. He bent down and looking deep into her eyes, said,

"I'm getting off at the next station, but I would love to meet you again. I think you are gorgeous. I know it is a risk, you don't know me from Adam, but if you would be brave, please take the risk of seeing me for a date, here's my number."

He took her hand in his and in biro ink, wrote his telephone number on the palm of her hand. He turned away from her, made his way through the standing passengers and walked out of the carriage door onto the platform. In that moment she felt a tingle down her spine and it was as if time stood still. Suddenly from this commuter train she felt transported back to the childhood fairy tale world of Cinderella, a story she had read many times. Perhaps now her childhood wish might come true and she had become the chosen one, the one whom the glass slipper fitted. The crush of passengers in the train carriage caused the temperature to soar. Despite sitting on her seat her hands were sticky and her wrists damp with perspiration. In no time at all the numbers on her palm smudged and before she could copy it into her Filofax some of the numbers became unclear. Should she trust herself to a stranger on a train? When she arrived home she could not get the image of his good looking face out of her mind. Initially she did nothing but by the evening of the next day the tension she was feeling inside became unbearable, and so she decided to call him. She sat on her bed, dialed his number on her bedside phone and waited.

"The number you have dialed is not recognised. Please try again."
"Shit! Shit! No don't do this to me, you stupid, stupid, phone!"

Mary dialed again but got the same message. Exasperated she banged the receiver down on the base.

Later in her life when she told this story to her girlfriends, were usually entranced and envious of how romantic this meeting was; how they wished their romances had begun with such a brief encounter. Mary usually ended this part of her story by saying, "well that is only part of it. Why is it that in the movies such stories end at the beginning when the rest is yet to come? Ladies, I think we know why!"

Over the years, she had worked on her relationship with Mark. As with all relationships that last, they had experienced passionate times, when they could not keep their hands off each other, times when they saw in each other only those things they wanted to see. Then over time as it developed into a more mature partnership she had moments when they were together when she was not sure who the person she married was. Both of them realised that their view of each other was changing and the person they thought they had married, blinded by romantic love and desire, was not completely the person sitting across from them at the dinner table. By this stage in their relationship they were committed to each other and bound by possessions and children. But then she fell in love with him again. It was not the same kind of love, a more reflective love. This was a more separate kind of love.

In her marriage as Mark's career took off, Mary began to resent the feeling that she was no longer a person in her own right. She envied his other life and resented the fact that his job became a mistress whose attraction was something she could not compete with. At the beginning of their marriage she liked being looked after and she looked after Mark in return. Their division of labour was clear-cut. She grew into the role of being a wife, following in the footsteps of her own mother. She devoted herself to being a domestic goddess, and did everything she could to look after Mark, her 'knight' in shining armour. Each day he went out into the world of business to slay his dragons and accomplish his quest of building his own publishing business. She was the queen of the castle running their household, choosing the decorations, and the furnishings. She had her own struggles, fighting with builders, plumbers, the electricians from hell, carpet fitters, Aga installers, who invaded their domain. Simultaneously she cooked, shopped and designed the garden. She devoted herself to building the best nest she could, in which to become a mother. When Mark came home she did her best to stay attractive and satisfy his appetites both in and out of the bedroom. When she met Mark he was keen to have children and in the early years, parenthood was a novelty to him . He loved the children because they loved him, and the attention he needed he received. However as much as she tried Mary could not give Mark the same level of attention he had before they had the boys'. Mark was often absent from the home when the children were awake because of the demands of his business. Her life revolved around the timetable that her children and their growing minds and bodies set. Gradually Mark began to feel an outsider competing with his children for his wife's attention. His solution was to do what he once told Mary he would never do, send his young competitors away to boarding school.

"Darling it will do them good, look they won't be as young as I was, they will be fine. I know I moaned about it, but it will make a man out of both of them. Like my father said, it builds character. My father was so pleased about our decision when I told him; he said he would help us out with the fees!"

When each of the brothers reached the entry age of eight, they left for school. Mary felt separated from her children prematurely, particularly the younger one for whom she felt particularly protective. He wasn't as outgoing as his brother and not as athletic. She felt an ache in her chest that didn't subside until they were home again. She didn't let either of her children see her distress. Mark wanted them to show a happy united front, and so she put on a brave face as they dropped them off at their school. Her own mother supported Mark in his decision because, as she said to Mary, it gave them a chance to 'keep their marriage alive!"

Her mother both praised and criticised her as a homemaker. She would imagine that at any moment her mother could appear at the front door wearing a set of white cotton gloves with which to test the exposed edges in the house for dust. It felt like a competition at times, tinged with feelings of envy, admiration, and resentment, on her mother's part. But through it all Mary never doubted her mother's love for her. They became allies with a common purpose, queens of their domains, and Mary wished, in her quiet moments, that when she had children her mother could do what she was never able to do with her as a child which was to make time to play with them.

Her and her brother understood from a very young age that their father was the king of their castle, and his happiness was the focus of their mother's life. The routine of the house revolved around him leaving for work in the morning and getting ready for his return in the evening. He was the source of her contentment and his demeanor became the source of her and the children's' anxiety. Her father's moods dictated the atmosphere in the house because her mother seemed to become so hypersensitive when he was present. Mary did not know if her father demanded that it be like this, or her mother made it so, but she came to the conclusion that in their married life together he had come to expect it. Her mother was positive about everything and excluded from her awareness anything that challenged the perception of the world she had built. When they were young her mother would love to watch 'The Walton's' and 'Little House on the Prairie', and now she was able to record them on the planner of their satellite box and have afternoons watching her programmes, with scones and a cup of Earl Grey tea, a slice of lemon , never milk.

When they were little her mother did not work and spent a lot of time with the children, but from Mary's recollection she did not know how to let go of her adult persona and play with them. She was present but not available to them most of the time, as she found things to do that kept her busy around the children but not involving them. One exception to this was baking. This was one of the rare occasions where she and the children were allowed to get messy, spill flour, play 'mixy-mix' with water and end up laughing together. Mary likened her mother's 'attunement' to them as children to a radio that was not quite on their wavelength. She looked after and protected them but she stayed aloof. Her mother was content cleaning, cooking, sowing, and having her lady friends' visit for tea and cakes. The tea parties were a source of learning for Mary as they gave her an insight into an adult world. She was allowed to stay in the room and share in the tea and cake as long as she behaved as if she was a part of the furniture, sitting still, reading a book, drawing or playing quietly in a corner of the room. Listening intently, she heard the women talk about clothes, makeup, recipes, dress patterns, husbands, and things to do with their bodies that often she did not understand. They also gossiped about other people in the village, and sometimes they would lower their voices to a whisper, thinking that she could not hear. Once she heard a story that seemed to be of particular interest to them about the barmaid in the local pub and the woman who worked in the post office. Apparently they had been seen holding hands and kissing near the local tennis club. The next time she went with her mother to send a parcel to their aunt in London Mary found it difficult not to stare at the face of the lady behind the counter as she wondered what it would be like to kiss. A frequent topic of conversation was illness and visits to the doctor or other women's marriages with husbands far worse than theirs.

"Did you see her wearing sun glasses again and it's not summer. She should go to the police."

"Why doesn't she leave him?"

This question was asked frequently in their discussions. The usual response being; "Where would she go?" and, "How would she support herself? "And," What about the children?"

Sometimes to her surprise, she heard her mother tell a joke, particularly at Christmas.

"Why does Santa ask for nail clippers for Christmas?"

She asked the assembled friends at the tea party, sitting with a glass of Sherry in their hands. A moment of polite silence followed while they all fidgeted and looked down into their drinks.

"We don't know Mary, why?"

"So that he can trim his…. Santa-claws."

To which they all responded with a burst of polite but joyous laughter.

Mary learned her love of the garden and flowers from her mother and remembered following her along the flower beds while she was dead heading the flowers. Her mother told her that this process was necessary as it made way for new growth. This was similar to the answer she gave Mary when on one summer's day sitting on the back lawn drinking homemade lemonade; Mary asked her mother why animals had to die. Her mother didn't reply immediately, but while staring into the distance, eventually answered her.

"I suppose as we evolved, if we didn't eat the animals they would eat us. If things didn't die we would run out of room for everything and everyone, we have to make room for new growth. Like the plants we all have our seasons, darling. Don't you worry your little head about such things? For god sake don't become a vegetarian, you would get so thin and your father would not be happy. You could be like Wendy, find your

Peter Pan and fly off to Neverland; you don't have to worry about seasons there and you don't grow old."

At 38 years old Mary had an epiphany, and decided that she had been in the shadow of her husband for too long. She read an article in the Sunday Times magazine about 'Women who run with Wolves', getting in touch with their wild woman. At the time she felt like a plant in the shade, she needed to bathe in a new light and begin to blossom. She could not rely on Mark to boost her self-esteem any longer. In September of that year she signed up for some day workshops at the local college in personal development. She wanted to meet different people and to share a new experience with them. They started with trust exercises, and listening practice, and then in the middle of the term they had an all-day workshop. One of the exercises they were given as a group was to go outside, wander around the grounds and find an object that interested them and bring it back to the classroom. The first thing she found was a can-pull, the second was an old broken fountain pen, but the object she decided to take back to the classroom was a bird feather. When they returned to the classroom, they were asked to write a story describing their object, its history, its present and its future. Mary loved the chance to write, she had forgotten how much she enjoyed writing when she was a child. This was an opportunity to use her imagination. When they had finished writing their stories, each person was asked to read their work to the class. Mary was enthralled and enchanted by some of the stories she heard. When it came to her turn everyone listened in silence, following her every word. After each person had read their story to the group the tutor asked them to change the story from reading in the third person to the first person, and to change all the 'it is' to 'I am'. Then they were asked to read their stories to the group again, with this new context. Some refused and got angry with the tutor for the trick she had played on them, as it made them feel emotionally vulnerable and what this process may reveal. Mary took a deep breath, composed herself and began to read her story to the class.

"I am a rather beaten and frayed feather. I was once pure and white, and I was a beautiful female bird that could fly on the wind so high, and because of this other birds wanted to be like me. I had a partner who went off to find food while I sat on the nest and looked after our two eggs. One day he did not return and so I had to do things for myself. My chicks grew and left the nest as they should, and I returned to my love of flying as I was not content to be part of the flock, and I wanted to stand out from the crowd. This did not get the approval of the elders in the flock as I was a woman, and I needed to have another partner, produce more eggs for the survival of the flock, but that did not interest me, I wanted to fly. One day while I was showing off to some young birds, another bird collided with me and I felt a sharp pain in my wing. The freedom I so desperately wanted was threatened, by my broken wing; all I could do now was watch and beg for food, and to get that I would have to do what the elders wanted. I had to adapt, keep my beak shut to survive, and my so called friends and admirers left me alone. In a way they were happy to see me fall. I had to live off scraps and leftovers of food that I could find in the gardens of the monster creatures. One day while I was eating some bread in a garden I was eaten by a fox."

When Mary looked up from her papers some of the women in the class had tears in their eyes, and suddenly, as if a flood gate had opened she started sobbing.

Consumed by her daydream, the recollections of her past, and the memories of this experience, time seemed to stand still for Mary when suddenly her reverie was rudely interrupted. The petrol engine of the gardener's lawn mower burst into life outside her window. Through her glass patio doors into the rear garden she could see Steven their gardener walking slowly away from the window mowing the lawn. His back was turned towards her. She admired his muscular shoulders and arms, pushing the mower from side to side. His shaven head glistening in the sunshine, his brown weathered skin contrasting with the whiteness of the vest he wore, he reminded her of Bruce Willis in the 'Die Hard' films. His dirty tight blue jeans showed off his firm thighs and taught bottom. The sight of his body aroused her appetite for physical pleasure and she wanted him again, as she did two hours earlier when she met him at the kitchen door dressed in her towelling dressing gown. She had made herself ready for him. Hair and eyebrows plucked, body oiled, shaved, perfumed and powdered. Under her robe she wore her black Victoria Secrets lace panties that her husband had bought her as a birthday gift and nothing else. Steven never refused her when she wore these and it was Thursday, the last Thursday before the children came home from their schools for the summer vacation, and she became a mother again. This was her last opportunity to take Steven to bed and ride him until October, which seemed so far away.

Although she was cheating on her husband in the marital home, she had rules. They never did 'it' in the marital bed, but in the guest room. She led him to the bed, disrobed, kissed him on the lips, lay down, closed her eyes and made herself ready. He was her naked guest and when he entered her she would spread her legs wide and put the heel of each foot behind his back resting on his firm buttocks, and clasped him to her. It was as if she had mounted her favourite horse, to have an exciting ride, and it took her back to what was her favourite passion when she was younger. She remembered the sensual thrill she would get when she mounted her favourite fox hunting stallion. Sitting astride him on the leather saddle, feet in the stirrups, full of anticipation, and with one nudge of her heels they would take off. Later in life she would compare it to driving a finely tuned fuel injected sports car. She felt the power and strength between her thighs, the friction of her soft middle against the saddle when she sat down into a gallop, horse and rider swept up in a pulsing rhythm, a rosy glow creeping up her neck and a spasm of pleasure flooding through her body.

"Ouch! Jesus, Mary, my sweet, be careful, you could crack walnuts with those thighs."

"Sorry Steve, have I ridden you a bit too hard today? I'm sure you like it really."

Each time Steven left her she made sure he was happy and felt well compensated for his efforts. When she was in bed with Steven she felt a different woman, almost as though her body had been possessed by a different spirit. A year ago when she lost her deep trust in Mark she coped by self-medicating with alcohol. She found her relationship with the bottle unfulfilling as the emptiness inside her remained. She needed human contact and Steven the gardener, who became sensitive to her pain, offered her a service with no strings attached.

Their relationship began at a very low point in her life. It was after an office party, where she got very drunk, and met Jodie, the daughter of one of Mark's friends whom he had employed as his P.A. She was very sweet and good looking and she reminded Mary of how she was when she was younger. Mark had hardly mentioned her, but when he did he spoke highly of her work and commitment to the firm. It was something she learned from her women friends, who had observed a pattern in the choice of women their husbands had affairs with. In a conversation over tea and crumpets her friends explained that these women, chosen by men in their mid-life crisis, looked suspiciously like the way their wives looked when their husbands first desired and fell in love with them. This revelation pulled a veil from Mary's eyes as Jodie fitted this profile and her suspicions about Mark gathered speed.

Strange things happened after that evening at the office. For some unconscious reason she sought out a recording of a song that she first heard on the radio programme 'Desert Island Discs'. It was written and sung by Dorey Previn, and it was called 'Beware of Young Girls'. She found out that the lyrics of the song were written about Mia Farrow, an American television and film star who took Dorey's husband, Andre Previn, away from her. Her mother knew of the song and Mary discovered an old vinyl copy of the album in her record collection. Mary had no inkling of any infidelity in her mother's marriage but this song and others on the record seemed to affect her mother deeply. She visited her mother for tea and scones and put the record on the turntable. When there was a pause between tracks her mother spoke to Mary with the beginnings of tears in her eyes, and said;

"Darling I have always wanted the best for you, but now you have grown and lead your own life with Mark. I hope you will understand that real love comes with real pain, but the joy you will feel in the good times will make it all worthwhile. We always have our children."

Her mother, who was rarely demonstrative, got up out of her chair, sat down next to her, put her arms around her and hugged her for what seemed like an eternity. This rarely experienced expression of emotion between her mother and Mary became a moment she treasured. Mary was curious as to why her mother never listened to this music when her father was at home, but refrained from asking her. Perhaps she was frightened of what her mother might reveal and wanted to preserve the comforting recollections of her parenting that they both shared. Mary looked on the internet and discovered that Mia, eventually married Frank Sinatra and later Woody Allen? After listening to this record this song kept coming back to her, often when she was washing or cleaning her teeth. She had to buy the C.D. entitled, 'Mythical Kings and Iguanas' to record it on her iPhone player. There was another song on the album that she identified with entitled, 'Screaming in my Car'.

Mary took advice from the lyrics of this this song when driving home one day. It reminded her of an exercise she did in her self-awareness workshop. The tutor informed the class that they probably held a lot of their bodily tension in their shoulders and chin. This could be observed in each of the class participants by the way that they and others in general eat their food. The tutor then pretended to open a box and lift out of it an imaginary cake. He then went through the motions of cutting the cake into slices. The plate on which the cake sat was then passed from one group member to another and each of them were asked to take a bite from their slice of cake. In their imagination they could make the cake full of their most favourite ingredients and it could be made to their own special recipe. Mary imagined her mother's lemon drizzle cake because she was never allowed to eat as much of it as she wanted. When the cake came to her she wanted to open her mouth so wide that she could be in danger of dislocating her jaw, but when she glimpsed the others looking at her she changed her mind and took what she thought was a ladylike mouthful. When each person in the group had taken their turn they were asked to describe their cake and what associations the cake held for them. Then what went through their minds while the cake was getting closer to them and what influenced the way they bit into the cake. Mary found this discussion very informative. Why didn't she open her mouth wide and gobble up the cake? Only one person bit off more than they could chew and started choking. Some didn't open their mouth wide at all and seem to nibble round the edges. Some did not give the impression that the cake was at all appetizing, and kept their mouths tightly shut, as if there was a bad smell under their nose. The tutor then asked them if in their lives they felt they swallowed things whole, chewed them over, or spat them out. One of the ladies said she thought she took take large mouthfuls, overindulged and then ended up throwing it all up. The facilitator then asked the group to apply their insights to other areas of their life and relationships to see if it resonated as a metaphor for how they engaged with life. At this point one of the quietest and prim looking members of the group put her hand up to get the teacher's attention.

"Yes Jane, you have something you would like to say?"

"Does this include our sex lives?"

This concluded the workshop and they all went home tired but intrigued.

After the workshop Mary found herself noticing how closed or open her mouth was or how stiff her neck seemed to be, in various situations. For some reason, this often happened when she was driving in her car alone. One day while she was stationary at a traffic light she realised that the muscles in her shoulders and neck were tight, and her teeth were clenched. She tried to relieve this tension by opening her mouth as wide as she could and moving her jaw from side to side while at the same time making a loud "Aaah!" sound as if she was at the doctors. Then she thought of the person that was stressing her the most at that time. She began swearing and screaming at this person out loud, using the foulest language in her vocabulary. Mary was like the person in the song sitting alone in her car screaming. Then she happened to look to her right and realised that her window was wound down, and so was the window of the man in the car next to her. He was having a cigarette while waiting for the lights to change and was staring straight at her with his mouth wide open. At that moment the traffic lights changed and she put her foot down on the accelerator and drove away from the traffic lights as fast as she could.

Chapter Five: David

David hated golf. David loved golf. Standing on the 17th tee at Chapel Hill golf course waiting to take his shot, with the wind swirling around him, he smiled to himself as he thought of the famous writer who was quoted as believing that a round of golf was a nice walk spoiled. It was his turn to tee off and so he bent down to put his favourite tee into the turf between the blue marker blocks, and placed his favourite ball on top of it. He had played the entire round without losing this tee or ball, and he hoped this was a good omen for performing well on this hole. David had often thought that golf was a game that lent itself to those who were susceptible to obsessional thought and behaviour. Tennis players, darts players, footballers had the same susceptibility and could be observed giving in to superstition and ritual, in the vain hope that conjuring up their own magic would influence the random and uncontrollable variables that dictate the outcome of their actions. Tennis players could be seen to pull their shirt up off a particular shoulder and bounce the tennis ball a specific number of times before serving over the net. Darts players may pull an ear lobe and close their eyes a certain number of times before throwing their dart at the board. Footballers may insist on wearing a shirt with a specific number or could be observed crossing themselves and kissing the medallion they wore a specific number of times as they run on to the football pitch. David's golfing ritual was to put his golf shoes on in the same order before each round of golf. He used the same pitch marker that he had in his pocket when he played his best ever round of golf while on holiday in La Manga with the lads. He made sure that he wore the watch that his wife gave him for their wedding anniversary because he felt that this kept her close to him and helped to steady his nerves when he looked at it. David did not feel that these affectations were behaviours extreme enough to worry about and if he forgot one of them he did not have a panic attack over it, but in a game where chance played such a part these rituals gave him comfort. David empathised with others who also felt in the grip of a powerful fear of the randomness of what life might throw at them. Perhaps golf was a stupid metaphor to use, but it helped him understand how sensitive people who had been subject to unpredictable events like attacks to their safety, separation or loss, invent rituals and mind controlling thoughts in the hope of protecting themselves and their loved ones. For them it was like praying.

They had probably discovered to their cost that the good are not necessarily blessed with a long life and the bad a short one. David felt that no matter what we did the gods could still be unimpressed with our efforts. They will enjoy gambling with our lives, playing snakes and ladders with our emotions. Destiny will be determined by a random throw of the dice and to add to their pleasure the gods will not tell us the score. They leave us to discover for ourselves if we go up or slide down the slippery ladder of life.

David had the belief that no matter what the game of golf and the game of life were better played with honesty. He could not control the honesty of others but he could his own. Players had to trust each other to be honest about their scores, and trustworthy in competition. For David golf is a game of integrity and looks badly upon those who cheat the rules. Accidental hits or misses had to be declared, as did losing a ball because of a wayward swing of the club. Competitors must resist the temptation to miraculously find their ball, by secretly dropping another one where the first one should be. If they were devious enough players could, have a hole in their trouser pocket through which they could drop a ball, and let it run down the leg of their trousers to accomplish this objective. David had suspected this of some of his competitors but it had been proved to him many times over that no player benefited from this practice in the long run as they were only fooling themselves. Ultimately the self-esteem and respect to be gained from their fellow players would be sacrificed on the altar of winning. David knew he could not handle the guilt that this kind of deceit would cause, and it would haunt him to the point where all pleasure he took from the game would go. To this end he only carried one ball in his pocket, clearly marked with his symbol, an alligator.

He would no more cheat at golf than provide false accounts for his business, or fiddle his tax returns. He had never stolen anything, with the exception of one lapse somewhere between the ages of twelve to fourteen when his sexual hormones took control of his mind and body. This was a time in his pubescent life when he could get an erection while riding on a number twelve bus from the town to his home. Once he had to miss his bus stop because it would have been too embarrassing for him to stand up from his seat. Fortunately he was wearing a large pullover that he pulled down over his thighs to hide the bulge in his trousers and avoid embarrassment.

The one lapse he remembered was when he was on holiday with his parents and with the pocket money he had been given he went to buy a novel from a bookshop near where they were staying. He found a book by an author called Harold Robbins called, 'The Carpet Baggers' which on reading the blurb on the back cover and flicking through the pages, promised some arousing sexual episodes between its covers. He was too embarrassed to go to the counter to buy the book because of his age, his tendency to blush and the fact that the person behind the counter was an attractive young woman. He took the book from the shelf and hid it under his arm beneath his summer jacket. Looking straight ahead he walked out of the shop. By this time he was sweating and fuelled by a mixture of fear and excitement his heart was pounding. He walked away from the shop for about twenty five yards along the pavement and stood still, his mind racing. He had to come to terms with the enormity of what he had done, and he felt so guilty and ashamed of himself and his actions. He could not go through with this; he had to make it right. He turned around and walked back to the shop, went in, smiled at the girl behind the counter, hoping she would not see the drops of perspiration dripping from his eyebrows, made his way to the book stand and as swiftly as he could, without being seen, put the book back on the shelf from whence it came.

David had been terrified of doing anything wrong and giving in to his impulses ever since he attended the church Sunday school. One day at the Sunday school the priest announced to the class that they should be careful what they did because "God sees everything, even in the dark!"

David was anxious from that moment on. Suddenly there was no place to hide, no secrets, no privacy from this all 'Seeing Eye'. When he got older he could understand why some people suffering from paranoia might be driven to wrap themselves in tin foil, and put protective hats on their head to stop unwanted powers entering their mind.

However if he learned anything good about the Christian God from Sunday school it was that God, and mostly Jesus was also about forgiveness. His adult life had taught him that one evil act does not an evil man, or woman, make. He realised that this world can be kind and it can be cruel, that sometimes he could be wise but sometimes a fool. We can redeem ourselves from our foolishness. One of the things in the present he would seek forgiveness for was his foolish decision to introduce his daughter Jodie to Mark Finch, one of his golfing friends. He had discovered to his cost that Mark could not be trusted. Mark's morality was questionable as was his honesty.

On some days, probably when they were bored, the gods of golf played with your head on nearly every shot. The only consolation to the mere mortals of the golfing world was that the best golfers in the world who practiced every day and hit a thousand balls on the practice range can be humbled by the fate that awaits them on the golf course. In golf as in life chance and luck had a big influence on the direction your life could take. So many religions sold themselves to their followers by promising to give them access to a divine power that could influence their destiny.

David gave up his religious faith a long time ago, he no longer believed in a divine power that punished or rewarded people for showing devotion to it. David believed that destiny was created by the choices that we made or avoided making. It was obvious to him that we cannot choose everything as much is determined by the accident of our birth. Who we are born to, what we looked like and what gender we were. However much of what we become is the sum of our choices. He wasn't too sure about illness. Illness could be the product of wrong choices but not all of them. What he was convinced about was that illness could not be cured by religion and prayer, and he loved no God that inflicted pain on young babies and children who had not lived long enough to deserve such punishment. Illness could only be cured by brilliantly educated doctors and nurses having the resources, the creativity and scientific knowledge to heal the sick. He did not always believe this. He wanted to believe in magic, he loved magicians and magic tricks and being amazed by what he saw. On two of his birthdays, his parents employed a magician to perform at his party. At a relatives wedding reception, he witnessed close up card tricks first hand and this increased his sense of wonder of the illusion that this magician created. For his childhood self, Jesus was a magician who performed miracles. David's grandiose self, the unfettered soul inside him, did not wish to be constrained by the limited abilities of his human body and mind. He needed to believe in the possibility of something greater. When he was young his parents sent him to church to get religion, every Sunday morning, and for a short while he was in his church choir. He was terrified of the Choir Master because he shouted at the choristers who failed to follow the music parts written for them. David was not proficient at sight reading and so he was often the target of this choir masters ridicule. The boys had to call him, 'Master Bates', which was hard for the pubescent boys to say and keep a straight face. David left the choir after singing the solo part in 'We Three Kings' at a Christmas carol service. He was praised for his effort but felt that the joy and fun he had from singing had vanished. When he thought about his time in the church now, he was suspicious about his parent's motives. He used to imagine that they probably got rid of him, each week, so they could have sex on a Sunday morning and indulge in a different kind of human worship. Little did he know?

His scepticism about the power of prayer and a belief in miracles gained ground when he witnessed what happened with a colleague he knew through work. She thought she would never get married, but she met a quantity surveyor whom she fell in love with and they got married. She didn't want children and devoted herself to her new found happiness with her partner. Only three years after they married he was diagnosed with leukaemia, and they were devastated. They went through all manner of treatments and various specialists but the N.H.S could do no more. They began praying with a friend of theirs who was a devoted Christian and they were both baptised, and held on to the lifeline of divine intervention. They went to a healing ministry that existed in Suffolk and he went up to the priest to have a 'laying on of hands', and be healed. They found some consolation in this activity as they were doing something to fight off the inevitable, and prolong the time left to them. They then heard of a mystic, shamanistic healer in Mexico, and used their savings to go out to his clinic on the outskirts of Mexico City. They stayed there for two months and for a while it seemed her husband's life improved. They came back to England and within six months he was dead. David went through this living nightmare of a journey with her as she shared with him her worst fears and greatest hopes. Many days and evenings spent with her in coffee shops or walking in a park as a shoulder to cry on when each new hope for treatment faded. He raised money for her by organising a charity match at the golf club which gave her some financial assistance to return to Mexico and buy what was needed. He went to the funeral. He decided there and then to give money to cancer research on a regular basis because his faith was now invested in the search for new knowledge and scientific discovery. Scientists became his God of life. It was a hard for his friend to recover from the trauma of her loss and initially she sold the home she and her husband shared together and moved out of the area. About a year later he received a letter from her letting him know her new address and telling him that she had found consolation and happiness again with a woman partner whom she had fallen in love with. She had found no magical solution to the illness of her husband but her hurt had a chance of being eased by this new love in her life. David often imagined what the impact of medical discovery would have been on past generations. All the people who died from infection before penicillin was available would marvel at its power. They would have witnessed a miracle performed by humans and what a magician their doctors would have seemed to them.

At this moment in David's round of golf he realised that he needed a manmade miracle to get the ball on the green and near the pin. The wind had got up and was blowing from right to left which meant that on this island golf hole surrounded by water, his ball could drift on the air and fall into the 'drink'. He chose a '9' iron from his golf bag, as with his swing it should propel the ball about 130 yards over the water and land softly onto the putting surface. He took aim, settled his stance, focused on the back of the ball, swung the club, made sure he followed through with his hips and ended his swing with his belt buckle facing the pin. When he looked up the ball was in the air on its way to the green, and Des the person standing near to him, shouted; "Great shot, straight at it!" At that moment the god of weather decided to intervene and from his right came a gust of wind. The ball seemed to be held in the air by some invisible hand, pushed sideways to his left, and dropped to the ground like a stone. The ball could have dropped into the water with a splash but instead it landed on the semi rough grass to the left edge of the green about fifteen feet away from the flag. The gods of golf had decided, in that split second, to be kind to David. Then he chipped the ball onto the green and putted it in a straight line towards the hole. The ball did a lap of honour around the cup and then dropped into the hole. They left the seventeenth green and walked on the path to the eighteenth tee. David hit a good drive landing the ball to the right of the tree a third of the way down the fairway. This shot set him up to hit a three wood aimed to the left of the final green where it would roll down a slope to the pin. One chip and a put and his round would be over. All that was left was to check his score with his partners, put his golf bag on the rack ready for him to take to his car, and then take a short walk to into the clubhouse bar and a refreshing glass of red wine. The walk between golf shots gave David plenty of time to think about the next shot he would play and the next choice of club he would use, but it also gave time for his mind to wander to other things that concerned him and that demanded his attention. On a round that lasted four and a half hours he often found himself dipping in and out of being present on the golf course. He would often find himself thinking of work or other scenarios and having private conversations with himself or others in his head. In many ways he preferred to play squash because there was little time to think between shots and his mind was kept occupied, whereas with golf there was time to think and reflect.

Soon in the club bar, after dissecting the round with his golfing buddies, talking about the shots that got away, the great escapes from misfortune, the putts and chips that were sunk from great distance on tricky greens, any doubts he had about his ability and his love for the game faded. Before they all left for home, they made an arrangement to repeat the same heroic adventure the following week.

David's golf buddies were a collection of guys from different occupations, backgrounds and education, and who had joined the club at different times. Depending on work and family commitments they all took part in the 'Saturday Swindle' as they called it. They all played on Saturday morning at 8.30, put £10 in the kitty and then had partners chosen at random with a mix of handicaps enabling them to play with a variety of members. Whoever came into the clubhouse with the lowest score won the money in the kitty and bought the drinks and snacks for the others participating in the competition. The regular players in the swindle were, Steven the gardener, a young man in good physical shape, who worked for himself, and also did David's odd jobs around his house. Steven was a good golfer who had played since he was a teenager. Mark, who worked in the City, was a partner in his own publishing firm. Phil, a local builder who was known for his excellent extensions, had the nick name 'Trigger'. When David joined the Swindle, he had asked how he got this name and the gardener Steven explained. "You see he likes, 'Only Fools and Horses'. Do you know that programme? Anyway remember there's this bloke called 'Trigger' that 'Del Boy' knows. Phil looks a bit like him and he can be a bit of an idiot sometimes, so he's a bit of a 'donkey'? Then one of the lads saw him coming out of the shower in the changing room and said he was built like a horse, well that was it, the name 'Trigger' stuck. Sometimes, to piss him off, we call him Roy or Roger, but he never gets it."

Then there were the Milligan brothers who had considerable wealth. David found them fascinating and generous, but a bit of an enigma. He put together details about their life from snatched conversations with each of them, and information given him by Mark Finch.

The remaining members of the Swindle group included Reginald, an engineer who once worked on oil rigs in the North Sea. He was widowed as his wife died from cancer. Des, who worked on a national newspaper buying photographs from the Paparazzi, and who, based on his consumption of alcohol, was training to drink for England. Lastly there is Danny who was a manager in the health service until he was made redundant and now works for a drug company selling them to the N.H.S. Danny, proud of his northern roots is married and is a keep fit fanatic. No matter what the weather or course condition throws at him, he insists on carrying his golf bag and refuses to use a golf trolley or buggy as, "They are for the old farts!"

All of these men loved golf in their own way and were serious competitors, but never lost sight of the social friendship and comradery that membership of this group gave them. David couldn't help but think that it was like being back at school with his gang of schoolmates. Some openly admitted that they preferred male company because relationships were less complicated. Over half of the guys went to all boy schools, some to private school, where women and girls were perceived as an alien race. David, whose closest friend was his wife, often felt the odd one out. However the group had experienced some great golfing holidays together. They all agreed that stories of drunken exploits, schoolboy pranks and other improprieties would not be talked about to others outside of the group when they got home. This secrecy formed a bond between them, becoming the stuff of legend and group myth. The swindle travelled all over the world to play golf on courses in fantastic locations such as Thailand, America, South Africa, Cyprus and Spain. They found that in most of these locations sex was a commodity. Where to go to find this trade became shared knowledge amongst the golfing fraternity of travellers. The Milligan brothers had collated a trip advisors guide to the best locations. In certain bars and clubs at home and abroad women swarmed around men on these vacations like bees around a honey pot. When they visited Marbella, in the south of Spain, some of the girls in the well-known Nautical Navy Club were local, but most were Russian, eastern European, or Brazilian. All were there to use their bodily asset's to make money and flatter men's egos. That tourist's with money, free from the fear of sexually transmitted infections, and a sweet tooth for sex, discovered that these places where like a sexual candy shop. On their plane trip to Thailand the Milligan brothers handed all of them an envelope. In the envelope was a card with a picture of one of their porn channel 'stars' on the front. When they opened their card, inside they found two hundred pounds of Thai currency and four Viagra tablets, with the inscription, 'Enjoy yourself it's later than you think!'

It was in these moments when David often felt at odds with the attitudes of his golf buddies. The maleness of the golf club and the behaviour of his golf buddies away from home was a throw-back to a different era. He wanted his daughter to grow up in a less sexist, more modern and equal world. Not the one they inhabited. When they were together there existed a crudity about the opposite sex that belonged in a school or a factory floor at a time when there was a greater division between the sexes than the world outside of golf they now inhabited. This attitude was accompanied by an active disapproval of political correctness when it came to the language they used about women or those from different cultures. If he 'shaved the hole' with a putt he still might be called a gynaecologist. He found it quite funny for the first time but the joke quickly wore thin. None of it was said with malice. This group subculture bound them together and to be one of the lads David went along with it. He was given the nickname 'Smiler' because he rarely laughed at crude texts or video clips sent to his mobile phone and often didn't open them. He didn't hold it against them or believe that any of the lads would behave with a lack of respect to his wife or daughter, or their own wives or girlfriends; if they were present. It simply reasserted old ways and attitudes at a time when the balance of power between men and women was being renegotiated. Like David, and perhaps all male children who began life depending on their mothers, they were born on the cross of the love they seek.

Of course David had no idea if when female golfers were alone and separate from the company of men, they spoke or behaved in the same way? He might soon find out because his wife Claire had decided to have golfing lessons at the club. She told David that she was fed up of being a golfing widow and wanted something that they could enjoy together. When she felt skilled enough, and had gained an official handicap, she wanted to go on a golfing holiday, staying in a good Hotel with a Spa. Recently she had joined forces with a group of women club members who played regularly on a Thursday. David was self-aware enough to know that he was no angel and could also be sexist, it was in his D.N.A to objectify women some of the time. Women were not innocent in this regard and they behaved the same way at 'Hen Parties' with male strippers and the like.

David had to be true to himself and tried to be consistent and congruent in his values and behaviour. His dislike of crudity went back to his school days, half of which he spent in an all-boys school. On the bus coming home after a schoolboy rugby or football match and listening to the popular boys with girlfriends boasting about how 'far' they had got in touching them made him cringe. He didn't want to admit to himself that perhaps his time spent at church and in Sunday school had made a bigger impact on him than he thought. He wasn't naïve enough to think that crude behaviour was the sole prerogative of boys, but girls who swore or talked dirty were not attractive to him. However a shadow side of him wanted what naughty girls might offer. His limited experience with nice decent girls, whom he dated from the girls' school next door, had taught him that they didn't mind kissing, but would not allow him to explore their body as much as he wanted to. They certainly didn't want to explore his.

When he was fifteen a friend of David's in the basketball team broke up with his girlfriend. David liked her and after about a week he thought he would ask her out. David remembered his friend confiding in him that his girlfriend rode horses and winked at him; it obviously had some significance which was lost on David because he had never been on a horse and had no intention of having riding lessons. His hope was that she was more sexually 'experienced' than David and wasn't shy about showing off her body. David knew from what his friend had intimated that he and she had, 'got up to something'. Her friend Christine agreed to give her a message he wrote asking her to meet him at the entrance to the local park at 7pm. Full of anticipation and with a box of chocolates in his hand he waited by the gate. She did not arrive at seven. An hour later, David walked home alone. Next day she was back in a relationship with his friend. David felt as if he had been kicked in the stomach. However, within a year he heard that she had to leave school prematurely because it was said that she was suffering from anaemia. He never renewed his friendship with the basketball player who also mysteriously left school in the middle of the lower sixth. David was informed by his mother's cleaner, who also happened to clean for the basketballer's family that he had got his girlfriend pregnant. David felt lucky.

He gradually realised that a lot of his guilt about sex came from his mother. He desperately wanted his mother's approval and often had to care for her when she was ill and his father was at work. Once, when he sat by her bed mopping her forehead with a cold flannel because she was suffering from a high temperature, she told him something he wished she had not confided. She probably thought she was offering him advice but it made David anxious.

"David, there is a responsibility, a duty, in marriage that every woman has to endure. You can't help it, you are a man. It is a sacrifice I made for the sake of my marriage and affection of your father. I never wanted to get pregnant but in a moment of weakness I gave in. I am glad I did because I had you but David don't expect too much, you know, in the future."

David wondered if she was a bit delirious.

"I said to your father that if ever I got pregnant again I will put my head in the gas oven. David, be sure to control yourself because should you get a girl pregnant before you are married, God help you!"

He had no idea that his parents were not happy together. After this conversation with his mother, if he saw them hold hands or occasionally kiss in front of him, he couldn't help but feel sorry for his father. Did his father know of the emptiness of his mother's emotions behind her painted smile?

David also wondered if he had been strongly affected by the fairy tale of the 'Beauty and the Beast'. It was a story his mother read to him a number of times when he was a young child. When he got older he discovered that in the original Grimm's fairy tale the man who was transformed into the Beast was being punished by a witch for satisfying his sexual desire on a young girl who had wandered into the forest. Somehow David got the message that being a sexual creature was ugly and beast like. However, in this fairy tale the beasts animalistic impulses become transformed by the love, acceptance and understanding of a courageous, young, pure, virginal woman.

When testosterone started playing havoc with David's body, he could not ignore his biological destiny. His voice dropped, his hair grew, and his face erupted in spots. He blushed in the presence of girls he was attracted to, and he woke up with rock hard erections. At night alone in the darkness of his bedroom, he was forced to give in to the pressing demand of his engorged organ straining against the front of his pyjamas and quickly brought himself to an explosive orgasm under the bedcovers. He wiped himself clean, flushed the evidence down the toilet, checked the bottom sheet to make sure no evidence of his activity would be found by his mother, and only then he could allow himself to relax and fall asleep. While he rested his head on the pillow waiting to drift away he would pray. He began with the Lord's Prayer. He hoped that this might open a communication with any saint listening. He needed to ask for forgiveness, and some help. Despite being a teenager being made ugly and beastly by his developing lust and pulsing sexual desire he desperately needed to find a woman like 'beauty' in the fable. This woman could enjoy and accept this ugly part of him. Then, with a love and desire equal in power to his, transform him into a prince. David had no way of knowing at this time that it would take him seventeen years and more than one princess to achieve his goal. When he found 'the one', she became his wife, and the mother of his children.

David's first sexual experience at nineteen was initiated by a girl that he met at a party who could not understand why he was not all over her, and literally led him to a vacant bedroom. It seemed odd to David that as he was about to make love for the first time the warning voice of his mother was in his head. It was this relationship that began his sexual education. It liberated him from some of the guilt his mother had instilled. They stayed together for a year. However it ended after she went on holiday to Spain with her girlfriends. Influenced by the warmth of the sun, copious amounts of alcohol and the promiscuous behaviour of her girlfriends, she cheated on him with a Spanish waiter. He was so hurt by her betrayal that he could not forgive her, even though she begged him to. He did not have another relationship for a year. He did not hate her, but remembered their time together with warmth and affection. She had given him his window in the sky.

David was not totally innocent of objectifying women. His thoughts were encouraged to lean towards those of his golfing mates. These days, it often occurred while watching a female golf tournament on the television, particularly if they were American. He could not help but to initially focus on the women's legs and figures and how sexy they looked in their short skirts with their hair up and threaded through the back of their golf hat. He fantasised about what it would be like to touch their tanned thighs, plant soft kisses on their bare neck below their pony tail, slowly undress them, and then massage their aching body with scented oil before making love. Once that initial response was out of the way he could concentrate on their golf game. A popular myth spread by envious men about female tennis players and golfers was that a lot of them were gay. Perhaps this thinly evidenced assertion was the product of a schoolboy fantasy about what they hoped might be happening in their showers and changing rooms. All this deviance could be put right as some men believed by a good 'seeing to'. One night spent with a 'real man' would cause any lipstick lesbian to change her sexual preference. Fortunately David wasn't stupid or arrogant enough now to believe in such nonsense but once in the past he was tempted to try.

Before he married Claire, he had a work colleague and drinking partner who was a female quantity surveyor, and whom he found very attractive. They frequently went out for drinks after work and got on very well together. On one such evening, after consuming a reasonable amount of alcohol, David plucked up the courage to tell her how he felt about her and ask her out on a date. She put down her drink, kissed him on the cheek, took his hand in hers and said; "David you are a sweet man and I appreciate what you just said, we have so much fun together and I can talk to you about most things, but you need to know, I need to tell you, that I like men, but I don't want to have sex with them."

David was not exactly sure what she was saying,

"I'm sorry; I didn't mean to be pushy. I don't want to pry but did something happen, were you hurt by a man?"

She briefly looked away, and then looking him in the eyes, in a calm and caring voice she continued speaking. "No it isn't that. I know some women turn away from men after some hurt or trauma, some of us come to hate and fear men. That's not me. In my life I have never tried to be straight, and I am not a tattoo wearing, beer drinking feminist. To be honest, like you, I just fancy the bits that women have, not the ones you've got to offer. Sorry David, please don't feel too rejected."

For a moment David did not know how to respond. He did feel a little bit hurt and rejected because he had hoped that something more than friendship could develop between them and he had felt exposed telling her of his feelings for her. He felt stupid for not suspecting that she felt this way towards women and up to this point had kept this part of her life secret from him.

He let go of her hand and took a handkerchief out of his trouser pocket and started to dab his eyes as if he was beginning to cry.

She had a look of concern on her face, and put her arm on his shoulder. "Oh David I'm sorry I..."

David lowered his handkerchief and she could see he was not crying but smiling.

"So, you know those bits that you have, I don't suppose you'd let me have a go at changing your mind?"

"David you're terrible!" and she punched him on his arm, forcefully enough to make him wince slightly.

They remained friends, and she came to his wedding, but work and life events caused them to see less and less of each other over time. David spent a lot of his time commuting to London from Kent. Often it was to meet financiers and property developers. They would invite him for lunch at the Bucks Club in Clifford Street or the Garrick Club with it's fabulous art collection, in the heart of the West end. Both of which were gentlemen only establishments. On these journeys he would wear earphones to block out the sounds in the carriage and listen to the music of Mozart. He hoped that this would also discourage any commuter sharing the small first class area of the carriage from beginning a conversation with him. David looked out of the window at the scenery flashing by and allowed his mind to wander. Perhaps it was because by chance rather than design he had spent a lot more time at work in the company of men rather than women that he became fascinated by issues of gender equality. He and Claire cared deeply about their daughter Jodie and were concerned for her future. David knew that the 'glass ceiling' women complained about did exist and attitudes in the board room about women often mirrored those in the wider society. David knew quite a lot about Jodie's current employer and worried that she may experience the same narrow prejudice. The clubs he visited for meetings with his business associates shared similar restrictions to some golf clubs. These golf clubs resisted the equal membership of women and if they were not barred completely, restricted the times they could play. He didn't know if women only golf clubs existed and applied the same rules to men. After all, David was aware of whole countries where men and women were still segregated in many areas of those societies. David could accept that this could be a good thing for both men and women as it offered them an opportunity to be themselves without the prying eyes and interference of the opposite sex. Arab friends of his believed that this segregation of men and women on trains and buses, or in school and work protected the women. Attractive successful women who were hidden from men's gaze could be protected from unwanted attention and could not be accused of using their sexuality to gain favours and rise to the top within their work place.

David felt that this argument was different from one based on an idea of biological inferiority and superiority. He'd read somewhere that women's brains are wired differently, or that they speak in a different voice, but so what. He had educated his daughter Jodie to be a strong independent woman who was able to survive without a man and not believe that her fate was determined by her biology. David and Claire wanted to give her the best start possible and so they looked at the research available on the achievements of girls attending mixed or single sex schools and it seemed obvious to them that a single sex school would offer Jodie the best chance of doing well. They chose Bedgebury Private School for girls in Cranbrook. Jodie integrated in to her class from the very beginning and soon made friends. David did worry that the love and attention her mother Claire gave to him might give her the wrong impression of the role she should play in life. He tried to share stories with Jodie about her mother in the early days of their marriage when she helped in his fledgling business and encouraged Claire to do the same. In those very important early years her mother was a formidable woman, enterprising partner and excellent organiser. She could get on with all the people on a building site from the labourer and brick layer to the architect and project manager. Without her dedication and support their business would not have pushed through the hard times and achieved the lifestyle that Jodie now enjoyed. He didn't know, and had not asked if Claire had shared with Jodie the sadness and trauma of her two miscarriages, or the desperate, lonely, terrifying, and heart breaking journey's she made by emergency ambulance to the hospital. One of these devastating losses happened while David was on a golfing trip with business associates, and the other happened when his homecoming train to Marden was unnecessarily delayed because of leaves on the track. These emotionally wounding experiences, which both of them shared, had a sobering effect on him. He had to accept that despite being the expectant father and caught up in the euphoria of this, he was still ultimately an outsider when it came to Claire's pregnancy. It was as if in the act of making her pregnant he had given something away, and from that moment it was hers to carry. He hadn't told Claire about this feeling, but it was Claire who endured these physical and psychological sensations within her body. When the loss of the babies happened and this connection was broken it was she alone that felt a deep pain within her. David had cried, took a short time off work to be with her and they tried to find some ritual they could enact to help with their grief, but soon he had to return to work for the sake of his business.

After this happened Claire's commitment to work changed and they decided that they would do everything humanly possible to preserve her next pregnancy. The mixture of joy and trepidation they felt when she became pregnant with Jodie was something people would have to experience to understand. David employed both a secretary and a cleaner to make sure she would not be stressed. He limited his work schedule to make sure he was at home around the time of the due date. Their daughter Jodie was delivered by caesarean section one week premature and immediately she became their pride and joy.

On a Friday night standing at the bar of his local alehouse with three pints of beer inside him, he would listen to the assembled locals and regular drinkers argue about these issues. On rare occasions he took the risk of sharing his views on topics that fed their predisposed attitudes and prejudices, but if he did do this he was most likely to be at odds with the majority opinion. Some of the regulars had worked abroad in Arab countries and did not think much of 'Rag Heads' as they named the locals. Nor did they appreciate the flood of immigrants from Eastern Europe who had replaced those from the Indian continent as the focus of their disapproval. But despite disagreeing with their views he could admire the consistency of their prejudice towards foreigners, people of colour, 'do-gooder's' and the simplicity of their argument. Interestingly, these blinkered views, did not encompass those they were familiar with and who served them in the local shops or restaurants. Sharon the wife of the village postmaster who was downing her fourth Gin and Tonic grabbed David's arm to stop him speaking.

"David, my dear man, let's face it, blacks are better at running. Look at the British athletic squad, my God look at the women, they hardly wear any Lycra and the men leave nothing to the imagination. You tell me a good white boxer. Come on, if I want a decent bit of gold or a diamond I go to a Jewish shop, they run Hatton Garden. The last time I had the bathroom done I had Polish plumbers, and they worked so hard. I went to the Hospital the other week and saw this doctor and I couldn't understand what he said to me. He might be good but he couldn't bloody well speak English!"

David did not want to argue with Sharon and so he nodded his head in agreement and signalling to Max the barman to order another drink; "Let me get you another G and T?"

It was not uncommon that one of his golf buddies, Reginald, would come off the mobile phone after talking to his wife and turn to him and say, "Women, you can't live with them and you can't live without them! Marriage! You only get fifteen years for murder!" Reginald and his wife had a routine established in the week where he would go to the local pub each night after work and get home in time for his evening meal to be served to him. Saturday and Sundays were exceptions to the routine as he played golf and they visited their children and grandchildren or her parents.

"My wife is addicted to cooking programmes on the television in the same way that people get addicted to watching porn on the internet. She watches them doing all sorts of amazing things but she doesn't try it at home. Don't get me wrong I love her to bits and she is a home maker. She cleans, decorates, does the garden, knits, sews, watches soaps and reads. She doesn't like any sport on the T.V apart from Wimbledon in the summer. In that respect she is amazing, and I tell her that she can watch what she likes on the television while I am at work or at the pub but when I get home we see what I want to see."

David smiled and nodded, as if in agreement, but in truth it was a sentiment that David did not share. Why didn't they buy another television? Neither was he totally convinced, that behind all of his bluster, Reginald fully agreed with it either. It was as if Reginald needed David to hear him complain. After all, a man with such strong opinions of what men and women could or should do in a relationship would not wish David to know that he occasionally depended on his wife, and therefore did not always have the upper hand. Reginald valued the concept of family and would do the best he could for them. Recently David overheard him in conversation with a young man called Nick who was a regular drinker in the pub. He was about thirty years old and worked for himself buying and selling this and that. He had a young wife with a small baby at home whom the regulars rarely saw. This particular Saturday night it was about eight in the evening and the young man had been in the pub for an hour. This was long enough to consume enough draught beer to show signs of 'being a bit pissed'. He had heavy eyelids with slightly blood shot eyes, and a lost look on his face. He had begun to slur his words.

"Reginald, I need to off load some stuff. Do you know anyone who might be in the market for it? I've got a garage full of bits; look some of it's not bad." Nick got out his mobile and thumbed through some pictures to show Reginald a couple of choice items.

"Not really Nick, I can ask around, but anyway, is that Chinese on the floor there yours, in that bag?"

"Yeah it's a Saturday night take away."

"Mate, I bet that's cold by now. Your missus will be wondering where you are. Why don't you take that home to her and the little one?"

"Yes, mate, you're probably right I should go, yeah I should go, but, time flies. I'm a dad now you know, but they don't come with instructions. Anyway I hate mess and the place looks like a wreck, but what does that matter. I don't think he needs his daddy when he's got his mum and she's probably crashed out on the sofa by now."

Nick reached for his car keys which were resting on the bar in front of him. He leant down to pick up his plastic bag from the floor but he overbalanced and nearly fell forward. He straightened up and slowly headed for the door of the pub. Reginald put his pint of beer down on the bar and quickly caught up to him at the door.

"Why don't I give you a lift home, we don't want anything to happen to you and your dear lady wouldn't forgive us. It's on my way and you can pick your car up in the morning."

David looked through the pub window and watched the pair weave their way through the parked cars to where Reginald's Range Rover stood. He wondered why Nick chose to spend time with drinking acquaintances in the pub than be with his wife and child who really cared for him. Nick was a young man who liked the company of 'the lads' and was finding it difficult to integrate sharing time with his wife and baby into his old lifestyle. From what David had witnessed in the pub he seemed to be mourning the past rather than embracing the possibilities available in the present. Nick didn't seem convinced that the joy possible in this new phase of his life was worth him letting go of the old one. David had been married for well over fifteen years, and it was a commitment he had entered into willingly, he didn't see marriage as a sentence to be served.

In quiet moments sitting alone or standing at the bar with either a pint of beer or a large glass of red wine in his hand he thought about this sense of imprisonment that some men felt about marriage. When David got married it was as if a door had been opened for him rather than a cell door being slammed shut. David did not have time to read novels but he was an avid reader of quality Sunday papers as well as some of the sociology text books that Jodie brought home from school. David knew from this research that despite the woman's liberation movement in the 60's and 70's, changes in the law and improved access to education for men and women in both America and England, it was still a reality that men were conditioned to look after their wife and children, and be expected to work until they dropped dead.

Sharon, who propped up the bar at the Style Bridge at least four nights a week, was not a woman David would associate with feminism but she was vociferous in her dislike of those that lived on benefits. In her slightly inebriated state she would tell David why.

"I tell you David, not that I frequent McDonalds willingly, accept with my dear old mother who loves 'Happy Meals' and collects the figures for her mantelpiece, last week it was Mario. My point is that you see them all there at a lunch time with their prams. God knows how they can afford them but they gather together, just left school with babies and no doubt given a flat. No fathers, probably because they don't give a shit, pardon my language, and would have to get a bloody job to look after the little one and their stupid girlfriends. Not the same for those lazy cows, they have everything given to them on a plate and get to lay down on the job!"

David could not deny that there might be some truth in what Sharon said. David didn't agree with this kind of behaviour but he could understand how it occurred. The last time David was in the waiting room of his dentist preparing for his six monthly check-up he picked up the 'Psychology's' magazine and read an article about the rise in teenage pregnancies. The psychotherapist who wrote the article expressed the view that for some girls who have little interest in further education and have limited job prospects, getting pregnant became a career choice. State benefits secured them an income and also the possibility of being housed. This was dependent on proving that they could not stay at home with their parents due to limited space or irreconcilable differences. Pregnancy gave them a readymade status in life and a purpose which fulfilled their biological destiny. Men on the other hand did not have this choice available to them. They were men without a womb and so they had to work for a living to gain status and survive in the economic jungle.

Men who fathered children did not complete their destiny by the act of insemination.

David could imagine that if the Titanic sank in the present day and there were limited spaces in the lifeboats it would still be the men who would be expected to sacrifice themselves to save the women and children. That was what men were expected to do for women as part of this traditional bargain. In many countries and within many subcultures, women were still taught to be sexually available, subservient, unpaid servants to their husbands. Biology dictated that women gave birth to children, fed them and were expected look after them. However if they didn't die from complications in childbirth they still lived longer than men. There were still many societies around the globe where men and women continued to see each other as the enemy. Where this attitude prevailed then David understood how it became inevitable for one gender to try to dominate the other by using whatever weapons they had at their disposal. Neither sex wanted to be like the fly stuck in a spider's web having the life juices sucked out of them until they became a dry husk. To survive they had to dominate those they were frightened of and who might use them. David could not deny that there were some evil men and women out there in the world.

For whatever reason, David didn't share this attitude and was happy to look after his wife when she got pregnant. He felt pride in doing so, and even though they had been through times when they had little money, he never resented supporting his wife. Claire was his rock in turbulent times and she had been faithful to him over their years together. He trusted her implicitly and had good reason to. When he started his business Claire was his 'Girl Friday', his personal assistant, she helped him with his accounts, his meetings, and tolerated his drunken trips to Paris on the Eurostar with architects, lawyers, and financiers, oiling the wheels of business. She believed him when he said that he did not indulge in the sexual antics of some of his business acquaintances even though the temptation to conform was great. Eventually she gave up work when she was pregnant with Jodie, but it was a necessary decision. Wealth brought with it the opportunity for them to make choices. He felt she made the right ones for both of them.

When David thought about his own parents it was hard to imagine that his father resented his mother, even though David knew that things were not perfect between them. However, when his father was dying from a terminal illness in a hospice he had to stop his father from spending his savings and selling the family home. On a visit to his bedside one evening his father waited until his mother had left the ward beckoned

David to come closer to him. David did not know if it was the side effect of the morphine he was ingesting but he asked David to sell his car and put the family house on the market. This would have made his mother homeless. He explained to David that he couldn't bear to think of his wife living there after he was dead and benefitting from his hard earned money when she had done 'bugger all'.

At times of distress his mother had let slip that his parents intimate life together was not very harmonious or joyful. David wondered if this toxic resentment based on the politics of couples sexual relationship could be avoided if society ditched what might be the outmoded practice of sanctioned sexual monogamy. Perhaps the English should have adopted attitudes from the culture of the French and the Spanish. Traditionally men could lead a double life, and have more than one woman in their life and the idea of a mistress, or visiting a 'Bordello' was an accepted part of their culture. David felt that managed discretely, it gave the husband an outlet for his sexual demands if sex was in short supply at home, and because of the boundaries implicit in the arrangement it was able to preserve the marriage. The mistress had to be single and of course it was frowned upon if the wife took a lover as well. David felt fortunate that this lifestyle did not appeal to him but it did to some of his acquaintances.

David was convinced that even if men and women spoke in a different voice they needed to become friends. One author he read about in a magazine suggested that women were like creatures from Venus and men from the planet Mars. David loved the scene in 'Close Encounters of the Third Kind' where humans found a way to communicate with the aliens through music. David felt intuitively, as it seemed true of his and Claire's relationship, that even if men and women represented different notes on a scale, if they combined in the right way they could make beautiful harmonies together. However in his opinion this would not happen if men growing up were told that the best place for women was in the kitchen and the bedroom. It was beholden to both men and women to try to learn each other's language and to see each other outside of the prism created by an outmoded attitude.

David understood that he could have hated his own mother because he was dependent on her and when he was little and his father was at work she had total power over him. She could be cruel to him but got the impression that apart from his aunt she didn't have many friends. She hit him when she lost her temper and when by her standards he was 'naughty'. Somehow he sensed in all of this that she was a wounded person chased by her own demons. His father who obviously knew more about her past than David did must have known this and tried to comfort her and heal her because he stayed with her. One thing he did tell himself in his teenage years was to try to avoid marrying any woman who could be a version of his mother. He did not intend to play out his 'Oedipus complex' and as far as he was concerned his father was welcome to her. However on reflection in Claire he felt he had married someone similar in temperament to his father. The many hurts inflicted on a child by a father or mother could make them vow never to be controlled by a person of their gender again. However, how much of this process was conscious and how much was driven by unconscious repressed emotions he could not tell. One thing he had observed by looking at the faces of couples was the frequent similarity of facial features in each partner. Sometimes it was like they had married a mirror image of themselves but of the opposite sex. Perhaps Freud was right, and as he read in one of Jodie's psychology books, we fall in love with versions of ourselves.

Fortunately for David his daughter Jodie took a while to express a romantic interest in boys. Of course she could have developed an interest in girls and David would have adjusted to that but Jodie loved stories about princes and princesses and when she was little she usually wanted to be the princess. For many years the main love of her life was her pony and later her horse. David enjoyed spending time with his daughter and as she got older they had some interesting discussions. One of the ones he remembered was when he was enjoying a rare weekday at home. Jodie was in her teens, and she came back to the house directly after a sociology lesson at school. She was all fired up by the ideas they had been discussing in class and proceeded to give him a lecture. They sat in the kitchen together eating toast and crumpets.

"Dad, do you know that we live in a patriarchal society with a male God and male prophets the power of women has been controlled over centuries. Dad we are an oppressed class. Feminists have shown us that our physicality, legal rights, education, and economic position in society are controlled by men."

"Jodie do you want some Jam? Strawberry or plum, you're mum made both." David asked, while pouring tea into her cup.

"Dad you are not listening to me and that is a typical male chauvinist response, I am disappointed in you. Support your daughter. Wow, I could get a tee-shirt made with that logo on it!"

"What in pink? No sorry don't look at your poor dad like that. I will listen, Sweetheart I will listen. I cannot disagree with you but let me ask why your sisterhood put up with it for so long?" David decided to play devil's advocate.

"I thought you would ask that and I can say that they are suffering from false conscience, no I mean false consciousness. That's what my teacher Miss Henderson says. We have been brainwashed to not see our fellow women as sisters and members of an oppressed class but rivals, and this is done by the men who control the media, education and the church." Jodie replied, her face getting redder.

David took a large bite of crumpet topped with strawberry jam made from strawberries grown in their garden.

"Is Miss Henderson the one who has red hair, wears leathers and rides a motorcycle or the one that you're mum says comes to school on that Dutch pedal cycle with the basket at the front? Mum says she wears flowery socks and looks like she goes to music festivals."
David knew he was teasing his daughter but he couldn't resist the opportunity. Jodie was not going to be put off.

"That's typical and don't you smile at me I know what you're doing. Miss Henderson showed us a page from the Sun newspaper at the time where they reduced this really important message to women burning their bras. That is insulting and demeaning!"
David continued eating his crumpet with a serious look on his face. While nodding his head in agreement he was thinking about how he would respond to Jodie's remarks. "Yes I agree. You and Miss Henderson make a good point." David took another sip of his Earl Grey tea.

"Ok, I agree that is insulting. Your mother and I lived through it. If I remember rightly the fire brigade had to do overtime, burning bras is a dangerous business!
Jodie slaps David's arm nearly making him spill his tea. Then he says; "No, no, please don't hit me, I can't resist teasing you, but it's great that you are learning about this. At the time, women should have rebelled like they did in ancient Greece. They kicked their men out of bed and, I don't wish to be crude, but they denied them 'you know what' until the men agreed to give them what they wanted! But don't tell your mother I told you this!"

Jodie was not impressed by David's suggestion. "Dad that is gross, you make my point for me. Women must be listened to as intelligent equals, without bargaining with their bodies. That should be left in the past and if you're not careful I will tell mummy that you are a sexist dinosaur, but it won't make any difference because she will love you anyway. Miss Henderson our teacher said this would happen unless our fathers were 'new age men'. She said it would be reduced to that old chestnut beginning with 's' and ending in 'x'."

"Now just hold on a minute Jodie, I must object to being called an 'old chestnut' and my name start's with the letter, 'D'."

Jodie stood up with a mixture of laughter and annoyance showing on her face. She threw the remains of the crumpet she was eating at her father followed by a piece of dry toast from the plate on the table.

"It's no good, you won't be serious. You are in one of your winding up moods. I've got to get ready for my riding lesson."

Jodie kissed him on the cheek and left the kitchen to go upstairs and change her clothes. David followed Jodie out of the kitchen and shouted up the stairs after her.

"Love you! Let me know when you're ready to leave. I will take you, Mum's at the supermarket!"

Another memory David had of their chats together was when he read Jodie the tale of the 'Frog Prince' in which the beautiful young girl is playing by a well with her golden ball. In the story she had been told by her father the King that she was too young to venture into this part of the garden but she had disobeyed him, and by accident she drops the ball into the well. She is desperate to retrieve the golden ball. A slimy green frog appears out of nowhere and overcome by the beauty of the young princess it offers to dive into the mud and get the ball from the bottom of the well. However before he does this he asks her to agree to certain conditions. They are to promise to allow him to sit at her table, eat from her plate, sleep in her bed for a week, and finally, allow him one kiss. The princess has never met a frog before and certainly felt disgusted by the thought of touching one but she agrees to these conditions in order to get him to do what she wants. Secretly she has no intention of keeping her promise. The frog dives into the well and brings her the golden ball. Without saying thank you, she runs back to the safety of her palace. A day later, while she is having dinner in the castle with her father the frog appears at the door asking to see the princess. She refuses to admit him and instructs her father to keep the frog away from her. The King wants to protect his sweet and innocent daughter and so he faces the frog intending to frighten it away and if necessary squash it. However the frog explains politely what has occurred and the King asks the daughter if what the frog said was true. The daughter loves her father deeply as he has been her sole parent since her mother died in childbirth and so tells him the truth. The King decrees that she must not make promises she has no intention of keeping and therefore must honour her deal with the frog. At this point in the story David remembered asking Jodie if she thought the King did the right thing and whose side would she be on, the princess, the frog, or the King? He was surprised by her reply.

"Daddy this is not easy, because what if the frog was really disgusting and kissing it would make her sick, but then the poor frog liked her and wanted to help her, but he knew what he wanted, which is a bit creepy."

David smiled; "Yes I agree but what if it was you? What would you want me to do?"

"I don't think the ball is worth it, agreeing to something just for gold. I wouldn't agree to kiss a boy unless I loved him. Not if he gave me a gold bracelet or something, or bought me a pony. Mummy say's that would be cheating and she didn't marry you for your money."

David was impressed by the way Jodie thought about this and so he posed her another question.

"Let's say at some time in the future when you're old enough, a boy turns up at our front door to take you out on a date and I think he is spotty, smelly and a bit of a frog. Would you like me to 'squash' him?"

Jodie giggled. "Like that is ever going to happen, but if it did, then if I chose him I guess you would have to be all smiles, but I wouldn't do that anyway because by then you and mum would have taught me to have a better taste in animals."

David closed the book they were reading and put it down on the cushion of the sofa next to him.

"We certainly hope so but who knows? What would you do about the frog wanting to sleep in the bed and allowing it one kiss?"

David could see by the expression on his daughters face that this was not something she would be happy with.

"I can see why it wanted to be nice and warm in bed because a frog would be out in the rain and cold weather. My bed is quite big so it could sleep on one side of the bed and I could put a pillow between me and the frog, as long as it promised not to hop about." Jodie's expression changed to one of quiet satisfaction with the idea she had come up with.

"That solves that, but what about the kiss? I know it sounds a bit yucky but what if it's like 'Beauty and the Beast' and you turn the frog into a handsome prince."

David persisted. He could see Jodie struggling to come up with an answer she was happy with.

"Why would it want to kiss the princess anyway?" Jodie looked at David.

"I suppose the princess was pretty and maybe he had never been kissed before." David answered.

"I don't know if frogs actually kiss each other but, O.K. Well I suppose as long as it had a bath in mummy's bubbles and it cleaned its teeth really well. I would let it have one kiss, as long as you and mummy were there, and I kept my eyes closed, and didn't open them until it was a prince."

"If that is what you wanted my little princess then mummy and I would do exactly that. You are one clever little girl." David gave her a big hug and kissed her on the top of her head.

"Daddy, can I ask you something?"

"Absolutely, ask away."

"Were you a frog when mummy met you?"

David laughed out loud. "Oh, I think you'd better ask mummy that one."

Chapter Six: Jonathan Hope

Jonathan Hope had been a teacher since his mid-twenties; he loved English Literature and wanted to spread this passion to younger people and at the same time get paid for his interest. On leaving Bristol University and finding himself unemployed he tried his hand at writing plays. Initially he found limited success through a contact at the Bristol University drama department in Park Row whose students performed a play he had written at the Edinburgh Festival. It was given favourable reviews and attracted a good size audience in part because the actors had to remove their clothes during the play. It was entitled 'Bath' and consisted of five people having a bath in what were meant to be separate cubicles at a public bath house in the 1930's. It dealt with body image, homosexuality, class issues, feminism, and the rise of Fascism in England. At the wrap party after the last performance Jonathan was encouraged to get a literary agent by one of the festival judges. Another judge who had connections in broadcasting suggested that he sent the play to his contact who worked at Channel 4, as well as to a drama producer at the B.B.C. He did what he was advised to do but after six weeks he had heard nothing from them and then he received a letter informing him that they did not accept unsolicited scripts. Further attempts at getting an agent also met with failure and now he lived alone in his flat above a furniture shop in Clifton. To add to his misery his girlfriend Maria whom he met at University had gone abroad for a year to study the Italian language. She was younger than him and for a brief time they lived together after he finished his studies. It was the first time that he had lived with a girlfriend and it did not go well as she was messy and he was tidy. They had argued about fidelity and trust in their relationship because he felt she was too easily swayed by others. She was a people pleaser and found it difficult to say no to others even when it lead to unwanted attention from male students at the University. It had created awkward situations for her in her past, some of which she had told Jonathan about.

The flat was small and had drips of water coming through the ceiling above their bed, which he managed to divert into a bucket by the bed by making a trough of tin foil which he pinned to the ceiling with thumb tacks. They argued, they cried, they made love, but when she went away to study for the first time to Spain and later to Italy as part of her studies it was a relief for both of them. They did not part on good terms and a day after she departed he wrote her a letter in which he suggested that perhaps they should part. A month went by before he received a reply and when it came it was more like a chapter from a novel than a letter;

"A perfunctory glance at the words and she knew, and yet she experienced no shock or surprise, it was as if she had been handed a sentence by a judge based on her misdeeds. She had expected this when his hand written letter arrived. He had stated the truth and tears welled up in her eyes, like they had many times before in their relationship. These were not tears of rage, she was not angry with him; she did not care if he replaced her with another, even though she longed for him between her thighs and to feel his kisses on her body. He was living with a ghost who had little contact with reality and yet he was so reasonable. She was the woman/girl, so lost and confused who grasped at life trying to find a hold. For her life was not serious, her experience did not correspond to any of the long and noble words that he used to describe it. Life was a chess game, but not a game played according to the rules that he followed. It was full of time without obligation and emotional entanglement. He could not understand why she gave her virginity to a stranger she met on a holiday in Majorca just to get it over and done with. She said she was fed up of waiting, and in a masculine way, by taking the initiative she felt empowered. She regretted telling him as he could not understand her giving this away so cheaply and without meaning. Now she wants to escape before things get emotionally messy and yet she needs to be needed. She envied his need for security. She dreamt of someone who in true romantic fashion would be her soul mate and she would be accepted without unnecessary questions. She adapted to others and tried to think and be what others expected her to be, even if their ideas were preposterous. She would 'fit in' and do things to be accepted, like smoking 'pot' sitting crossed legged on the floor, even though it made her sick. She would complement people even if she detested them. Under his critical gaze he saw this and she felt a disappointment to him. She was a plump ghost of a woman but in her chess game like an invisible pawn she could enjoy a longer life that the handsome queen. The attention he lavished upon her made her glow with praise and recognition but how could she trust this knight in shining armour? To her he looked like someone who had unscrupulously bedded every available girl at the University. He had a kind of attractive lecherousness and a wildness that any young girl away from home admires, and he wrote plays and songs and poems. She had to protect herself by lying when she got into devious situations that she kept from him. He suspected her dishonesty once when he caught her in a restaurant with another man without telling him where she was. Her excuse, which he believed at first, was that it was a meeting about a student project. Later she told him that she had agreed to meet this person because she had inadvertently smiled at him and he invited her to dinner. She did not want to upset him and so she went along for the meal. She enjoyed building up her nebulous personality with bigger and bolder lies. Her deception was in relief to his white washed honesty. She had no qualms of conscience because in her game of emotional chess to lie was to escape from his black and white morality and his withering gaze. When he told her he loved her and he loved her smile she was shocked because her smile was her mask, her defence. How could love be the consequence of her deceit? To complicate things she fell in love with him. This was not her plan and when blurted this out in a drunken state at a student party she cried all the way back to her room. Now she could no longer treat him like the faceless nameless people she had met before. However living with him, his life force, his way of stripping away her façade, challenging her fragile ego, expecting her to be able to live up to his standards, share his passions, while ridiculing her inability to organise herself was not easy. It was a tsunami of criticism that she found hard to swim over or around. It was too much, too soon. She started to long for freedom without guilt. Now when she had her freedom away from him, and the opportunity to do as she pleased, experiment and sleep with whom she pleased, she felt disgusted at the thought of being picked up in some bar and screwing a stranger. She wanted him, but did she want what came with him? He was in her head. She flirted with the idea that like the tragic women of literature she should kill herself. This was like the schoolgirl in her, responding to her teacher's rejection when he firmly and politely rebuffed her protestation of affection on a school camping trip. He must do what he wished, after all she had left him alone for so long. He wasn't that great, he was too controlled, and he needed to loosen up!

Any way dearest I hope this has made things clearer, I shouldn't write when I'm a bit pissed. I LOVE YOU anyway, I hope this helps, and don't forget me.

From, you're confused, and maybe, a bit crazy love, Maria.

A month later another letter arrived.

'Jonathan, sorry about the last letter, I guess I was dazed and confused and I was a bit crazy. I do want to care for you and I need to understand you a bit more but you make it difficult because you don't show your vulnerabilities very often and I feel it's all me. I can see myself having your child even though I said I didn't want children. You can be a big kid, so you would be a good dad, but I wanted other things as I said. I want to travel and use my languages and so I guessed, unless you did too, we would be apart a lot. On another point, if you do live with anyone else let me give you a word of warning. You are not easy to live with. I

know I am guilty for some things, but I found you exceedingly exacting when it comes to my behaviour, without looking at your own! However you're endearing qualities and your abilities in bed, by this I don't mean the water thing; can make life bliss, even though it's hell elsewhere. However you will be pleased to know that I am much cleaner and tidier than I was and my room here is organised and so some of our little quarrels could be avoided. I am working hard in the school where I am an assistant and I am reading a lot. I had a bad stomach ache and I feel sick. Don't worry I'm not pregnant. I wanted to tell you that I love you and will see you in the holiday. If you want to sleep with someone else while I'm away don't feel guilty, but don't get involved in their emotional life or their problems, Shit! Why do I say these things, I wanted to make you love me and write a tender letter, and I want you to wait for me, but now you could hate me and be mad at me. I won't go with anyone else so don't worry, but I know your needs. Shit there I go again. I'm going to stop writing now and draw you lots of kisses.
  Love, Maria

Jonathan was not sure what to make of the letters. He thought she was a bit out of her mind, but it was the most honest she had been in the time he had known her. They made him uneasy, but they also made him smile. He felt sad that she had kept this all inside and part of him wanted to put his arms around her and tell her everything would be all right between them, however he wasn't certain that it would be. They survived this separation, and the feelings expressed in the letters were ignored when she returned. The pleasure they felt in exploring each other's bodies rekindled their appetite for each other. They no longer lived together as it was the end of term, and she went home to see her parents. All was well until Maria went to Italy.

He had known that Maria loved all things Italian especially the pasta, but as it turned out, she also loved the men, in particular one man.

Each time she came back from Italy to visit him he noticed she was gradually putting on weight. When he asked her about this change in her shape she replied that if she had indeed gained weight, it was the consequence of the children in her class at school who brought her presents of pastries each day which she found hard to refuse. The other reason she gave, and it was one that he liked much better, was that she missed him greatly, was starved of sex, and ate to make her happy. While living in Siena Italy, Maria sent him letters. She loved the period in the history of English Literature when English authors went on a European tour, visited health spas, ancient monuments and sent letters to each other about their travels. She told Jonathan that like them she would prefer to use old fashioned letters to share her thoughts and feelings with him, instead of more modern forms of communication. She asked him to return the favour and also correspond with her by letter, so that when she finally returned home they would have a bundle of letters to read and use to reminisce. In the previous letter he received she told him that she wanted to extend her stay in Italy and stay longer than she had first planned. For the sake of their relationship and for the health of his creative spirit she asked him to consider leaving Bristol and staying with her in Siena. They would be together in the Italian sun, dance under the stars, drink Valpolicella, and 'make sweet love' on the secluded balcony of her flat. When this letter arrived he hadn't seen Maria, or held her close, for about three months. He could imagine the warmth of this intimate embrace and savoured the touch of her skin as his hands caressed her body. However, as tempting as this request seemed it put Jonathan in a quandary. If he was brutally honest with himself, he had been without her for so long now he wasn't sure if being with her was still what he wanted. He spent sleepless nights tossing and turning in bed, staying awake, struggling with the idea of moving to Italy and living with Maria. Then in the midst of this emotional turmoil another letter from Maria dropped though the letter box of his flat. He made himself a cup of tea, sat down on a chair by the kitchen table and opened the envelope. Her previous letters to him usually began with an update of what she had been enjoying with the children in the school where she taught English. She also described to him what sightseeing she had done since her last letter. This description included some little drawings of any celebrations she had attended.

This letter came decorated with her normal doodles drawn in the margins, but there the similarity ended. It was not her usual chatty letter; instead it was to inform Jonathan that without planning, or intending to meet someone new, she had met 'Roberto'. This surprise encounter took place at a party in Siena where she got drunk on fizzy wine. This apparently lowered her defences so much that when she awoke in her bed the next morning Roberto was by her side. She went on to tell Jonathan that Roberto became infatuated with her, waited outside the school gates each day to give her flowers and gifts and to profess his love for her. He insisted that she met his mother and they both took her to an opera, 'Madam Butterfly' which made her feel more alive than she had felt in a long time. The Opera made her so emotional that she was tearful throughout the meal they had afterwards. Roberto's mother gave her a big hug and clasped Maria to her ample bosom. Roberto whisked her away for a weekend spent together, with his uncle in a beautiful converted farmhouse perched on a hill in the countryside. Then as if to remind him of their previous conversation she wrote; "Roberto tells me he loves every curve of me, and can't get enough of my 'pasta filled' body or my 'Venus like' hips, and wants to 'make babies' with me!"

Jonathan was surprised that the letter affected him as it did. He had tears in his eyes and an ache in his heart. Maria had rejected him. Luckily this feeling did not last long. In truth he was happy for her finding romance in a wonderful setting with a man who loved her curves and he hoped it would last to become the love of her life. It would have been selfish of him to try to hold on to her because his pride was hurt. His sadness was replaced with a sense of a new found freedom. At the end of her letter she wished Jonathan every success in the future, while at the same time realising that, in all probability, she would never see him again. To help him overcome his separation Jonathan went to the nearest record store and bought himself Beethoven's Ninth Symphony 'Ode to Freedom' recorded by Herbert Von Karajan and featured in Stanley Kubrick's 'A Clockwork Orange'. He returned to his flat, turned the volume on his Hi Fi up as loud as he dare, lie down on his sofa and let the sonic waves of the symphony wash over him.

One morning, not long after receiving Maria's letter, feeling alone and sad, he went for a walk in Clifton near the suspension bridge to visit his favourite café. He liked this coffee house because he could spend a long time sitting with his laptop writing without being troubled by the staff to buy more drinks or food. His current project was a novel about an out of work student, like himself, who, while writing a novel in a café, rather like the one he was sitting in, gets approached by a young woman who gives him a serviette with an address written on it in purple ink. She tells him that a fancy dress party will take place at this house that evening. He must wear a disguise and to gain admission he must use the phrase; 'Eyes wide shut'. She leaves the café without giving him her name but promises to meet him there; "Look for Marylyn Munro," she said.

Jonathan was excited by the premise of his story. He often came to this café to think, people watch, order a flat white coffee, and to eat jam and toast. He would have preferred a café like the one he imagined situated on the left bank of the Seine in the 1930's. Full of artistes' models, prostitutes, or authors like Henry Miller, John Paul Sartre, Simone de Beauvoir, or Ernest Hemmingway, all drinking coffee and cognac, talking loudly about their art, and smoking 'Gauloises Disque Bleu', cigarettes pulled from crushed blue packets. Instead of meeting this highly regarded assortment of literary talent he bumped into one of his old university professors.

"Jonathan, my playwriting success story, what is it almost three years now since I saw you last. How are you?"

"Surviving, but I must say it is good to see you!" He replied.

The professor smiled and patted him on his back as he sat down in the seat next to him.

"To be honest Professor I feel stuck with no direction to go."

"You can drop the Professor now, call me George."

George took a sip of his Americano coffee, and a bite of the sweet brown biscuit that came with it. Jonathan waited in anticipation to hear what he would say.

"My dear Jonathan, I will tell you what I think. What you need is money, and time to write, and a job that suits your morality. Remember what Siddhartha said, right speech, right livelihood, etc. Why don't you share your knowledge and passion for your subject with the masses and teach. I know a professor in the Education Department who would give you a reference, I know it's a bit late to apply for this year but, he could probably pull some strings, if you didn't mind doing a P.G.C.E in London."

"But George I would have to stop writing full time and I could get dragged into letting my dream of being an author go. You know George that if I do something I want to do it well."

"Writing a play or some novel is a great legacy, teaching young minds to enjoy literature is also a great legacy, a bid for immortality. Having children who themselves will carry your soul forward and maybe do great things in your footsteps is also a great legacy. Think Jonathan, you do not have to starve while you do that!"

Within six months he had left Bristol and was in halls of residence at the London Institute of Education starting his P.G.C.E. However, because his interview and enrolment happened so quickly he did not fully realise that training as a secondary school teacher meant that he had to be able to teach a broader range of subjects across the curriculum. For his first teaching practice in an inner London school in Stepney he had to teach History, Geography, and Religious studies to the lower school, while his icing on the cake was being allowed to teach GCSE and A level English to the older pupils. It was during this time that he realised teaching could be tough, gruelling, and hurtful. Some of his fellow graduate students left within the first term because of the fear they felt in the classroom, and their inability to deal with unruly pupils, or to find a sense of humour about their situation. There were four student teachers on placement in the school he was in and they likened the experience to being a soldier in the trenches in the First World War. When the school bell rang before assembly and they left the safety of the staff room to teach it was as if the whistle was being blown in the trenches to send them 'over the top into 'no man's land'. The trainee teachers soon discovered if, although they had the knowledge to do the job, they had the character needed. Jonathan discovered that to survive in the mostly hostile environment of this inner London Comprehensive and not breakdown or run away from the course, he had to find stamina, show courage, and possess a winning personality to make it through the teaching practice. Unfortunately for some of the trainees it was like trying to fit a square peg into a round hole. One of the friends he made on the on the course with him had a first in history from Cambridge. He was a gentle soul who wore thick glasses due to his poor eyesight, green cords and sandals to work. He could not impose discipline in his classrooms, which became a war zone and was crucified by the children in the school that he was sent to. After much heartache and tears he left the course. If he had been sent for his teaching practice to a private school, or a Grammar school, and taught 'A' level History he would have made a success of it. When he talked about his subject to Jonathan his eyes lit up, and his demeanour changed from that of a mouse to a lion. Unfortunately this was a part of him that his pupils never had the chance to experience because he left after the first teaching practice and was frightened to go back. This likeable and educated 'mouse', had been fed to the wolves of this comprehensive school classroom had his aspirations ripped to shreds.

For Jonathan that experience in his first school seemed so far away from him now. He had become the deputy head of English at Sherwood House mixed comprehensive school near Tyburn Corner in outer London. The school had one thousand two hundred pupils divided into an upper and lower school, plus a sixth form. In the early years at the school he loved teaching English to the eleven year olds, as they were like new untarnished, bright shiny buttons, which also followed orders. They arrived at the school with new uniforms, white shirts, and brushed hair; like new pennies from the mint before being in circulation and becoming scarred by the friction of school life. They were polite, they stood up when you entered the room, they said 'Sir', and 'Miss', they sat down when you asked them to, and didn't talk over you. That didn't last long.

In his first year of teaching English he taught a topic with the pupils called 'truth'. They were asked to do an experiment which was to spend a week without telling an untruth. They then had to keep a diary each day of what that was like, but the diary had to be truthful. He read them a poem by a Liverpool poet about a man on the bus who told everyone that he heard on the news that the world was going to end that evening. It turned out that what he heard was a mistake but he saw how he and others reacted to the news and particularly if the girl he was attracted to and who sat next to him every day on the way to work would lose her inhibitions and kiss him. While he was writing the task on the white board a sweet little girl called Mary who sat near the front of the class raised her arm.

"Yes Mary?"

"Sir, if we have to do this, do you have to do the same for a week?"

Jonathan thought about this for a moment. "Well I suppose I should Mary but I won't keep a diary."

"Sir, if I asked you a question now, would you promise to give me an honest answer?"

"It depends what the question is, but I would try to."

"Mum and dad tell me there are things called white lies. They say it is ok to lie if you want to protect someone, or not hurt their feelings, is that true?"

"Yes Mary there is what people call white lies, but I do not know if they are a good thing." Jonathan replied.

"My mum and dad told me there was a tooth fairy but there wasn't, and they told me about Santa Claus, and my mum told me that when my grandad died in a car accident he was still alive in heaven and he was happy. I asked them if he would still be bashed up or would he be like I remembered him. They said he would be made better and normal up there. They also told my sister that she looked great in her tight trousers, but I thought she looked like a tramp, and the first time she went out in them someone tried to touch her bum and she got really upset. They told me that having an injection at the dentist wouldn't hurt and it did."

Jonathan could see his pupil getting more emotional as she spoke, and the rest of the class were silent and appeared to be hanging on to her every word.

"Adults do try to spare their children knowing some truths that they think will upset them. That's true Mary, and I guess that they make a choice that suits them, because sometimes a truth can be as difficult for them to deal with or accept as their child. You, I, the rest of the class, we all might want to avoid what might be an uncomfortable truth."

Mary looked intently at him, Jonathan felt as if she wanted to say something but was afraid to ask.

"So, Mary, I suppose that you are wondering if I am going to be like your parents and perhaps tell a white lie. I think the only way you will find out is to ask me what you want to ask."

Mary paused for a moment, as if to gain some courage to ask her question and then she spoke.

"Ok, well, we all go to the toilet Sir." At the mention of toilet some in the class started to snigger, but the rest were transfixed on their teachers face.

"Yes we do."

"Well what hand do you use to wipe your bottom?"

At this the whole class broke out in laughter, and Jonathan tried to settle them down.

"Quiet, come on lets settle down. Right, Mary, this is a bit of a trick question and as your teacher I should tell you that you are being a bit naughty. But it is something we all do and we should not be ashamed of our bodies, I guess I made a deal, and just this once, I will answer you. I am right handed, and so I use my right hand."

"Oh Sir, that's disgusting! We use toilet paper!" Mary giggled and the rest of the class laughed out loud.

Mr Stevens, the deputy headmaster happened to be passing the classroom and witnessed the frivolity inside. He thought he should investigate and entered the classroom. All of the pupils shot to their feet and tried to be silent.

"What is going on in here Mr Hope you look a little red in the face?"

"Mr Stevens, welcome to my class, I was telling the class about the importance to our health of laughter, and I asked them about the comics they like from the T.V. They all like the comedy show 'Bottom', and I was telling them about Billy Connelly and one of his jokes."

"I preferred Tommy Cooper myself but, carry on, carry on, glad they are enjoying themselves, as long as they learn something." Mr Stevens smiled at the class gestured for them to sit down and left.

Jonathan Hope developed a relationship of respect with Mr Stevens, and was sad when he died, because despite of his stern exterior, he cared about the pupils and the staff if they worked hard and gave that bit extra. In John's second year as a form teacher he taught a year nine class on the ground floor of the school. For a week at the start of term in September, they were asked to get the students to remove the graffiti and names carved in the desks with compasses with sandpaper. The plan was for the caretakers to re-varnish the tops of the desks and remove the collection of chewing gum stuck to the underneath. To keep the tops clean John came up with a plan. He got the pupils to make a hardboard wall in technology which they painted as bricks in the art lesson. They put this up on the classroom wall with a sign that said, 'WRITE ON HERE AND NOT ON THE DESKS'. The wall was a great success and the desks remained clean for a month after the wall appeared. What the pupils wrote on the wall could not be controlled as the classroom was left open and there were at least ten different sets of students that used it in the week. John read some of the comments but felt that embarrassment and crudity was a small price to pay for the desks remaining clean. John walked into the classroom in the fifth week of the success of the wall to get ready to take the afternoon register and found Mr Stevens studying the graffiti.

"I must say I admire your idea Mr Hope and I like innovation, and your classroom has desks that are in better shape than others I have seen today, but you have to take the wall down. I am sure as an English teacher and one who appreciates the finer points of poetry you are disappointed in the limited vocabulary displayed on the wall. I am afraid I cannot allow 'Stevenson is a wanker' to survive any longer. Take it down today please."

Within two weeks the newly sandpapered and varnished desks of his form room were scratched with all manner of implements and covered in graffiti.

In his present position at the school Jonathan arrived in his office at seven forty five in the morning and rarely left before five thirty at night. This changed if he was rehearsing a play, running the poetry club or playing five a side football in the gymnasium with the staff and some upper school pupils on a Friday night after school. He also helped the pupils of the school to publish a digital newsletter every month which contained, news, computer game reviews, poems submitted, music and film revues plus any issue that they thought young people cared about. There was a lower and upper school section to give as many pupils the chance of getting into the paper. The regular five a side football competition between staff and pupils, which took place after lessons had finished on a Friday afternoon was a staff tradition which started twenty years ago. There was a break in playing of about three years when the head of P.E. died from a heart attack after diving to save a shot from a fellow staff member. The football ball hit him hard in the face and left an imprint on his cheek. The person who caused the injury by kicking the ball so hard so close to the goalkeeper left the school shortly after the tragedy. Out of respect for his wife and children the games were suspended. The staff decided to go for a swim in the school pool instead. For a short while they played water polo, but the numbers dwindled because this sport required participants to be a strong swimmer. The good swimmers didn't let the weaker players put their feet on the floor of the pool to give them a rest, when they could and this created a lot of antagonism between the staff. After the three year break Jonathan and the new P.E teachers resurrected the tradition and it grew from there. It pleased Jonathan that as he got older he was able to stay in shape and his skill as a footballer had not diminished.

It gave both teams the chance to enjoy football, get to know each other outside the classroom and 'kick the shit out of each other' when emotions ran high in the week. The pupils respected the fact that these teachers gave just that bit more than they were paid to do, and they could meet the staff in another setting. Sometimes problems with pupils would be sorted by a conversation after the match when the staff took them to a local café for a soft drink or a coffee, before the staff went down the pub to talk about the trauma and stupidities of the past week. It often ended up in joyous laughter, because just like the soldiers in the trenches they were all in it together. Once in his fifth year of teaching at Sherwood, John had lost his temper with a fifteen year old in his class who had told him to 'fuck off' when he reprimanded him for calling the girl sitting next to him a 'bike' who had been ridden by half the sixth form, and a 'slag'. She burst into tears before trying to stab him with her pencil. It was the last period on a Thursday, a day that he wished he could avoid each week because he had a year eleven religious studies class with a non–exam group, and no free periods, plus he had playground duty. Playground duty meant keeping those apart that wanted to fight; keeping those apart who wanted to spend their time 'sucking face', and separate the smokers from their 'fags'.

The class went silent waiting to see how Jonathan would react to this boy's abusive comment. If he had been in a more relaxed mood, he would have pretended not to hear what had been said, separated the pair of students and awarded a detention after school for the both of them. But the sound of contempt in the boy's voice triggered his anger. Jonathan turned quickly, grabbed the lapels on the pupil's blazer, and hoisted him out of his chair. Two of the buttons on the boy's shirt pinged off into the air in the process.

"What did you say to me? Do you think in any other place you'd get away with that? Get the hell out of this classroom, before ..."

The boy broke free of John's grip, ran to the classroom door, pulled it open, stared back at him and shouted; "My dad will be after you!"

He then threw his notebook at Jonathan, slammed the door shut and ran down the stairwell and all the way home.

Jonathan had to report what had happened to the deputy headmaster, who was primed to receive a complaint and an angry parent wanting blood. That Friday, while Jonathan was changing into his football kit for the weekly match, the boy's elder brother Simon walked in to the changing room.

"Mr Hope, Sir, I hear you had a bit of bother with Steven."

"Yes, I did Simon, and I went too far, even though he was behaving like a little shit. I wanted to speak to him but he had gone. He threatened me with your dad, and said he would come up the school and sort me out."
"Yeah, I know, my dad is a bit hard Sir, knows some shady characters…but I told him he was well out of order with you Sir, you're one of the good guys, any way he's too scared of my dad to tell him he got in trouble at school, he'd get a smack and lose the money my dad gives him. So don't worry yourself about my brother or my dad, it's sorted. You'd better watch out if you're in goal tonight Sir? No mercy."

Jonathan got involved with extra curriculum activities when he could, including school plays, and because he had a reasonable voice a couple of musicals, 'Oliver' and 'Half a Sixpence'. In the local press his sixth formers version of Hamlet gained great praise and it was entered into the local drama competition at the Queens Theatre, Hornchurch. The most recent outing in musical theatre was 'Joseph and the Technicolour Dream Coat', which was a particular favourite with the parents.

He loved being a teacher when he started, the first two years of any teachers life are tough, because they are writing and preparing lessons, finding the resources online, doing power points, marking at the weekends and most importantly, finding a way to make a relationship with the students and involve them their learning. In the first years in a school you have no 'street cred' and so some pupils will not be kind to you or automatically respect you. They may not give a damn about your subject and to them you are a prison guard stopping them living their life outside school. Some would rather work on the local market and get money by buying and selling, than study a subject which for them had no practical purpose and they saw no use for. One of the main pleasures available to them whilst at school was to disrupt the class. They used this to alleviate their boredom from what they considered to be forced imprisonment. It was hard to get a child excluded from his school and so Jonathan soon learned that control in the classroom for the none exam pupils was dependent on two main factors. Engaging the pupils by how you taught your subject. For the lower 'sets' in a subject, it meant finding ways to get the pupils to learn by doing as well as listening. If that didn't work the teacher could try instilling fear in them, or more likely try winning them over with humour. Some of the year eleven students were as big as Jonathan and a lot meaner. In confrontational situations he had to learn to control his fear as well as his temper and find ways of diffusing the conflict.

It was compulsory for the school to deliver a form of religious education. The head of this department was a lay preacher and when John first arrived he was expected to teach R.E. to a year eleven class, before lunch on a Thursday. The group were not interested in the salvation of their souls, nor the metaphors held in the parables of the bible. They did accept Jesus as a historical figure, but they thought that any father who could not save his son from being tortured and killed on the Cross was not a good one, especially as Jermaine pointed out;

"This geezer had all the powers of the 'X-men' put together! No man that's sad."

78

However their vision of Jesus was based on the pictures they had seen in their Bibles. He was white skinned with blue eyes and long brown hair. The class was a mixture of three African-Caribbean, two Asian students and the rest, like him, were white skinned. Jonathan had worked in a school in inner London before moving to this school. He remembered that his R.E. teacher in that school had an artist's picture of Jesus that was more in keeping with his Hebrew roots, the region he came from and the hairstyle and dress he may have worn. Jonathan photocopied the picture and handed it out in one of his lessons. The students were interested in the contrast, some were not open to this idea of Jesus and it stimulated a lively discussion. In the staffroom after the lesson the Head of R.E. came into the staff room, with a face like thunder.

"This takes the biscuit Mr Hope, I do not know what subversive intention you have but to tell the pupils that Jesus was black skinned is a step too far."

"Come on Peter, they are winding you up. Did you see the picture?"

"I did, and I want you to explain yourself to the Head."

"Certainly, no problem, lead the way, let the inquisition commence, I suppose you would like to apply the thumb screws yourself?"

Jonathan was so annoyed with this show of ignorance and prejudice, that he could not stop himself from saying what came next.

"Did they tell you the joke I told them about the man who went to hell and was given a choice of his punishment?"

"Don't make this worse for yourself Mr Hope; I suggest you remain silent until we get to the Heads office."

Jonathan continued;

"Well they took him along a corridor and opened the doors to various rooms in which sinners were being punished. In the first one as man was having his skin peeled from his flesh and was screaming loudly. In the second a woman was strapped to a rack and was being stretched, of course she was screaming very loudly. In the third was a group of six people standing naked up to their waist in what could only be described as foul smelling sewage, but they were drinking tea from china cups and eating a cream cup cake."

The two teachers turned a corner and the Headmasters office came into view at the end of a long corridor.

"The man asked his guide if he would get the tea and the cake if he opted for this punishment, and the guide promised that he would be treated the same as the others in the room. The man accepted his fate took off his clothes and climbed down the ladder, lowering himself into the foul smelling sludge. Miraculously the tea and cake appeared in his hand, and so he took a sip of tea and was just about to take a bite out of the cake when an announcement was made through the speaker hanging in the corner of the room. "Ok sinners, the tea breaks over, back on your heads!"

The head of R.E. looked at Jonathan Hope and did not laugh even though Jonathan smiled at him waiting for some favourable reaction to his story. Instead of returning Johns smile he opened the door to the Headmasters office, and then before stepping inside he paused and said;

"What was the point of telling me that?"

"Can I choose the tea and cake please?"

The pupils asked some good questions in R.E. that Jonathan did not have answers for because he was not a subscriber to any faith other than a search for the truth. He remembered when he had to teach the creation of the Ten Commandments to the same class. Simon who was sitting next to his friends at the back of the class was pretending to pour out pints of beer and then he passes them along the row.

"Would you like one Sir? Quench your thirst."

"Thank you not now, maybe later. Can you please put your feet down off the desk and open up the book in front of you at page twenty six. You are not old enough to drink alcohol anyway, and we don't have a licence to serve it."

"Ok Sir, I don't want to get in any trouble with the law, and so I will close the bar, though shalt drink no more."

"Thankyou Simon, we will now look at the story of Moses"

"Sorry Sir?"
"Yes Jermaine?"

"Well we know about this from primary school. This bloke goes up a mountain, gets spoken to by some voice, and comes back with these tablets of stone with the Ten Commandments cut into them."

"Yes that's broadly it."

"Well how do we know he didn't chisel them into the stone himself?" Jonathan noticed that Patience, one of his girl pupils looked up from her mobile.

"Patience do you want to say something, you look like you do?"

"Yes Sir I do. Why did all this happen so long ago, and nothing has happened since apart from space men and aliens coming here and taking us up into their ships and doing weird things to us. And another thing, why did it happen in this place and not in China, or America? This God who spoke to these men seems to have left us alone with all the crap that has happened in the world."

"My dad says Bob Marley, and Nelson Mandela is prophets" said Winston, who rarely spoke in the lesson. "He says all the answers we want are in Mr Marley's songs and we live in Babylon under the white oppressors who made us slaves, except for his Royal Highness, the Lion of Africa, King of Ethiopia, and he wants to go back there, and take me with him, when he can afford to leave his job on London transport. I told him, no way, no signal for the internet, no MTV, too hot, and no MacDonald's."

"Way to go Winston!" Simon said, clicking his fingers together by shaking his hand in the air.

"I get why he knows things," said Simon, "Ganja."

Then Patience spoke up.

"What about the women in these stories, they don't get the credit, it's always the men. I feel sorry for Joseph, he had this young wife and he gets no credit for the baby. My mum and my Gran brought me up and she says Mary should get more props. She must have been a great mum, she helped make a great man and how did she feel when he went away without telling her where he was going. My dad just went back to Trinidad and left us."

"Good point Patience. Why don't you read 'The Da Vinci Code', you may like it. There is one book of the Bible that is not in the version of the Bible we all read called the 'Infant Gospel of James' which claims that Mary was divine, and when she was examined by a midwife who did not believe that she was pregnant with the son of God her arm was set on fire. In England before Christianity came here, about four hundred years after the death of Jesus we had religions with male and female gods, but anyway folks, that's for another time."

The school bell rang for the end of the period which John felt was timely because he did not want a repeat of the previous situation with the head of R.E. He did not wish to be accused of trying to recruit devotees to paganism. Fortunately, for Jonathan the school bell rang for the end of the period and they left the classroom for their lunchbreak singing, 'Your Sex is on Fire!'

Jonathan Hope was thankful that he stopped teaching this subject some years ago, and that he was able to focus on the subject he loved and teach it at a level that he enjoyed. He had also been able to write again, and recently he had sent a manuscript of a crime novel to Finch and Faber a publishing house in London, and to his surprise had been invited to a meeting with one of the top people, Mark Finch, to discuss his book. He had arranged with the head teacher to get the day off to travel in to London for the interview, and he felt that perhaps this was the break he had been waiting for, and coming in his thirties it was not too late in his life to capitalise on the opportunity. It could mean a chance to give up his job as a teacher and write for his living as he had wanted to all those years before.

Jonathan accepted that he went into teaching as a vocation, not to become rich, but he felt he had served his time. He had given enough of himself to the job. What he had achieved with his pupils in his school was despite the education department, not because of it. He knew his experience was not unique. Teachers, nurses, social workers, health visitors, care workers, probation officers, mental health outreach workers, and lots of other dedicated people working for councils and central government were undervalued by their employers. They were the soft target when cuts in budgets had to be made by central government, and as long as their clients did not revolt, turn nasty, or commit any shocking crime that got into the papers the rulers were happy. His present school had to sell off half of the playing field for housing development, which now meant that with an increase in the school population, they had to hire another field and bus the children to it for their sports afternoon. Institutions, like the ones these public service people work for, function effectively to stop a revolution amongst the masses by controlling the level of social discontent.

Jonathan had to take the time to research, and then teach social history, to the pupils, as one of his curriculum subjects in school, but he remembered reading 'The Ragged Trousered Philanthropist' when he was doing Advanced levels at eighteen, and it had a profound impact on him. He knew that if he wanted to become an author he had to read widely and so at university, in addition to the books on his English syllabus he read books on slavery, the history of Churchill's battle with the miners in Wales, Keynesian economics and books that explained the benefits as well as the exploitation of workers due to the Capitalist ideology worldwide. He was quite politically motivated at University and was active in the students' union. For a short while he was the union representative for the teachers in his school, but he soon realised that this would hinder his chances of promotion.

In another life where he imagined himself to be more courageous and less conforming Jonathan would be a politician. In fact his mother often told him that when he was born he cried so much and so loudly that the midwife predicted he would become Prime Minister one day. He did toy with the idea of being a political journalist while he was in his last year at university, but he wanted to be a feature writer and a political commentator, not one of those reporters who have to cover births deaths and marriages or the local fete. He wanted to be a reporter who exposed local corruption and fight for the rights of the common man, and if that wasn't possible, at least write the reviews of the new films or plays. Jonathan felt that it was only now, with the chasing of internet companies for their taxes that the general public had become incensed by the practice of companies moving profits around the world. Jonathan argued politics with anyone who would listen, and tried to tell them what was obvious to him and clear to any student of economics, that multinational companies were no longer loyal to their own nations but loyal only to their shareholders. He became incensed over the fact that these companies shed their workforce without compassion when they decided it would be cheaper to provide a service or a manufacturing base elsewhere, dumping the responsibility for the care of the unemployed on the government that they evaded paying tax to. He hated hearing a television news report informing a passive public that "so and so are shedding one thousand employees," without the interviewer asking a representative of the company, why they did not have transition payments in place for the workers they had made redundant? The government would have to pick up the tab for unemployment benefits while the company protected their profits. The latest enemy to blame for the government's austerity measures were the old. Articles appeared in the right wing press stating that the young must pay for the pensions of the old. The old and retired were now portrayed as the enemy of the people, a drain on the wealth of society. They tried to incite resentment in the young for the financial income of the older generation. Jonathan did not begrudge the older generation a dignified retirement. He was comfortable with the fact that the old created the wealth in society for the present generation and should not be overlooked. How that wealth was managed was the responsibility of previous governments and the financial sector. Jonathan could see that a myth was being constructed to support policies of austerity, increase the retirement age and reduce taxation. The old were an easy target to blame. For Jonathan this attitude was a return to a time when employers did not have to provide pensions to the old and got rid of them when they could no longer work. He remembered visiting his grandfather when he was too ill to sleep in his bedroom upstairs because of the pain he was suffering. His grandfather had a manual job into his late sixties and put up with the pain of a hernia because he had to go to work. The younger workers on his team used to cover for him on the job when the foreman came looking around but eventually he asked for a less strenuous job and they sacked him. Jonathan was certain that the majority of citizens forgot that governments are their servants, elected by them, distributing their taxes, and if they want things to be different it was in their power to make it so. Jonathan did not believe that a citizen, who had worked for forty five years and paid their National Insurance, should be forced to work until they drop dead! Jonathan was perceptive enough to see how the right wing media, who represented the wealthy and business classes, tried to persuade the less informed that these changes were an irreversible fact rather than a politically biased agenda. If taxes and National Insurance payments continued to be reduced, the elderly would be deprived of a decent state pension and the time to enjoy it. The responsibility for this provision would fall to private pension providers who as businesses have profit as their primary motive. Jonathan knew of a friend's father who invested in a private pension for years, but when he cashed it in, it was worth half the value of what he expected. This was the result of the mistakes of the fund managers and the fall in the value of investments. Over the years the company had continued to take its costs and bonuses out of the funds, but the investors pensions suffered. He was left having to rely on his state pension. Jonathan had heard various politicians compare running the national economy to running a household budget, but these politicians forgot to mention one important difference between the treasury and a family's budget. Mother and father did not have the ability to print their own money! From 1931 Britain, like many other countries around the world, were no longer restricted to printing bank notes based on the amount of gold we had in our treasury. The value of our currency, like any other product that was bought and sold was based on the forces of supply and demand. Jonathan feared that in the future our society would become like a science fiction film he once watched called 'Soylent Green' where no one was allowed to live past a certain age. When they reached this magic age they were euthanized to make room for the young and their bodies made into green food for the population.

Jonathan was not a supporter of any totalitarian regime, he liked the possibilities, the social mobility and freedoms that the Capitalist system offered to those people who could take advantage of it. He supported proportional representation, individual enterprise and a freedom to choose. He did not like the idea of 'scroungers', who could not be bothered to make the effort to contribute to a system that will support them. However he also knew that to have an ethical and liberal capitalism in society those in the wealthy and economically powerful class must be constantly persuaded to assist and support those people that did not have the same share of the systems wealth that they expropriated. Before the first and second world wars and the growth of organised labour this class had been contained, but human sacrifice, political representation and changes in the law, made this more difficult. Post War governments realised this, and council housing programmes, state education, a national health service, offered hope to men who had come home from the war. They had served their country and their sacrifice protected their own homes but also the wealth of a class they were excluded from by their birth. If they were to be pacified they had to be given more avenues for social mobility. These soldiers knew how to fight, shoot guns, use explosives, and could be a dangerous group for politicians to alienate. They had to be offered a future for them and their children that was better than their past, and after rationing ended they needed to be promised that a time would come in the not too distant future where they, 'never had it so good!'

In the recent past Jonathan felt things had gone backwards for the young people in his care. Jonathan studied political history and was well aware that after Thatcher and Major everyone was encouraged to climb the ladder of wealth and success, get 'loads of money' and look out for themselves. The poor were portrayed as lazy, and Trade Unions were seen in the media as envious of other's success, or were 'reds under the beds' out to spoil the party and burst the 'Cities' balloon. Even the Labour governments got in bed with the City of London and eased controls on them gambling with people's money. The American system of a minimal state seemed to be replacing the British one as the model to be admired and adopted for health and social care. This attitude fermented a sea change in the relationship between the government and it's aspiring, capable young people. The government introduced an American type system of student loans for all and as a consequence the sense of duty and loyalty for teachers, doctors, and those in the caring services allied to the previous system of student grants was broken. When Jonathan went to university he was one of the last cohorts of students to get a grant from his local authority, and because of this he felt that a covenant existed between him and the society that had supported and trained him. He felt an obligation to the system that supported him and a duty to commit his early career choice to work in areas where he might make things better for those that followed. This sense of duty which he felt seemed less present amongst the graduates of today, but who could blame them. He knew first-hand how a student came out of University with loads of debt and who could criticise them if their loyalty was to find a way of reducing their financial burden. If they needed a mortgage or wanted to have a child in their twenties this debt was a big barrier to that happening. Yet again the system favoured the wealthy. Jonathan had an interesting conversation with his local G.P on his last visit to the surgery. His G.P. had been on duty since early in the morning and had not had a day off work for ten days. In his allocated eight minutes his doctor explained that he was overworked because they could not fill five vacancies for doctors at his practice. He believed that graduates finishing medical school with at least five years of debt did not find the N.H.S. an attractive prospect. They would get their student debt reduced much quicker if they went overseas to work. The G.P. stated the obvious; "Why should they serve in the system that trained them, do ridiculous hours, and for what? Just to end up like me, tired, stressed and drinking too much alcohol."

Shortages in teaching and the N.H.S. could be reduced if the government followed Jonathan's plan to pay off half of their student loan in return for a guaranteed period of service from them. He also felt that it would help in schools if they cut class sizes, cut paperwork, reduced the number of inspections, and focus on inspiring the subject teachers, not threatening them.

Some of the pupils he taught in school could not see the need for education once they could read write and do basic arithmetic. They worked in the large market that the local town was proud of and which attracted customers from all over Essex. Their attendance at school may have been erratic but they worked on the market from six in the morning until it closed in the evening. They made money from an early age. Bradley, one of Jonathan's non-exam fifth form pupils, was in line to take over his uncle's cake stall. Bradley came to school late on market days and despite numerous letters home nothing changed. He also played with Jonathan after school in the five a side football games and sometimes gave Jonathan his particular insight into life.

"Sir I don't mean to be rude, but all this stuff you teach us don't make us money. I don't need to know about algebra or some old dead geezer who writes plays. My uncle left school at fourteen and he's got a villa near Benidorm. He knows how to make money, like he says to me, usually when he's had a couple, 'all you've got to do Brett is buy something cheap and flog it rich and if you don't have to buy it in the first place, sweet!' It don't take no degrees to do that. I bet he makes more in a day down the market than you do in a week trying to teach us difficult bastards. Sorry sir didn't mean to swear."

"No offence taken. Brad it's nice to get your take on things." Jonathan smiled.

He was immediately reminded of a lift in a car he took when he had to hitch hike back to University, because he'd run out of money. A white BMW three series stopped at the roundabout and offered him a ride. The driver looked about twenty five with short hair and wearing a red polo shirt. Jonathan could see that he had a tattoo on each of his forearms. In the rear of the car was his small child in a flowery dress strapped into a car seat.

"Her names Lily, you can call me Al, it's not my real name, in case you turn out to be the 'old bill'. I hope you don't mind fast driving, I hate hangin' about. Just sit tight and enjoy the ride. What's your name and where do you live, in case I have to hunt you down? I am only joking mate!" With a wry smile on his face he rammed the car into first gear, pushed his foot down on the accelerator and took off at speed. His goal seemed to be to pass as many cars on the motor way as he could while singing with Lily at the top of his voice.

"Come on Jonathan, mate join in." Then looking in the rear view mirror at Lily said, "Lily, clap your hands if you want Johnno to sing with us. If he doesn't sing do you want me to throw him out of the car? Yeah, well that's my girl!"

Jonathan thought it better to sing than risk the alternative. When they got to Clacket Lane Services, Al told him that he had to do some business, change his daughter's nappy and take a 'whizz'. Al bought Jonathan a coke and a sandwich and asked him to sit with Lily while he went to talk to a man at a table on the opposite side of the restaurant.

Jonathan saw him give the older man with a shaved head and a tattoo on his arm a fat brown envelope. The man said his goodbyes to Al and left. Al seemed a little on edge but also pleased with himself. Al picked up Lily and said; "Come on the ladies let's get out of this place and I hope it's not the last thing we'll ever do, Jonathan you must know that one, an oldie and a goody, something for all us animals."

As they drove at speed along the motorway Al looked sideways at Jonathan, and then looked ahead. He obviously wanted to say something to him and couldn't make up his mind. In the end he could contain himself no longer.

"I will hopefully never see you again after the good deed I have done for you today and so I might as well tell about what you saw back there. That diamond geezer is a lorry driver with whom I have an arrangement, and as of now I am the proud owner of a container of tins of John West tuna and salmon. It is in a lockup, but very shortly it will be on its way to my buyer and I'll have made a tidy bundle."

"Al I know I shouldn't ask, but how's it done? Don't tell me if you don't want to." Jonathan asked tentatively. Al swerved the car into the outside lane of the motorway to overtake an Audi Jonathan could see that his head was buzzing.

"No, no that's cool. It's all covered by insurance, so no one loses. He stops at a service station, leaves his lorry in the carpark. I give him an incentive to take his time and look the other way. We come along, unhitch the trailer, and put it on our tractor and 'Bobs your uncle'. My uncle is not called Bob in case you are wondering Now I've told you, and of course should you tell anyone, it will bring you a world of pain!" Jonathan was not sure whether Al was joking at this point or being serious, but he thought he would risk one more question. "What if someone does talk, or say a driver gets cold feet?"

"Well, they would have to be taught a lesson by my associates and persuaded that it was in their interests to shut their mouths. If that did not work then they might have to disappear but nothing too suspicious; probably some accidents, to make it look like bad luck. They could trip and fall into some cement, get hit by a bus crossing a road, or fall in front of a train. You ok Lily my love? Give daddy a wave."

Jonathan felt his stomach clench which gave him a sudden need to go to the toilet. He wished he hadn't asked the question. Al could see that his answer had affected Jonathan more than he expected.

"Come on Johnno I'm just pulling your chain. You look a bit pale mate. I wouldn't do none of that, I would politely tell them that their employment was terminated and ask them to sign a confidentiality agreement…..probably in blood!" Al burst out laughing.

The car screeched to a halt. "This is your stop I think, time to leave, good bye and good luck. Have a good life. Lily, give him a wave, say bye, bye, to the nice man."

Jonathan got out of the car and stood by the side of the road. Al lent across the passenger seat and spoke to him through the open window of the car door. "Remember, Johnno, confidentiality agreement." With a spin of the wheels the car zoomed off down the inside lane of the motorway leaving him standing in the pouring rain waiting for his next lift.

Jonathan remembered that when he left the car he felt emotionally drained and yet excited, as if he had accidentally been parachuted into some crime drama on television. He had actually met a criminal and was fascinated by the carefree way in which Al seemed to ignore being apprehended and sent to prison. Jonathan could see the loving bond between Al and his daughter and yet he was prepared to risk watching her grow up from behind bars.

"You ok Sir? You look miles away." Bradley had packed away his football kit into his sports bag and was ready to leave the changing room.

"I'm fine Brad, I was daydreaming. Have a good night and maybe I'll see you in school Monday?" He wondered if Bradley would end up doing the same as Al to get his villa in Spain. After all, 'buy it cheap, sell rich, and if you don't have to buy it in the first place, sweet!" was his uncles motto and could have been Al's as well.

Jonathan did not want to be on the wrong side of the law. He had always struggled with his desire to see change for the better but at the same time the need to have a comfortable and conflict free existence. He did not like protest marches, and hated the thought of being arrested. He had thought about standing for the local council but there was not a political party that he wanted to join. He was not a joiner and hated being one of the crowds, but he needed to find some way to express his views. He was an avid watcher of Question Time and News Night on the B.B.C. and would have loved to be a presenter on a programme like that with the chance to put politicians on the spot.

In the local pub on a Friday evening, after the regular five a side football match, and the consumption of four pints of Guinness and at least two scotches, Jonathan found his audience. He would stand on his 'soap Box', usually an upturned beer crate on the floor next to bar and near to the pool table and 'orate'. Sometimes he would begin by talking to his opponent playing pool and as he potted successive balls his voice would get louder and louder. His friends and the somewhat startled customers in the saloon bar would cheer, some would leave, and some would tell him to go and live in China, or encourage him to become the potential Member of Parliament for the Coach and Horses Public House. Some were amazed at his ability to deliver these speeches while walking around the pool table potting balls with apparent ease and winning each game.

"Listen! All of you, I have just received my electricity bill and like you my alcoholic brethren I am somewhat in the dark about what it all means. It is like potting shots on this pool table there are so many angles to work out. Their bloody monopoly of the energy supply has us by the balls!"

"Oh no he's off again, get him a beer and shut him up." One of the regulars in the pub gave the barmaid a five pound note to buy Jonathan a drink. Jonathan would not be put off and continued speaking.

"Thank you for your kindness but I think you will all agree that Thatcher's gift to her mates was crazy. What do we want; we want energy prices to come down and less energy to be used. Energy efficient, that's what we want, but they won't do that because if they sell less energy to us, then the profits will go down and the prices will go up."

Frank Carpenter a local builder standing at the bar could contain himself no longer,

"You call yourself a teacher but I think what you say is a load of crap. You live in a bubble mate, it was the 'Iron Lady', bless her heart, who allowed me to buy my council house, and I bought shares in one of those companies. I'm not going to give them back. And why shouldn't me and people like me have a bit of the cake? I do the lottery every week and I want to be rich. Fuck those who say the money wouldn't change them; I'd want it to change me. Good bye to this shit hole and hello to the south of France, or Mallorca."

Jonathan knew that he had consumed too much alcohol and did not want his evening to end in unpleasantness. One of his colleagues from school tugged at his arm to get his attention.

"Time to leave now, let's say our farewells and go, I think they get the idea and we don't want the landlord to bar us from here."

Jonathan heeded his advice.
"Sir, I can appreciate what you are saying, I wish you a great weekend, and my best wishes to you and yours, but I have just been informed that my taxi awaits, and I you could take bets on whether I can walk in a straight line to the door. I thank you all for indulging me." With this parting speech Jonathan left the 'Coach and Horses' never to return.

After climbing down from the bench he was standing on in the public bar that Friday, and recovering from a massive hangover the following day, he entered a period of contemplation. His partner was pleased that he would moderate his drinking and give up trying to tell those who would listen how he would right the wrongs of the world. She had been frightened that someday she would get a call from accident and emergency at the local hospital because he had been beaten up by an angry listener. Jonathan came to the realisation that the fire in his belly fuelled by alcohol, a strong sense of social injustice, and sexual frustration, had a lot to do with a feeling that his life and relationships had not progressed as he wanted them to. He felt he was in a rut, and he had lost touch with the creative part of himself that he enjoyed in Bristol. It was about two months after that evening in the pub that he began to write again. Firstly he tried poems, then the beginnings of a play, followed by a brief attempt to complete the novel he had thought of in Bristol. He found a copy of the play he had written in a box in his loft and beside it the outline for the book he thought about writing. Sometimes he felt more confident in his abilities than others and so it took him a while to find what he wanted to write about. He had let go of the feeling of responsibility he felt to talk about social injustices affecting others to focus on the work he had to do on himself. He was able to accept that politicians would continue to use education as a political football and that would never change no matter what complexion of political party was in power. What he could do was to change his future and getting a novel published would achieve that. He also decided to end his relationship with Gill his live in partner.

Whenever Jonathan looked back at this time of change in his life, it seemed to be a world away from where he was now. All the upheaval he went through then had been worthwhile, because the end result of it was to free him up enough to write, and make a space in his heart for a special someone with whom he fell in love. Although the love he found came with complications of its own, he was fortunate it was a slow burning love which evolved over time. He consoled himself with the thought that, as with all things worthwhile, it was worth the wait.

Eventually, after toying with various genres for his first novel he settled on writing a crime novel. Initially this style was not something he thought he would choose because with his political obsessions he was more inclined to write a novel exposing political intrigue and corruption. However he needed to do something completely different, outside of his comfort zone and more likely to be popular fiction. He researched the works of successful authors like Jeffrey Deaver, Peter James, or Thomas Harris the creator of Hannibal Lecter to get an idea of what he should compare his own creation with. He also wanted to have fun writing the book. It had to be something that would engage his imagination and he could have fun and play with. If it got published and sold in its thousands, then perhaps made into a film or television series the consequences would be life changing for him and his young family. He developed his story over a period of two years, mostly in school holidays, when he was free from the distractions and responsibilities of teaching. When he felt that his writing was as polished as he could get it and despite his historical fears of rejection, he sent extracts of his manuscript to three publishers whose addresses he obtained from the inside pages of crime novels. He did not let the love of his life read it or give it to a friend for their opinion. He was mindful of a reflection that Henry Miller shared in one of his novels about being a struggling author in Paris. He advised authors not show manuscripts to friends because friendship is based on similarities of interest and ability. If you are a creative artist and they are not, your effort makes you different to them and in some ways more special. If they are jealous of your ability or competitive in their relationship with you then they will criticise, ignore, and withhold praise. If they are frightened that your success will cause you to leave them behind then they will want to keep you close by diminishing your achievement. They may easily give praise and admiration to others who do the same thing as you but at the same time withhold praise and support from you. They will not wish to acknowledge the talent close to them but only those at a distance. It takes an evolved personality who feels fulfilled within to be able to recognise such ability in one close to them.

One of the publishers that replied was Finch and Faber. Mark Finch asked him to send additional chapters of his novel in the post after his initial submission sent to the publisher by e-mail. Recently Jonathan received an e-mail inviting him to meet with Mark Finch at their offices near Russell Square in London. Jonathan was so excited by this opportunity he accepted immediately but not soon after he began to worry. He remembered what happened to him in Bristol. He hated the fact that these people had so much power over him. His fate would be decided by a stranger to whom he meant nothing. This man would decide whether his novel 'The Gardener' would be published and his life as an author could begin.

He sat alone in the sixth form common room. A slowly aging teacher desperate for a change of career, but this was in the hands of Mark Finch, someone who was probably public school, Oxbridge educated, who with one signature on a contract could make his dreams come true. He was unmarried with responsibilities' waiting at a crossroads in his life; he felt he had sacrificed enough for his vocation.

This sixth form block had so many good memories for him. It was where he taught 'A' level English Grammar and Literature to eager students who wanted to be inspired and grew to love his subject as much as he did. It also held memories of great sadness, internal torment, beauty and hope. His thoughts drew him back to times gone by. He had been teaching for about six years and he was 29 years of age. One afternoon he was teaching his students in the sixth form common room, and they were sitting around a table in the alcove of the large bay window. He was caught up in the poem he was reading aloud to them. It was ' The Wasteland' by T.S. Eliot, one of the most important modernist poems, and an 'A' level text. He looked up from the page to realise that they were not taking a blind bit of interest, with the exception of Jasmine who seemed to be listening intently with her eyes shut. To the side of the alcove, on the floor, there stood a wicker waste paper basket which was hidden from the students view. While he read to the students he had been pacing back and forth in front of the table. When he got to his next turn he picked up the bin and quickly placed it over his head, and continued reading and walking. He wanted to find out how long it would take them to notice his headwear. Jasmine spotted it first and started to giggle; it took six lines of verse before they all looked up from whatever they were doing and joined in the laughter.

The students' attention to the poem was restored but the problem for Jonathan was that when he took the basket off his head he noticed that Mr Relish the Head of the Sixth Form was watching him through the common room window. They smiled at each other.

While he was having his cup of tea at afternoon break in the staff room Mr Relish walked over to where he was sitting.

"A unique approach to teaching poetry, John, seemed like fun. The students told me it was 'The Wasteland', very apt!"

Jonathan went to sleep that night and for the first time dreamt about Jasmine. It was not Jasmine as she was in class, she had the body of his last girlfriend, and they were running towards each other at the edge of the water on a beach somewhere. When they got close he saw that it was Jasmine's face. Then, as often happens in dreams, something weird happened, as he kissed her passionately on the mouth, and her tongue gently flicked between his lips, his teeth came loose in his gums and filled his mouth like a handful of Tick-Tac mints. To stop himself choking he was forced to spit them out and watched as they flew through the air in slow motion landing on the sand at her feet. He woke up in a sweat and sat up in bed breathing heavily. This was wrong, he thought, he should not have these thoughts about a pupil, but like it or not, approve of it or not, he did. He must do nothing and certainly not give Jasmine any reason to suspect that may have these feelings for her. He knew that another teacher had been removed from the school after he was seen and reported to the headmaster for meeting a sixth form pupil in a bar after school. They swore that there was nothing inappropriate happening between them at the time but he knew from overhearing one of her friends still at school that after the student left for university the teacher had visited her there. He was critical of that teacher at the time and cut of contact with him. Surely he could not be that hypocritical and follow in his footsteps.

Jasmine struck him as a lonely soul, who kept herself to herself, and seemed older for her years than the other girls of her age. It helped his positive feelings towards her because she seemed to love his lessons and share in his sense of humour. She was an intelligent eighteen year old girl. She was one of the hardest working of his students and wanted to study English and Drama at Bristol University, after her 'A' levels. She had heard him talk about his time at the university and what a great student friendly city Bristol was. From what he knew of her over her years at the school, her parents had separated when she was six years old and her brother had joined the Navy. Jasmine told him in a tutorial that her brother had a rapid series of promotions in the Navy but now felt very unhappy. He wanted to buy himself out of the Navy but didn't have the money and he was desperate not to be posted to the Gulf.

The contemporary author they had to study for their A level exam was D.H. Lawrence. The novel chosen was 'Sons and Lovers', a favourite book for Jonathan to teach. Jasmine asked Mr Hope if he would give her some additional coaching for her exam. He thought deeply about this as he knew that time spent alone with her may intensify the feelings that he was frightened of having towards her. He told himself that he was a professional and that what he felt amounted to a teenage crush should not spoil her chances of good grades and University entrance. He agreed to the extra lessons, as long as her mother approved and payed for his extra time at school. He wanted this to be on a proper basis and did not want her to feel grateful for the extra teaching.

They met in a small room in the sixth form block after school; he made sure that they were not alone in the building and that other school staff were still around and on the premises. She sat next to him while they looked at her exam texts and her assignments. Jonathan thought she dressed well, quite demurely compared to some others in the group, she didn't wear much makeup, and he felt that there was an inner strength about her which made Jonathan calm when he was with her. If he looked at her in the class when she was sitting quietly reading or writing she seemed noble in her demeanour, sweet and attractive. She had short brown hair cut with a bias, deep brown eyes and a petite figure which looked great in jeans. She wore a perfume that reminded him of summer flowers, particularly if the central heating in the room was too high. Initially she came to his notice because she actually wanted to learn from him and know more and more about the subjects they studied. He looked forward to their time together and began to listen for any hint of a boyfriend in her conversation. He was well aware of the age gap between them, and his responsibility to her and her parent as a teacher. He did not think for one moment that she reciprocated any of the feelings he felt for her towards her, towards him. He rationalised his interest in Jasmine as being a substitute parent. He was someone for her to rely on in the absence of her real father and someone who took a kind and benevolent interest in her wellbeing. Try as he might he could not control his unconscious and he did have more wish fulfilment dreams of a sexual nature and this feeling of arousal bothered him. This was something that had not happened since he was twelve. He also had dreams of them walking in a park with what he assumed was their baby in a pushchair. He also dreamt of them shopping in Marks and Spencer's food hall together.

Jasmine never took advantage of their closeness or familiarity bred by the extra lessons in his classes and she was careful in company to keep an appropriate distance between them. Some of the students made comments about her privileged relationship with 'Sir', but Jasmine attributed these to their envy of her gaining knowledge, more than to anything else. Then that Christmas she sent him a card which she signed 'Love Jasmine' with two kisses underneath. His heart skipped a beat when he read this, but he wondered what had prompted this sign of affection at this time. Jonathan tried to connect the dots in his memory and then rightly or wrongly he connected it to a recent tutorial they had in which he told her of D. H. Lawrence's affair with the wife of his university professor. They ran off to Switzerland together, deserting and sacrificing the ones who loved and depended upon them on the altar of the passion they felt for each other. He remembered telling her that this real life event was the basis for Lawrence's other great novel, 'Women in Love'. This great novel, dealt with characters who loved too much, wanted sexual freedom, compared love between men to the love of a man for a female, and others in the novel who, sadly were so damaged by their tormented early relationships that they could not love at all. He told her that 'Women in love' was a bitter sweet story of unfulfilled attachments.

"Gerald, in the book really wanted the closeness with a woman that he felt with his male friend, but the woman he unconsciously became paired with despised his maleness and wanted to compete with it. He was like a stallion whose will she had to break. Some men are born on the cross of the love they seek, maybe we all are."

"Sir, don't you think women are as well, you told us about the John Lennon song lyric, 'Women are the niggers of the world', about women's subservience to men and male chauvinism in all cultures around the world. I hate to use that word but in terms of class and power, in history, below the most exploited man is his woman. I don't think I want to be married or be a wife who must love and obey."

Mr Hope looked at Jasmine and smiled.

"I admire your passion Jasmine, and you should be choosey if you have a relationship, when you want a close relationship. There are too many men who actually want women but don't like them, and too many women who need men but don't like them. If I love someone I want them to be happy and I want them to feel that I will help them fulfil themselves the best that I can, and I want them to feel that way about me too. But sometimes, after the honeymoon time is over, when you're love bubble bursts, you start to see people for who they actually are, and not what you wanted them to be. When you start seeing the differences, rather than the similarities between you and them, then the real love starts."

When Jonathan stopped talking he was aware that Jasmine was staring at him with a look on her face that made him feel slightly embarrassed and as a consequence he started to blush.

"It's hot in this room; Jasmine would you like me to open a window?"

"No Sir, I'm fine. I think what you say is special. Having seen what happens with my mum and dad I think they married when they were too young. They never seem happy."

Mr Hope thought he could see a tear in the corner of one her eyes. He recollected that from the moment she joined his class he had always thought she had beautiful dark brown eyes.

"Jasmine the characters in the novel, you, me, your mum and dad, we are all people who need to be able to give love and feel love in return."

"I see that Sir, but like you said, it's what kind of love we give and get that matters."

It was then he noticed this was the first time she had broken the distance between them by gently, almost accidently touching his arm. She could see he was getting emotional. She leant forward resting, her hand on his arm and asked;

"Sir, do you think love and desire like that is worth such a sacrifice? I mean they risked hurting themselves and others, shame and social disapproval."

When she spoke she held him in her gaze and for a moment it passed through his mind that his answer could in some way dictate her future. He looked away, cleared his throat, blew his nose and weighed up his answer carefully before replying.

"Jasmine that was a different time. It was a time before sexual equality. Freud's ideas were making an impact on Lawrence, in that time women probably made the biggest sacrifice because society had different standards for them than it did for men. Not that it is so different now; women are still expected to hold the best and worst values for society. It was before reliable contraception, when pregnancy held a fifty percent chance of women dying in childbirth. There was greater sexual tension in relationships because of ignorance around lovemaking and the guilt that religion spread surrounding sexual expression. Remember all this happened before twenty four hour news, social media and all that stuff which makes it harder for couples to escape scrutiny and be found. They escaped to the mountains, and it was nearly a year before they surfaced, then they communicated by letter. If you are interested you should see the Ken Russell movie of the book, Alan Bates plays a teacher in it, with

Glenda Jackson, Oliver Reed and another actress whom I never remember."

"Yes, but Sir, would you give everything up for love, and take that risk with someone?"

"I know it sounds so romantic to you now Jasmine, but we all have responsibilities, and we must be prepared to live with the consequences of our actions. I guess I'm a bit more cautious than Lawrence; I would like to think I might but I would probably go for a run and think about it. No, if I felt that much in love, I think I would take a risk."

"There you go Sir; you are a romantic at heart. My friends think that Lawrence was sex mad because of the book about the game keeper and the lady. They watched the programme on the television. I felt sorry for the lady because she loved her husband but he was emotionally scared and physically wounded. His wife needed to feel alive and that was where the game keeper came in. He was connected to the earth and nature and had no shame about his body or sex. Do you think love and sex have to go together for people to be happy? My mother said my Dad left her because she wasn't enough for him. What do you think Sir?"
"I can't speak about your mum and dad because I don't know much about them but for me , I think if you love someone you should try to work things out, and if that takes time, well it could be frustrating but in the end, worth the wait."

Jonathan was not sure how the conversation had got to this place, but he needed to change the subject and get back to what he felt would be safer ground.

"Anyway let's get back to the book."

"Didn't Lawrence die in Mexico? I watched a great documentary about his house there."

Jonathan felt it was time to cut the conversation short. "Yes he did, anyway, it's time for us to go, and I've got a lot of marking tonight. Is your Mum picking you up from school?"

"Yes she is, she'll probably be outside waiting, and I had better go. Thanks Sir, very much, I loved the lesson." Jasmine got up and left the room closing the door behind her. John watched her back as she left leaving him with the smell of summer flowers.

Jasmine did not know that in his private life he was without a relationship as he had broken up with his girlfriend of three years, six months before. They had met when he came to the school and she was the drama teacher whom he had helped with her school theatre productions. They were happy for a couple of years but after the first few dates she told him that she did not believe in sex before marriage. He father and mother were devoted Christians and they wanted her to have a white wedding. She wore a ring of chastity which they had given her when she went up to university. Jonathan liked her, she was attractive, fun, had a 'fit' body as the kids would say, and loved the movies in the same way he did. He did not want to come across to her as a man who wanted her for her sexy body and not for her other qualities and so he agreed to abide by her wishes. She could do the physical things in their relationship at her own because he wanted to be with her. It wasn't that they didn't learn to gratify each other with certain sexual practices that were on her 'to do' list. They got naked and slept with each other in the same bed, they had orgasms, but for Gill intercourse or other forms of penetration were not on the agenda. He understood that she was saving herself for her wedding night. He felt under a constant pressure to propose, and he was not happy that he felt in an inferior position in their partnership. More and more he found himself begging her for some sexual gratification. He would go to her flat after work and find her in the kitchen preparing a meal. He had been thinking about this moment on the drive home and the movement of the car had got him aroused. After saying his usual "Honey I'm home," which was a joke between them, he walked into the kitchen went up behind her and put his arms around her then a kissed her on her lovely neck.

"God you smell great, in case you wonder, that is not a gun in my pocket, I am just pleased to see you. Come to the bedroom and let us work our magic."

"Is there anything you would like for a starter?"
Jonathan knew it was a corny reply but he could not help himself.

"Could I have you, naked on my plate?"

"Not now, Jonathan really I've got the food on, maybe tomorrow after we go to swimming."

Jonathan felt she did not wish to appreciate what it was like for him to have an itch that needed scratching immediately to be told to wait until tomorrow. What could he do, if he got angry with her it would not happen tomorrow, he could not force himself upon her like a caveman,

99

because he respected her too much? There were times in the last few months when he had come close to doing just that. He could go into another room, turn on the internet and masturbate to some erotic video clip showing women who were always available. That wasn't a choice because he would feel sad and embarrassed, even though it was her fault. "I'm going for a run; I'll be back in half an hour."

He could relieve his sexual tension by pounding the pavements rather than his manhood which he felt had been castrated by pasta.

"Ok, enjoy your run; I won't put the pasta in the pot until you're having your shower." Gill shouted after him as he went out of the back door.

There was no big dramatic scene to end their relationship; they had separate accommodation, even though he had spent most of the last year sleeping at hers, there were few personal possessions to take back to his flat. The time between seeing each other gradually increased until one Thursday evening after their curry at a restaurant in Brentwood high street, she drank the last gulp of her Chardonnay, looked him in the eye and said;

"Jonathan, sweetheart, are you ever going to propose to me? I need to know now. My biological clock is ticking louder by the day and I need to find someone who wants to be a father to the children I want to have. You never tell me that's what you want. I need to know."

"Gill, I'm really sorry to let you down, I do feel bad that I can't offer you what you need. In the end I guess we want different things. I know you think I can't wait forever, but I still think there is a novel in me, and I have to try, that's my biological clock, and it's ticking just as loud as yours."

He moved out the following weekend. At school they were civil, and friendly with each other in the staffroom. The rest of the staff were divided between those that said they saw it coming, and those that told him he was stupid to let go of a woman like Gill. Jonathan agreed to continue helping her with the production of the school plays. It was about eight weeks after his conversation with Gill at the Indian restaurant that Jasmine arrived for her tutorial with him in floods of tears. She told Jonathan that she had received a text message from her brother to say that he had been arrested by Navy Police and charged with desertion. She had looked up the penalties for deserting the armed forces on her phone and found out that he could be in prison for a long time.

"My mum will be destroyed, she feels so guilty because she was going to borrow money on the house to get him out. We all told him to give himself up, because before this he had a great record, he just had a breakdown."

"Come on Jasmine this is a shock for you. Here look have some water, you can talk to me say whatever you want and it won't go any further."

"No! No, I've got to go home; I've got to find out where he is."

With this declaration she turned away from Mr Hope and moved towards the door, paused and started sobbing again. Jonathan could see her shoulders rise and fall with each gasp of breath; she seemed so hurt and vulnerable. He wasn't sure what to do, did he respond from a place of her mentor, her friend, her substitute father, or someone who had feelings for her he knew he should not have, love? He walked up behind her and put his arms around her shoulders to hold her, so that she did not feel so alone. She turned and melted into his chest. He held her close, quietly stroking her hair to reassure her. He told himself that this was no different from what any feeling person faced with someone distressed.

"Ok you feel calmer now, would you like to tell me what your brother did, sometimes talking helps find some direction, here, sit down by me. Here's a clean handkerchief to wipe your face."

With a blotched red face and runny nose she told Mr Hope what had happened.

"He was very good at computer games and they soon noticed this, and so he was trained in tracking missiles and missile defence systems. He also learned how to fly drones for recognisance. He was posted to a cruiser and went on patrol. While he was in the Gulf, or Iraq, or somewhere like that a missile was fired at the ship they were guarding. Well, practice in the base and computer games are one thing, but the pressure he felt to defend lives really got to him. He said he realised that his computers and anti-missile machinery was positioned at the front of the ship. It didn't take a genius to work out that any enemy who wanted to disable his ship would target the front of the ship first. He said it dawned on him that he had actually signed up to die. He couldn't get on another ship and so after his shore leave he didn't go back. He had talked to the Chaplin on the ship about his fears and to his credit he offered to write a letter for my brother to his admiral, or whoever it was, to support his early exit from the Navy, but nothing happened."

Jonathan could see that she had calmed down as she talked and was no longer tearful.

"At least he has someone on his side, what about you?"

"I'll be O.K. it was the shock of the text, I did not know who to go to and I knew you would be waiting for me, I'm so thankful, you are kind."

"That's O.K. Is your mother picking you up?

"Yes in about ten minutes, but I'll go and wash my face in the loo."

With this she got up out of her chair and moved towards the door. Jonathan followed her a second afterwards to hold the door open for her, and as he leant forward to turn the handle on the door, Jasmine turned towards him, leaned in close, and kissed him on his cheek.

In no time Jasmine was gone from the room leaving the scent of summer flowers behind her.

The cleaner switched on her vacuum machine, and the sound of it interrupted Jonathan's trance-like reverie. With a jolt similar to an electric shock being applied to his body his attention was brought back into the common room. He felt as if he had been time travelling and the years between Jasmine passing her exams, leaving school for Bristol University, getting a first class degree, doing her M.A., her brother getting out of the Navy, and her mother getting remarried, were all accelerated through space and time. Years had passed. Jasmine had visited the Swiss Alps and Mexico. It was before he was inspired to write his book. She contacted him by e-mail at the school and then skyped him while on her travels. When she returned to England she asked him to meet her. She told him that on her travels she had been approached by a number of men, young and old but that none of them compared to him. She felt that she had waited long enough, and it would break her heart if he did not feel the same, but she knew from their conversations that there was no woman in his life, and she had to tell him. She asked him if he still saw her as this stupid schoolgirl or as a woman he could love.

He listened with tears rolling down his face as if a dam of emotion suddenly broke inside him. Jasmine knew at that moment that her wait had been worthwhile.

"Of course I love you; all this time I could not let myself go. I could not let myself hope. But yes, my beautiful scent of summer, yes, I do."

They both sobbed and hugged in the middle of the café with the other customers looking on, and then one customer started clapping and the others joined in.

Jasmine qualified as a teacher, and as soon as it was possible, they had a baby.

"Evening Shirley, am I in your way?"

"You are staying long Mr Hope? Please excuse me I've got to get on."

"No you work around me I just need to read something on the laptop before tomorrow. I have a big day ahead." Jonathan opened the laptop and chapter FIVE of his manuscript 'The Gardener 'appeared.

Chapter Seven: What Happens on Holiday

David sat at the large panoramic window of the club house overlooking the eighteenth green waiting for the rest of the lads to finish their rounds of golf. David's golfing partners had left him there to go up to the driving range with a bucket of range balls hoping to iron out any faults in their swing before the others arrived at the clubhouse. Left to his own devices, and with only a glass of red wine and a packet of dry roasted peanuts to distract him, his thoughts about the relationship between the sexes continued to rampage through his mind. Just below him on the pathway where the golf buggies were parked he recognised Stanley, another member of the golf club with whom he had recently played a mid-week medal with. Stanley's wife had just given birth to boy twins. Stanley was finding sleepless nights with the babies and the demands of his job in a city bank overwhelming. David had exhausted his thoughts on mothers and inevitably this vacuum was filled by the question of the role of fathers. "What about our fathers in all of this?" The answer seemed depressingly obvious, because as David observed, for the most part in his growing up the chances were that dad was not around. They were at work and for this reason all sons are virtually abandoned by their fathers. That could be their excuse for not taking any responsibility for how their child's attitudes or personalities were formed. Their father abandoned them to the mercy of their mother and they had to survive, so why shouldn't their sons just get on with it and stop winging. On the other hand perhaps the son simply copied how their father behaved towards their mother. Maybe Dad saw their son as competition for his wife's affections and slapped him down. Eventually, boys are old enough and big enough, to break free from their mother's apron strings and strike out alone. Like Hansel and Gretel they may be pushed out of the family nest too soon, and be left in the forest by their mother. Or their mother may have held on to them too long to avoid a life alone with their father which has lost its appeal. Eventually they get free. However just as the drive for independence from one woman becomes possible, their hormones kick in and they are directed to find a romantic and sexual partner. For men, suddenly their penis behaves as if it is a divining rod finding water in a desert. Now it's not their mother they need but a new and younger version of her gender. Their logic and ability to make rational choices is clouded by a magnetic and potentially fatal attraction, the desperate need to be loved, and to feel special returns. It doesn't matter if they are a man or a woman, or up to this point in their lives, they have behaved like an angel or a demon, they now become a slave to love. David thought of the millions of love songs that had been written by men to girls. Each one telling them how much they adored them, wanted them by their side forever, and would run through fire to find them. David had often thought it funny that in these songs men and women lovers were referred to as 'babies'. Baby love; Love to love you baby; Baby where did our love go? He imagined women in makeup and high heel shoes wearing nappies, dating men dressed the same. When he mentioned to one of his golf buddies that he was fed up of the use of the word baby in songs and told him of his vision the guy showed him a clip from a fetish website where this actually happened.

David didn't want to be Claire's baby and she wasn't his but they did look after each other in sickness and in health. He comforted himself in the knowledge that unlike a lot of couples, he never had a baby nickname for Claire, or she for him, even when they were dating. They didn't indulge in baby talk with each other like some couples do. She called him, love, darling, honey, or sweet, but when she was angry with him she called him David.

When David left his childhood home and first lived alone he was faced with the problem of having no one to look after his needs. How will the cooking, cleaning, shopping laundry, ironing, etc. get done? David had either lived at home, with a girlfriend, or for the brief periods when he had a small flat, he discovered the benefits of the laundrette and takeaway food. When he first moved away from home to another town, because of a promotion at work, he was encouraged to take his washing home to his mother in large black plastic bags. This practice continued until one month when she unpacked the bag she found that his tee shirts and underpants had green mould growing on them.

It took David a while to find the love he sought, to find a soul mate. On a Friday night after work it was a ritual that his boss took them out for a drink at a pub near the office. He usually drank too much and was prone to giving the younger members of the staff advice, whether they wanted it or not.
"David my boy, you could go far in this business and what you need is a good woman behind you. Not too good, mind you, if you get my meaning. You need someone like my dear wife. I swear to you she is a domestic goddess in the kitchen, and thank god! And this is not to insult her in any way, but a whore in the bedroom. That David has a lot going for it."

105

David read somewhere, probably in a magazine at his Dentist, that when you found the right woman you felt that you were reunited with a part of yourself that you had lost. David thought that it must be the same for women. He had also remembered a line from a card he had read which said, "We are born on the cross of the love we seek." In moments of loneliness and doubt in his search for love he definitely felt like this. The right woman would make you feel as if you were finally complete. Claire had this effect on him. However he was well aware that on his journey to find his soul mate, and as much as he had tried not to be hurt by, or hurt anyone, this quest for love had brought out the best and worst in his character. This was one of the main reasons that he felt so protective of his daughter Jodie. This was the reason why he had finally come to the decision that Mark Finch was no good for her, and why he felt that introducing Jodie to him was like leading a lamb to the slaughter. This was one aspect of the unfinished business with Mark he intended to sort out when he travelled to London to see him. David knew he would be at his office on his wedding anniversary. His wife Mary had told Claire she was going to surprise him there. David knew it was a priority that he spoke to Mark alone in case things got nasty. He did not want Jodie to be present when this happened and to witness what could become an unpleasant confrontation. She could see a side to her father's character that she had not seen before. The whole issue of the relationship between daughters and fathers was something else he had given a great amount of thought to.

The flag hanging on the pole just in David's eye line fluttered and this movement was enough to interrupt his concentration on the weighty thoughts in his head and make him aware of his surroundings. He realised that in the time that had elapsed since he sat down he had not touched his drink or his peanuts and so he took a large swig of the wine and a mouthful of nuts.

"David, my old Buddy. Get the drinks in!"

The Milligan brothers walked off the last hole and into the clubhouse with the highest points score for the round. Then, as was the custom they treated everyone to a few drinks, some French fries, followed by the sight of them eating an enormous bowl of mussels cooked in garlic, crème and white wine. They loved food as much as they loved sex, and they indulged themselves in both when their wives were not around. This meal was their faithful contribution to the strict calorie controlled diet that their wives had put them on after their last medical which showed their cholesterol to be dangerously high. They were told that they needed to do more exercise and so they bought a gym, and gave all of their friend's free membership. The only problem was that the gym they belonged to was in Soho near to their favourite restaurant and their office. They solved the problem of their erratic attendance for exercise at the gym by deciding to rename the toilet in their office, previously referred to as 'the John', as the 'the gym', and hung a sign to this effect over the entrance. This meant that they could say to their wives, if asked, that that had visited the gym regularly or at least once a day. Their wives could spend what money they wanted when they came to London to do shopping. It was their custom to collect rolled up banknotes in elastic bands that magically appeared at the front desk of their husband accountants' office situated near Leicester Square.

The brothers had an economic view of relationships with the opposite sex. On the plane to Las Vegas David sat next to the eldest brother Patrick who explained this point of view to him.

"I look at relationships as if they were a bank account, because you have to make sure that your relationship with your wife is always in credit. If it is the bank manager leaves you alone. I try to make sure that with my wife I am always in credit in the current account, and not only that I have a bit saved up in her deposit account in case I do something that makes me overdrawn. I do what most men do, I look after my wife and I keep her in a comfortable home with her own car and credit card. She doesn't have to work; she has a job looking after me and the kids. She likes skiing, so we go to the Alps once a year, she likes the sun so we've got our villa in Portugal and one in Cyprus. She is the same with me; I need her to be in credit with me emotionally and sexually, because then I don't feel hard up if she wants to make a withdrawal. By that I mean, let's say she wants to go away with my sister in-law and leave me to my own devices, and I do not want to worry about what she gets up to. Well if I feel that she has invested enough in me in terms of giving me attention, looking after my needs, kept me happy, if you know what I mean? If my demand has not exceeded her supply, I am happy and I can trust her. Then I'm fine about it. Now, say this happens too often or for too long a time, then she may go into an overdraft situation and I have to call in the loan. We have to make sure that my demand does not exceed her supply, or vice versa. For example, I know she can't be available for sex whenever I want it, and so I do not put that pressure on her, I stock up on the deposit account somewhere else, but I do not rub her nose in it. My brother and me we are the same, we do not have anything to do with our 'Babes' as hot as they are, we keep it professional, as unbelievable as it may seem. We sell the fantasy of available sex, men want it and we make a lot of money doing it. Our girls make good money as well and we don't force them to do anything on the T.V. that they do not want to do. Sex is a product like anything else, it is a commodity, and it has a price, whether you are married or not. Come on David you know this, every man does, and so do the women. Sex is part of a bargain you make with the woman you're with. It may not be out in the open but it is part of the deal for any couple. Like all business nothing is free, it all depends on supply and demand. In the paper they reported that the two things that couples argue most about in a relationship is money and sex .The arguments in marriage about sex come down to the fact that once you get married the bloke has a monopoly of supply for the wife and she has a monopoly of supply over him. They vow to be faithful each other, and so it's like agreeing to buy your electricity from one supplier and not switch if the price gets too high or the service is crap. So the price you are prepared to pay for sex depends on the supply of it and the demand you have for it. If one person needs it more than the other then the price goes up, the deal is more expensive to one person than the other. What people go through to pay this price in their relationships is fucking ridiculous, in terms of all the feelings of pain and hurt that people go through. A wife or the husband holding out on each other to get a price they want for the service they give and fucking with the other one's head. Just think of the frustration, the anger, and the boozing, fucking exercise, winding each other up, prick teasing, and fucking rape, which is like an armed bank robbery. Fuck that! Find another supplier, someone who appreciates your demand! A monopoly of supply seems great to begin with, but competition is the basis of great capitalism and we are capitalists."

"You could have an affair?"

"No, no, David you are missing the point, affairs fuck up your marriage, too messy. We go for the free market."

"What if you catch something and bring it back home?"

"Rules, don't go with trash, and wear something. You get what you pay for."

"But what about what happened to Phil in Thailand?"

"Phil's a 'donkey' there was no way that girl in Bangkok was actually in love with him. He wouldn't listen; I told him he was a commodity to her as much as she was to him. It was a deal, a trade they made. It was her job to make him feel special, to give him the best blow job he had ever had, to make him feel wanted. He was her cash cow and they worship cows in that country. I'm not saying that she didn't feel anything for him, he had her for the week and she probably appreciated the fact that she didn't have to find other work that treated her worse. The fact that he fell in love with her, well, love was the bonus. This is the same for all of us, if you're led by your dick, love, money; the only thing that changes is the currency we use. Don't get me wrong, I like the guy, I want him to be happy, I warned him, like you did, but he was fucking sad and lonely, and believed what he wanted to believe. She was probably giving the money he sent to her family. I saw a documentary about families getting rid of their girls because they cost them money. Don't get me wrong I do feel for her, but they do it to make a living and stay alive. The money he sent for the lap top so he could see her on line was just the start, and money for the plane ticket was never going to get her on a plane. I told Phil he was stupid, but he was obsessed with her, and he had no one at home."

David paused for thought;

"I think I might be a bit like him if I gave in to temptation. The problem with me is that I think of the parents of these women. I can't divorce myself from the idea that they have fathers and mothers. How would I feel if my daughter Jodie had to sell her body to survive? I find it hard to put things in compartments like you. It's why I could never be a surgeon because I can't separate their body parts from the person. I'm not making out that I'm better than you or anything like that, it's just that I don't think that it's worth lying to Claire or myself and betraying her trust for sex with a stranger. No matter how desirable they are. I'm no saint, it's really hard, no pun intended, and there have been times when I wished I could just say to myself, sod it! I do get frustrated and I wish I could let go. I can't say I haven't envied you. To be honest it's never made sense to me why I'm the one feeling the guilt when you're the Catholic."

Patrick raised his airline plastic cup filled with whisky and dry ginger as if to toast David. Then, in his Southern Irish accent which he used infrequently and had learned from his father said; "Forgiveness, penance and confession David, it's never too late."

"Well as Phil would say, it is what it is, it is what it is." David replied.

David felt a tap on his shoulder. Mark Finch seated behind him leant forward to speak so that David could hear him;

"You OK, David? I heard a bit of that. If Paddy could write as well as he talks I could have a best seller. I would have to change names to protect the innocent. Nothing in there for you to worry about, but it could cause a few embarrassed faces. They might go home one day and find their child's bunny being boiled in a saucepan on the cooker, like in that movie."

"What Movie?"

"The movie where, Clint Eastwood or it might be Michael Douglas has an affair with this woman, who turns out to be an obsessive psycho."

"What 'Play Misty for Me'?"

"That was Clint Eastwood and he was a D.J. great film."

"It wasn't that film", said Patrick interrupting. "He was working in an office and it was that actress who married our boy Bruce."
"What Demi Moore?"

"I know that film." David said. "It was 'Disclosure'. I remember I watched that with Claire and she was funny with me for about a week afterwards."

"Come on David, get real, she knows that you are a saint. Patrick you must know, you love your movies. Who is it?"

"I try not to think of it too much, as you may imagine, knowing what saintly lives my brother and I lead, but well anyway, let it be a lesson to all those poor souls who cannot keep their dick in their pants, keep silent as the grave and the wife and the bit on the side very far apart. It was Douglas and Glen Close, and the movie was 'Fatal Attraction'. Now, for 'feck sake', leave me alone, I want a large glass of the good stuff, and to get some sleep."

He reached up above his head and pressed the button to attract the attention of the stewardess.

They were five hours into their journey and David had lost interest in watching any movie on the plane and so he took a Sominex and settled down to sleep.
In Las Vegas they stayed at the MGM Grand and Casino, they had booked West Wing Tower rooms because the Milligan brothers had been there before, and said that the beds were great; it had easy access to the

strip, and a 50 inch plus T.V., not that they intended to spend time watching it. The great lion outside the hotel, and the giant L.C.D. screen that was on the side of the tower advertising shows gave them all the feeling that they were really in Las Vegas, the gambling and showbiz centre of the wold. David had offered to take Claire on a vacation there a couple of times but she had refused. Her reasons were not what David may have predicted; "Thank you David but to be honest I find that place a bit too plastic for my taste. I wouldn't feel safe. You only have to watch C.S.I. to know that it seems to be the murder capital of America, as they have to solve at least one a week."

David smiled. "Sweetheart, don't believe what you see on T.V. that is a fiction, and Las Vegas is the fastest growing city in the U.S."

"That doesn't surprise me, with all those murders, the house prices must have fallen dramatically!"

They both began to giggle.

On their first night in Las Vegas they had been to eat at the extremely large buffet in the hotel, but tonight they had grabbed a pizza because the Milligan brothers had other plans for those that wanted some female company. That afternoon they had played their second game of golf at the Nevada Golf Course. The course was beautifully manicured and the scenery spectacular. They all played well and David had beaten the competition with the best individual score. He holed a 15 yard putt on the last hole to win and to put Mark into second place.
It was now 8.30 in the evening and David found himself alone on one of the casino's gambling floors. The place was busy, lively and beautifully decorated with a large plaster moulded gold ceiling. He made his mind up that he would try the one armed bandits that were lined up around the edge of the gambling tables. Playing these took no thought, it was pure luck, and it would keep him occupied while his friends were in their hotel rooms with the escort, or escorts that the Milligan's had arranged for them. Patrick and Nico had booked the escorts for tonight on line before they left England as they had done the last time that they stayed at the hotel. The brothers had two each, as did Steven while Mark and the rest had one sent up to their rooms. David felt lonely, and abandoned by his 'buddies', who made him angry, although he would not tell them this, instead he would gradually get drunk. An attractive black woman sat at the machine beside him.

"How you doing, any luck?"

"Not yet, just keep feeding the coins in the slot."

"You English, I love that accent, sounds very cool and sexy!"

"Very nice of you to say but I don't feel that sexy, more like a spare part."

"Sorry honey, I don't get that, must be an English thing."

"Yes, I'm sorry, I don't know your name, and mine is David."

"David, that's a nice biblical name. Would you like to buy me a drink David, and maybe we could get to know each other better. My name is Cherry, and I am all yours for as long as you like."

"Oh, I'm a bit slow at this, I think you may have the wrong idea Cherry, I just want to sit here alone and waste money and then go back to my room."

"Well you do not have to do that alone, we are very friendly here in Las Vegas. This is the town that never sleeps, and there are other things we could do in your room than sleep…if you get my drift."

"Well Cherry you are sweet and friendly, and I am sure, very flexible, but I have to say no to your company."

"If you don't want me, honey, I know a guy who could take my place, we have all sorts in Vegas and we aim to please, whatever your choice of pleasure, I can help."

David felt his anger rising along with the level of his voice.

"No, thanks I'm not interested so please move on, just leave me alone, don't make a scene, just go, I am not interested, please go."

"OK, OK, stay cool, Mr David, I just thought you looked like you wanted company, I'm going, you don't want to taste my sweetness then stay hungry cracker, you put your dollar in my slot babe and I guarantee you win every time. You want to stay with them machines; you don't hit no jackpot tonight!"

Watching Cherry waddle away in her short skirt and high heels, David's heart was pumping and his stomach churning, he needed the toilet and he felt a desperate need to telephone home and speak to Claire. It didn't matter that by the sound of his voice she would know he was emotional and under the influence of alcohol, he wanted to tell her that he loved her. He needed to hear her voice, the love of his life, his closest friend, the mother of his children, the person who cared for him, and would make him feel real in this town of plastic and hollow dreams. He took his mobile out of his pocket and found the number. He was about to press the screen and dial when he remembered the time difference. He couldn't be that selfish and interrupt her sleep, worry her unnecessarily, just because he felt lonely and abandoned by his mates who were in their hotel rooms satisfying their sexual appetites. David wondered to himself, if under his thoughts of disapproval he was actually jealous and envious of their actions. Claire would never know and he repeated the mantra of the brotherhood to himself; "What happens on a golf holiday away from home, stays on holiday."

He knew he was not free of guilt, but he could not believe that one evil act could make an evil man. He had given in to desire once and he deeply regretted the choice he made at that time. He would tell himself that it was not a choice and that he was in the control of his instincts. Only one of his fellow travellers knew of his indiscretion and he had paid for it since then. It happened in South Africa after a brilliant day's golf and he was feeling on top of the world. Claire was not happy that he left her for another golf holiday when he had been away with the lads two months before. He had just closed a difficult property development with one of his investors, and they had sold units to major retailers, making them a tidy profit. He wanted a change of scenery and so he agreed to go with the gang. He and Claire had not been 'together' for a while because the stress of the work had impacted on his sleeping pattern and the level of his whisky intake. He was having long days, getting up at three in the morning and going to bed late, and so he would sleep in the guest room so as not to disturb her. She was not a woman to seduce him spontaneously and so their usual timetable had been interrupted. He was sitting in a comfortable leather armchair in the bar of the golf club, drinking a cold beer and chatting to Mark about the golf. Mark pointed out a young black African woman sitting at the bar with her equally attractive friend.

"Her friend told me that the one on the left finds you attractive and would like to meet you if you are interested?"

David looked at her more closely; she had her hair naturally short and curly and was not wearing a wig like her friend, which David liked. She was long limbed and her face had exquisite bone structure, which probably came from some European ancestor in the past. For David she sat like an exotic sweet at a magical counter which he was tempted to taste. He played well that day for little reward until now and perhaps this was his prize. The alcohol and the heat made him feel sensations in his body that he could not deny, and the sight of her long brown legs, smooth thighs barely covered by her white short skirt, her pillow like lips and flashing smile, rocked his defences. At the age he was how else would he have the chance to feel the body of a woman like her and not threaten his marriage. No one would know, and it would bring back memories of how lithe and lovely Claire was in the first years of their relationship. He always tried to live in the now, and be grateful for those memories, those peak experiences, when their bodies were so wrapped up in each other, he could not tell where his body ended and hers began. His appetite was aroused and it was a hunger that demanded to be fed. He gave in to his desire, put his morality to one side, went over to her at the bar, introduced himself to her while Mark entertained her friend, bought her a drink, and found himself chatting to her with an ease he thought he had lost. Within thirty minutes he led her outside and into the coach that transported them to the golf course. She led him to the back seat where she took his trousers off, and he helped her take off of her panties. He started to explore her body, but she pushed him back onto the seat and took control. From that moment it was as if this experience happened in slow motion and to someone else while he was watching. What she was doing to him was amazing, he remembered a comment that one of the Milligan brothers had made about a woman in Thailand;

"She could suck a golf ball down a hose pipe."

Crude as this sounded, it was as if this was happening to him now. He was being totally and exquisitely excited.

The door of the coach yanked open and Mark appeared standing by the driver's seat.

"For Christ's sake there you are! Get out now! The police are here, something about illegals."

The woman got up quickly, adjusted her clothes and ran down the aisle of the coach, out of the door and into the darkness. David put his trousers back on and walked back to the clubhouse with Mark.

"Mark please forget what you interrupted and please don't tell the others what you may have seen, I don't know what came over me."

"Come on David; don't beat yourself up about it. She and her friend were absolutely gorgeous; we were just getting down to it when the guy behind the bar sent someone to knock on the door. It seems like the girls were independent and had some deal going with the barman. I think he upset someone or didn't pay the right policeman; the warning was as much for the girls as us."

"No but I'm not like you, I never do that kind of thing."

"I know but you do now, and don't worry, your secret is safe with me!"

Mark was true to his word, he told the group that he found David outside being sick, "too much booze." David was known as a lightweight as far as drinking was concerned and so it all passed off without unwanted questions, only a few knowing winks from Mark.

This event occurred before Jodie, David's daughter, went to work for Mark in his publishing firm. Jodie broke up with her then boyfriend because she said he was too immature and asked her father if he knew anyone who could give her a job in the City to get her away from Marden, and to do something where she could use her German language, her love of literature, and gain some knowledge of business. One Saturday after a competition at the club, David happened to mention this to Des because he worked in print, and Des told Mark. This coincided with his previous secretary getting pregnant and moving to Canada with her partner, a client of Marks who distributed his books there. Jodie went up to town and had an interview at Finch and Faber and got the job. Mark really valued her work and soon she became his 'Girl Friday' doing a range of things for the partners and taking on more and more responsibility in the firm. All went well, until Mark needed money to finance the interest on a loan he had taken out with a merchant bank to expand his business in Europe. The time for the repayment of the loan was up and they wanted their money back or they would charge his firm extortionate interest. He had negotiated a stage payment but he needed money for the first instalment. Mark told David that when it was completed it would be a great opportunity for Jodie to travel and she may end up as the marketing manager for those countries.

"I wouldn't ask David but I feel we have a special bond, with Jodie, and well we have history, and you know you can trust me."

David was not sure if the last part of the sentence ended with a quick wink of his right eye, or if it was the sun shining through the club house window. David asked Mark for time to talk to his accountant and his bank, and to make up his mind. This process took longer than David expected, and Mark kept phoning him, understandably anxious and under pressure from his creditors. Then one day in the post, David received a small unsigned greetings card with a picture of a 'Stagecoach' bus on one side and on the other an inscription which read, "Memories are made of this!" David transferred the money into Mark's business account online within twenty four hours and nothing more was said about the loan, or as Mark liked to call it 'an investment'. David disliked Mark from that moment on, but he did not let his wife or his daughter know this, and tried to show no outward sign of his feelings. His daughter got on with Mark and seemed to really like him but recently when she came home to stay for the weekend, David was sure he saw sadness in her eyes, and whenever her employers name was mentioned she changed the subject. Claire had noticed this change in her mood as well, and had tried to ease her round to this subject in conversation, but she would not be drawn. David knew something was not right in her world, and if it had anything to do with that 'snake in the grass' Finch, he would sort him out.

His own anger towards Mark had festered since becoming beholden to him in South Africa, and the money he owed him which had little prospect of being returned. He was not a violent man but he adored his daughter and would not stand by and see her hurt. He knew people, or rather had had dealings with people who knew people, who were grateful for the money he had made them, and the chance to put money from certain less that legal sources to good use. He owned a shotgun which he had a licence for and he knew that in the country it was perfectly legal to shoot vermin. Perhaps he could persuade Mark to go shooting with him and arrange for a loaded gun to blow up in his face. He'd had enough of Mark feeling that he was untouchable and having conversations at the club after games as if nothing was wrong between them. He had asked Steven, one of his golfing partners, and his gardener to see what he could find out about Mark and get back to him. It was time to sort things out; he had got away with this blackmail for too long, Mark had to pay for his deeds in one way or another. David decided to ask him for the money back and make a surprise visit to his London office. He knew that Jodie was left to lock up the office after Mark left for the tube and so he would intercept him as he left. He had to be certain that Claire would not know of his intentions, he would tell her that he would be home late. David would tell her that as he had to meet his company lawyer for a business lunch at Lagan's Brasserie near the Ritz. This was their normal meeting place, and she had been there with him for their anniversary the year before. He recalled that he booked a table on the ground floor so that they could eat the savoury Soufflé`, which they both loved. At the time they both agreed that Lagan's Soufflé came second only to the raspberry soufflé they had eaten at the Waterside Inn in Bray near Windsor. "What was he thinking of? Forget soufflés!" David told himself, "This business with Mark had to be sorted out and now was the time to do it."

Chapter Eight: The Milligans

The Milligans had an Irish father and a Cypriot mother. Their parents met when their father came from Ireland to make his fortune in England and found work in a burger restaurant called 'Wimpey'. The brothers told him that their father fell in love with the part time waitress who worked there, who also happened to be the daughter of the owner. The couple's relationship flourished despite coming from a different background and religious denominations. Her father and mother were against the relationship at first but their father won them over because of the respect he showed their daughter and by working hard in their restaurant. The fact that a Cypriot and an Irishman were both immigrants made some common ground between them. Eventually the couple gained the blessing of both sets of parents and were married in both a Catholic and Greek Orthodox ceremony. It wasn't long after the wedding that their father was helped by her parents to buy his own Burger franchise and his mother became pregnant with their first child. This took place when Wimpey was the main burger chain of shops in England and before McDonalds invaded from America to set up their first burger restaurant in Woolwich on the outskirts of London. While growing up, both of the Milligan brothers worked in their parents' restaurants and this gave them an understanding of what was involved in owning your own business. Their parents insisted that despite working in the burger business, they should value education and sent them to private school for their secondary education. They both graduated from university. Patrick gained a degree in Economics and Nico one in Computer Science. Mark told him that after university they travelled around the world together and on returning to England went back into the family business. The brothers wanted to expand their business interests and persuaded their father to invest in property development and renovation. It was at this point in their lives when they started making 'serious money'. This coincided with them taking up golf for the first time. They joined a local golf club where one of their playing partners was a lawyer. Nico had been introduced to him by David, another of his golfing friends, in the bar at the golf club while they were drinking a pint of 'Gunners' in the 'nineteenth hole'. The lawyer asked if they knew anyone who wanted to buy eighty acres of land that his client wanted to sell quickly. Initially they said no, but on reflection it seemed too good an opportunity for them to waste and so within a couple of weeks, they got together all the money they could raise. They borrowed money from the bank against the property they owned, as well as persuading their father to become an investor, and were able to purchase the land at what turned out to be a tenth of its market value. With the help of the lawyer it took them a further two years to get through the planning process, but eventually, after partnering up with a construction company who built houses on the land, sold the development for twenty times the value of their initial investment. To show their gratitude to David they gave him a 'finder's fee' and treated him and his wife to a holiday in Cyprus.

With the money their company made from this deal, the family sold the burger bars. Their parents retired and moved back to Cyprus where they bought a large house at Aphrodite Hills. The brothers bought a nightclub and bar in Paphos as well as one in Dublin, then eventually a club in London. Both brothers were married. On their trips to Ireland they met and married two Irish sisters from Galway whose parents were involved with the racing fraternity. This encouraged them to invest in owning and breeding race horses. Due to their business commitments, as well as the fact that they preferred each other's company they spent a lot of time away from their families. It was as if they were married but behaved as single men. It was not long before the female escorts they allowed to frequent their bars in Paphos and Dublin to pick up clients eventually led them astray. Their friend David, who believed in the sanctity of marriage, disapproved of their behaviour and initially tried to influence them to uphold their vows, but soon gave up. The attraction of their secret lifestyle was too great. He and their golfing partners visited the bar and club they owned in Cyprus and saw this process in person. David witnessed the local escorts of different nationalities plying their trade, tempting the moneyed English tourists with their offer of an uncomplicated sexual service. Single and married men away from home, full of bravado, testosterone and alcohol, found the offer of an anonymous encounter hard to refuse. In the high season for golf, the influx of all male societies provided big business for the brothers and a constant supply of clients for the women. The police were nowhere to be seen and seemed to ignore what was taking place. The Milligans had spoken to a selection of the girls in the bar on arrival, and made it clear to their golfing buddies that they could expect special treatment from these chosen ones. They made sure to remind David and the rest of their guests from home of their mantra;

"Remember David, 'What happens on holiday stays on holiday!'.

Eventually, Patrick and Nico diversified their business into broadcasting and became the owners of an adult soft porn satellite channel. After their first very successful year in business they invited their golfing buddies to their Christmas party. On arrival, they were met by some of the actresses that starred in their programmes. During the evening all the guests were served champagne and mince pies by topless waitresses. As the party got going and the alcohol flowed, one buxom woman approached Phil and David and invited them to lick a substance that looked like sherbet powder from her naked breasts. David, taken by surprise and slightly embarrassed, replied in a slightly shaky voice;

"Sorry, my dear I don't do sherbet, indigestion, loved sherbet tits, sorry dips, when I was young but, but, thanks, for the offer. Nice breasts, by the way!"

Phil tried in vain to find somewhere else to focus his gaze but mesmerised by what was in front of him bent down to taste what was on offer. When she turned away to find other guests and restock her supply of powder, Phil followed in her wake.

On this day in London the Milligan brothers sat across from each other on a comfortable couch in an alcove of their favourite bar in Soho. They had a more recent problem to deal with that concerned their friend David, and another golfing acquaintance, Mark Finch. After a brief discussion about the money they had made, and their conservative estimate of what their wives could have spent during their weekly shopping trip to Oxford Street, their topic of conversation focused on Mark Finch.

"Nico what do we do about Mark?"

"I don't know Patrick; he's as slippery as an eel. He owes us money and he's made no attempt to give us anything, and as much as I like him when he's sober, he's a loose cannon when he's had a few."

"You know David doesn't trust him and when we were in Vegas he let slip that he wasn't happy about his daughter working for him anymore."

Nico nodded in agreement. "To be sure he's a dark horse and he has form, but who are we to talk, after all we're no saints."

Nico raised his glass as if to toast that fact. "To the both of us, may our sins be forgiven, when and if, we meet the great man upstairs?"

"Well my dear brother, maybe the blacker our souls the more worth saving. Who knows?"

They both downed the glass of Irish whiskey they had in their hand.

"It's a fact he owes us money and there is something going on between him and David which we know nothing about. Steven, the gardener is doing something extra for David, but I don't know what."

Patrick thought for a moment. "I think that if he takes us for fools we should remind him who he is dealing with and give him a serious warning, and maybe put the frightener's on him a bit. He still owes us for Las Vegas."
"Then there's the Dimitri factor." Nico shifted in his seat and signalled the waitress to bring two more whiskies.

Patrick looked surprised, "What about Dimitri?"

"Well, he owes them money also, and we know they take no prisoners."

"Nico when did he tell you that? How the hell did he get involved with those dangerous foreign bastards?"

"Sorry Patrick, I thought you knew. It was on the last golf trip. You know he gets invited to various things through his contacts, well; he got an asked to some gambling party near the docks. Some fucking big place and he got pissed as usual, lost a lot of cash and ended up giving them an I.O.U."

Patrick couldn't believe how stupid Mark Finch had been, "What an arrogant prick he can be. He thinks he can get away with anything. They will want payback."

"He says they are being reasonable and they are giving him time to get the money together. He says he just needs a couple of new novels to publish that he can make money from and it will be O.K."

Patrick wasn't convinced by what he heard, "No, there's something else going on, what is it?"

"He says that he has something on them that they will want kept quiet. I don't know the details but it's something about underage girls being offered as escorts. At the party there was a kind of menu with pictures of women and girls that he thought were of questionable age, maybe just legal. He wondered if they had been smuggled into the country. You could choose one and for a fee they would take you upstairs. I'm glad we keep well away from that crap here. It's like the stuff you see on the T.V."

Nico took a big gulp of his whisky. Patrick was struggling to control his emotions.

"Come on, he's not into that shit. His 'fecking' gambling gets him into trouble. We know he finds it hard to keep his dick in his trousers, but even he draws the line at that."

"To be sure Patrick he would be no friend of ours if he was into that, we may stray but we have our standards. The thing is, these gatherings happen quite regularly and he thinks that a tip off to the police is something Dimitri wants to avoid."

Patrick could contain himself no longer.

"Jesus, fucking, Joseph, the man's a fucking idiot! They'd crucify him. They would chop off his head, hands and feet, and throw him in the river. Even more likely, and much less likely to cause suspicion, they could shove him under a train."

Nico felt that now they had no alternative but to act urgently to clear Mark's debt.
"That makes it even more important that we get our money back before anything happens to him. Why don't I pay him a visit at his office, keep it away from the golf club, arrive unexpected?"

"O.K. but Nico remember he has a lot of stuff that he could tell about our trips away that he could use against us." Patrick commented.

"Come on Paddy he's not that stupid, that would really get our backs up and knowing who we know, and what we know, he would be too scared to go there."

Paddy didn't seem convinced by his brothers attempt to reassure him. "I guess it depends if he thinks he's bigger and tougher than he is."

Nico replied," Listen he can act like a playboy in one of the novels he publishes but he is no James Bond."

Patrick smiled at Nico, "Ok, so do it, or we send someone to follow him and confront him when he's least expecting it so he knows he can't "feck" us about. Look, let's put a tail on him and find out what he's up to, and maybe we can give David a helping hand. Now drink up, we're out of here!"

Chapter Nine: Tony and the Therapist

From the outside, the building in Ladbroke Grove looked like it was a
residential nursing home. In fact it used to be a small residential home
for the elderly until the funding from the council for residential care was
reduced and the flow of potential elderly who could afford the homes
fee's ceased. It then became a Counselling and Psychotherapy service
which was originally funded by lottery money to promote access to
mental health services in a multi-ethnic community. The staff who
delivered the therapy consisted of a mixture of qualified professionals and
trainee students on placements from college and university courses across
that part of London. Some of the rooms still had hand basins with hot
and cold running water, and some of the therapy rooms were adjacent to
toilets which if used while a session was in progress, could provide added
sound effects which could be heard through the thin walls of the therapy
rooms during the therapist or clients moments of silent contemplation.

Nigel Clifton, one of the experienced therapists who worked there tried
to get the toilet next to the room he regularly used closed for use while he
was working. As the toilet was on the ground floor and was used by the
receptionists and the clients who were waiting, this proved difficult. His
solution was to have an 'out of order' sign made which he stuck on the
entrance door to the lobby where the toilet was while he was seeing
clients. This reduced the toilets use to only the receptionists who were
able to use it in the fifteen minutes between his sessions. However it was
a constant source of anxiety to Nigel while a session was in progress as he
wanted to provide his clients with a secure safe and private space in
which to do the work of therapy. In the past it had caused some
restrained laughter when one of his clients commented that he did not
expect to have Handel's Water Music as the backing track to his life story.
Nigel commented that at least it wasn't the 'Fireworks Music'.

"Thank God it wasn't the 1812 Overture;" his client replied.

While Nigel waited for his three pm client, Tony, he looked at the brief
notes he had made after his last session. He did not believe in making
lots of clinical notes on his clients as he wanted to be in the 'here and
now' with the client and not be influenced by what had happened the

previous week. He found that once the client was sitting in front of him his memory of past interactions came flooding back, and more often than not he was able to recall who had said what, when and to whom in the time they had spent together. This habit of not visibly taking notes, and not having an agenda for their meetings, annoyed Tony, because as a soldier he marched to time and orders. He needed to know where they were going and what was expected of him in the sessions so that he could make the most of their time together. Tony would often begin the session by asking Nigel what they were going to talk about that week, and how was he doing? Nigel explained that he did not know until Tony told him.

"Imagine your mind; your personality is a house with many rooms, including a basement and a loft. When you arrive each week I do not know which room, or which floor of your house you want to explore. I wait for you to give me clues as to where you wish to explore and off we go."
"Come on, you must have an idea, you're the expert!"

"Ok, I might have an idea where we may want to go based on what you have said before, but it is still better that you lead me, rather than I take you, at least to begin with."

"Yeah, but you have taken me into rooms where I would rather not go, but I suppose it was like exploring the furniture, opening draws and cupboards."

Nigel had been seeing Tony for six months. In the early weeks he had seen him twice a week, because he was distressed and trying to hold on to his reality and deal with high anxiety caused by flashbacks from his time in the army. He had seen service in Ireland in the 90's and Iraq in 2003 with 3 Commando Brigade. He had joined the army when he was 18 and had served over seventeen years in the armed service. He was grateful to get away from his home and his father. Like many soldiers the army was his family, it gave him everything in return for his loyalty and his willingness to die for his country. It was the biggest and strongest attachment in Tony's life but when he left the army family it felt like he had been abandoned by them. His problems seemed like an embarrassment to them, and not the image of a serving soldier that they wanted to be advertised. Afghanistan had changed the view of society with regards to injured soldiers, and documentaries showing the terrifying effect of I.E.D's, with the 'Help for Heroes' campaigns, had got public sympathy on the side of soldiers coming home from that theatre of war.

But Tony still felt that those suffering from mental injuries were less accepted or understood by the general public.

He kept in touch with some mates he was on tours of duty with. They met up for a curry and a drink near their old barracks once a year. Usually they got very drunk, were very sad about the friends they had seen killed or wounded and then some of them found an excuse to pick a fight with a local civilian who 'knew fuck all about what they did over there to keep them safe'. They just had to look in a certain way towards the group or say something that could be misinterpreted as an anti-war or anti soldier comment and it kicked off. He had decided not to go to the meeting this year; he had to find some way to move on with his life.

When Tony was discharged from the army he tried to join the police force but his interviewer told Nigel that at thirty five he was too old, and that despite his honourable service record, they did not want him.

This rejection made him even more determined to prove that they were wrong and so he managed to get a job as a civilian in a police headquarters in the radio communications centre. He sat at a computer screen wearing a headset through which he heard the communications from police officers on patrol connected to him by their radio intercom attached to their uniform. He dispatched officers to scenes of crime and reported incidents, or requests from officers for back up or assistance. He felt that this job was worthwhile and although he was not a police officer he was connected to the front line of policing. It wasn't long before his military training and beliefs about how things should be done, and the support that one soldier was expected to give to another in the field made him disgusted with the attitude of some of the officers he dealt with. They seemed to want an easy ride when they were on shift. They seemed happy to park their patrol car somewhere, eat their rolls or donuts, and be reluctant to respond quickly to his communications. The paperwork they had to do to record each incident they attended could, if they played it right, stretch their time on the job to the end of their shift. He complained to his manager about this but his protests fell on deaf ears. One evening when he was at work he dispatched an officer to a reported domestic argument in a flat in a known trouble spot in the city. The officer whose name was Mike got to the incident and through his radio requested assistance. Tony put out a call for any cars in the area to attend, and he knew that there should be at least two within two or three miles of the location. Mike had left his radio on and Tony could hear the level of anger and dispute rising over the airwaves. Mike the officer was trying to calm the situation down when a friend and neighbour of the man involved came on the scene. Things escalated quickly and Tony heard something breaking, he found out later that the woman involved had hit the man on the head with a table lamp. Mike shouted into his intercom;

"Where is the fucking backup, how long?"

Tony could hear what sounded like a scuffle taking place and the officer was breathing more heavily.

"Get back Sir, and put that down or I may have to arrest you….."

Tony opened the radio channels, so that the patrol officers who should have been speeding to the address could hear Mike's pleas for help.

There was a thud, a crackle of electrical disturbance, and then radio silence. By the time the patrol cars got to the flat the P.C. was unconscious and he had suffered serious head injuries. He was rushed to the City Hospital, but he had suffered brain damage and ended up paralysed on the left side of his body with impaired speech.

Tony was angry and disgusted with the behaviour of Mike's fellow officers who could have got there within minutes of the call going out but didn't, and despite their excuses and justifications, Tony knew and they knew, that they had put their colleague in harm's way. He put in a formal complaint which was not received well and he felt made him a target for his managers. They began to find fault with his work and he felt under increasing scrutiny. He did not respond well to this added pressure and started having dreams about the incident and flashbacks from his army days.

Tony felt responsible, because he felt he should have been able to do more and not have to listen passively to an officer being brutalised. It played on his mind. He found it harder and harder to go to work and put on the headset. He started to take more breaks at work, take time off, and drink more alcohol. Things started to get difficult with his partner Jade at home and they began arguing about money and the lack of affection he showed her, and his disinterest in making love. Jade tried to be understanding but because he would not tell her what was going on in his head, she got frustrated and angry with him. She was frightened that he would 'do something stupid'. In the end she told him to leave the job with the police.

He resigned his job, took his notice period as holiday he had owing to him. Jade and he went away for two weeks to Marbella in Spain, where the all-inclusive hotel holiday seemed to give Tony the rest and recuperation he needed. Jade felt that she was desirable again as he rediscovered his ability to make love and they could satisfy each other's needs. By the time they returned home it was as if they had found each other again and Jade was more relaxed in his company.

Three weeks after they returned he took a job as a security guard. He did well for a while but was accused of being heavy handed with a shop lifter, and later he was suspended from the company after he had tackled a robber at a container storage facility and in the process injured him, but he did make a citizen's arrest. Tony thought it was a strange world where criminals who threaten to sue a security firm protecting the premises of the people they tried to rob, could get an employee sacked. According to Tony that is why he was asked to leave. At this time in his life his demons were getting the upper hand and it became harder and harder to drown out their voices with drink, loud music, exercise and his X-box games.

At the time of his referral to therapy he was living in a local hostel. However before he was found by a Salvation Army officer and offered a place in his present accommodation Tony had been homeless and sleeping under bridges and in gardens. In previous sessions with Nigel he had explained how he had made his way to London from Brighton where he previously lived. Nigel discovered that Tony ran away from his pregnant fiancée because of his 'crazy mind'. He believed that he would be a failure as a father and a danger to the mother and the child. He could not tell his partner Jade about his terrible thoughts or the bad things he had done in the past and so he drank heavily to numb his pain, usually Vodka as it smelt less on his breath. What if he hurt the child? What if he hurt Jade?

Not long after moving in with his partner; his night terrors became more florid. He would wake up shouting and find the bedsheets soaking wet because he was dripping with sweat from the dreams he was experiencing. Because of this he had not been able to sleep in a bed for some time, preferring to sleep on the sofa in their lounge in his camouflage sleeping bag. He pulled the bag up his body and over his head to hide, but also he had to stay alert to any sound outside so that he could be ready to protect his loved ones from intruders. His anxiety reached a tipping point and he ran away from Jade and a child that he had never seen.

Tony told Nigel in one of the early sessions that this was what he had to do when he was on foot patrol in Ireland. They would wait overnight in hedge rows where they expected the Provisional I.R.A. or the U.D.R, or U.D.A. to dig up hidden weapons, then to capture or ambush them.

Tony sold the 'Big Issue' at his pitch which was the entrance to Russell Square tube station. Next to where he stood, sitting on small fold away stool was a girl busker called Selina, who sang and played guitar to the passers-by. Her companion was an Alsatian Puppy dog called 'Chip' who sat or slept at her feet. Since arriving in London to escape the things that troubled him, he had realised that where ever he went his troubles would go with him. He still drank a lot and he was quick to lose his temper, particularly when triggered by anyone whom he thought was disrespecting the armed services. It was hard to watch people living their smug lives oblivious of the reality of the human suffering he had witnessed and inhumanity that people inflicted on their fellow men and woman. They slept in their beds at night oblivious of the horror that could be waiting for them around any corner. He had seen the evil that is done, in the name of a God, a religion, and political belief, the desire for land, wealth and power. Since he had moved to London he had been arrested twice by the police. He explained about the first time to Nigel;

"I got fed up listening to some jumped up young city twat talking about oil, Afghanistan, the size of their bonuses, when my mates lost fucking legs, keeping them safe, or making their investors rich on the back of the blood that is being spilt over there."

Fortunately for Tony the policeman who dealt with him the first time was an ex-serviceman who let him off with a caution and told him to get help. The second offence, which was only two weeks ago, was at the hostel. He had caught another occupant going through his things and lost his temper with him. The homeless person had pulled a knife from somewhere, and due to his training, Tony had reacted instinctively, but with too much aggression and had fractured the assailants wrist. The police were called and because of other witnesses to the event, Tony was given a caution at the police station and the other man was arrested.

After the first incident in the bar, a member of staff at the hostel who knew of a veterans' charity that would pay for some mental health support for people like Tony, helped him fill in an application, which was successful and so after a wait of about three weeks the therapy sessions with Nigel were arranged.

The room where the therapy took place was typical of a therapy room. It was painted in neutral colours, two comfortable arm chairs, not leather in case clients were vegetarians, an impressionist painting on the wall by Vincent Van Gogh of a starry night, a window which overlooked an empty garden, and the small wash basin. There were two clocks in the room. One clock was fixed to the wall in between the two chairs and was visible by both Nigel and the client. The other smaller electric clock belonged to Nigel and he placed this on the window sill behind the client so that he could see the time without looking up at the wall. Nigel saw clients on the hour with a fifteen minute gap between each appointment. He never saw more than seven clients in a day because he found that his concentration lapsed as the day went on and for some reason that years of therapy had unveiled he liked the number seven.

Nigel did not provide a jug of water or tissues that were visible. He did not want to give the impression to a first time client that this was a room in which people cried a lot or caught colds, and so his box of tissues were placed discretely out of sight. He had observed that women tended to bring their own tissues to their sessions in their bag, but men who were less prepared used their sleeve, or asked for a tissue if they did not have a handkerchief in their pocket. Nigel had observed that the use of handkerchiefs was on the decline and this worried him, because he hated the habit of spitting in the street, and he hated runny noses in adults and children. Nigel did carry a handkerchief, a habit instilled in him by his mother who like Nigel hated children to have 'snot' on their faces. He used a clean cotton handkerchief every day and felt uneasy if he left his house without one. It was his security blanket, and his transitional object to his attachments at home. His wife ironed his handkerchiefs for him and folded them neatly, and when he opened a clean one for the first time it smelt of her and home.

When Nigel first met Tony he had worked with him on his night terrors and the flashbacks of the incident with the police officer. In his dreams he either ran to the block of flats from the call centre, burst into the room in time to save the police constable and take out the attacker with one kick to his head. In the other scenario he arrived to find the P.C. slumped on the floor next to a woman, his throat cut, and the attacker laughing at him repeating the phrase; "It's all a joke, it's all a joke."

Nigel asked Tony to try to actively remember this event and recall the feelings he had at the time and the details of the conversation that took place with the police constable. Nigel asked Tony to focus on the part of his thought that triggered his anxiety, and asked Tony to say that out loud.

"I was useless, I let him die!"

He then asked him to measure the intensity of his feelings on a scale of one to ten where one is no distress and 10 is strong distress. Tony rated his distress at ten, and so Nigel asked him to concentrate on the phrase but this time to say out loud;

"I was useless and I completely and deeply forgive myself, I completely and deeply forgive myself for carrying this around with me for so long, I completely and deeply forgive myself for carrying this around for so long."

Nigel then asked Tony to think of a shortened version of the phrase that meant something to Tony while he began to tap on the top of his head with two fingers. Then Nigel showed him how to tap near the top of his nose where his eyebrow ended, ten times while recalling the event, then ten times on the side of his eye, under his eye, then under his nose, under his lip, on his collarbone and then cross his arms and tap under his armpits. When he had completed this round of tapping Nigel asked Tony to tap the forefinger of his right hand on the back of his left hand just below the knuckle of his third finger. While he did this he asked Tony to close his eyes then open them. Point his eyes down to the left then to the right. Make a big circle with his eyes one way and then the other, hum 'Happy Birthday', count to five aloud and lastly he asked him to hum 'Happy Birthday', again. After the first sequence of tapping and getting over the strangeness of what he was being asked to do, Tony got into the swing of things. After a few rounds of recalling his traumatic memory while tapping, something seemed to change in his consciousness. He could think of the event without getting the feeling of panic that was always associated with it.

In the session the following week he asked Nigel what he had done to him. He told Nigel that he went away thinking that he was some kind of magician, like Paul McKenna.

"Whatever that was I had the best night's sleep I have had in a long while. But now I feel a bit guilty, because I seem to have lost the panic, but a bit of the connection with him too."

Nigel felt pleased that his intervention had worked on one level and decided that he would not use this technique with Tony again until he knew more about the dynamics of his personality. He had chosen to relieve his client of what seemed like a disabling terror, but maybe the desire to act quickly was as much about the distress that hearing Tony's story had evoked in him. They both needed to tolerate the anxiety they felt a bit longer.

There was a knock on the therapy room door, it opened and Tony walked in and sat down in the armchair he had chosen at the start of his counselling.

"Hello Mr Clifton, are you feeling better, you had a cold last week?"

"I'm O.K. Tony, how has it been for you, you were not happy with the others in the house last week and you felt you were lucky to get away with a caution?"

Nigel studied Tony's face intently to see if he showed any residual anger left over from what he had talked about in the previous week's session. "When you look at me like that, I wonder what you're thinking. I did lose it, I was lucky. I guess I have to accept that I am one of them, and I am living where I'm living, maybe I don't see myself as bad as them. I'm not as far down the slope as them but, maybe I am, I am homeless. But there is no excuse for stealing from someone. They may be poor but some of them should have seen and been where I have been, and they wouldn't think their life was so bad."

Nigel was silent for a couple of minutes,

"I suppose the problem for all of us to accept, is that we all have our own experience, what we feel or think is what we feel or think, and so it is hard to compare one person's existence to another, it's all relative."

Tony was not happy with what he heard Nigel say;

"Come on, you're saying that because you're one of the 'love all humanity' crowd. You cannot sit there and tell me that some experiences, some things that happen to people are worse than others and that some people make a lot out of nothing."

"What I am saying is that how we feel about things, how we react to things depends on our own perceptions, what sense we make of it. We make a judgement of how big or small an impact something has on us, but it does depend on various factors, that we may or may not be able to control."

Tony was still not happy with Nigel's attitude and did not want to let his point of view be lost on Nigel.

"So in your world losing a leg is the same a cutting your finger, it just depends on how you think about it? That is crazy. Being shot at is not the same as someone throwing a stone at you, and you would know that if you lived in the real world!"

"I can hear that you're starting to get annoyed with me, and maybe I'm starting to remind you of those 'twats' who make you angry in the pub, and who have no appreciation of the fear, suffering and human sacrifice that you have faced in conflict. You are right I have never been in your shoes, and that is my point, only you can tell me what being in your shoes is like. I imagine your pain threshold is going to be different to mine because from what you have told me you have had to soldier on with injuries that would floor someone else. It was your mind and your training that allowed you to do that."

Nigel could see Tony weighing this up in his thoughts.

"One of the things I remember you saying to me when I told you about my fears of having the baby was a question you asked me. You said; "Do you have your thoughts, or do your thoughts have you?" I thought that was a load of crap when you said that, you sounded like Yoda in Star Wars, but when I went away from here it did make me think. It was true that my thoughts had control over me then, I treated them like an unwelcome intruder in my house, and I tried to bar the doors and windows, I fought them as best I could, but unless I was unconscious, or angry, the bastards got in. I know since I have been coming here to see you, and we have been inviting them in to have their say, I am less frightened about what they are saying about me. Now I'm starting to feel, and I am worried about saying this in case they come back stronger to punish me, I now feel I have them, more than they have me."

"So there are still things that you are frightened will breach your defences and take you over? These things will want to punish you, and so I am wondering if there are things that I do not know about that you feel you deserve punishment for. Our unconscious can be a cruel persecutor and if yours thinks you've done things to escape punishment; your mind can get you to feel like you have to punish yourself. Does that make any sense to you?"

Tony remained silent and Nigel noticed that in the silence his gaze rested on his shoes.

"One of the things that I saw when I first came to see you was that you polished your shoes, and I have never seen you when you have dirty or dull shoes. It made me wonder if you had been in the services like me."

"I have noticed how shiny your shoes are, and even though you had been sleeping rough, you kept them so shiny that I guess you could see your face in them." Nigel replied.

"Attention to detail, spit and polish, and a toothbrush, it's a habit I picked up in the army, and I think you can tell something about a man by his shoes. Is that a Van Gogh on the wall?"

Nigel paused before answering his client. Nigel never wanted to answer a question from a client immediately without finding out what made the client ask him that question at that time.

"Before I answer I would like to know what made you ask me about it now."

"I have just realised what it was and it reminded me of Jade and our flat, because she bought a couple of prints to put on the wall at home. One like that as well as one of a sunflower if I remember, and she downloaded the song 'Vincent' to her phone, she used to listen to it a lot at one time, it made her cry. We watched a film together one Sunday afternoon, I think it had Kirk Douglas in it, it was old, but it was about Vincent. He went mad over some woman and cut his ear off didn't he?"

Tony stared at Nigel waiting for his reply.

"I have to be honest, until now I haven't paid much attention to it. It was here when I started working in the room, but now you draw my attention to it I think you're right. It is one of his, and yes he did seem to go crazy, but they reckon now that it was because of lead poisoning. It wasn't love that drove him mad but paint. He used to lick his brushes and the paint on them had lead in it. He also had paternal affection for a girl who worked in the brothel he frequented and wanted to look after her. Some researchers say it was this girl he sent his ear to, the same day that his brother told him he was getting married, and Gauguin left him because he was too difficult to live with. Rejection is hard to take, and so is too much Absinthe, which they all seemed to drink in those days. It makes me sad that in the past behaviour that was considered bad or mad was punished and the people treated cruelly, because it wasn't understood."

"Do you think you could have helped him?" Tony asked Nigel.

"I don't honestly know, but I would do my best, if he would trust me."

Nigel and Tony sat looking at each other and then Tony shifted his gaze to look down at the floor. They sat together in silence, which for Tony seemed like an eternity, but actually was not more than two minutes.

"I don't think it's that much different now. Poor bastard, he didn't know the thing that he loved doing was driving him mad. In the army things had to be black or white, I didn't have time for 'nutters'; I thought they were weak, making excuses to get out of things. If someone wants to kill you, you don't have time to find out if their dad had beaten them up, or their mother left them. No offence, you wouldn't last long."

"Black and white is not easy for us therapists, as you have gathered, I guess I would have to think differently, or not think at all. I imagine that for you, a second thought could mean a bullet in the head. I went paint balling a couple of times, and we were divided into teams and we had to capture a wooden castle. The first game I managed to crawl in a ditch all the way to the castle without being splattered and when I got there I could see the person from the other team, who I didn't know defending the place. I took aim and shot him. I was in the castle feeling excited, exhilarated, pretty tired, but I had to get a flag. Anyway, I waited, my team were getting shot all around the castle and so I peeked out from behind this hardboard door to see where the flag was, and splat I got hit in the forehead with blue paint. I did not know where it came from, but I was dead. It made me think how terrible that would be if it were real and not a game."

Tony was looking at him intently, then took a pound coin from his pocket and started to role it between the fingers of his left hand. Nigel saw that he still wore his wedding ring.

"You mentioned Jade, and I see you still have your ring, do you think of her much?"

Nigel could see that Tony was not happy with this question as he moved in his chair and held his left hand with his right one, to stop himself playing with the coin.

"I try not to but since coming here, not drinking so much, I find I sometimes dream of her and the child, and she's with someone else on a beach by the sea, and they look happy, and I wake up in a sweat, feeling sad and angry with her at the same time."
Tony's eyes looked watery.

"I wonder who you are angry with, her or perhaps with yourself."

"She thought I was going crazy, I can't blame her for being scared of me for Christ's sake she found me trying to dig up the kitchen floor with my bare hands one night, because I thought I was in Iraq getting a squaddie out of a wreck of a bombed building because I thought he was buried alive. The bloody Americans couldn't be trusted to drop a bomb in the right place. She is better off without me, I am a killer, that was my job, and I could end up hurting her and her baby."

"Her baby, is it only her baby?"

Nigel could see Tony was visualising something in his thoughts, as if he was looking far away.

"Did I tell you about the dream I keep having?"

"Would you like to, I would like to hear about it." Nigel replied.

"I am walking down a sandy street with terraced houses on both sides. I am on patrol, and there are six of us, three one side of the street and three the other. I have my rifle at the ready and it is on repeat fire. I am looking at the doorways and the windows of the houses for any sign of movement, because it could be a trap. It is very hot and dusty and my mouth is dry. I can taste the salt on my lips from the sweat running down my face. I look up to the right above me and suddenly the wind swirls along the road causing the curtains in a window to flutter. I see a shape behind the curtain move, I fire a burst of bullets into the window and a body falls out of the window on to the ground ten feet in front of me. I run to the body and it is a pregnant woman in an orange dress, lying face down in her own blood which is soaking into the sand of the road. I turn her over and it is Jade. I scream out loud, and I wake up, covered in sweat and all I can think is, I did that."

"You tell me you did that to Jade in the dream, or are you telling me you did that at some point in the army?"

Nigel looked at Tony and held his gaze.

"I did that, I haven't told anyone, only my patrol knew, and they did not tell. They all said that it could have been them, dead on the ground if it was someone with a machine gun, but I shot an unarmed woman, say what you like, I took her life."

"You took her life, and in the dream you took not only Jade's life, but your child's life as well, and so by leaving them you feel you are protecting them from you and some terrible fate?"

Tony started to sob, deep chest heaving sobs and Nigel sat quietly with him, witnessing his guilt and his pain, holding him with the invisible arms of his respectful, silent, attention.

Tony wiped his eyes with the sleeve of his shirt; "Have you got a paper handkerchief, something I can use?"
Without thinking, Nigel took his newly ironed and folded white handkerchief from his pocket and offered it to Tony.

"Are you sure, don't you need it?"

"No it's fine, I've got another one."

Tony wiped his eyes and blew his nose. Nigel felt his muscles tighten in his stomach for a brief second, but let the feeling pass.

"When I was in Ireland for the second time, we were sent to a house where our commander told us there was an I.R.A. hit squad that had carried out knee-capping, torture, executions and protection rackets. We went to the house out of uniform so that we could not be identified. We were told to capture or kill anyone we found inside, so that they could be interrogated. It was at night, we were blacked up, and we knew we had to go in hard and quick. Three of us went in from the rear and three from the front. I crashed through the back door into the kitchen where someone was making food. He tried to pick up his pistol but I stabbed him in the neck so that he could not make a sound and warn the others. My mate Daz rushed passed me into the hallway and went upstairs. The people downstairs were dealt with quickly, but the two upstairs had time to get to their weapons. Daz was shot in the chest, but he had a vest on so he was badly bruised but not fatal. By the time I got upstairs in the back bedroom, the other soldier and this big fella were wrestling on the floor and both their faces were covered in blood. They were screaming and cursing at each other, suddenly the Provo had a knife in his hand. Luckily for me they rolled over so he was on top. I had both hands on the knife which was cutting through my fingers, sorry I mean our guy had his hand on the knife, it was slicing his fingers and so I shot the Irish in the back three times with my automatic. One of the bullets went through his body and into our blokes shoulder. We did not capture anyone, none of us were killed, and we all got back into the vehicles and left. We were there and gone in under an hour."

Nigel was silent for a moment; "I heard you say that you had both hands on the knife."

Tony looked at him with a puzzled expression; "Did I? No, it wasn't me, it could have been me, but it wasn't me."

"Another time we were ambushed in a street that they had blocked with a burning car. Following our normal drill, my squad started to get out of the back of the vehicle as quickly as we could. Then they opened fire on us. I was the last man to get to the hatch, and the guy in front of me, Taff, got a sniper bullet in his face, under his helmet, and he was propelled backwards on to me, and we fell down between the seats. He was gurgling, drowning in his own blood and I could do nothing, because he was about sixteen stone of muscle, and he pinned me down,"

Tony was looking out of the window into the distance, in full flow telling his memories, as if a dam had broken in his mind. Nigel started to fidget because he could see the clock and it was time for Tony's session to end, and so he moved forward in his seat hoping that Tony would sense the movement and bring his awareness back into the room.

"You know Nigel, a lot of the guys prayed before they went out on patrol, or they had rituals that they thought could protect them on the streets. Some put clothes on in a certain order, some had jewellery that they wore, kissed their wedding ring, those kinds of things. Poor bastards they died anyway. If everyone prays, the good and the bad, how can this supernatural power choose who is going to be blown to pieces or get the bullet? If I survive and you don't, does it mean that God loves me more than he loves you? Perhaps I've got the right religion and you have the crap one? For Christ's sake, six million Jewish people in the concentration camps chose the wrong one…. all the prayers in the world did not turn the gas off, or some sick bastard randomly shooting a prisoner for the fun of it. The poor people massacred and dumped in a pit in Bosnia just couldn't get through, didn't get heard, and got put on hold, on some overloaded prayer call line. Maybe God, whoever and whatever, which ever, one it is, takes a nap every now and then."

Nigel took a breath, moved in his chair, summarised as best he could what Tony had just said, then waited to see if Tony would continue talking. Tony took a deep breath, looked past Nigel towards the room window, and began again.

"If God doesn't exist then there can be no forgiveness. We're all damned and we have to live with what we do."

"I guess we are responsible for what we do, at least that's the idea, but what made you say that we are all damned, because if there is no God, then there is no hell to go to?"

Nigel paused looking at Tony, waiting to see his reaction.

"If hell is a place then I suppose your right, but we can be in a living hell…like in war. Nigel, whether you like it or not there is a double standard about killing someone. People who kill people in civilian life can be monsters and get sent to prison or executed, but if we kill someone in war for King and country then we can be heroes. To take a life is a terrible thing and in the beginning it hurts you, but then, then, it doesn't. Nigel it matters that it doesn't, for your own and your mates' survival."

Tony paused briefly and Nigel took the opportunity to make an observation.

"I can see that this is a contradiction for you, where your feelings become a liability."
Nigel wasn't sure that Tony heard his intervention, but Tony continued speaking anyway, still avoiding Nigel's gaze.

"When I was little I used to go and visit my auntie and uncle quite a lot. They are both dead now. I knew that he was in the army in the Second World War, and in history at school we had a project on it. I asked him what he had done, and he got out his army belt, his Captains cap, and then his dagger. He let me put the hat on and look at his dagger but I wasn't allowed to touch it, until one day when I was in the front room alone I opened the cupboard where it was kept and took it out of its sheath. It was sharp on both sides of the blade. Later I found out that he was in the commandoes and used to be sent on missions behind enemy lines. They would take them by submarine, then in boats they would row to the target, do what they had to do and get back to the sub. He showed me his medals one day. I think my dad was a bit fed up of me talking about him, and one day when I asked what the knife was for, he said; "Slitting throats!" My kind uncle, who took me fishing when I was older, was a killer. This was a normal man whom I never saw lose his temper, but who had killed the enemy. I knew he drank a lot, whisky mostly, but that was it."

Nigel waited to see if Tony wanted to say more, then he spoke.

"So normal men can do some extraordinary things in different and difficult circumstances, things that seem morally reprehensible, and outside of those circumstances, still lead a regular life."

"I guess so, but wouldn't you ask if it is possible that once you have crossed that line, taken a life, you may be conditioned to cross it again?"

Tony looked at Nigel waiting for his answer.

"Is that something that troubles you Tony, a fear you have when you get angry and see red?" Nigel asked.
"I wasn't talking about me, I was thinking about my uncle, but I only saw him kill a fish. Some of the guys who I served with had to go back into a war zone, private security, and mercenary work. It was in their blood."

Nigel wondered if Tony felt he had said too much and wanted to bring the subject to a close. Nigel wanted to give him another chance to talk about his own experience, his own thoughts and feelings.

"I supposed soldiers can be proud of what they have done, or on the other hand feel guilty, and want to hide amongst others who did, and continue to do the same. We know it is hard to fit back into normal society, and you know, you have experienced this at first hand."

"So which one am I then? I wouldn't say my life is exactly normal, would you?"

Nigel did not want to answer this direct question at this time, but he did wish to offer the opportunity for Tony to see a connection between trauma and coping behaviours.
"Your uncle found whisky, and fishing as well as meeting your auntie, the others you mentioned found it difficult to detach from that life and went back. It is well documented that a lot of those who were the victims of brutality, the survivors of the death camps for example have survivors' guilt. Those that survive disasters, like plane crashes, can develop similar extreme symptoms where they take risks to see if they can still cheat death. It is as if they were testing or daring fate to kill them or harm them. Pardon my language but I guess they are saying; "Fuck you!" to fate, destiny, the God's, or the dark angel, that seem to take pleasure in playing with the lives of us mere mortals. I had a client once who couldn't eat strawberries without going into shock, and after their crash they felt compelled to take a strawberry and eat it if one was available. I

guess they wanted to keep testing if their immunity to death was still active. Another client felt compelled to run into the road without looking left or right after they had walked away from an accident on New Year's Eve where four friends had died. They switched seats in the car at the last minute."

Nigel paused briefly and added;

"There are some who get drunk and pick fights with strangers in bars......However, there are some who cope in a different way and decide to pay their tribute to those who have been hurt in a more positive way. They come to realise that living well in the present is the best revenge they can have on the grim reaper. It is also, probably, the best gift they can give, and the best respect they can show to those who unfortunately, died."

Tony had listened intently to what Nigel had been saying. He shifted in his chair, uncrossed his legs, took a fleeting glance at the old scratched divers watch on his wrist and started to talk.

"I was in intelligence then and my job was to spot 'faces' in Belfast and other places nearby. They knew we were watching them and they would sort us out if we got too close. By that time they had intelligence on us, we tried to rotate surveillance, but we were informed that they had photos of some of us. I was not on duty, but for some reason I took a wrong turn in my car and got stuck at a traffic light. This 'face' crossed the road in front of me and briefly glanced at the car. I panicked, I thought I had been 'made', and so without turning round, I watched him in my car wing mirror walking down the other side of the street.
After about thirty yards he stopped, turned around and started walking back towards my car. I could see he was reaching behind his waist to get something.
I was really panicked by then, and my heart could have leapt out of my chest. I couldn't move forward because I was at a crossroads and the light was on red. I reached down beside me into the pocket of the car door where I kept my automatic pistol, and it wasn't there. I was so angry with myself I thumped the dashboard with my clenched fist because I was so stupid to leave it at the barracks, even if it was a day off. He was getting closer, and I was certain that in a split second he would shoot me through the offside window of my car. I revved the engine and shot forward as fast as I could without looking left or right. How I didn't hit something or someone hit me I don't know, if I did believe in a God, he helped me then."

Nigel leant forward in his chair and raised his right hand slightly with the palm facing Tony; "I've got to stop you there Tony we've come to the end of our time today."

"Really, sorry, have I kept you, I'm sorry if I ran over, you should have stopped me sooner."

Nigel smiled softly; "Don't worry, that is my problem not yours. You needed to tell me and I wanted to listen. I'll see you next week at the same time."

"Nigel, what if I need to see you before then, I feel knackered at the moment and yet I feel bit out of it, I guess I'll come down, but I'm a bit worried how I will be."

"Tony, if you need some time to get yourself together before leaving the centre then you can sit in the waiting room and I'm sure the receptionist can find you a cup of tea or coffee. If you need to see me before next week then get in touch with the centre and they will call me, and I will see when I can give you an appointment. Don't be afraid to do that if you need to."

Tony got up from his chair and let himself out of the room. Nigel sat back in his armchair and closed his eyes. He felt a familiar combination of fatigue, apprehension and excitement washing over him. This usually happened when something significant happened with a client, and intuitively he sensed that Tony had turned a corner in his therapy, but Nigel knew from experience with traumatised clients, that things could get a lot worse as the coiled spring of Tony's defences started to unwind. He liked Tony as he liked most of his clients, but he knew that at some point Tony would have to deal with the issue of the partner and child he had deserted, and the feelings that he had managed to repress in relation to this. Then there was the relationship with the girl singer whom he had mentioned briefly in a previous session and whom he cleverly avoided speaking about when Nigel had asked him how he felt about her. Nigel knew that eventually these things would come to the surface and Tony would speak of them, when he was ready to. He knew from experience that as a client's trust in him increased, so did their honesty.

When Tony had calmed down after his session he walked out of the building into the street. One thing troubled him; he needed to tell Nigel about the traffic lights at the rail crossing. He had intended to talk about it to Nigel in this session, but for some reason, it slipped his memory or had he avoided it?

He had been waiting in his car at a railway crossing at a town near the Sussex Coast. The London train had arrived and it was so long that the carriages did not all fit next to the platform. The barriers were down and he was impatient for the train to leave so he could to get going. The battery in his mobile phone was out of juice and so he could not contact Jade. Unless the train left the station and the barriers were raised soon he knew he would be late home and Jade would worry. He had taken a chance deciding to drive home along the coastal road in order to avoid long delays on the A road and avoid the build-up of traffic that occurred at that time. He looked in his rear view mirror and saw these lads messing about on the pavement with some cans of beer in a plastic bag that they were swinging about trying to hit each other. As they got closer and closer to the rear of Tony's car he could feel his heart rate rising and he started to sweat and his hands gripping the driving wheel started shaking. He desperately wanted the lights to change and the barrier to go up, but it did not move. He had to get out of the car. He opened his car door, got out and ran to the pavement, and threw up in the gutter. The lights changed, the barrier went up, but his car was stuck at the front of the line of traffic without a driver. The line of traffic skirted round his car, some beeped their horns, and some of them rolled down their windows and swore at him. He didn't give a fuck, in his mind he wasn't in this Sussex town at that moment in time, he was in Ireland.

Chapter Ten: Selina

Selina really liked Tony. He was kind, protective of her while she was busking and sometimes escorted her back to her bedsit at the end of the day. She lived on the Euston Road and based on what little information she could glean from Tony, he lived somewhere between the Edgeware Road and Paddington station, but he kept the exact location to himself. He went out of his way to make sure she was safe and not bothered by any unwanted attention from those he called 'lowlife'. He was quite a bit older than her but in good physical shape, with short hair, a trimmed beard, clean teeth, kissable lips and a face that looked lived in. She had to admit to herself that for an older man, she did find him attractive. She had dreamt about Tony and on more than one occasion, in her dreams he had rescued her from a terrible monster. In another dream they had been marooned on a desert island with only each other for company. They helped each other to survive and as the days passed the age difference between them seemed less important as they grew closer together. In the tropical sun, sea and surf with no room for false modesty it became obvious that they needed to be more than just friends. However despite sleeping by the campfire together and keeping each other warm when the nights were cold Tony would not give in. He felt that he was her guardian and did not want to take advantage of their situation. In her dream she emerged from the sea naked and Tony ran into the surf, picked her up in his arms and kissed her. The dream ended with them rolling around on the beach in a passionate embrace.

In her waking life Tony showed no indication that he thought of her as a potential girlfriend. He treated her more as a friend or younger sister, which she respected him for, but couldn't help feeling like 'Sabrina' a character in an old film portrayed by one of her favourite actresses Audrey Hepburn with Humphrey Bogart as her co-star. As things stood she felt invisible to Tony as a woman and she wasn't sure that she could or should change this.

Selina was nearly twenty six years old, had been privately educated at Roedean School near the Marina in Brighton. Her mother was the daughter of a Canadian oil magnate and during the time they had been married her father was at first a Captain and then a Commodore in the

British Navy and destined to be an Admiral. When she reached the age of twenty five she and her younger sister would inherit a large number of oil shares that had been put in trust for her since she was five years old. She would be a very wealthy young woman, exactly how wealthy she was not sure, and she was still frightened to find out. Her parents lived in a large thatched cottage with two acres of ground in the Sussex countryside, and her childhood seemed idyllic. She had a pony called 'Flower', she sailed a Mirror dingy with her father in the Isle of Wight and competed in junior races during Cowes week. When she was about five and her father was on leave from his ship he read her a bedtime story about a female pirate who when captured pretended to be a boy. Just as he was about to leave her bedroom she asked him about something that had been troubling her.

"Daddy, would you have been happier if I was a boy?"

Her father paused at the door and then sat down beside her on the bed.

"Selina, what's got into that little head of yours? No my precious don't be so silly, of course not. You wait, in the story, she has a great adventure. I love you and you're my little shipmate. I love that you are a girl, and we will have great fun together."

Her father kissed her on her forehead and left the room. Every year the family spent part her school holidays at a house they rented in Seaview, overlooking Seagrove Bay, in the Isle of White, where her father socialised with members of parliament and business folk. Selina played pirates with the children of the English upper crust who like her were home from private school for their long summer break. Her sister Ruth was nine years younger than her. She was a cute baby, blond and cherubic. When she was slightly inebriated one Sunday afternoon her mother confided to Selina, that her sister was the result of a drunken reconciliation between her and her father when he returned from a long voyage at sea as the captain of a Royal Navy Aircraft carrier. Her relationship with her sister Ruth remained distant. Parents were not supposed to have a favourite child, but it had been clear to Selina for a long time that her mother and her sister had a special bond. Her mother suffered from depression after her sister was born. Both her sister and her mother stayed in hospital until the doctors and a psychiatrist felt it was safe for her mother to be allowed home. At the time Selina was told that her mother had caught an infection in hospital and had to stay until the all clear was given. It wasn't until one weekend when she home from boarding school, sitting down at breakfast with her father he confided the truth to her. Her father didn't seem interested in the food in front of him and he kept pushing the one sausage on his plate from side to side with his fork.

"Daddy is there anything the matter? You look worried, is there anything I can do?" Selina asked.

"Selina, poppet, you know me well. Look I don't want to worry you, and I am sure it is just a phase but I'm a bit concerned about your mother's drinking at the moment. She is also spending an increasing amount of time away from me with her so called 'friends'." He used his fingers to put the word friends in parenthesis.

"I am worried that the 'the black dog' of depression is snapping at your mother's heels again, like it did before when Ruth was born."

"I didn't know Mummy suffered like that Daddy. I thought it was having Ruth that made her ill."

"No poppet we told you that because Mummy didn't want you to worry at the time but now you're old enough to know the truth and it might explain some of your mother's erratic behaviour in the past."

Selina didn't respond immediately and seemed lost in her thoughts. Her father put his hand gently on top of Selina's which was resting on the table.

"Are you Ok? You shouldn't worry I'm only being silly." He squeezed her hand.

"No, I'm fine, it makes perfect sense really. I have always sensed Mummy and Ruth had something special between them and now I know."

"Your mother loves you, please don't doubt that. She may not show it all the time but it is something you can be sure of. At this moment in time it's me, I'm not sure how your mother feels about me, but grownups go through this from time to time, so don't worry."

Selina looked at her father sitting at his table, in his kitchen, in his lovely house but looking so alone. She got up from her seat, put her arms around her father and gave him a big hug.

Her sister went with her mother on trips to Canada to be with her Grandmother and loved the life there. Ruth refused to follow Selina and go to boarding school in England and so she was enrolled in a private all-girls school near their home. She made it clear to her parents that she wanted to be educated in Canada and eventually live there. This suited her grandmother who had felt lonely since their grandfather died. When she was old enough Ruth moved to Canada to live with her grandmother and complete her education.

When Ruth was born her mother decided that she would bring her up without a nanny. The nanny was let go without a word being said to Selina. This greatly upset her, because Nanny Williams was more of a mother to her than her biological mother. Selina found this sudden separation almost unbearable and on the day nanny left Selina grabbed hold of coat and would not let her go. Nanny Williams had to push her away then set off down the drive with her suitcase in her hand. Selina had to be stopped from running after her. Nanny Williams invited her to visit her at home in the local village anytime she wanted to. For a while they met together and chatted over cream teas but the magic had gone, soon Nanny Williams found another family who needed her services and moved away. Selina was left to cry alone. It was this kind and compassionate woman who had looked after Selina when she was sick, bathed her, dressed her wounds, held her when she cried and read her stories at bedtime. It was Nanny Williams who had reassured her when she doubted the love of her mother and father because they were often away from home working or socialising and ignoring her. Her father spent many months at sea on duty with the navy. Nanny Williams was the one whom Selina felt attached to and whom seemed to show selfless devotion to Selina rather than focusing on her own needs. It was Nanny Williams who explained the facts of life to Selina and when she began her periods, calmed her fears and assured her that all was normal. She would not bleed to death, and she was becoming a grown woman, a giver of life, and a guardian of morality. Selina only understood some of this but Nanny finished by saying,

"Selina, grow into a strong woman who can find your own way in the world. Love can be fleeting and life can be lost in a heartbeat. Get a job that's worthwhile and for god sake don't marry before your thirty. Time can be a healing friend but we all need to find a purpose in life."

Selina knew very little about Nanny Williams's life before she met her but she assumed that it may have been tragic and romantic. She had probably been engaged to marry an explorer who disappeared in the jungles of South America a month before they were to be married. Heartbroken she devoted herself to raising the children of others in place of the family she lost with the death of her lover.

When Nanny left her home Selina cried for a week and refused to eat or leave her bedroom. Selina begged her father to intervene and get her mother to change her mind, but her father said it was more than his marriage was worth to try to change her mother's decision. It was sad to realise that her father was a weak man when it came to his relationship with her mother. He was a commander of a fleet of ships in the navy, but in the home her mother commanded him. She wondered what magical and mysterious power her mother had over her father. She knew her grandfather was a wealthy oil man, whatever that meant and wondered if that made the difference in their relationship. For much of her late childhood her mother and father slept in separate bedrooms. Her mother's room was the first one at the top of the stairs, and her father's was situated downstairs next to the study. Sometimes they emerged from the same room for breakfast, and when they did things were happier for a while, but at that time in her life Selina knew of no obvious reason why things between her parents became more cordial overnight. In the evening it was a custom in their house for her mother and father to have drinks before dinner in the large sitting room that went across the length of one side of the house from the front to the back garden. The sitting room was furnished with two faded Knole sofa's with yellow rope ties at each corner and an assortment of arm chairs, some of which were antique. The décor of the room paid homage to her parents' upper middle class taste and its contents lacked the brashness of new money. They did have a relatively small Sony T.V. that was kept in a cabinet in the corner of the room. No one admitted to watching television for any length of time unless they watched documentaries. It was a family tradition liberally enforced by her father that no alcohol was to be consumed in the house until, as her father would say; "The sun has sunk below the yard arm". They would sit in the lounge and pour their favourite tipple from cut glass decanters. Her mother would drink pale Sherry or a 'proper' Martini with two thirds gin and one third dry vermouth. Her father would drink dark navy rum, malt whisky or sometimes brandy.

Her mother was a tall woman with a good facial bone structure, an athletic body with a medium size bust which 'did not get in the way' as her mother would say. She remembered her father trying to pay her mother a compliment once by telling her she reminded him of the English tennis player Sue Barker. Her mother made it clear to her father that she had no intention of dressing up in a short white tennis skirt just to please him. Selina thought this odd at the time as she had never seen her father playing tennis. Her mother was not a 'girly' woman. She preferred wearing jodhpurs to skirts, ski pants or jeans around the house in the daytime, with one of her favourite cashmere sweaters. Often she would wear a string of slightly pink Victorian pearls with a diamond clasp, plus a set of matching earrings inherited from her grandmother. When she went out during the day she threw on her well- oiled green Barbour coat, climbed into her car and was gone in a flash. Selina rarely saw her without her 'face on', but her makeup enhanced her natural complexion rather than covering it. She wore her hair up or in a ponytail when it was the right length. Her mother drove a beat up Range Rover capable of pulling a horse box which she named "Annie", while her father owned and drove an old style Jaguar nicknamed "Morse", which he had lovingly restored.

Her parents lived a busy social life and had many weekend guests who would come up from town on Friday evening in time for drinks, to stay for the weekend. When she was young, before nanny took her up to bed, she was allowed to sit quietly with, what was at first, a non-alcoholic drink and some nibbles in her hand and listen to the adult conversations. As she grew older she would be allowed to mingle with the visitors and sit where she could. Sometimes she would be asked to give her opinion, "… and what does the lovely Selina think we should do?"

The conversation would stop and all eyes would focus on her waiting for a reply that may add some humour to their evening. She never felt humiliated or criticised, but was often challenged to give the rationale for her answer. Her parents' guests were all fascinating. They were people who had travelled and lived abroad, their opinions were mostly conservative, altogether they drank copious amounts of champagne, wine and spirits. The more they drank the looser their tongues became and the conversation got louder and bawdier. Some had served in British Consuls in Pakistan, Africa and Russia, and had strong views about the politicians who had visited them there. On the whole they did not have a good word to say about Tony Blair, or Jonathan Major. Most of them had met the Queen at one time or another in a formal capacity and told Selina that the Queen never pressed skin, but wore white cotton gloves when she shook hands with those they introduced to her at ceremonies. They all loved the Queen and admired her for her calmness and diplomacy when dealing with strangers, which some had witnessed personally. Needless to say they did not approve of cuts to the armed services because as her father said; "We should get the public to think of the armed forces in the same way they think about firemen or the police. If your house was set on fire you would need enough of them to put the fire out and also make sure someone doesn't do it again. They have got to be there ready and prepared to save your home, your possessions and your life. If you wait until disaster strikes, it is too late. We can all sleep safe in our beds at night because our way of life is being protected twenty four hours a day by someone else."

"The trouble is father, they're cutting the police and the fire brigade, doctors and nurses as well as the armed services and just like these things, we rarely value them until we use them." Selina replied.

"Very true my sweet, sad times, sad times, still we must fight the good fight, and hope it doesn't take another tragedy on our streets or an invading army sitting the other side of the English Channel to bring them to their senses."

Selina got into the habit of reading her father's collection of the Sunday Times and the Telegraph newspapers which he kept in his study, and when she could, watching 'Newsnight' or Question Time, on her laptop when she was alone in her bedroom at night. She looked forward to these gatherings and wanted to be prepared for them. The one issue that they all agreed on was the threat to the nation if the independent nuclear deterrent was abandoned. Being a high ranking officer in the navy her father was personally involved with N.A.T.O. Manoeuvres and the U.K's defence capability.

"Our submariners do a great job and if we didn't have that ultimate threat during the cold war we'd might all be speaking Russian or Chinese by now. Politicians can try diplomacy but it didn't stop Hitler or the Japs because the pen is not mightier than the sword when it comes to unhinged dictators. Look at North Korea now for example, brainwashed and dangerous!" Her father took a gulp of liquid from his glass of dark rum.

Sitting on the edge of a sofa the wife of a newspaper editor whom Selina had met before looked up from stirring her Martini with an olive stick and spoke to Selina directly.

"Come on Selina let's hear what you think about what your father said? You are going to be here after we've gone, if there is still a 'here' to inherit."

Selina felt the yes in the room focus on her, waiting for her response. Her mind was racing and was not sure what to say that would not embarrass her father. She looked at the lady and then at her father who was standing by the drinks tray. He raised his half-filled glass, smiled and winked at her. Selina took a deep breath and spoke.

"Well I'm sure that daddy knows a lot more about this than I do, but in history at school we were taught about the bomb the Americans dropped in the last World War, and I've seen on the computer about deformed babies and the illness caused by that power station in Russia which they covered in concrete. So if there was that kind of war, then what would be left for anybody? I read the 'War of the Worlds' in English at school recently as well as listening to the record. Did you know that David Essex was in the original "Evita" and my teacher told us that the singer with the lovely voice is in a group called the "Blue Moods", or it might be the "Moody Blues"? Any way I think H.G. Wells had a point. In the story they tried to bomb and shoot the invaders, but in the end they died from an infection and not a bomb. Afterwards we had a discussion in the class about this and Bethany said that her uncle, who worked at a chemical research institute, told her, terrorists or someone could poison our water if they wanted to kill us and take over the country. They could make us so ill we could not fight. Perhaps we need more money spent on medicines to protect us from biological attack than bombs."

By the time Selina had given her answer the room had gone silent and all the adults were looking at her. The lady with the Martini swiftly downed the contents of her glass.

"My God, what a gem you have here Admiral. Just like Selina say's your big toys would be useless. Thank God I only drink bottled water. I think I need a refill, Derick another Martini please!"

One Sunday lunch, when Selina was much older, before she had met Tony and before she was busking, her parents had the foreign correspondent of the Telegraph visiting. At lunch she entered into a discussion about Communism while they were drinking the Port and eating Stilton with crackers. She passed the solid silver serving spoon for the wheel of cheese to this rosy cheeked and slightly inebriated gentleman while commenting that in her opinion the fall of the Berlin Wall was 'great' for East Germans and how the Russian people were better off "freed from the yoke of Communism". There was an awkward pause in the conversation as the correspondent nearly choked on his mouthful of cheese, before gulping down a swig of age old Port from his crystal glass and fixing Selina in his sight with his puffy red eyes.

"My dear child, I doubt you have met Mr Putin as I have, nor dear Yeltsin the leader of the white revolution before him. Both of them were crooks in different ways, and stole Russia and its assets from a great people. They gave whole industries to their friends, who became billionaires. Putin is not a democrat; he is ex KGB, and in bed with the

Generals who really have the power in Russia. Mark my words he will become a cult figure who has t-shirts, plates and mugs sold with his image on. The Russian people are a wonderful lot, they have produced fantastic authors and composers but, after so many years of a one party state and the power of the Soviet Union they don't know how to work a democracy. They will support a strong leader even if it means the loss of hard won freedoms and isolation. The press and television stations are not free to say what they want. He wants to be like Stalin, and bring back a cold war. You watch my dear, give him time; any way let's not let him spoil our lunch. I hope this leopard can change his spots but my darling, who knows? "

It was very hard for Selina to argue with a man of his experience and who had inside knowledge of his subject. Someone who spoke Russian, had visited the country, and met so many people. She did the only thing she thought would be helpful; she passed the port.

"More cheese anyone?"

Growing up Selina became an intelligent, forthright and strong willed child who did not simply do what she was told. Later in her life she wondered if this was partly the reason why she was sent to boarding school, or whether being nine years older than her sister, her mother could not cope with the stress of having both her and her sister at home at the same time. Selina was a child who constantly asked "why?" Why do I have to do this or behave in a certain way? Initially this put her at odds with her father when he was on leave from his warship, as he was not used to his authority being questioned, especially by a small person. When he was at work, his word was law and those who did not obey could be punished for insubordination. Selina came to realise that her relationship with her father was special to him and that behind his bluster he admired her for not taking things at face value and standing up to him or her mother. At times when relationships with her mother became fraught they became allies, and supported each other. Selina often felt that her mother did not give her father the respect he deserved and could not understand why he let her get away with some of the comments she made about him, particularly when they were entertaining outsiders to the family. It was not until she developed physically and became the focus of unwanted attention from the opposite sex that the hidden power her gender and the use of her sexuality gave her. This awareness gave her a missing piece of the marital puzzle that helped explain the mysterious dynamics of her parent's relationship. Her father desired and wanted her mother more than she wanted him. Her mother she was a vibrant woman and it became clear to Selina that when her father was desperate for affection she kept him like a puppy on a lead begging to be stroked and given a treat. Selina could see that her father loved her mother desperately, but at times during their marriage she sensed a fear in him. He was scared that her mother might leave him for another. When she was younger it caused her to have sleepless nights and dreams of witches tapping at her window. Her mother was young rich and desirable when they met and her father often said to his friends,

'She was quite a catch and I'm not sure what she saw in me but I'm glad she did see something!'

When Selina was sent to boarding school leaving her father and mother alone, she worried that their marriage might explode and bring about an inevitable separation between them. She was surprised when this did not happen. In fact, for a short while her father seemed to have a spring in his step and her mother talked of them both re-visiting the place of their honeymoon. This new dawn in their relationship only lasted for the length of time it took for Selina to complete the first two terms at her new school.

Selina hated boarding school and viewed her time there as a prison sentence. The school itself was a lovely place to be. It had wood panelled walls, plaster pillars, good food, and great common rooms. Situated above the Marina in Brighton, it also had great views of the sea. It owned lovely grounds with its own indoor swimming pool, a theatre and a wonderful library with internet facilities. In all there were about four hundred girls attending the school from all over the world between the ages of eleven to eighteen. She played hockey, loved swimming and horse riding, studied the piano, the violin, and sang in the choir. Like a lot of the girls she had a crush on the choir master, as well as the girl captain of her school year hockey team, with whom she shared a room. Rosy was a free spirited American who came from San Francisco. Her father was an ex-captain in the American Marines who now worked for a security firm in Iraq and Afghanistan providing protection for important people. Rosy told Selina that she did not know exactly what he did but it was stressful enough to cause problems between her mother and father. She witnessed some fighting between them when her father was drunk and they got divorced when she was ten. Her father tried to see her at least twice a year but although he said he loved her he always seemed to have more important things to do. Her Mother was now a successful corporate lawyer and was too busy to have her at home all the time and so she sent her to an expensive school in Europe where she might rub shoulders with royalty. There were aristocratic girls at the school and some from royal families, but not the English one. Selina thought she was a fascinating, athletic, and attractive girl with light blond hair, tanned skin, and worldly wise. Rosy told her that she had smoked cigarettes, drank alcohol and tried 'weed'. She intended to 'drop out' and 'do her own thing' when she escaped from college. Selina was entranced by her accent and most things about her as if she had fallen under her spell and they soon became close friends. At night they would eat midnight feasts with snacks and sweets they bought from the tuck shop or from food parcels sent by Rosie's mother. Selina tried Oreos with milk, Twinkies, which she hated, peanut butter and 'jello', all for the first time. In return she introduced Rosy to crumpets with butter, teacakes, strawberries, scones and clotted cream. Then when they were in the dark, feeling lonely and homesick, they would slip into each other's bed at night to comfort each other. Rosy introduced Selina to a kind of fiction she had not read before. The first was 'Forever Amber', which told the story of orphaned Amber St Clare, who made her way up through the ranks of 17th Century English society by sleeping with the gentry, including King Charles. The second was a saucy book by Jackie Collins about the secret life of film stars in Hollywood. They read passages to each other and giggled, but more importantly for Selina they stirred up in her physical sensations in her body she had not experienced before. When she was at home for the weekend Selina found a book on her parent's bookshelf at home called 'Riders' by Jilly Cooper, and smuggled it back to school in her bag. This book was a 'find' because it was about horses and their riders, which they both loved, but it also introduced them to a naughty side of the horsey set that they knew nothing about. It was full of steamy desire and romance and a new form of "riding" common to adults that stirred new feelings within them.

At night, under the bed covers they pretended to be the characters from the novel. They began to enact little episodes of what they read with each other while they were reading it. Rosy was more aware than Selina of the parts of her body that excited her and showed Selina where to rub herself in a certain place while squeezing her legs together in a particular way, so that Selina could feel what Rosy felt. The sensation between Selina's legs grew in intensity and then like a wave crashing on a shore she was overtaken by a strong throbbing spasm which caused her to arch her back and tighten her stomach muscles. Rosy told her that she had experienced her first orgasm, which she found to be both wonderful and frightening at the same time. Selina wanted to find out more about this amazing experience and so she went to the school library and looked up 'orgasm' and then 'masturbation' in a dictionary. She discovered that the French called female orgasms 'little deaths'. Her appetite for this new found feeling increased and became an obsession to the point where she could hardly go a day without pleasuring herself. To keep her compulsion a secret from Rosy, Selina made excuses so that she could sleep alone and for a while they seemed to grow apart. Rosy accepted this rejection and put no pressure on Selina to continue their mutual physical exploration. Then one day when she was browsing through books in the psychology section of the library she found a book with descriptions of psychiatric disorders. There was a picture from Victorian times of a female hysteric, strapped to a chair, drooling at the mouth, with a description of her symptoms. One of the symptoms attached to the picture leapt out at her from the page. The patient Emma Eckstein suffered from extended periods of menstruation, hysterical coughing and compulsive masturbation. To cure this, her doctor Fliess did an operation to remove a bone from her nose, which he thought at the time, was linked to obsessive sexual compulsion. He incorrectly left a strip of gauze in her nasal cavity which Freud found after it had become infected. The surgery for its removal left her disfigured.

A wave of anxiety flooded over Selina, she began to perspire and felt sick. She immediately became anxious that she would become a victim of this recent compulsion and so decided to control her secret pleasure immediately. He had to find other ways to decrease this new found appetite. At first she ate, but that gave her spots and so she distracted herself by putting her energy into sport, dissipating her energy and practicing her musical instruments. Even when she felt lonely she avoided sharing her bed with Rosy telling her that she had to get used to being alone, and she didn't want to run the risk of them getting a reputation in school like Bridget and Helen who were seen kissing and were definitely a 'couple'. Her newly discovered appetite was subjected to a strict diet. Self-denial had to be practiced and her appetite satisfied on special occasions or times when she became so sensitive she could resist no longer.

On her next visit home, while she and her father were tucking into a full English breakfast on Sunday morning, she slipped a mention of Freud into their conversation. She pretended that someone at school had been to the Freud Museum in Vienna and wondered what her father knew anything about him.

"Not much, darling rather obsessed about sex, and a bit of a cocaine addict, if I remember rightly. He did identify war neurosis which is both a good and bad thing for the chaps on board who have been under fire. Some do go A.W.O.L. when they get home on leave, anyway that's another matter, and a bit heavy weather for breakfast, don't you think?"

"I only wondered if what he said about things had any meaning today."

Selina looked down at her plate and cut into her vegetarian sausage. Her father looked at Selina, and then began piling food on his fork ready for his next mouthful. While doing this he spoke.

"I don't really know my sweet, I mean people still do have psychoanalysis, but it's not my area of expertise. Some people think he's great and some think he's 'Quacker's'.

"Oh daddy you don't think he had a thing about ducks do you?"

Her father grinned.

"Tell you what Selina, one thing I am grateful to that chap for was the invention of the... "Freud- egg!"

"Oh Dad that's terrible, or was it.... "Egg-cellent ?"

"Egg-cuse me!" He replied.

They both chuckled while they stacked their plates into the dishwasher.

One of the good things about her school was that it was a bus ride away from Brighton. Her close friendship with Rosy rekindled when Rosy was given a guitar and began her two year struggle to master the instrument.

The music staff at school wanted Rosy to have Spanish guitar lessons and learn to play like Segovia or Jonathan Williams, but she wanted to play folk music like her mother and fathers heroes, Bob Dylan, Joni Mitchel, James Taylor, Paul Simon, and Leonard Cohen. Her father sent her Paul Simon's first solo album on cd, and the book of the songs with guitar chords to go with it. Selina heard the 'Paul Simon Song Book', over and over again on her friend's iPod dock. She loved, 'I am a Rock', and 'April Come She will', and helped Rosy write out the chord charts and overcome the soreness of her fingers on her left hand, by finding a liquid that would harden the skin on her fingertips.

It was not long before Selina joined Rosy in her new musical passion and bought an Epiphone acoustic guitar and began learning to play it. Selina had an advantage in their efforts to play guitar because she could read music from her study of the violin and piano, and had excellent hand co-ordination. She could also work out the finger picking styles of the artists by listening to a song on a record. Then practiced the sequence in which the strings of the guitar were being plucked. They both learned to play

'Both Sides Now', by Joni Mitchell, and by accident they came across a record by Donovan, a British songwriter who was popular in England around the same time as the American folk revival spread across the Atlantic. He had written two songs they loved and decided to learn on the guitar, 'Colours' and 'Catch the wind'. They had to learn how to copy his style of playing which involved using a plectrum to pluck the base note of the melody while strumming the chords. Once they could do this they realised that Bob Dylan had a similar style and so they learned two of his songs, 'Blowing in the wind', and 'The times they are a changing'. Selina found Joni Mitchell's guitar parts difficult to fathom because when she got the chord symbols off the internet and played them they still didn't sound like the record. Then she read on Wikipedia that Joni retuned her guitar to an 'open chord' like 'E' or 'A'. Selina told Rosy, who looked up how to do this on line and it worked. They suddenly discovered that with this tuning, one of their favourite Joni songs, 'Big Yellow Taxi' was easy to play. They watched 'Woodstock' the movie, and loved the close harmonies of Crosby Stills Nash and Young, and so they learned 'The Marrakesh express', and 'Woodstock'. On the radio they heard 'Monday, Monday,' and discovered the Mama's and Papa's, and then taught themselves 'California Dreaming'. They would spend every spare moment singing and refining their harmonies and soon the other girls in their house block heard them and told them they sounded 'totes amaze' or 'unreal', and encouraged by this they auditioned to perform at one of the school concerts that Christmas. Selina invited Rosy home for a couple of weekends and they performed to her parents and some of the weekend guests. Despite the fact that her father and mother only listened to classical music and wanted Selina to become a concert pianist or solo violinist playing the concertos of Beethoven or Tchaikovsky they applauded and respected their talent. When they reached the age of sixteen and were studying 'A' levels, Rosy and Selina decided to try busking in Brighton. It was important for them to get the reaction of the public to their duo performance and perhaps make some additional pocket money. They took themselves down to Churchill Square on a Saturday, put down one of their guitar cases for passers-by to put money in and started to sing their repertoire of ten songs, over and over again. They dressed themselves like the pictures of the hippy girls of Haight-Ashbury in San Francisco that they saw on the internet, and found their outfits in the second hand clothes shops around Kensington Gardens and Sidney Street in the Lanes of Brighton. In just one day busking they made fifty two pounds and felt they had hit the jackpot. They invested in a set of bongo drums and a tambourine purchased from Amazon, which added variety and rhythm to their sound. They also began performing on the pedestrian walkway in front of the Theatre Royal near to the Pavilion Gardens. In the beginning they would set up and sing for about an hour and then go for a coffee or move on so that they did not get in trouble with the police. Then in conversation with another busker they discovered how to get a buskers permit enabling them to perform during the Brighton Festival. Every moment of their spare time from classes and studying for exams was spent rehearsing their set.

Selina took the common entrance exam for Oxford and Cambridge because her parents expected her to attend this traditional institution, like her father, and his father before him. If she did not get in to one of the colleges at these Universities she was expected to attend St Andrews, Durham, or Exeter. Selina had no intention of actually going up to any of these Universities because her first calling was music, and now with Rosy as her partner this seemed possible. Rosy and Selina would become the female "Simon and Garfunkel".

The Housemother at her school was not impressed with their plans and tried to stop their trips to Brighton, but the pair made it clear that what they did in their free time was up to them. The headmistress wrote to both their parents for support in controlling these musical mavericks. Rosie's mother was involved in a
Patent dispute at the time and simply said that she trusted her daughter to do the right thing, and would skype her when she could. Selina's parents demanded that she went home for the weekend to discuss the headmistress's letter. Selina told them that there was no point to their visit as she was perfectly safe, and making money. She invited them to come to Brighton to see her perform as soon as they could, but her mother was off on a skiing holiday with friends in Zermatt, and her father was involved in a naval exercise at sea, with the French, American, and Spanish Navy. They gave her their blessing for showing initiative and wrote to the school to let them know of their approval.
 One day, after nearly a year of busking they were playing and singing their version of, 'Mr Tambourine Man' in Churchill Square, when a tall young man with a square jaw, blue eyes, in jeans, a leather jacket, red Dr Martin boots, very pale skin, and hair in dreadlocks, stopped to listen to them perform. He sat on the floor in front of them with his eyes closed as if he was in a trance, then after the fifth song ended he introduced himself to Rosy.

"Hi, my names Mick, you chicks are very cool. No, sorry I'm in the 70's vibe there, let me start again, you young ladies are great! Have you been recorded? I would love to record you in my studio. If you wanted I could get you work as backing singers to the guys that come to record their stuff. I could help you produce a video and put it on 'You -Tube', get your songs on Napster, you could do X-factor or Britain's Got Talent and I could help. I bet you, your video would go viral you've got something, very cool, great harmonies, retro stuff, and real attractive talented babes. How about it, are you interested, come on you have got to say yes?"

Selina could see by the look on her face that Rosy was interested in him let alone the offer he made to record them.

Rosy seemed to have lost her voice, her mouth was moving but no sound was coming out, and so Selina talked for them;

"Yeah, that sounds fantastic, Mick, don't get me wrong, we are flattered, but we don't know you, you could say that to all the girls, and how do we know you're not some slave trader who wants to capture us and sell us to some Russian mobster?"

"Look, let me give you my card, it's got my mobile on it, ask around and I think you will find that people know 'Pink Dog' records, it's our independent label. Our studio is in Hove under what used to be a bank, across the road from an Indian restaurant. Give me a call and come and see me, you can get a bus to Hove, or walk to the King Alfred and turn right. Don't let me down; see you soon, bye for now."

Mick waved to them both and walked away.

"Oh my god Selina, how fucking great is he, I mean that. What a chance, we've got to go to the studio!"

"O.K. we will go, but we must tell someone in house where we are going, we have to tell the House Mother."

"Are you crazy 'C', she won't let us go, I will give the address and the number to Rachel in the next room, we can trust her because we didn't tell on her about that boy she met at the fair ride."

It was a week later Rosy and Selina entered the haloed ground of Mayfair Studio's in Hove. It was a dark cavern that they descended to by a flight of stone steps to be met by a large black door with an intercom and a sign that said: 'Press Here and Wait'. Mick opened the door and led them down a corridor with posters of rock stars on the walls, and a picture of Mick playing guitar in a band in front of a large crowd.

"Come in ladies, welcome to the place where the magic happens. Please don't mind the mess but we were recording and mixing until late last night and my butler has not had time to clear up."

Selina saw two soundproof booths with mic's and headphones at the back of the room and then to the left was a larger room with a drum kit, an electric keyboard and a guitar amp in it. To their right was what she later found out to be the control room with a large mixing desk, monitor speakers, and Apple computers.
Mick invited them into the minimally lighted control room where they sat down on the leather sofa that rested against the rear wall.

"Well my special friends, what do you think of what you see, are you ready to let me do my magic on your lovely voices? I have come up with a couple of names for your duo, 'Free Spirit' or 'Angels of Mercy', what do you think?"

Rosy looked into Mick's eyes and sat on the edge of the sofa with her short skirt, white boots, showing a bit too much of her thighs for Selina's taste.

"I think it's just so cool, but I don't know about the names, we have to think about that. When do we start, we have our guitars with us? Can we do something now, it's a real studio. Selina, a real studio, God I'm so excited."
"Yeah sure why not, let's get started, no one is booked in until tomorrow, get yourself ready and we will do a sound check to get the levels right."

Mick pressed switches, fired up the computer to set the sequencing programme for new tracks, balanced the microphones in the booth, let the girls have a run through of the song they had chosen for their first recording, set the click track running, gave them the thumbs up, and off they went.

The studio was Mick's place of work and also frequently his place to stay. He had a mattress on which he slept propped up against the wall in one of the recording booths. There was a small galley kitchen with a sink, kettle and microwave. From the amount of metal trays in the waste bin it seemed that Mick lived on takeaway food from the Indian restaurant on the other side of the road, opposite the studio. From what they discovered in the kitchen fridge he would save any leftover food and heat it up the next day. If he didn't fancy Indian food he ordered Pizza to be delivered or he walked to George Street and bought a coffee and sandwich in a café. His pale skin was the result of his work schedule, spending many hours in the dark studio, working all night mixing tracks for his customers. When they asked him about the sweet perfume like smell that permeated the studio he informed them that he smoked a lot of cannabis. He showed them his own potent imported plants from Amsterdam which sparkled under the electric light because of crystals growing on its leaves. These crystals he mixed with tobacco and smoked in joints. Some days when they went to the studio to record he would be sitting in a drug induced trance for hours. Mick believed that the high this drug produced gave him extra sensitive hearing which helped him get a special sound from his recordings. It was this sound he was convinced made the studio unique in Brighton and East Sussex. Some of his customers questioned that this was in fact true, especially when he would waste their expensive studio time listening to the same sound, for example a high hat cymbal, over and over again, until it had 'that' sound. However all the musicians the girls met agreed that Mick was a talented guitarist and producer who used the mixing desk like an instrument and manipulated 'Pro Tools' the sequencing programme like a magician.

The studio was also a place for parties. Over the following three months of recording and hanging out at the studio, Rosy became obsessed with Mick. She stopped wearing a bra to be a real hippy and encouraged Selina to do the same. It was obvious to Selina that Rosy was in love with Mick, and would text him every day and converse with him on the phone for as long as she could. At the parties there would be other musicians and their girlfriends, Mick's drug dealer, and other people that they knew who hired the studio. The parties were often in the day because they worked at night, and this meant Selina and Rosy could attend without being absent from the school house at night. Rosy thought it was like California in the sixties, with booze, brownies, pot, magic mushrooms and great loud music. Selina was not as comfortable at these parties as her loose limbed friend, because there was no one she was attracted to, and part of her resented the expectation to take drugs because she liked to stay in control of her mind and body. Rosy told her she was, 'too English', and to 'live a little'. The guys she met at the studio were reasonably attractive and all right to talk to but not her cup of Tea, which when she said it sounded so like her mother, but it was how she felt. She tried to 'loosen up' and sometimes the drug she tried aroused her feelings, but even though she had kissed a couple of 'frogs' when she felt warmed by eating the brownies, or sucked in cannabis smoke from a bong, while she sitting in a circle on the floor of the studio, none of these 'frogs' had turned into 'princes'. What the guys wanted was for her to relax, chill out. This meant her being 'cool when they got high together and wanted to explore her body, put their hand down her top to feel her breasts or slide their hands up her thighs under her skirt hoping that she might rub the growing bulge in their trousers. Resisting their initial attempts, slapping or pushing their hands away, they soon became too stoned to bother with sex. They focused on the pulsating music pumping out from the studio speakers and floated away in a drug fuelled trance. She hated being the only one in the room neither stoned nor drunk. Mick and Rosy were making out together on his mattress or the sofa, their mouths and thighs glued together by the heat of their passion, while she was left alone. She felt like a spectator at an orgy. Mick and Rosy were an 'item' but still followed a Hippy lifestyle, as Rosy insisted telling Selina.

"Ours is not an exclusive relationship, that crap is too ordinary. The seventies were about free love, like Mick says. I mean it might be one day but I am cool with it as it is. Really Selina I am!"

"Whatever you say, just don't get hurt or pregnant. Remember that "-a rock can feel no pain and an island never dies!" Selina replied.

Selina felt concerned for her friend. As far as Selina could make out Rosy had not yet had full sex with Mick, but from what they got up to in the studio and with the competition for Mick's attention from older girls, that day was fast approaching. Mick's relationship with Rosy did not inhibit him from occasionally sleeping with a couple of the other girls that came to the studio. Particularly a girl called Sky. Selina could see that although she tried to ignore his behaviour Rosy was hurt by this. Selina continued to impress on Rosy that she needed to be careful and not catch something horrible from Mick, whose dental hygiene left a lot to be desired. Rosy told her to not worry because she was taking a contraceptive pill that the school doctor had prescribed for her spots. She also had a supply of 'things' her mother gave her and would make Mick 'put one on'. She had practiced this on a banana and had followed a video clip on 'You Tube'. She made it clear to Selina that she should stop acting like her stupid mother;

"So, Selina just, back off! I am not stupid."

In one of their intimate conversations while they were in bed together Rosy told Selina that she had made out with a college kid in the States during her Easter break. She went to a pool party that this 'jerk' threw at the house of a lawyer friend of her mothers. She got drunk and ended up in a hot tub with this really good looking drummer who played in a local band. It got late, she felt horny, hot and steamy and they 'did it' in the tub, but it was disappointing.

"When we got it on and he touched me down there, he whispered in my ear; Jesus you're so smooth! Then just after I eased myself down on him, I felt him quiver, and pop! He 'came' straight away. What a loser. He was so embarrassed and I was left high and dry."
She went on to say that he kept apologising to her, asking her not to tell his friends.

"That was easy because I didn't know anyone anyway, I was so glad when my mother came to pick me up." She added, "I will never get into a hot tub at a party again and take my advice, don't you Selina. You can't be sure what's floating in the water."

One afternoon in the studio, sitting with a group of musicians who were between sessions, the air was thick with the scent of 'pot'. They started talking about the tattoos and piercings they had. Mick had a ring in his lip and his nose, another guy showed them a tattoo of an eagle that he had on his back, and another had a silver bar through an eyebrow and the back of his neck. In a pause in the conversation Sky stood up, undid the straps to her dress and let it fall to the ground. She had a lithe body with small breasts and her protruding nipples seemed to stand to attention. "I got this yesterday." She pointed to a nipple ring and a ring in her belly button where the skin looked inflamed and red and then pointed below to where she had shaved her pubic hair.

"I might get one there as well."

Not to be outdone and to get Micks attention Rosy suddenly stood up and let her dress fall to the ground. She was totally naked underneath, showing off her tanned athletic body, with her equally pert upward pointing breasts to those in the room.

"Look guys, no piercings."

Everyone laughed, Mick pulled her down to the floor in an embrace and they started kissing and rolling about. Sky sat down in her partner Bruno's lap guiding his hand to her thigh and kissing him on the lips. Soon everyone who had the opportunity to get hold of someone near to them began caressing each other, going into a side room, the sound booth, or sliding to the floor. Selina sat still, forgotten and alone. Once again felt like a voyeur at a 'happening' where she was not included. The atmosphere in the studio soon became oppressive for her and so she got up from her seat and walked down the dimly lit corridor that led from the studio to the street entrance. Suddenly, and without warning she was grabbed from behind. Someone put an arm around her neck, while another wrapped around her waist. The strength of the attacker momentarily lifted her off the floor which left her feet kicking in mid-air. Her heart was pumping harder sending adrenalin flooding through her veins as she began to panic. Thoughts raced into her mind, 'What the fuck do you think you're doing? Attack me! Assault me? Fuck you, for God's sake! My dad's in the bloody Navy! You don't know who you're fucking dealing with!' She shouted out loud. "Get your fucking hands off my body, you shit! Get your fucking hands off me!"

Then her body responded in the way her father had taught her. She remembered what her father said,

"Selina, someday you are going to have to fight. When you do, don't be a lady, fight dirty!"

 She let her body sag, increasing her weight, and changing her centre of gravity. This threw the assailant off balance and the grip round her neck loosened slightly but enough for her to grab their wrist and pull the arm away from her neck with her free hand. Then she bit down as hard as she could into the flesh of the arm as hard hoping to draw blood. This loosened the attackers grip enough for her body to drop down a fraction so that she could put her two feet firmly on the floor and with then all the force she could muster quickly push her body upward, hitting the attacker on the chin with the back of her head. Whoever it was, let out a yelp and loosened their grip so that her body came free from his grip.

"You bitch!" The attacker shouted out loud.

Then, as if by instinct and without turning to face the attacker, jabbed her right elbow back into their body causing them to gasp out loud. Then she stepped back, brought the knee of her right leg up as far as she could and stomped down on their foot with the heel of her boot.

"Fuck you!" Her attacker yelled at her and who by this time had let go of her body and was hopping backwards down the corridor. Selina made a break for the exit and ran along the dark corridor to the studio entrance, pulled the door open and ran up the stone steps leading into the street. She did not stop running until she reached the King Alfred swimming pool on the sea front and she felt safe.

This was the beginning of the end of her singing relationship with Rosy. Rosy was genuinely mortified to hear about what happened to her at the party, and Mick was very apologetic. Despite their video of 'California Dreaming' getting over 800 hits on You-Tube, and their song getting interest on Myspace and Sound Cloud, Selina could not bring herself to go back to the studio. Mick texted Selina and told her that he guessed that the person who attacked her was a friend of Jonathan, a bass player in a group he was recording, and who had got into the party uninvited. He told Selina that he had banned him from the studio and threatened to get a friend to sort him out if he ever showed his face there again. Mick and Rosy begged Selina not to go to the police as they could shut down the studio, and if it got into the paper the studio could get a bad reputation it would reduce studio bookings. Selina reassured them both that she wouldn't involve the police and wanted to forget the whole thing, but things could not be the same between them. Her recording career was over and she intended to concentrate on her school work and getting into University.

For a while after the attack she had nightmares replaying the scene in her head, trying to get away from her assailant. Once she woke up screaming and had to be comforted by Rosy who, on this rare occasion, did get into her bed and cuddled her until she went back to sleep. They continued playing music together for fun but stopped busking in Brighton. Rosy spent time away from the school house with Mick and on these occasions asked Selina to cover for her, but her interest in him began to wane. One afternoon when they were sharing tea and crumpets she told Selina that Mick was 'an experience', interesting, a great guitarist and producer, not a very good lover, and probably going nowhere.

"He reckons he played my body like his Fender guitar, but in truth Selina most of the time I had to make my own music. He was so stoned most of the time he couldn't perform."

Mick continued to live in the twilight world of the studio. It was his kingdom. Rosy tried to get him out of the studio into the sunlight but he preferred the dark and to live at night. Rosy and Selina imagined that he slept upside down hanging from the ceiling. They imagined that he was a descendent of 'Count Dracula', a vampire with skin so sensitive it would burn and ignite into flames if he exposed it to sunlight. About seven weeks after the party Selina found Rosy sitting on her bed crying, in their shared room. She had gone to the studio on the day of Mick's birthday to give him a present. She found him on the mattress in the sound booth with Sky and they were both naked. They were not put out by her arrival, instead, Sky asked her to join them on the mattress to,' get it on together'.
  That incident put the nail in the coffin of the relationship between Mick and Rosy. That evening she sent him a text making it clear to him that she never wanted to see him again. In amongst the expletives she told him that he deserved to catch some horrible S.T.D. From Sky, 'the slut',

and his 'dick will fall off!' Rosy stayed in her room all the next day, but after that it was as if nothing had happened.
Emerging from her room she told Selina that had decided to go to U.C.L.A. her mother's old University, to study film and psychology. She had contacted her mother and asked her to arrange for her to take the S.A.T and the A.C.T assessments. She had no doubt that she would get accepted at the University because of her mother and father's contacts. In addition to this she would have three 'A' levels from this top British private school.

Selina was 'gob smacked' by the speed of her friends decision to concentrate on her education. Once Rosy made the decision to go to University she went for it, full steam ahead. She asked her mother if she could have extra lessons in her weak subjects and promised to help Selina with any revision for exams they could do together. Selina was pleased to have her best friend back supporting her, especially because it meant that the two of them could study together. From that moment, boy's and music had to take a back seat.

Rosy went to U.C.L.A. as planned and Selina waved goodbye to her from the departure lounge at Gatwick Airport. Rosy promised Selina she would keep in touch by all electronic means available and begged Selina to come and visit her in Los Angeles. Selina passed her three 'A' levels and her common entrance exam to Oxford and Cambridge. However on her eighteenth birthday she received a letter on quality paper in a large envelope from her grandfather's solicitor telling her the terms of her inheritance. She decided not to share the contents of the letter with anyone other than her parents who had prior knowledge of her large fortune. Her sister, who lived in the States with her eighty year old Grandmother, would get a similar inheritance when she came of age. Neither she nor her younger sister could remember seeing their Grandmother alive despite knowing that they had met when she was five years old. This memory had faded. There was a picture of her sitting on the knee of her grandfather on the veranda of his very large house in Canada, with her proud mother and father standing behind them. This picture had pride of place on a wall in the hall of their house at home. She knew her mother was an oil heiress, a wealthy woman. A friend of her mother's made a comment at a tea party that stuck in Selina's memory,

"Old money is never 'showy' Poppet. Wealth like you mother's just sits and breathes. No need to flaunt it."

She found it important to follow that advice now; suddenly she had become a woman of substance, like her mother. Money could change her life but she needed time to think of the consequences. The letter explained how she could take an allowance from her trust fund each year until she reached the age of twenty five when she would inherit the bulk of her oil fortune. However the solicitor advised her to consult financial experts, and the executers of the will, including her mother, before any large expenditure. The letter concluded,

"Money hard won can be easily lost!"

Selina realised she had choices to make about her immediate future. After much thought and a few sleepless nights she decided not to go straight up to university from school. Her money gave her time to pursue options others did not have. She could produce her own album of songs and form a record label of her own, to which she could discover and sign new artists. She could contact Rosy in America and resurrect their singing duo. This freedom to do something or nothing with her life brought more problems than she expected. She hoped the attitude of her father, mother and younger sister would not change towards her now that she was financially independent. Her sister would get her inheritance when she reached twenty five but her father was still a professional working man. He remained an Admiral in the Navy, which is a very important occupation but he had little inherited wealth. Selina was now in a position to give him money but would he resent such a gift. She realised that the balance of power between her father and mother must have been affected by the inequality of wealth between them. It wasn't as if her father was a kept man. He could command a decent lifestyle on his own but would it be the same?

Selina felt certain that her mother had occasional affairs but managed them discretely so as not to embarrass or humiliate her father. Selina had suspected her riding instructor, one of her ski instructors, as well as a very handsome hotel manager her mother met in Zermatt, while they were without their father on their annual winter holiday. At one time Selina became anxious that her mother would leave her father when they moved into separate bedrooms, but nothing happened; it seemed more likely to her that her mother and father had an implicit arrangement between them which allowed these romantic dalliance's to take place, on the understanding that they were discreet, and did not upset or invade family life.

After giving her possibilities much thought she decided to travel for a year. However she had no intention of back packing around the world, or working as a chalet maid to the randy rich and infamous in an alpine ski resort. She heard stories of this life from other girls at school whose elder sisters had done this. The job specification apparently included a willingness to get drunk, jump into hot tubs naked, and have sex with older rich men or arrogant, self-obsessed, snow seeking city traders. This did not appeal to Selina in any way shape or form. Her desire to experience love and sex was as present as it had always been but now she was a wealthy woman. She felt she had more to lose and she needed to control her desire to take a bite out of that particular cherry. She had set her mind on exploring America the home of the music she loved when out of the blue her father tempted her with a much better offer.

A friend of his had ordered a motor cruiser to be built by 'Sun Seekers' based in Poole Dorset. This boat had to be delivered to his friends mooring at a marina in Mykonos, Greece, and they needed crew for the voyage. Her father made the opportunity sound very interesting and tried hard to sell this idea to her;

"My darling 'C' just think you will go across the channel to France, then Lisbon, through the Strait of Gibraltar to Algiers, then Sardinia, Palermo in Sicily, Athens, and then east in the Aegean Sea to the old port on the windy island of Mykonos. Did you know it was where they filmed one of your mother's favourite films, 'Shirley Valentine', in about eighty nine? She loved Tom Conti in that film."

This convinced Selina and she found herself getting very excited about the trip. There remained the small thing of actually being offered a job on the boat. Her father contacted his friend immediately Selina said she was interested and on the basis of her father's recommendation she was offered a place in the crew. Her father insisted that she be given no special favours in terms of what she did on the boat but without telling Selina he did ask his friend to look after her when they docked and went on shore. Selina had no worries about being a sea as she had crewed with her father on their yacht at Cowes week on the Isle of Wight. This boat had no sails to worry about. On this adventure she would 'sail' the 'Med', see the sights and perhaps meet an intriguing beautifully handsome man. "Daddy I know I will love it, when do we depart?"

"In September I think. You can give him a call. You have to take it out for some test runs before you leave. I am so glad you are going but you haven't asked me how you get back." Her father looked at her with a big smile on his face.

"I will miss you and so will your mother."

"Do I need to come back?" There was a pause in which she could see her father looking uncomfortable.

"Oh come on Daddy, don't get upset, it's my adventure and you helped me get it!"
Selina and her father hugged. Then he spoke quietly into her ear.

"Come back when you're ready, and my lovely sailor daughter, make sure you do."

Chapter Eleven: The Anniversary

While cleaning her teeth on this sunny morning she started humming a song to herself. When she focused on the tune she recognised it as 'The Winner Takes it All' from the musical 'Mamma Mia'. She had seen the musical twice on stage in London and had bought the D.V.D. When Meryl Streep sang this to Peirce Brosnan in the film version, tears rolled down her cheeks. Mary wondered if her unconscious was sending her a message.

The secret arrangement she had with Steven was risky but at least she had taken control. She was fed up of being the dutiful wife especially if she had become the second choice in his affections. She was not without a moral code. Her philandering had strict rules. Steven must wear a condom, one that could stand the strain of their exertions, not one of those things that could break and get lost inside her as it had on her honeymoon with Mark. This was not to stop her getting pregnant as she was on the pill, but to protect herself from any sexually transmitted infection that Steven could give her from any other contact he might have. Steven was not allowed to stay after they had finished having sex and get all 'lovey-dovey' with her. She wanted him gone so that she could shower her guilt away, check for tell-tale marks on her body, change the bedclothes, change her underwear, and wash them with the sheets. Then she would freshen up her makeup, blow dry her hair, put on presentable clothes, then pour herself a stiff gin and dry vermouth to steady her nerves. She would pretend to herself that nothing of significance had happened. She told herself that it was the equivalent of taking her favourite pony for a ride across the fields, the pony that her father had bought her when she was ten years old.

She wondered what her father would think of her now. Would he be able to hold her close and tell her it was O.K. and that no matter what she did she was not an evil woman? She knew he didn't want her to marry Mark anyway. When she thought of this lovely man's death it brought tears to her eyes and she began to sob out loud. It was a day of heightened emotions.

"Bugger I've spoiled my makeup" she said to herself.

The alarm on her mobile phone burst into song and brought her back to the demands of the present. It was a reminder for her to get to the station in Marden, as she did most days, to pick up Mark from the London train. She looked at the time on the clock and realised that it was too early for her to depart from the house and it would not be the right train. Lost in her reminiscences she had temporarily forgotten that today was not an ordinary day. She had planned to surprise Mark at his office in London, because the next day was their wedding anniversary and she had booked tickets to see 'le Miserable' for the sixth time. She had arranged for them to stay in the 'Lillie Langtree' suite of rooms at the Berners Hotel, just off Oxford Street. This is the hotel and the very room where one of the Kings of England used to meet his mistress Lillie Langtree a star of the stage. She and Mark would have their dinner in the ornately decorated dining room with its plaster cornices, but save their pudding from their meal to eat when they returned from the theatre. He would have a glass of malt whisky and she would order cocktails until she felt drunk enough to go up to their bedroom and participate in celebratory sex. She would try her hardest to make him think all was fine between them. For a brief drink fuelled moment in his arms she could pretend that their love conquered all. While gathering her things together she began to humming a tune from the musical they were going to see, then softly began to sing the words,

"I dreamed a dream in times gone by, when hope was high and life worth living. I dreamed that love would never die,"

Mary stopped singing and made a wish from the bottom of her heart that if there was a God looking down on this poor woman, whichever God it was, could find a way to be forgiving.

Mary changed into her travel clothes, picked up the case that she had packed earlier in the day for Mark and herself, locked the front door and ran to her car in the driveway. Sitting in the car she made sure that the train tickets were in her purse, and in no time she was at the station, parking her car. While she waited on the platform it started to rain, she had no umbrella and nowhere to shelter. Soon the train to Charing Cross would arrive. The rain running down her face reminded her of Mark proposing to her in Regents Park, by the lake.

All those years ago Mary had given up hope of contacting the attractive man who found her purse on the train. The number she dialled was not recognised and she did not catch another glimpse of him on her commuter train. Then as if by magic, two months later they met again at a party thrown by a friend of hers who was in advertising.

She had gone to the party with a date, a man named Christopher, someone she knew through an estate agent friend of hers who made money from property development and had been involved with a deal of her fathers. Mary stood in the kitchen trying to open a bottle of wine with an old style cork screw; she needed to refill her glass and to get some alcohol inside her. She needed something, anything, to take the edge off the boredom she was feeling. Christopher had left her on her own while he mingled with the party guests. He probably sensed from Mary's body language that there was no chemistry between them, and no hope of any intimacy developing between them. She wandered into the kitchen and stood by the table festooned with all manner of alcoholic drinks. She picked up the nearest bottle of white wine. A young man with a cork screw in his hand offered to help her open the bottle and complimented her on her choice of white wine.

"I love Pouilly Fume, delicious, like gooseberries in summer."

"I don't care; just tell me its alcoholic."

"Come on, taste some with me, let it roll around your tongue, and then drink it down, nectar, pure nectar!"

She looked at the handsome gentleman, who had come to her rescue, she was sure she knew him from somewhere.
"Who are you anyway and why, prey sir, are you talking to me in this godforsaken kitchen".

Her heart beat faster in her chest and her bosom heaved, and she felt a queasy feeling in her tummy.

"Well, my lady, I have been watching you from the other side of yonder room, and I could tell you were a girl of good standing and fine breeding. Actually I was waiting for you to drop something, but failing that, and coping with the panicky feelings due to my previous rejection by your good self, I thought I would speak to you anyway. Furthermore, I love the fact that you have put your hair up showing your beautiful neck. I would love to plant a row of gentle kisses there, which I hope would make you tingle. However, sadly, I am aware that you came with a gentleman escort. Sorry I don't mean an escort, I mean someone has escorted you here. Anyway, my lady, I am speaking out of turn, please forgive me?"

"My God you're him, my prince on the train, sorry the man on the train who found my purse, I'm so sorry, I tried, I lost your number, I didn't mean to…"

Mark ignored her protestations and continued speaking. Despite being in a daze at the time, she still remembered what he went on to say.

"I must warn you I have the same reaction with babies. My sister has a baby boy, who, if served up on toast, I would eat. I hold him close to my cheek and smell his neck."
"I bet sometimes you smell other things as well." They both laughed.

"Do you want to have babies?" he asked, but before she could reply, he continued talking.

He told her that whatever happened, in the future with marriage and children he would not send his children to private school. He would not inflict on them what his parents did to him. He said that on the first night, in the dorm, and for the rest of the week, he cried himself to sleep. He showed no emotion when they left him at the school with his trunk of clothes and provisions. He watched as his parents drove down the long school road in their Jaguar car and disappeared into the distance. His father told him that public school would make a man of him, and that he would make contacts and friends that would last him a lifetime, just as it had for him.

"Whether you like it or not son, money still buys privilege, and your times here will open doors for you in the future." He also said something to him that did not make sense until his later years;

"Try not to get too close to any of the older boys, don't accept favours, and do lots of sport. It served me well."

Mark told Mary that he hated the fact that in his business, publishing, the first part of his father's advice had been proven right. The second part was not so useful, but his own experience at school had not changed what he wanted for his own children. He wanted to be there while they grew up and not farm them out to someone else. He seemed so passionate, and yet there was a little boy charm to him. She felt a reaction in her stomach, which at first she put down to the lack of food she had eaten before drinking alcohol, but in the kitchen, she forgot the person she had arrived with. She interrupted Mark in full flow to say that she had to go to the loo. His parting comment as she walked away was,

"Someday across a crowded room......I should not let you go, but needs must, I guess."

Sitting on the seat in the loo her thoughts were racing and her heart was a flutter. Cupid's arrow had pierced her defences. She decided that she would make some lame excuse to her present companion, tell him she had to go to work early in the morning, or that she had a stomach upset. She took her pink lipstick from her bag and wrote down her first name and telephone number on a strip of toilet paper. She left the toilet to the great relief of the line of people waiting outside and went back into the crowded living room where the party goers had started dancing. She walked over to where Mark was chatting with some other guests, tapped him on the shoulder and when he turned towards her, leant forward, whispered in his ear, "This is for you!" Without the others seeing, slipped the note into the breast pocket of his jacket, turned on her high heels, and left the party.

From that moment, their relationship developed rapidly, spending weekends away together as well as holidays abroad. They talked of moving in together. Then one evening after work, standing by the lake in Regents Park in the rain, watching the ducks, Mark kissed her, held her close, and said,

"I will never let you go because I love you. You are my special treat and I know we will be perfect together. Let us make babies and have a home together."

At this moment Mark stopped talking. He ignored the puddles on the path made by the rain water, knelt down on one knee and looking up into her eyes said;

"Please say yes, I love you, please will you marry me?"

Looking down at her rain soaked Prince Charming, with a smile that stretched from ear to ear she said yes. It was a magical moment she still treasured. The following weekend, Mark asked her father for her hand in marriage. Her father replied with a question in his typically witty fashion.

"Well Mark if it's her hand you want, that's fine, but what do you expect me to do with the rest of her?"

Her father continued speaking.
"Mark, I can see that my daughter loves you. I will to give you my blessing but it comes with a health warning. Treat her with the love and

respect that she deserves and when you say the wedding vows, listen to them, and mean what you say because if you don't you will have me to deal with."

Mark smiled and shook his hand, but as he did her father pulled him closer and spoke quietly in his ear.

"I do know people you would not like to become acquainted with."

Mark let out a nervous laugh and her father smiled.

Why torture herself with these memories now, Mary asked herself. Standing on the platform at Marden train station, she was no longer in in a fog of blissful ignorance. Recently she had been to see a divorce lawyer recommended by one of her friends. He advised her that she was entitled to half of everything they owned and half of the worth of the business that Mark had built up. She was also entitled to half of his private pension. Their children still existed in a world where their parents apparently loved each other but if she went ahead with this separation their idea of family was about to be shattered up. Being away at private school they had learned some degree of self-sufficiency. Some of their friends had survived their own parents divorcing but they prided themselves that their family was different. How could she break their hearts? They had no idea of their father's infidelity.

Although attitudes had changed somewhat in recent years Mary felt society still set a higher standard for a mother's morality than a husbands. Historically women were seen as responsible for carrying the standards of morality for the society. They were still portrayed as the archetypes of the Madonna or the whore. What would her children and friends call her? Whatever happened, it would have to wait until after their annual family holiday.

Mark would not take her bid for independence lying down; he would fight, as it would cost him too much financially and emotionally. He was a 'have his cake and eat it' personality. He loved the idea of family and the security that this family structure gave him. He would not want to admit that his behaviour mirrored that of his father in many ways. He provided for his family and this gave him the right to behave as he did. Perhaps he would take this opportunity to make a life with his young mistress who could be a trophy on his arm and in his bed. She could blame herself for becoming less attractive, less interesting, less like the person he married. She could do nothing and eventually become a crazy housewife deeply depressed as her anger and hope imploded. She remembered that the teacher on her awareness course told the group how depression was often linked to despair and that while neurotics blame themselves for their ills, psychotics blame everyone else but themselves. Mark certainly had narcissistic tendencies. What if her independent actions caused him to become controlling and violent? In her scariest moments she had crazy thoughts. She imagined that he would make plans to get rid of her and claim the insurance they had on their lives. She dreamed of a headline in the local paper accusing Mark of cutting her up into pieces and throwing her down the well in their garden. She thought it more likely that Mark would exert his financial power over her by cancelling her credit cards, removing her name from their joint bank account and change the locks on the doors of her house making her homeless. This bombardment of her most negative thoughts left Mary feeling anxious and sick to the pit of her stomach. Perhaps she focused too much on bad things happening to her. What if something happened to Mark, like a heart attack on the golf course, or a road traffic accident. If the Old Testament God of the bible existed and could read her thoughts, it wouldn't surprise her if a lightning bolt struck her dead for wishing Mark harm. Try as she might, she couldn't stop herself thinking, what if he missed and it struck Mark instead?

The guard on the station shouted at her.

"Miss, are you getting on this train! Stand clear of the doors watch the gap!"

Dripping wet, Mary picked up her case climbed, onto the train, and made her way to the first class seats. She decided not to text Mark or to phone him about her departure, she wanted to keep her arrival, and their meeting as a surprise, after all, it was their anniversary.

Chapter Twelve: Steven the Gardener

In his own way Steven loved Mary, even though he knew she was using him as a distraction to ease her boredom and loneliness. This sadness weighing on Mary was the result of a gradual realisation that her husband had lost interest in her. Over the previous six months she felt that he had been showing less and less attention to her changing needs. Steven had also noticed a difference in her mood as she had become more demanding of his time but also more distant and introspective. As a gardener working in Marden and the surrounding area he had an opportunity to observe the behaviour of the local inhabitants and pick up gossip about those who lived in the local area. He had a unique opportunity to see what went on in the various homes he visited when partners and children were not at home. He also became a shoulder to cry on for some of his regular customers when they were going through hard times. In doing the work he did in the gardens he visited locally, he had heard seen things about her husband Mark that he vowed to keep to himself. Steven was in a difficult position as he belonged to the same golf club as Mark and had been on holiday with him. He was also employed by Mark as his gardener. Steven did not wish to be the one adding to Mary's misery by telling her more about her husband's misdeeds. Steven was not an innocent in this situation as he was not free from guilt himself and so his relationship with both Mark and Mary remained complicated. He had to be careful not to let Mary know his true feelings for her as this deeper affection was not part of the bargain between them. His honesty would blur the emotional boundary existing between them. The love he felt for this mature attractive woman was not a possessive one; when they had sex he wanted her to feel that it was his gift to her, as one human being caring affectionately for another. It was as if they were like two isolated humans on planet earth. Lonely little specs of carbon floating in a vast universe, hoping to find some happiness and meaning in their world. It was a description he had heard his mother use in a self-reflective moment during her illness. From the very beginning, Steven felt that if he could help Mary heal her emotional wound he had found a worthwhile purpose. He could offer a warming connection in what could sometimes feel a barren and hostile world.

Mary was not the only woman in Marden, Staplehurst, or Headcorn, that he shared his gardening expertise, a bed and his body with. Of the forty or so gardens where he cut the grass, dug the herbaceous borders, planted vegetables and fruit, trimmed the trees and hedges, or put up fences; eleven of his clients benefited from the extra attention that he offered. The ages of his special ladies ranged from those in their late twenties to one lady in her sixties. All of these women customers he found attractive in different ways. His clientele had increased in number by word of mouth or circumstance. He offered all his ladies absolute discretion and it was agreed that if he should bump into them in the shops, high street, local pubs, like the Unicorn or the Style Bridge, or any other establishment he frequented, he promised to ignore them. If they happened to meet by accident when they were out with their partner or husband, Steven would engage in polite conversation and try to focus on the work he did in their gardens. Some of his employers were also members of his golf club, and so he made sure that these limited conversations were unlikely to cause suspicion about Steven's other duties. There was however the constant risk of one of his special clients getting drunk, depressed, and angry with their spouse in one of the pubs they drank in and blurting out details of their liaison. Steven knew that this was a real threat to keeping the secret relationship they had between them. In some cases the situation between his lady client and their spouse became so toxic, and the struggle between them so vicious, that she may want to find a way to hurt and punish them. Shoving her infidelity with Steven in their face would certainly enable them to take some revenge for their partner's hurtful, unfaithful and abusive behaviour. Not surprisingly Steven was very worried about the possible violent consequences towards him if this took place. Therefore he became very careful in choosing the clients to whom he'd offer his special services. Until now Steven had managed to choose 'clients' who were mature enough to deal with the secrecy required and able to keep a degree of separation between them. If this arrangement was to work boundaries had to be maintained. From the beginning of his 'therapeutic' service he made a decision not to formally charge his clients for the extras he provided. They paid him for his gardening work and grateful clients, which included most of his lady friends ,gave him an extra cash donation towards his 'social fund', as it was called.

Steven's guiding philosophy in his ministry of love was that during the time he was with them would try to love and appreciate each of his female clients for the special individual people they are. He made it his mission to be open to help women of all varieties of age, shapes, size, hair and skin colour. Often his client doubted her beauty and had low self-esteem because of ageing or operations she had undergone due to

necessity or vanity. He reassured them of their desirability and hoped that because of his ministrations they became less ashamed of their naked bodies and able to express their sexuality.
If they showed their insecurity, Steven would try to reassure them;

"You have earned each memory that every line, every crease, every wrinkle on your skin, represents. Just relax and let me enjoy each curve of your body. Let me help you, because to me you are beautiful sexy and perfect. You need to know the unique and incredible woman that you are."

He helped them relax into this way of being by becoming their personal masseuse. Techniques he had learned over the years observing his mother massaging friends and then practicing on her when she became ill. The massage he gave his lady friends differed in many respects from that practiced on his mother. In the beginning he gradually and delicately removed their clothes and then invited them to lay face down on their bed naked, while he massaged their muscles from head to toe with their favourite fragrant oil. Sometimes they had candles burning and peaceful music playing of the kind his mother played when she did reflexology on him and her girlfriends. They soon relaxed, and as the tension flowed from their body and Steven ran his rough hands over the skin of their thighs, bottom, back and breasts they often became aroused. He would ask them to turn over; keeping their eyes closed, continue his sensual massage over the front of their body. He watched their response to his touch, lingering on the areas that seemed the most sensitive and gained the most physical response. They would sometimes moan, arch their back, take his hand and place it where they wanted it to be. It could culminate in a sexual act of some kind, or his soothing massage might send them into a peaceful sleep. Steven would cover them with a blanket and leave quietly.

His encounters with each of these women with fragile egos evolved his understanding of their plight and helped him relate to his other clients. The emotional and physical pleasure that he provided for them was food for their soul. It helped them to restore energy which was absent from their lives, and helped rebalance their personality. They had been starved of intimacy and in most cases physical release. From her traveller days his mother was a great believer in the balance between the body and the mind or 'psyche' as she would call it. He remembered her saying;

"Steven, if your energy gets blocked from flowing in your body then you will end up ill, neurotic, or both. You have got to let your 'Orgone' energy flow. That is a big problem with the world and Reich knew it. He made a device to accumulate it, hoping to heal people with it. Poor bastard they put him in jail, even though Einstein gave him a hearing. The energy of the orgasm is part of it, and if more people had more of them, the Fascists, the Communists, the fundamentalist terrorists would all disappear!"

At the time Steven was too young and ill-informed to understand what his mother was talking about. He was also not ready to talk to his mother about orgasms.
Over time, Steven had come to see his role with his special clients as therapeutic, nurturing the seeds of hope, self-love, and enjoyment in each of them. Some women had invested money in counselling and therapy of various kinds before meeting Steven but he doubted that a talking cure could offer the intimacy and physical release he gave his clients. If life's hardships had left them in the shadows feeling lost and abandoned, it was his job to be their ray of light, helping them grow from a shy caterpillar into a beautiful butterfly.

Steven also took pride in his occupation as a gardener. He studied for a degree in landscape gardening from the University of East Anglia in Norwich. After graduating and a brief spell working in Norfolk he moved to Kent to be near his mother. He remembered the day when he had been told by the doctor that she had a terminal illness and would probably not last longer than a year after her diagnosis. At the time he had his own flat but made the decision to move back home and look after her. He continued to earn money from local gardening jobs, but not on the scale of those he did now. Gradually, and over time word spread about his good work. While he lived in Staplehurst, his gardening business had grown and grown. Apart from carer's in the later stages of her illness he was her only support as the father who adopted him had died. Steven had never known his biological father.

His mother told him she had met his biological father at a rock festival in the Isle of Wight. According to his mother's story of his conception he was the proud product of three days of free love, cannabis consumption, homemade alcohol and crystal magic. She found out she was pregnant a couple of months later and could not remember exactly who his father could have been. By the time she became certain she was pregnant she was on the road to France in a camper van with other travellers heading for the grape or olive harvest. The group of women that his mother lived with in the pagan community promised to support her in giving this new life to the universe. The group insisted on an initiation ceremony before she could become a fully accepted member of their 'tribe'. It took the form of a ritual rebirthing ceremony requiring her to be naked and painted white from head to toe. Then, accompanied by her birth sister and space guide Echo, she slept in a small tent, heated by hot stones and steam for a night to be purified prior to being reborn. The tent was meant to represent a mystical womb. She was encouraged to take a tab of L.S.D. to heighten her journey of enlightenment. Then in the morning, after her journey through the mystical birth canal her tent was unzipped and she emerged back into the world. She was then ceremonially washed by the other women of the group who emptied buckets of cold water over her head while singing 'Good Morning Star Shine' from the musical 'Hair'. From the moment of rebirth she answered to the name Stardust, or Star for short. This was the name Steven knew his mother by as he lived and grew up in this community for four years. He had only happy memories of his life with the other children and mothers. His early childhood was free and adventurous and the camp followers co-parented their children sharing caring duties between them. Later in life his mother told him that their child rearing bible was a book called the 'Continuum Concept', by Jean Liedloff. The author of the book left her sophisticated life in the New York literary world to live for two and a half years with the Yequena Indians who were a tribe in the heart of the Venezuelan jungle and who reared their children in a natural, good humoured and unfussy way, sharing the duties of childcare between them. The children were carried by their parents until they asked to be put down, and they slept in the same bed or sleeping space with their parents until they chose not to. The Yequena loved children and so did the members of the commune. It was a contained freedom that other people he met later in life had not experienced. He was picked up and held by the nearest loving arms if he cried and was allowed to crawl and explore with the other children the rest of the time. One day, and he couldn't remember exactly what age he was, his mother sat him down on the floor of their travellers van and said;

"Son you are a child of a Yequena upbringing, independent, happy, inwardly secure, physically and emotionally balanced, and loving the universe. That is how I know you will be able to survive on your own and understand why I cannot be tied down. I need to be a free spirit. I am going on a trip with Gino but I know you will be fine."

While picking olives in Italy she met Gino, the son of the owner of the estate where the olives grew. She said he swept her off her feet and asked her to go to Sicily with him for a week of passion free from the demands of work, the world, and the demands of her child. Steven was left in the capable hands of Echo and her partner Jed. His mother's week away became a month and despite the hugs and cuddles that Echo gave him, as well as the companionship of her children, he began to pine for his mother's smile and her infectious laughter. He wanted the smell of her and the comfort of her body close to him at night. He needed to know where his Star was in the night sky was. After five weeks with no news from his mother, Gino's father arrived at Jed and Echo's camper van. He informed them that Gino had been arrested by the Italian customs for smuggling dope, what kind it was he was not sure, but Steven's mother had been arrested as an accomplice.

Gino had used his mother, a foreigner, and someone who could be seen by the authorities as a tourist, as a cover for his drug importing expedition, and to hide his meetings with bandits in the mountains of Sicily. Gino's father told them not to worry as he had contacts in the police and if necessary bribes could be payed to smooth everything over. Then he left. Unfortunately the police investigation revealed that the olive grove and the vineyard owned by his father was part of a money laundering operation financed by a crime family linked to the Mafiosi. Gino's father was arrested. In later years when he was older, his mother told Steven that the Italian police offered her a deal. Tell them everything she did, everywhere she went, and everyone she met in Sicily who had a Sardinian connection. If she co-operated with them they offered to deport her without trial. She would not be allowed to return to Italy for ten years, but she would be free and able to return to England with her son. She accepted their offer, arrived back at the camp with a police escort, where she met Echo, Jed and Steven who were waiting, packed their belongings into her travel bag, swept Steven up into her arms and then escorted by the police, they were taken to the nearest airport.

Steven found himself at five years old, back in England, living with his mother and his grandparents in their farm house near Sproughton in Suffolk. His mother decided it was time for a change of lifestyle in order to become more respectable. Supported by her parents who helped with childcare she decided to train as a primary school teacher. This became the vocation she was to practice for the rest of her life. 'Star', who now reverted to her actual name Sarah, discovered that she loved teaching. It gave her new opportunities to be creative and express both her academic and artistic side in the classroom. The children adored her because her lessons were instructive, fun and sometimes wacky. Eventually she became the Head Teacher of a primary school in Ipswich and then later in Maidstone from where she retired.

Life with his mother was going smoothly until she met Gordon the Dentist. After a whirlwind romance his mother made the decision that they should move in to Gordon's house. Gordon had no children of his own. Steven tried to find out about him from dental receptionists and anyone he could speak to but not much was forthcoming. All he discovered was that Gordon had devoted himself to preserving teeth and having brief relationships with a series of adoring dental nurses or hygienists whom he then sacked. Gordon's parents were both dead and his father had been a surgeon at the local hospital. By all accounts Gordon was an excellent dentist. Steven and his mother became patients at his practice and they had Gordon to thank for their excellently cared for teeth, cavity free, with no amalgam fillings. Steven was fourteen at the time his mother met Gordon. He hated the intrusion that Gordon brought to his and his mother's happy life. His mother had dated other men since returning from Italy, and Steven had no objection to this because he understood that she was a vibrant, attractive, healthy, physical woman who needed adult company. Until Gordon she kept her love life away from Steven and their home, preferring to spend time with her lovers in a different environment. She was careful to keep them separate from her home life. The exceptions to this rule were those men she was involved with for longer periods of time. One of these, Peter, another teacher, Steven got to know quite well, and for a time they both supported the local football team. They went together to see Ipswich Town football team play at Portman Road football ground about ten times in total. Peter was also a musician and he helped Steven learn to play the drums on his drum kit in the basement of his house. His mother and Peter stayed together for about two years, during which time Steven saw him regularly. Then without warning he didn't see him for a month. He asked his mother when he was likely to see Peter to practice the drums again. She explained that Peter had left his job as a teacher to travel on a cruise ship to Latin America as a drummer in the resident band. His mother did not seem at all phased by the loss of her boyfriend and life continued as normal. However Steven felt hurt and abandoned. For a while he would get angry with his mother over the smallest of things and without realising it he would find himself passing Peters house in the village and being close to tears. Peter was someone he had become attached to. In one of his outbursts over burnt toast he ended up asking his mother why she was not showing any feelings. Surely Peter meant something to her. She put her arm around his shoulders and said,

"Steven darling, we have to follow our dreams, I used to, and so it wouldn't be right for me to stand in his way now."

What she didn't say to Steven at the time, but Peter explained later in a letter, was that he did ask his mother to go with him but she had refused. She told Peter she wanted stability in her life and she was finished with her nomadic ways. It was not long after Peter left that his mother met Gordon. He came to her school to talk to the children about teeth hygiene and dental awareness as part of a health education programme she had organised. In the staff room over tea and biscuits she mentioned the trouble she was experiencing from a tooth that was sensitive to hot and cold liquid. Gordon offered her a free appointment at his surgery. Not long after this she became his patient and their romance blossomed.

"I fell in love with your mother when I looked into her eyes as I was polishing her teeth. I guess you could say it was love at first bite. She had a lovely mouth, kissable lips, hardly any fillings and a healthy set of gums! I asked if I could take her out, instead of one of her teeth."

Gordon hoped he would make Steven laugh at this but his joke fell on stony ground. Steven was far from convinced that Gordon was the right match for his mother. Steven could not understand why his mother needed to give up her freedom for such a small improvement in her circumstances. Surely her independence was worth more than a detached house in the Tuddenham Road, just off the Valley Road, north of the Ipswich town centre. The house had six bedrooms, en-suite bathrooms, a medium sized horseshoe shaped drive at the front, a swimming pool in the back garden. Gordon also owned a BMW car, golf and gym membership, plus the promise of foreign holidays (excluding Italy of course). He inherited a villa in Mallorca from his parents when they died.

To gain his mother's approval and to avoid conflict Steven adapted to Gordon's rules and routine and fitted in with Gordon's lifestyle. He felt he owed it to his mother to do the best he could to fit in to this respectable middle class existence. It had its perks. He could save for and buy any games console and games he wanted with the allowance he was given each week. Eventually he learned to ski and became a brown belt in Judo, as well as enjoying amazing surfing holidays in the sun where he could meet girls and start to appreciate the female form at close range. It was on a skiing holiday in Switzerland that he met Heidi a Swiss German girl with a 'fit' body, soft lips and a curious attitude to all things English, which she spoke fluently. Her father terrified Steven at first glance, because he wore a black leather coat and looked like a gestapo officer from a war film he had seen. He also had a duelling scar across his nose and left cheek which Heidi explained was from a sword fight he participated in at military school. Fortunately for Steven he and Heidi were left to their own devices most of the time. She was the first girlfriend he had been with who did not shave under her arms. This caught him by surprise the first time they went swimming together in a heated infinity pool at the resort hotel with a spectacular view of the mountains. When, later on in the holiday they became more intimate and were alone in her father's chalet she allowed him to fondle her breasts.

He was sixteen at the time and though he didn't ask, he assumed she was the same age. She appeared confident, physically well developed, forward in her actions, and seemed socially sophisticated for her age. Extricating herself from their passionate embrace, still with the blush of excitement on her cheeks from the heat of their kissing and cuddling, she looked him in the eyes and asked him if he loved her. Steven, who was visibly aroused by their heavy petting grabbed a cushion to cover his groin and retain some modesty, knew in that moment that she was offering herself to him. If he answered yes he felt certain they would end up in bed together naked. Up to this point in his life he had seen porn on the internet but now, here it was, his opportunity to actually do what he had seen and read about. To actually do 'it'!

Steven sat back in his seat on the leather sofa, trying to calm down. He took a deep breath, thought for a moment, then, he leant forward and took her hand in his. Looking into her eyes and gently stroking her hand he said;

"Heidi, please don't be upset, I am really flattered, I want to, and I can only guess how much this means to you, but as much as I want to say yes, I have to say no. Please don't cry, don't hate me, because I think you are gorgeous, but I can't lie to you. It wouldn't be love, not that I know what love is yet, but I don't deserve what you might give me. I am on holiday; I don't want you to feel used, I want to be sincere in what I say to you. You know my body is telling me one thing but my conscience another. Look, I am really confused. I think I know what saying yes could mean but, to be honest, I think you should wait."

Steven could see from the look in her eyes that he had hurt her feelings and probably had blown any chance of her being interested in him over the rest of his holiday. She let go of his hand and moved away from him on the sofa.

"Why do you English only think of yourselves? You sound like my father. What about me? What about what I want! You think you are the spider and I am the fly? Think again! Ich kann nicht verstehen! I'm not so stupid."

Steven was taken aback by her response, her mood changed so quickly from sadness to anger at his rejection.

"I know you are going away, 'dummkopf', that is the point."
He stuttered out his answer, "I, I, I'm sorry, I didn't mean..."

She looked at him and with fire in her eyes shouted, "Well, how you say-'fuck you', you had your chance with me now get out, get out!"

When he left the chalet she was sobbing, he never looked back, and she never spoke to him again. For the rest of the holiday he became paranoid that her father may challenge him to a duel for upsetting his daughter, or tell his parents that he had done something wrong. Nothing happened.

The holidays abroad were enjoyable but for Steven the best outcome of his mother's time with Gordon was that he helped him to become a junior member of the Ipswich golf club at Purdis Heath, where he was a member. Steven took lessons from the professional who worked there and he progressed quickly due to his natural ability and feel for the game. All seemed well as Steven went to Northgate Grammar school and studied for his 'A' levels while working part time at the golf club doing anything he was asked to do. Then the party happened.

One Easter his mother and Gordon decided to go away for a week to the South of France. He asked them if he could have a few friends over for a games night. They said yes with two conditions, no alcohol and the bedrooms were out of bounds. Steven could have sworn that when his mother said this to him she winked and said, "Don't do anything I wouldn't do."

Steve thought at the time this offered him quite a bit of scope, but Gordon shook his hand firmly, looked him straight in the eyes and said, "I trust you son." At that time in their relationship he hated Gordon calling him son.

Steven text and e-mailed his friends from college, "Party on for Thursday, bring your swimwear, cool pool, fun and games."

Steven expected to have fun with the six friends he invited, but not the thirty other people that turned up. What started out as a fun party with loud music, drink, party games, and swimming in the pool turned into a chaotic alcohol and drug fuelled mess. Steven tried to turn people away at the door but some got very aggressive and so it was easier to let them in. He tried to stop them roaming around the house by locking the upstairs rooms but the increased numbers meant they needed to use more than the ground floor toilet. In his haste he left the key in the door of the toilet forgetting that there was a master key on the keyring. The girl who he was attracted to in his class at school and whom he had a crush on for the last six months arrived at the door with a gorgeous looking friend whom he guessed was in her twenties. From the moment they met she made it clear to Steven that she found him attractive. She pulled him close to her in a welcome embrace and after saying, "How lovely it is to meet you." She kissed him fully on the lips and slipped her soft wet tongue in his mouth. This sent a shiver through Stevens's body and caused a slight swelling down below. From the moment of that kiss Steven's rational brain took a vacation and the one residing in his pants took control. He became so obsessed with this girl that all the other party goers seem to fade into the background as he followed her about the house from room to room. He resembled a puppy dog walking with his tongue hanging out. His attention to her did not go unnoticed. Every now and then she looked at him and smiled. When she stopped at the drinks table in the kitchen he quickly stood by her side and offered to pour her a drink.

"What would you like? I have most things. Beer, wine, spirits, do you like Prosecco?"

"I would like ......you." And with this she took his hand and led him out of the kitchen onto the patio and stood by the pool.

"It would be a shame to waste this lovely pool. Can you swim?"

Standing at the poolside she pulled her dress over her head to reveal the bikini she wore underneath. The she took her bikini top off, dropped it on the floor and dived into the pool. For a moment Steven watched her gliding under the water, and then as soon as she surfaced and turned to face him, he jumped fully clothed into the pool. He swam up to her, grabbed her around the waist pulling her body close to his and planted a kiss on her inviting lips. For the next hour it was as if Steven was living in a dream. He became oblivious to the mayhem taking place around him. It wasn't until Jim, one of his friends, ran into the pool area shouting his name and urging him to get to the living room as fast as he could that reality kicked in. Later it became clear that a girl who crashed the party and with whom he was not acquainted had taken ecstasy, become dehydrated, and collapsed in the living room. Another party crasher who said she was a nurse began to checking her pulse and airway, while someone else phoned for an ambulance. Other people were too drunk to notice the girl on the floor or so wrapped up in the music and dance to take this collapse seriously and continued dancing. Steven turned off the electric to the music system and shouted for everyone to leave. He then heard the sound of the ambulance arriving in the drive, followed by a police car with its siren wailing. The moment the ambulance crew and the police entered the house panic ensued. There was a mass exodus of party-goers, leaving the house by any means possible. Some went out the front door, some the back door and some over the garden fence. Others climbed out of the bedroom windows and jumped to the ground from the roof of the conservatory extension. Others hid under the beds in the upstairs bedrooms until the police had departed.

Fortunately for Steven the girl who collapsed regained consciousness before being taken away in the ambulance and told the police it was her fault. She confirmed that Steven knew nothing about the drugs found in her purse. The police constable took a statement from Steven, as well as his friend Jim and despite being in the clear, warned Steven that they would be contacting his parents about the incident on their return from France. Steven apologised profusely, explaining to the police how the party had spiralled out of his control, eventually shaking hands with the officers as they left, and closing the front door behind them.

He stood in the living room surveying the mess his so called 'friends' left behind. The gorgeous girl, whom he now knew as Claire, had stayed behind to support him while he was interviewed by the police. She came up behind him and put her arms around his waist. She kissed him on the cheek, then without speaking took his hand to lead him into the kitchen to find the rubbish bags. Jim, Steven and Claire moved from room to room, cleaning as they went. They filled one waste bin with enough bottles to stock a pub; they mopped up vomit from the bathroom floor and pee from the side of the toilet seat where drunken revellers had lost the ability or care to take aim. In the bedrooms they found used condoms. Steven picked them up with kitchen tongs, wearing the yellow rubber gloves he found under the sink. They also surprised a naked boy and girl who had fallen asleep in his parent's bed. They made them get up and dressed quickly and ushered them out of the house. In the lounge, to Stevens's horror, Gordon's pride and joy, his very expensive Mark Levinson amplifier had been splashed with beer. One of the grills of his B. and W. Hi-Fi speakers had been slit and on close inspection it looked like one of the speaker cones was perforated. Luckily his mother's ornaments survived intact, but someone had drawn a moustache on the print of Gordons graduation picture hanging on the wall by the stairs. On the carpets were various food and drink stains, all of which they tried to remove with detergent and other products but with limited success. Claire removed all the sheets from the beds and put them in the washing machine. Steven would remake the beds the next day before his parents arrived home. They were all tired and weary from the drink, excitement and anxiety of the previous evening. Jim crashed out on the sofa while Claire and Steven stood in the kitchen drinking a large glass of water.

"I want to thank you for all you have done, you didn't need to, and you were fantastic."

"No, its fine, that's what friends are for anyway, and you needed support. I kind of feel a bit responsible."

"No, why, no, you were in the pool, it was the other idiots, no if it is anybody's fault it's mine, I took my eye off the ball."

"Yes, well that was my fault I guess because I know you didn't take your eyes off me earlier, I mean when I stripped by the pool."

"Umm, well yes you are gorgeous and I wasn't expecting to feel the way I did."

"Yeah but I was a bit full on, I'm not really like that but I did enjoy the attention you gave me, and I was flirting with you."

"Really, I wouldn't have known….." Steven looked longing into her eyes. You have lovely teeth you know, sorry sounds stupid, my mum's partner is a dentist, and he would love your teeth."

"Really, you like my teeth? I thought you were going to say that my teeth are like stars, they come out at night!"

Steven smiled. "Never, well …. Do they?"

"That's cheeky. Ok what about my mouth, is it a nice mouth?

Steven moved closer to Claire, and put his drink down on the draining board.

"If you don't mind I would love to kiss your mouth," and before she could answer their lips met.

Holding hands they walked upstairs to his bedroom. Being older than Steven, he soon discovered she had more experience in the art of love making. He felt excited, aroused, and nervous all at the same time. The warmth and completeness of the sensation he felt when she first opened herself up to him and he entered her was so overwhelming that he climaxed in no time at all. He apologised to her for what he felt was his failure to give her any pleasure but she simply kissed him and directed his hand between her legs. Steven knew what she wanted him to do. With her guidance and patience he tried again later that night for a second and third time, he was successful. He felt things, and learned things, he would remember for the rest of his life. For Steven it was both a physical and spiritual experience during which he felt connected to another, similar to how he felt as a child. Held in the magic of this velvet glove he had been transported to another realm. It was for him a peak experience that he longed to repeat as soon as he could. It was midday before they finally disentangled themselves from each other's body and climbed out of bed to have a cup of tea and make breakfast.

During breakfast little was said about the previous night. They made polite conversation about the weather and what Steven might say to his parents when they returned. Stevens's friend Jim left before they got out of bed. Steven needed to tell Clair how much he had fallen for her, how much their night together had meant to him and how desperately wanted to meet her again. He was just about to make the speech he had been preparing in his mind while munching toast and marmalade when her mobile phone rang.

"I'm sorry Steven I have to take this. She got up from the table and went outside to take the call. Through the kitchen window Steven could see her demeanour change as she seemed to be arguing with the caller. Claire came in from the patio, put her phone in her bag and said,

"Sorry Steven, I am sorry, but I have to go. I can't explain why right now but please don't think badly of me. You are lovely, I know where you live. I just have to go."

Before Steven could get up from the breakfast table she ran out of the room, opened the front door of the house and slammed it shut. By the time Steven got to the front porch she had disappeared from view. Steven was in shock. His hopes had been shattered and it was as if he had lost his window in the sky, his vision of a new horizon.

When Gordon and his mother came home they were in a good mood. Steven thought all would be ok until the next door neighbour knocked on the front door and proceeded to complain loudly to his parents about the raucous and wild behaviour that took place in the house while they were away.

"Do you know Mr Prentis that the Police were called and a young girl was taken away in an ambulance? There were also young girls swimming topless in your pool. Well so my wife told me. This is not the kind of road in where such behaviour can be tolerated."

Then the police turned up wishing to caution Steven about the drugs found and the complaints about the noise that they had received from the locals who obviously did not enjoy the party.

Steven had no inclination to argue or defend himself. He was suffering pains in his stomach and a real feeling of anxiety that he had seen the last of Claire. Steven knew that Gordon would be mortified by the complaint and also the police visit. His standing in the community meant a lot to him. Even though Gordon encouraged his patients to open their mouths as wide as possible, he himself was tight lipped. Steven's mother had loosened him up a bit since she had known him, but his idea of a party involved six people at most, a buffet and a game of Trivial Pursuit, or if he went wild, Charades or Canasta. After the police left Steven was summoned to the dining room by his mother. When he entered the room Gordon and his mother were sitting at one end of the table with a chair opposite in which he was expected to sit. Gordon sat next to his mother holding her hand. He looked at Steven, his face stern, like a judge wearing a black cap ready to pass sentence on a prisoner for his crimes. He leant forward in his chair and began to speak,

"Your mother and I have had a long conversation. We are disappointed with your behaviour and you have dented my reputation with the neighbour's. To be honest with you, your mother and I don't like them anyway. However we have decided that you will pay for the service of my amplifier and the repair of my very expensive speaker from your savings. We will also stop your allowance for three weeks. During which time you are officially grounded, to use an American term that I can't stand, but it will serve here. Concentrate on your academic work. In addition to this, and this was mainly my suggestion, but your mother has come round to my point of view. I am a dentist and belong to the, some say, secret 'Order of Dentistry' which has its own code and certain standards to uphold. Therefore under this code I must demand payback for your outrageous behaviour and lack of respect. We have imposed a fine, however in addition I decided that you must give me something I value. In keeping with the rules of this sacred order, we feel that it is only fitting that I remove ….just one of your teeth."

The colour drained from Steven's face. He went white as he sat gripping the arms of his chair. Everyone was silent for what seemed an eternity to Steven. His mother and Gordon looked at each other, and then down at the floor, then at Steven's pale face. Then unable to keep a straight face any longer, they both lost their composure and burst out laughing.

From that moment his feelings towards Gordon changed. He could see that his mother had lightened his stepfather's mood and introduced a more 'chilled out' Gordon to the world. Steven responded to this new attitude by doing as he was asked, focusing on his work, playing golf, and thinking about going to University in the future. His hurt and sadness caused by his inability to be with Claire eased gradually but he still did not know why she hadn't contacted him. He asked the girl at the sixth form who brought her to the party to pass a letter to her. In it he wrote a poem based on a song lyric from one of his mother's CD's, hoping it would prompt her to contact him. He had dreams where he saw her walking along a road while he was riding on a bus, or in his mothers and tried to get the vehicle to stop so that he could run after her, but it was always too late, and she was gone. The lyric went;

'Tell me what you feel that's all I ask, your words can drive my doubts away.
Close this open wound, come heal my past. Please tell me what to do or say.
Now is the time to open up your mind. Put your trust in me and I won't hurt you. Lovers in your past too scared to ask. Why turn me on then push me away?
One night making love can't be the last, too much to learn, too much to say.
 I'm caught in your tangled web and there seems like there's no way out. Please won't you tell me what it's all about?'

The girl assured Steven that she passed the letter on but he had no reply. Later she told him that Claire had "got back" with a previous boyfriend. He was a trainee P.E. teacher at a college in London and she had moved there to be with him.

 Steven found this rejection hard to accept. How could she be the same person he had been so intimate with? His confusion was such that he had to confide in his mother. He needed some reason for her behaviour to hang on to. Sitting on his bed in the privacy of his room he told her his feelings. She listened and put her arm on his shoulder to comfort him as tears formed in his eyes.

"It's fine to let it out darling, this is a real hurt for you. I can't take away the way you are feeling but in this life if you don't take the risk of opening yourself up to loving someone it becomes a cold grey world. Look at me I'm a fool for love. Maybe, and I don't really know, but it is a possibility, that she was on some kind of rebound. Maybe she had broken up with him for some reason and was trying to forget by using you to fill this void in her emotions. I hate to say this but us girls can do this, as do boys."

"What, so I was some kind of try out?" Steven asked.

"I know it sounds callous, but I don't think she thought so at the time. Look love you are a lovely person and your looks aren't exactly shabby, so I think she genuinely felt something for you at the time but it was the wrong timing. Perhaps you comforted her but she was undecided. If she had been with him for a while and she still had feelings for him then unfortunately this one adventure with you was not enough to tip the balance."

This wasn't what Steven wanted to hear but his mother's hypothesis did make sense to him.

"But mum she was so gorgeous and so sexy and she wanted me!"

"I know darling, and it's hard, but console yourself with the knowledge that if she found you attractive, others will as well."

His mother's assurances were fine but having opened a new chapter of experience with Claire he became very sexually frustrated. His penis seemed to have a mind of its own, constantly reminding him of his desire. The memory of his encounter with Claire could be summoned up to gratify masturbatory satisfaction for a while but this faded. He was a healthy teenager who felt like someone obsessed with a food he had tasted in an exquisite restaurant and now, not only had the cook left but they had closed the restaurant. He had no idea where his next meal was coming from. Like a starving man constantly dreaming of food sex was never far from his thoughts. One afternoon, coming home from the sixth form early, he was alone in the house and being bored wandered into Gordon's office. By the wall behind the door was a bookshelf and he browsed the books on the shelves. When he got to the shelf one up from the bottom he found some books by Freud, one of which was 'Three Contributions to the Theory of Sex', which sparked an interest as it had sex in the title. Next to this volume were other books that interested him and he realised that this was a collection of erotic fiction. He took each book off the shelf and read the blurbs on the back. They included 'My Secret Garden' and 'Women on Top' by Nancy Friday,' Sexus', by Henry Miller, 'The Pearl" a collection of Victorian erotic stories, 'Lady Chatterley's Lover,' by D.H. Lawrence, and a large thick autobiography called 'My life and Loves', by Frank Harris.

Steven felt a mixture of erotic excitement and mild distaste at the thought that his mother or Gordon read this literature in secret. It was a bit more sophisticated than porn magazines in the news agent and explicit video's available on the internet. From his travels with his mother and her liberal attitudes to sexuality he should not have been surprised, but Gordon seemed so straight laced and inhibited. However despite his early reservations about his mother's choice of partner Gordon and his mother seemed relaxed in each other's company and they enjoyed a comfortable lifestyle. This may well have transferred to the bedroom. Alternatively it could be that Gordon purchased these books in secret and read them in the office when he was supposed to be working. Whatever the reason for their presence this discovery was the beginning of a sexual education that enabled Steven to become an informed and practiced lover over the years ahead. Eventually putting the techniques he learned from his studies of erotic literature into practice. Later in life he had wondered if reading 'Lady Chatterley's Lover' had inspired his love of gardening and the connection he felt between the earth, nature and human sexuality. He believed what his mother told him about the connection between our mind and our body. If either one became starved of nourishment, either one could suffer. He did imagine himself as Mellor's the gamekeeper and it was not too greater stretch of his imagination to conclude that later in life as a gardener, each lady he developed a relationship with became a version of Constance from that story. Freeing up their sexual energy, a force of nature, liberating them from previous relationships where they felt their sex life and pregnancy had in some way oppressed them. He had pruned many fig trees in his work but a reading 'Women in Love', another of Lawrence's novels, and watching the film on D.V.D. he certainly never thought of figs in the same way again.

By the time he slept with another woman in the second year of University he had completed 'My Life and Loves', and was keen to demonstrate his expanded knowledge of the female anatomy. When he insisted on giving her pleasure before taking his own, her arousal became so intense that she fainted. He felt so pleased with himself; he had a smile that went from ear to ear. It was like he had passed a practical examination. When she resurfaced she took one look at his satisfied smile and hit him across the head with a pillow.

He decided not to look for another relationship while at university and work on his degree. He took comfort in the literature of sex, rather than the complications of the real thing perhaps because he knew that at least the books would not leave him.

Chapter Thirteen: Hope

The Gardener by Jonathan Hope; Chapter Five

"Inspector Kane, phone call for you, line two. P.C. Jones"

"Hello, constable, I mean Sophie, anything to report?"

Bob Kane had seen Sophie at the scene of the last killing, but had not heard from her since asking her to maintain the perimeter around the area of the crime. He was still unsure of his feelings for her after their brief but warm encounter.

The voice he heard was not Sophie's;

"I think she would like to tell you that she is tied up at this minute, or rather, that she is in a bit of a 'pickle', or in hot water, or that she does not want to keep you in suspense. All of these things if I would let her talk to you, but for now you will have to put up with me."

Kane felt a chill run through his body. This was not what he expected, Sophie was obviously in danger. He started to wave frantically at the detectives sitting at their desks in the outer office. His office had a sound proofed and bullet proof glass window dividing him from them. He couldn't put the phone down and he was too far from the office door to open it. No one looked his way.

"Ok, well you have my attention, and I guess that asking you to release her would be a waste of time?"

"Not entirely, I do have a heart, and so does your precious Constable Sophie, and it would be good for you and her to let her keep it."

Bob Kane paused for a moment, listening intently for background noise or any clues as to the whereabouts of the caller's location.

"This is the bit where you expect me to lose my temper, shout at you, tell you that if you do anything to her, touch a hair on her head, I will rip your throat out with my bare hands, etc. etc.?"

The voice on the other end of the phone line sounded as if it had been disguised by some electronic device.

"It would not be her head I would be touching, Mr Kane, oh no, there, there, you have got me behaving to type which is not what I intend to do. I am not interested in your plaything Mr Kane, shame on you, and if you want to behave like a Neanderthal then go ahead."

Bob Kane could feel his anger rising inside him but he needed time to act.

"I see, so you are an educated and sophisticated psychopathic serial killer. Why don't you walk into my police station and surrender like that bloke in 'Seven', or are you more of a 'Scream' person, but I don't have any popcorn with me, and you would need a more original mask because you would not want to be a pathetic copycat. No wait, I know what you are. I think you, my seriously disturbed person, are more of a 'I Know What You Did Last Summer', kind of freak with a fisherman's cape and a fucking great hook, to make up for the small appendage that no doubt my profilers will tell me about."

While he was delivering his monologue Inspector Kane grabbed a sheet of paper on his desk and wrote in large black felt tip letters, TRACE THIS CALL KILLER! On it and pressed it against the office window. One of the detectives spotted the note and quickly started the trace on the phone call. He held up five fingers to indicate that it could take five minutes to track.

"Don't insult my intelligence Mr Kane, great speech by the way, I fancy myself as a bit of a Tommy Lee Jones character, but with bombs there is too much collateral damage and that would not follow my beliefs. Some people live in tree's to stop them being cut down; I on the other hand, prefer to nail the people I don't like to them. You won't trace me, a pigeon will arrive soon. Do what I ask and she will be returned safely to you."

The caller hung up his phone.

Bob pulled open his office door and shouted at Lavender, the detective who had started the trace,

"Did you find that bastard?"

"No Sir, sorry Sir, not enough time."

"Shit, it never works now, they know what we would do, and they've all seen the bloody 'Wire'."

As he was speaking the Desk Sergeant came into the room.

"This is for you Inspector, a boy dressed in bicycle gear delivered it and said I have to give it to you and say 'the Gardener' sent it. He scarpered before I could grab him."

"Was he wearing a hat, and did it have an emblem on it?" Kane asked.

"Some stupid bird I think." The desk sergeant replied.

"Put it on the desk please. Thanks Dixon you can go. You lot gather round, this is a letter from our killer."

Inspector Kane put on blue rubber gloves, picked up some tweezers and a letter opener. He held the letter still with the tweezers and cut along the sealed edge. He then retrieved the sheet of paper from the inside of the envelope with the tweezers and began to read what was printed on it.

'This country and its politicians are stealing money from pensioners by making them work until they drop. People who were made a promise many years ago are now having their retirement stolen from them. The rich get richer, they exploit the poor in this country and abroad that make cheap goods in factories that kill people. They have blood on their hands, but because the people that die are in foreign countries they get away with it. If they do not do what I ask then they will have the blood of a policewoman on their hands this week. Place my demands in the local paper and on the news. In four days, two well-known high-street stores, Debenhams and M&S will open their stores to pensioners between the hours of 5pm and 8pm. On the production of proof that they are 60 years old or above they can take anything they want from the store for free. This means food, clothing, whatever, they want or need. They must bring their own bags for life. This event will happen on two consecutive days in the week and on Sunday as well. When they do this, and I want it covered by the local T.V. and radio, to prove that it is no hoax, I will release your precious police constable complete and intact.

Fail and I will send a bit of her to you for every day you do not comply. Reap what ye sow!"

At the bottom of the page in green ink they had signed it '**The Gardener**'.

"Bastard, who does he think I am? Get this letter down to forensics. Lavender, get me the C.C.T.V. footage of the front of the building and the roads around and get Dixon to identify the cyclist and see if we can pick up a trail. I need to speak to the Chief Superintendent to see what our response can be. One of you, get in touch with the top person at each of these stores, I need to talk to them and they need to talk to their head office."

Inspector Kane ran out of the office and headed for the stairs.

The Superintendent's office was at the top of the building, and it was unusual because it had a low coffee table and a sofa with an armchair in one corner. The chair came to be known as the 'executioner's chair' because if you were asked to go to the office and sit in the chair it usually meant you were for the high jump or the sack. When Inspector Kane arrived at the office having asked for an emergency meeting he was sure that he could hear classical music playing in the office. When he knocked on the door the music stopped.

"Enter!"

"Thank you for seeing me at such short notice Sir, but I need your help and we have a serial killer who is making a demand. Was that Mozart Sir?"

"Yes Inspector, Clarinet Concerto in A. Are you a lover of great music? I find it soothes the soul."

"Yes I like Mozart Sir, piano music usually, twenty first concerto, I also like "The Magic Flute."
"Freemason mythology, something for you to consider Kane if you are interested, anyway, now is not the time. What is it I can help you with?"
Kane quickly outlined the situation to the Superintendent.

"We cannot be seen to give in to blackmail and threats, but I want nothing to happen to the constable. I will speak to the regional managers of the stores and their head office if needs be, and I will speak to the Chief Constable. Try and keep this quiet and away from any reporters until I have a chance to see what is possible. I'll get back to you in the next three hours."

"Thankyou Sir, I really appreciate anything you can do, I will not tell her mother until I hear from you, and perhaps she can be let in on any plan we come up with."

The superintendent thought for a moment.

"Yes, yes, she's a good officer she deserves to be informed and to help us do something. It's her daughter for God's sake, terrible business."

"Contact me on my mobile I'll be out and about."

Bob Kane left the office and made his way back to the squad room. Lavender ran up to him with a smile on his face.

"Got the footage and Dixon picked out the kid on the bike, we followed him from road to road and we saw him handed the letter by a man in a pin striped suit outside a Tesco Express in the row of shops near the station. Problem was he had an umbrella shielding his face."
"Great work, but what does it tell us?"

"We have a problem Sir, and if we want Sophie back in one piece, we need the Super to do some magic, and a lucky break."

The telephone rang in Inspector Kane's office. Kane rushed back to his desk and picked up the receiver; "Bob Kane here…"
"Hello Bob, Forensics, we have some saliva from the envelope, checking the data base now. Whoever it was likes garlic."

"Thanks, great work."

Bob Kane thought for a moment. . The 'Gardener' likes garlic. He could be someone who eats garlic, cooks garlic, or perhaps grows garlic. Surely it cannot be that simple. 'The Gardener' is a gardener? Why not check the garden centres and the gardens and allotments in the area, for somewhere a person could be held and harmed without anyone hearing or seeing.

"Lavender, get me an ordinance survey map of the area, and what are you like with Google maps?"

Jonathan Hope closed the laptop, put it in his bag along with the marking he had to take home and do at the weekend. He wondered what it would be like if like 'The Gardener' in his story people could be afraid of him, and he could take revenge on those that offended or hurt his feelings without remorse or hesitation. How liberating that would be. He had been in a few fights at school, but they were brief skirmishes, between him and bullies, whom he could not stand. The last actual punch he threw in anger was when he was training to be a teacher. He was sitting in the underground bar at the University, having a pint of beer, when one of the other students whom he did not know well started an argument about the Conservative's selling off the state owned utilities. The argument became heated, and fuelled by alcohol, this person, sitting at arm's length from Jonathan staggered to his feet.

"How would you like it if I smashed this glass into your stupid communist face, you wanker!"

Without thinking Jonathan reacted, he punched him in the solar plexus with his clenched fist. The beer glass the student held in his hand dropped to the floor, he sank back onto his seat gasping for breath, and then threw up over the table in front of him. Jonathan turned away from the scene of the attack and headed for the door of the bar, strode up the stairs and out into the night air. Jonathan felt a mixture of elation and fear that he may have seriously hurt this idiot but for once he was not going to apologise. He had a sleepless night waiting for the campus security to knock on his door, or even worse the police, but no one came. In the morning he went down to breakfast in the student cafeteria and sitting at a table in the distance with his girlfriend was his antagonist from the night before. For the remaining time on his course they never spoke and apart from sitting in large lecture rooms with other students, avoided each other.

Tomorrow when he had the verdict of the publisher on his book, how life affirming for him it would be if the publisher was as worried about his reaction to the decision, as he was about theirs. He did not want to cry or lose his temper, he wanted to accept rejection with dignity, but it may depend on how he was treated, and that he could not predict. It was no longer just about him.

The door of the sixth form common room opened. His lift home had arrived.

"Hi, are you ready, sweetheart, it's time to go home, vegetarian Spaghetti Bolognese tonight, and if you speak to me nicely, a bottle of Chianti.

Please don't eat my liver? Kiss me on the cheek, I could be persuaded to make some garlic bread."

For Jasmine this common room still had wonderful memories for her. It was where she fell in love with literature; it was where she fell in love with the man who would eventually become her partner for life and the father of her child.

"Jasmine my sweet you had me at hello, I cannot wait. Let's get out of here. Is Charlie in the car? Goodnight Shirley!" Jonathan shouted at the cleaner.

"Night Mr Hope!" She shouted back," Don't you worry, I'll lock up."

Jonathan and Jasmine left the building.

Chapter Fourteen: Life Goes On

Stevens's stepfather, Gordon, died of a heart attack during a charity event at the golf club in which he tried to break a Guinness Book of Record's record. Gordon was attempting to play as many holes of golf possible with the lowest number of strokes and thus the lowest total score, between eight in the morning and eight at night. To make this more strenuous he had to carry his golf bag, adhering to the P.G.A. rules. Following his shocking and untimely death his mother sold her property in Ipswich and moved to Kent with Steven. Live moved on for both of them, his mother progressed in her teaching career and Steven developed his gardening and landscape design business. He met a young lady and was engaged to be married.

In the year his mother died Stevens's relationship to his then fiancée, Josephine, ended. He met Josephine in the off-licence in Marden while buying his mother a bottle of Tanqueray No 10 gin and some tonic water. Since she became ill drinking alcohol helped with his mother's pain control and once or twice a day a glass of gin or brandy became a treat she looked forward to. His fiancée Josephine never wore much makeup, and to accompany her natural complexion she had blond hair, blue eyes, a trim figure, plump lips, a lovely smile, and a love of animals, particularly horses. When he met her in the off- licence she wore jeans, riding boots and a Hounds Tooth hacking jacket. Accompanying this there was a slight earthy aroma of horse stables about her which made her even more attractive to Steven. Much later he realised his immediate attraction to her could have been triggered by her similarities to his long lost girlfriend Claire. They both bought lottery tickets. Steven noticed her ticket and made a comment about never winning more than another ticket.

She heard his remark, brushed her hair away from her face and said,

 "You could be someone who is unlucky gambling, but lucky in love. Which would you choose?"

To which he replied spontaneously;

"Love, obviously! No Money! No love! Well maybe, you could help me make my mind up. Please agree to come to dinner with me, right here, right now. It would be better than winning the lottery."

She seemed a little embarrassed, smiled, then turned away and took one step nearer towards the exit from the shop. She stopped by the sweet stand turned to face him with a slight pink blush on her cheek but a smile on her face and spoke;

"I'm sorry but are you seriously trying to pick me up in an off-licence, having just met me?"

The other customers standing in the queue either looked down at the floor and pretended not to see what was happening, or continued buying their food and drink over the counter.

Steven took a step towards her with his bag of groceries in hand and said,

"Look I know it is a bit of a cheek but I may never see you again. Who can explain this mystery? I hope you feel you would like to get to know me. I promise I am not a serial killer, though I have to confess I do eat shredded wheat, muesli and other 'cereals', if that counts. I also promise not to sell you into slavery in Kent, for endless apple picking."

The woman serving behind the counter could contain herself no longer.

"Go on love, give him a chance."

With their attention focused on each other Steven and Josephine had temporarily forgotten that they had an audience.

Josephine smiled at Steven, "Looks like you have a supporter."

"Ok, then I will. It's a deal. Where and when?"

"What about the 'Style Bridge' tomorrow night at 7.30.? We could have a drink and perhaps a meal at, eight o'clock?"

"Great, see you then." With that she turned and walked out of the door of the off-licence.

They met for the meal and by the time they had consumed their pudding and coffee mints they had fallen in love. For the following six weeks they were inseparable, their desire for each other seemed insatiable. Steven's mother adored Josephine and for Steven 'all in his garden was rosy'. Steven proposed to her after a meal at the Style Bridge. When the group entertaining that evening took their break from performing, he got down on one knee and asked Josephine to marry him. The crowded bar, filled with regulars and those on their Saturday night outing, noticed this man on one knee and fell quiet. When she kissed him and said yes, the customers gave him a round of applause and the publican gave them a free bottle of 'bubbly' to celebrate.

Plans were made for the wedding and reception at the Chapel Hill Golf club where Steven was member. Everything went smoothly until Steven had a nightmare and woke up covered in sweat. In his dream, Claire the girl he met in Ipswich, turned up at his house with a child and accused him of being the father. Next they were in a clinic of some kind at which he was to have a D.N.A. test. Steven, dressed in a hospital gown was arguing with Josephine who was accusing him of being unfaithful and threatening to cancel the wedding. The doctor came into the room and spoke to them all, saying that it was impossible for Steven to be the father and he could show them why. He walked over to Steven, pulled open his gown and invited Claire and Josephine to look. They both gasped in amazement. Steven looked down at his stomach, only to discover his penis was missing.

Steven had made love with women many times since Claire. Something he was not particularly proud of. Now he had found the person he wanted to be with he was content and his search was over. Somehow, in the same way that a computer gets infected with a virus, Stevens's thoughts became infected with a doubt. None of his sexual partners had experienced a pregnancy scare. Steven had been careful not to knowingly put his partners at risk. However, frequently he had unprotected sex, not knowing if his partner had used any form of contraception. Up until this time he assumed that he had dodged a bullet but now that he was to be married and actively try to have a baby this anxiety would not go away. His recent frequent activity with Josephine added to his worry as he had assumed that she was using an oral contraceptive pill. Recently, when talking about a girlfriend of hers, she mentioned that she could not do this because it made her put on weight and feel ill. He assumed, rightly or wrongly that some other form of prevention was being used. They both said they wanted children. After all this time making certain he would not get anyone pregnant things had changed, now he was expected to father a child.

In the moments while he was planting seeds or hoeing borders this doubt plagued his thoughts and so he decided the only way to stop his obsession was to ask his GP to arrange for his sperm to be tested. The G.P. was sceptical at first because Steven appeared to be a fit and healthy man, but Steven insisted that he needed to know and if it couldn't be done on the N.H.S. quickly then he would pay for private testing. The G.P. made the arrangements for Steven to go to a private clinic. Five days later, putting aside his embarrassment, Steven was shown to a private room where stimulated by the choice of literature available managed to give a sample of his sperm to the consultant. The test results came back quite quickly and Steven rushed to the G.P. surgery after work to hear the results and put his mind to rest. It wasn't long in the waiting room before he was called into the doctor's office.

"Well, Steven, let's get down to it, I imagine this has been a tough time for you. Now we may need to do further tests to be certain, but it seems, based on this sample, that your sperm have low motility. This means that many of them are not strong swimmers. There are things we can do about this to build up their vitality, and so it's not conclusive."

"So you're saying my sperm are slow swimmers. Would it help if my fiancé had fast eggs?"

The doctor looked unmoved by what he interpreted as Steven's gallows humour. He did not smile and continued speaking.

"I cannot say conclusively that you would not be able to father a child but the possibility could be hit and miss and I would not want to offer you false hope."

Steven sat bolt upright in his chair in a stunned silence. The bottom had dropped out of his world. Why did he say such a stupid thing? All he could think of was that it reminded him of the moment when his stepfather Gordon announced his punishment for having the disastrous party when he lived in Ipswich. Like then he was waiting for the doctor to suddenly burst out laughing, like his parents did, and tell him this news was a cruel tease. The doctor did not laugh. Instead inside Steven a wave of emotion spread from his stomach into his chest. His jaw dropped open and Steven began crying. He struggled to contain his emotions as painful thoughts raced through his head. The doctor suggested that he saw a fertility specialist and arranged an appointment at the nearest hospital in Maidstone. His second test came back with the same results as the first. He clung on to the hope and perhaps one little super sperm could be like an Olympic swimmer. He didn't care if it chose front crawl, breaststroke, butterfly, or backstroke, anything it could do to win the race and get the finish line, win the 'Golden Egg' and make Josephine pregnant.

He didn't tell Josephine of his investigations. Lying in bed together after making love they talked about their future. Steven became frightened that If he told her now she might reject him, or worse still, feel sorry for him and just to make him feel better, say it did not matter. It was a possibility they could have fun trying to get her pregnant but how long before what started as fun turned into a duty, a burden they both carried. If she did this for him he knew that he could be depriving her of the one thing she wanted most in her future. He would feel incredibly guilty about it and despite her protestations she would begin to resent him. This problem taunted him night and day, and for the first time in his life he couldn't face making love to her, and made excuses to avoid being in her company. She was occupied organising the wedding and he had many gardens to look after telling her that they needed the money for their honeymoon.

It was three weeks before they were to be married. Steven decided he could no longer deal with his anxiety. He had to be honest and tell Josephine his secret. He took her for a walk in a local orchard; they talked about their work which passed the time until, on the way back to his car stopped on the small bridge that spanned the railway line. Holding her hands and looking her in the face he summoned all the courage he could muster and told Josephine about his problem. Her immediate response was to be silent while Steven studied her face waiting for a reaction. She took a step backwards; half turned away from him and began to cry, brushing tears away from her cheeks with her fingers. He stepped forward putting his arms around her trying to hold her close but she pushed him away. When she stopped crying she turned to look at him. She looked angry.

"Did you know when you proposed? What the fuck were you thinking? Why didn't you tell me you were worried? We said we would not keep secrets from each other. What did you think would happen? Were you ever going to tell me before we were married? Why now? Why now for god's sake, we've made all these fucking arrangements!"

"I'm so, so, sorry. It's a poor excuse but it's been like torture for me. I wanted to tell you but I was afraid."

Josephine knew by the look on his face and the tone of his voice that this secret and his need to confess had played on his mind. Her initial anger was now softened by her compassion for his predicament.

"Oh Steven just listen to me, I'm so fucking selfish, sanctimonious cow, what about you sweetheart how do you feel going through all this this?"

"I feel shattered, and I feel like something has been taken from me. I can't help but think I'm being punished in some way for something I have done, and I don't believe in that shit. I thought nature might reward me. Everything I do is about growing things, planting things and now I've been told that I probably can't plant the one fucking thing that would be special for the both of us."

"Oh love I am so sorry. Look this isn't the end Steve, we can try I.V.F." Josephine took his head in her hands and kissed him on a cheek to reassure him.

"Things could change, for Christ's sake we've got time and medicine gets better, it's not hopeless."

"Yes I know, I hope for some miracle but we cannot be sure and I cannot be the one to deprive you of the one thing that I know you really want. I could not live with myself if I did that."
Josephine said all the things Steven expected her to say to try to make him feel better about their situation but none of it penetrated his increasingly bleak mood. None of her words could shine a light at the end of this dark tunnel. They got back into the car, and hardly spoke on the journey back to her parent's house where he dropped her off before returning home to his mother.

In the days that followed his work suffered, his golf suffered, and the interaction between Josephine and Steven was stilted and confined to short e-mail or text messages. They both threw themselves into their respective occupations. Steven still had his mother to care for. After about a week, Josephine texted him at work asking to meet at the bridge near the orchard. On his way there his heart was pumping and his nerves were jangling. When he arrived and saw her standing by the bridge she reminded him of how she looked when he first met her. She looked gorgeous, but he could see she had been crying.

"Steven, in this time we've had apart I have thought long and hard about our future, I talked to my father and mother who you know really like you, but they asked me some difficult questions that perhaps I didn't want to think about. I came to realise that despite the fact that I love you to death, I don't think it would be fair to you to hold on to you. I think I would harbour some resentment. I'm sorry, I am really sorry, but I have to let this go. I expect you hate me for this but I can't marry you."

Steven felt his stomach churn and a desperate and sudden need to go to the toilet, but he stood his ground and did not run away.
"Listen Josephine, I'm hurting, but I expected it might be something like this when you asked to meet. It's ok Jo, I kind of knew, before I got here

what you might say. In some strange way I feel relieved. I understand. I couldn't live with it either and that's why I had to give you a choice."

"Hug, for old times?" Josephine put her arms out towards him inviting him close.

"Well why not." Steven put his arms around her and they hugged as tears rolled down their cheeks. This was to be the last time they were together.

Steven contacted the Golf club and cancelled the reception while Josephine took on the responsibility of sending back to their owners those wedding gifts people had already given them.

Steven coped as well as he could with the knowledge that he may not become a father. In each subsequent relationship there would probably come a time when he would have to tell his then girlfriend the same information he had to tell Josephine. He resigned himself to this fate, and got on with work and enjoyed the friendship of the Saturday golfers he had met since he moved to the area. He still enjoyed golf, and thanks to Gordon, it was something he was good at. He won club competitions, got his name on the boards in the club house, and represented the club in the Kent regional competitions. However at night alone with his dreams, one kept repeating. In this dream it didn't matter how much he tried to putt his golf ball into the cup, he couldn't. Either because the green tilted, the hole moved unexpectedly, or his ball raced straight towards the edge of the hole then stopped abruptly before dropping in. In these moments he often woke up bathed in sweat from the tension he felt. He didn't want his anxiety to become apparent to his mother and spoil the time they had left together. She suffered enough with her illness. Then like a shooting 'Star' flying across the heavens in the night sky, his mother died peacefully in the night. He forgot his worries and arranged her funeral in the way she wanted. She asked to be cremated in a 'green coffin', the address at the funeral to be given by a humanistic celebrant and then her ashes scattered in the air from a plane or a balloon so that she could 'fly with the birds'. Steven spoke to the local balloonists at Headcorn airfield and they helped him to fulfil his mother's wish.

After the funeral and the small gathering of friends and acquaintances had left his mother's detached country cottage Steven found himself alone. He had a job, a reasonable inheritance, no girlfriend and no bigger purpose. He pulled out a C.D. from his mother's collection. It was one he recognised because it was given to him by a builder friend in Marden. It was an unknown singer songwriter but on this album called 'Come and Go' was a song entitled 'Be like me', which she played loud in the kitchen and danced to. The lyrics also had meaning for her. Steven sometimes hummed the tune without thinking and remembered a part of the lyric;

There is always one special morning that won't let you feel the same.
It comes in like the tide on the Ocean but never goes out again.
One morning I walked down the main street and met a man from another time, like
some ion drawn to a magnet something told me his fate was mine.
Be who you are if you learn to and like stars shine it calm clear and bright.
Do only those things that you want to while knowing that like attracts like.

For Steven it was not a mystic prophet he met that changed his life but a woman, named Lucy. Her garden had been damaged by a storm and she needed a gardener. A friend of Lucy happened to be having a drink in the Unicorn in Marden where Steven sat at the bar with his pint of Harvey's working out the Daily Mail crossword. He looked over Stevens shoulder and offered him a clue to seven down which fitted. Then he overheard Steven telling the barmaid the satisfaction he felt about the work he had completed in the garden he had been working in that day. John, asked Steven if he had space for another client and if so, to contact his friend Lucy because she needed urgent help cutting up and removing her fallen trees. The next day Steven visited her large double aspect square looking house, situated in an acre of land with a fish pond at the front and a small duck pond in the rear, to give an estimate of the cost of the work she needed Steven to do.

When he arrived in his beaten up Land Rover with trailer attached, Lucy met him in the driveway. She was taller than Steven expected and wore a tight fitting pullover and jeans that accentuated her figure. She wore no makeup but her well defined cheekbones defied her age as did her tanned skin, brown eyes and long reddish hair tied back with a scarf. Steven was not put off by women who were taller than him. He remembered what a drunk friend at University said to him when they were discussing tall women they both found attractive, "Steven, just remember, women are all the same height when they are lying down!" He climbed out of the cab of his truck to greet Lucy.

"Hello, pleased to meet you and thank you for coming at such short notice, please call me Lucy, and you're Steven? Please come round the back into the garden and I will show you the mess the storm made. It's so sad; one of these trees must be centuries old, but then we all fall over at some point."

With this she walked away and Steven followed her into the rear garden. Then she stopped walking and stood in front of the first large uprooted tree.

"Well there it is, what do you think, is it possible to do something with it? My husband is away, well he nearly always is and he leaves me to deal with this stuff, which is fine but I want to tell him that I can handle it. I sent him pictures on my phone and he told me to get it sorted before he came back as he would not have the time. Well surprise, surprise, he never has the time. Oh, I'm sorry I am rambling on, how silly of me. Anyway Steven, can I call you Steve? What do you think?
Steven could feel the nervous tension emanating from her body, and he sensed that she was close to tears despite the efficient front she presented.

"Yes, please call me Steve, that's fine. I can do this for you so please try not to worry. I can get some help and we can cut the tree up and dispose of the wood, unless you and your husband need any wood to use."

"Yes, you can leave some wood for logs if it is dry enough and put them in that shed over there. He likes cutting up logs with an axe, he says it helps him get rid of his tension. He is an angry man most of the time but that's something else. So how soon can you start?"

"Well it will cost a bit as it will take two of us for some of the time, but I usually charge by the hour, and I can pop my estimate through the door tomorrow. I could start in three days."

Steven watched Lucy thinking and waited for her response. "Oh, three days any chance of getting it started sooner? I would like to send a picture to my husband showing him I have got it moving as soon as possible and that would keep him happy, and I always like to keep him happy."

Lucy stood looking at the tree with her arms across her chest rubbing her upper arms as if she was soothing herself.

"Look, I can start tomorrow afternoon, if you like, I just have to tidy something up and then I can come straight here. I need to get a chain saw from the tool hire company, but that should be fine."

"Oh Steve really, that is so lovely of you!" Lucy launched herself at Steven and gave him a hug.

"Would you like to come in the house and have a cup of tea and a scone, it's the least I can do."

Steven felt that it would upset her if he said no. He followed her into the kitchen, leaving his muddy boots just inside the door. While Lucy made the tea and got the cups, plates and saucers out of the cupboard, he enquired about her husband's occupation.

"He is in Afghanistan at the moment looking after some important politician. It is all quite hush, hush, but he is a partner in a private security firm which is part owned by Americans. They are all ex-military like my husband. We've been together for twelve years. I used to live out there with him. I have lived in Iraq, Thailand and in Mexico, when he worked out there but this last contract seems to have got to him. Maybe it is just time, he has seen too much, been involved in activities he is not proud of. He will not talk about it because he says he does not want to contaminate my mind, but it has contaminated him... and... us." With this admission tears filled her eyes and rolled down her cheek, she turned to look out of the window towards the garden so that Steven would not see her dab her eyes with her sleeve.

"What made you stop living out there?" Steven asked.

"He tried to kill me." She replied to his question in a surprisingly matter of fact tone.

Steven remained silent and for a moment thought about saying something to lighten the mood and change the subject, but before he could speak Lucy continued talking.

"When you live out there the community is very tight and small and with the work the men do the tensions can run high. Why am I excusing him? Even now, sorry this is something I am working on! For some reason he thought I wanted to have an affair with this American we met in the ex-pat's club. Out there we had little to do after six, go to the club, play tennis, go the services gym and watch satellite T.V. oh and have sex, lots of it, to help relieve the tension of the boredom you feel being hemmed in, or being shot or blown up which is what the security guys faced each day. I am a friendly person and I would go to the club alone when he was in country or on a detail for a longer time than usual. Like an idiot I mentioned I had talked to this single guy in the club about films and favourite moments in movies. We sat there compiling our top ten horror movies and our top ten war films. My husband likes movies and when he asked what I had been up to while he was at work I told him. He went into a rage and forbade me from going to the club without him. Then he stopped me going to the gym, and then even shopping, if he was not with me. This got worse and I put up with it for about a month and then I decided that I had to go out, which I did, but the wife of a colleague of his saw me walking to the gym within the camp. When he came home I was in the kitchen at the sink, I turned towards him to say hello and give him a kiss but he punched me in the face. I fell on the floor and he got on top of me, put his hands around my throat and tried to strangle me. All the time he was shouting in my face, "You bitch! You unfaithful cow! You fucking slut!" His face was bright red and the veins in his neck were bulging. He had wild eyes. He said all these vile things. I thought I was about to die. I couldn't breath and so I couldn't shout out or say anything. When he knocked me over my arm had pushed a metal saucepan onto the floor, it was one my mother gave me, a 'le Creuset', a heavy one. I managed to get hold of the handle and wacked him on the side of the head with it. I think he was more startled than hurt because his adrenaline was pumping through his body but it made him shift his weight and I could get my legs up enough to push him off and I got up and ran out of the kitchen door. I headed for the club, because I knew he would not embarrass himself in front of other security guys or soldiers. When I got there I bumped into Randy an American nurse from the infirmary. He could see I was bruised and I had a small cut on my cheek bone and he looked after me. After I told him that I had hit my husband he assured me that he would check to see that he was ok, but he would take care of me first. I gave my husband a lump on the side of his head but he didn't lose consciousness and came looking for me later but thank God, they kept him away from me. Anyway to cut a long story short, I did not go home for two days, until my husband and I were seen by his boss we decided that I should come home. He was reprimanded, but I was so relieved to get away. That was two, nearly three years ago."

"How are you now?"

"Truthfully, I still don't trust him and I am still scared."

"Why don't you leave him?"

"I think he will leave me, eventually. I know he has had other women since I left him alone out there. I think he is the kind of man who would be a stalker, I've learned that men like him are narcissists and he doesn't see me as a separate person. I am a part of him and I belong to him. If I act for myself he gets anxious jealous and violent because he can't cope with it. I've read a lot of self-help stuff for women since I've been at home, and I know where the women's refuge is in Maidstone. I have an escape plan ready if he goes crazy again but for now I want to keep him sweet. He has all the money we saved together, and I would get half the house."

"It's not my place to comment, but it seems a bit risky to me."

"Look, how remiss of me your tea must be cold, would you like another one?"

"No thanks, sorry if I spoke out of turn."

Steven could sense that his comment had made her uncomfortable.

"No, no that's fine, I'm sure you must be going now, you have things to do and so do I for that matter, so see you tomorrow then."

He got up from the kitchen table went to the back door, put on his boots, walked to his Land Rover and drove off. However, as much as he tried he could not get her face out of his mind. He wanted to help her in her lonely desperation but what could he do to make her feel better without making the situation worse between her and her husband. If he was religious he would have prayed for her but he didn't have the comfort of a faith. He watched his mother wither away with cancer and the pain that Gordon's death had caused her and this cured him of a belief in a benevolent God. Did Lucy deserve to be married to a crazy person who tried to kill her? Was this her punishment for not believing enough? Steven had come to believe that life for humans was the sum of the choices they could make, and what he and everyone else had to do, was to get to a place where they could actually make good choices and then act upon them. The notion that there existed a divine power we call God, the father of us all, whom we could get to favour us with good or bad experiences if we did certain things for him, seemed an infantile idea to Steven. It was human arrogance to assume that this God was a person, and male arrogance to assume that it was a man not a woman who gives birth to us all. The pagans had things more balanced with many gods rather than one. It seemed just as likely to Steven that gods could be insects, plants or fishes as they had existed longer than human kind. He smiled when he thought of religious worshippers getting to their heaven and finding a big tree or a fish sitting on the throne of a God. He thought vegetarians would get a shock if the plant God said to them; "Why on earth did you eat me and my brothers and sister plants when I provided you with all those animals to eat?"

Steven wanted to ease Lucy's pain, of this he was sure, but he could not have predicted that the events of the next day would set him on a new path, with a new set of clients that needed more of him than his expertise in the garden. He trimmed the branches off the tree first and then began the job of cutting the tree trunk into sections for disposal. He saw Lucy watching him from the kitchen window and after a while he needed to go to the toilet and felt embarrassed to pee behind a tree in the garden and so he knocked on the kitchen door. Lucy must have been in the kitchen because the door opened quickly and there she was looking the same as the day before but he noticed she had pink lipstick on her lips.

"High Lucy, sorry to trouble you but can I use the loo, I'm bursting."

"No please do, it's just here, help yourself."

Steven used the toilet, washed his hands, closed the door and was about to leave when Lucy called out from the kitchen.

"Are you at all peckish, I have some scones and tea ready if you would like a little break?"

Steven thought for a moment contemplating the possible outcome of accepting the offer Lucy made. He doubted he could deal with another emotional outburst from her without wanting to take her in his arms and hold her until she felt comforted and not alone. His attitude to the situation she was in had changed overnight. He knew in his mind and his heart that despite Lucy being a slightly older woman, with a husband that could kill him; her vulnerability made her very attractive and something hard to resist.

"Thanks Lucy that would be lovely, I fancy a break and scones would be great. The ones I had yesterday were delicious."

Steven walked into the kitchen and sat down at the table. Lucy brought a plate, knife and spoon over to where he was sitting and lent over to place it on the table in front of him. While she did this, Lucy placed her hand on Steven's shoulder and let it linger while she put the cutlery on the table. He inhaled a slight whiff of her perfume as she stood next to him and then she moved back over to the oven to remove the scones. Steven felt a tingle run down the back of his neck and it reminded him of the feeling he had when his mother gently ruffled his hair and caressed his neck when he was little. Lucy was gentle, warm and inviting, but at the same time determined. Steven thought Lucy seemed to be wearing an even more closely contoured top this afternoon, and as she bent over to take the scones out of the oven he was convinced that her jeans to hugged her bottom and thighs even more tightly than the day before.

"I hope these are to your liking Steven, there is butter and strawberry jam to have with them."

As Lucy spoke she leant forward over the large wooden kitchen table to push the butter and jam towards where Steven sat. Steven could not help but look at her cleavage and as he did she caught him looking and he felt himself blush.

"Sorry, so un- P.C. of me, I'm really …" Steven apologised.

"I hope you like what you see, it's a while since anyone looked at me the way you just did and to be honest I found it quite alluring."

He wondered what she meant, but did not move, trapped like a rabbit in headlights as she slowly edged her way around the table to where he sat. She spoke calmly with a voice that sounded assured and sincere.

"I know I may have scared you yesterday, and I did not mean to, but I could not stop thinking about how kind you were to me and how empathic you were. I don't find that in many men, not that I have known many men, but I want to get to know you. I'm not looking for love, and I don't want anything too complicated, because as you know, I am not free of my husband."

Steven felt the brush of her hand on his neck and the warmth of her body standing next to him. She leant down to speak softly in his ear.

"I feel under nourished and scones and jam just aren't enough. I need to feel the comfort of a warm body next to me and you inside of me. I want to feel that again but with someone I actually desire, not as a duty. I hoped this person could be, you."

Lucy put her hands on his cheeks turned his face upward towards hers and kissed him fully on the lips, her tongue darting out between his lips and into his open mouth. Steven responded by simultaneously pushing his chair back from the table and putting his arms around her back and waist. She straddled him with her legs and sat on his lap, continuing to kiss Steven and run her hands through his hair.
Steven turned his head away.

"Wait! Lucy, please stop what you're doing, just for a minute."

"What's wrong? Have I come on too strong, oh God I must be stupid, of course it's the married thing, my age, you're frightened, it's ok, I understand."

Lucy shifted on his lap and started to get off him.

"No don't be silly, listen to me, I really want you, I couldn't stop thinking about you since yesterday, but I have to get things straight before we get into this and we go further. I need to ask, I know it may seem strange but, do you have children?"

"Um, no, my bastard husband did not want anything to spoil our relationship. Well, that is what he said, but I know now, he probably didn't want anyone else to take my attention away from him. Steven I don't understand why that matters."

"I'm sorry but I needed to ask you. I don't want you to let you down. I don't want to be that guy again. I know you say you're not looking for love and all that, but if this goes anywhere, you might have a change of heart. I need to be honest. So do you think you will want children in the future? I know it may sound crazy to you, but please indulge me."

Lucy could see that Steven was deadly serious. Steven could see from the expression on her face that Lucy was troubled by his strange outburst and paused for thought before she answered.
"I don't think I'm in the right place to think about that now. I guess it's a decision I will have to make sometime before it gets too late for me, but that kind of thing is changing all the time. Darling, come on, I don't want you to father a child I have secretly longed for. Right now, I don't want to close doors, I want to open them. When you're near and I need you, I just know what I want now, right now, and that is you."

"Look if you did, I mean, if you changed your mind, I have to tell you, I can't give you a child, I mean I don't know if I can, if you wanted one, this is hard for me to own but I have to be upfront with you from the start, and it's nothing about you. It is a medical thing."

"Oh Steven I'm sorry, that must have been so hard for you to say. Look if we can't have sex, that doesn't matter, we can find other ways."

"No, it's not that, things work fine, I will love to make love to you, I want to touch and kiss every bit of your body that is not the thing; God this is awkward! It's the fact that, and I can't believe I am saying this, my sperm are not great swimmers."

Steven felt so silly saying this and waited for Lucy's reaction. Lucy began to smile and then stopped herself. She grabbed his shirt and pulled him close to kiss him again.

"Oh my darling, don't you know how much of my life I have spent worrying about getting pregnant. This is great, great! We can have sex without any worries, when and where we like. You make me feel as if, at last, I can break out of this prison I'm in. You can set me free."

By the end of her sentence Lucy was laughing in a playful way. Her laughter was infectious and Steven's mood lifted, his face broke into a smile and he pulled her to him. That night Lucy and Steven made a meal of their love making. Lucy was insatiable. Her appetite was ravenous; she had been emotionally and sexually starved for a long time. Their bodies covered in perspiration, slid against each other, glistening in the candlelight that illuminated the bedroom. Steven worked hard to give Lucy the pleasure he felt she deserved and probably had been denied. He put the needs of her body and its pleasure before the needs of his own, and by his touch and kind words, encouraged her to guide him and her own hands to the places on her body that excited her the most. Steven lost himself in Lucy's soft, warm and responsive flesh. At one point in their lovemaking she pushed him over onto his back and lowered herself onto him as if to say, enough is enough, now it was her turn to give to him pleasure. In her increasingly loveless marriage sex with her husband had become more of a duty than a pleasure. Lucy had never experienced the intense heights of sensation she felt with Steven that night.

Steven finished the clearance of the fallen trees, and their relationship continued regularly while her husband was abroad. It stopped for about two months when he returned home between contracts. Steven told Lucy that this would be a terrible time for him and he hated to think of Lucy having sex with her husband. She tried to reassure him that her sexual relationship with her husband was functional, keeping him happy, but she would not be a willing participant.

"Steven I promise you, I may be there in body, but not in my mind."

Then a strange thing happened one afternoon after they had finished making love, sitting up in bed, sipping a cold glass of Chablis and eating a lettuce and Marmite sandwich. Lucy stopped eating and started talking.

"I have been thinking. Don't interrupt until I've finished. Just let me explain what I am about to suggest. You know I adore you and we have a great time when my husband is away and it kills you when he comes home. I think you are incredible about that, I love you for it, and without making you big headed, you are also great in bed, but I think I am being selfish, and so I have an idea that will make those times easier for you. I have a friend who is a little bit older than me. We go riding together. Now she lost her divorced her husband about a year ago and she has quite a bit of money from him in alimony. She does not want a live in boyfriend but she is getting very frustrated on her own and wearing out the batteries on her little toy. She is a lovely person and she is very attractive. She is a woman of Chinese origin. She met her husband in Hong Kong when he was working for this international investment bank. I have told her about you and I have told her how unselfish you are in bed. She would like to meet you and I think you will want to sleep with her once you see her and get to know her. I hope you won't mind but I have invited her over for lunch tomorrow and I would like you to accidentally drop in to give her the once over. What do you think?"

Steven felt complimented by Lucy's proposal and didn't know how to respond. On the one hand Lucy had obviously thought this through, but he felt a bit like he was some kind of sex pill that had been prescribed to an unknown woman. He didn't want to feel degraded and treated like a male prostitute but on the other hand he felt flattered and intrigued by the possibility of the sexual experience on offer. He knew that Lucy would not offer him to someone she did not like and whom she thought would not benefit from his talents in the bedroom. This opportunity that Lucy presented would make the times when her husband came home much more bearable. This arrangement with her Chinese friend would distract him and give him a purpose. He concluded that he would be selfish to refuse her offer.

"This sounds crazy but if you are happy with this solution, and you want to help your friend then, I will come by and check her out tomorrow." The following day Steven went to lunch at Lucy's house where he met Juan, which he was told means 'graciousness' in Chinese. She informed him of this definition of her name while she laid cradled Steven's arms, wrapped in red satin sheets in her opulent six foot bed after making love. Lucy had knowingly opened a doorway to a new era of Steven's life that added meaning to his existence as well as beginning a journey of discovery lasting to the present day. His arrangement with Juan and Lucy continued happily, and then Juan introduced him to a widowed friend of hers, in her forties who needed some fencing in her garden repaired or replaced. Juan indicated the possibility that she may benefit from Stevens special abilities as she seemed depressed and had been without a man in her life for over three years. Her friend thought of internet dating but was frightened of meeting weird people on line that may exploit her wealth. She wanted to have a relationship with someone that could be tailored to her needs and have her privacy respected. Steven mended her fences and in the process helped her lower her defences. Now he had another client added to his list.

Steven had learned a lot from the books he found in Gordon's study all those years ago but he knew he needed continuing professional development. Steven wanted to bring pleasure to the women he provided his service for and to this end he became an amateur sexologist taking every opportunity to learn from the women he had relationships with. This growing area of study and his desire to learn eventually infiltrated his other hobby, golf.

On a golfing trip to Las Vegas with Mark Finch, David, and the Milligan brothers Steven took a golden opportunity to further his research. While the other men on the golfing holiday were having sex in their hotel rooms with the girls provided by the Milligan brother's contact there, he decided to interview the two call girls sent to his room about their sex lives and techniques. Ever since he left University he had regretted not taking a Masters in horticulture and doing academic research.

The Milligan's arranged for him to be sent a black prostitute and a white one. The black girl called herself Candy Spice and the white girl went by the name Black. When they first entered his room they asked him to pay them the money up front then went through the menu of what was on offer. This included any sex act he wanted including anal with Black as 'Candy wasn't in to that', or he could watch some 'girl on girl action' and join in if that turned him on. Steven raised his hand palm outwards to politely stopped their pitch, asked them to stop taking their clothes off, sit on the bed, and listen to what he had to say.

"I guess this sounds a bit odd to you but in England I sort of do a bit of a job like you. I'm not a male prostitute but more of a sex helper to women who need my attention. I'm kind of a gardener with benefits and want to be better at what I do, so I want to ask you about your knowledge of having sex. Look, relax and have a drink from the mini bar if you want. I know this is unusual, but I would really appreciate your insight. Don't worry; I will pay you for your time. I don't want to insult you, you are attractive sexy ladies but I don't want to sample the goods today. Is that ok? Oh yea, and I will make some notes, is that ok too?"

They both looked at each other and shrugged their shoulders.

Candy spoke first. "This ain't no secret documentary thing? I don't want my picture seen.

"No it's just me, weird English guy." Steven assured her.

"Shoot man, you're one weird dude, but if that's what you want, yeah, go ahead ask what you want. What do you think Black?"

"Yeah, sure why not, maybe we can help some of our sisters in the U.K. get more from giving it up."

Steven sat in the hotel chair next to the bed and waited for them to begin their stories. Candy Spice took the lead as she did previously.

"Man are you a cook, have you ever baked a cake? Well honey let me tell you that to be a good lover you need to know the best ingredients to use and how to put them together in the right proportions and in the right order. Then add a bit of friction to turn up the heat and that, 'cake' will rise up out of the tin. Get that sugar?"

Black looked at Candy as if she was spaced out and from another planet.

"Don't take any notice of that crap. Let's get down to it. Don't waist this man's time. First forget all the penis crap. I've had big dicks and small ones and the length don't matter, but if it get used right then fine. Men get hung up on the size of their dicks, well feelin' full is ok, but some guy bangin' away on top of me for a fucking hour does nothing for me. If you want exercise then I say go to the gym. If they use their mouths or their fingers more than their dicks it's so much better for us sisters. I like my breasts, mouth and inside my thighs touched and then I like my little man rubbed and I start to come alive. When I come my little friend seems to vibrate and my muscles in my stomach and back just squeeze really hard. My whole body seems to throb along with my clit and vagina. I hate that "V" word, that is no word from a sister, bet some guy probably thought that up, it's so cold. My man called it his 'pussy' cause he liked to stroke it all the time, but you can take my word for it. It don't look like cat I've ever seen. I call it 'honey.'"

Steven smiled but stayed silent. He was entranced, listening to the insider knowledge of these professionals and recording their experience in his note book.
Candy seemed inspired by Black's honesty and joined in with her own narrative.

"Honey don't you worry your pretty head about lookin' for all the right moves. That's crap. Sex by numbers babe, not good, they want you to do things to stir them up! They want your sweet touch, but you got to look and listen. I say it's like making music, when you hit the right groove, hear them moan, then babe you bet, you're playing the right tune. But listen here, you got to tell them, don't fake it. All that, "yes baby, yea!" It's shit, because they lie.
Candy was on a roll and didn't want to be interrupted.

"Take this 'G' spot thing. Man, some guy invented that just so he could sell the maps! I've been poked by many 'John's', one after another. I used to turn maybe twenty tricks a night and if I had a 'G' spot one of them would have hit it. Shoot! I know that was work but sure as hell my girlfriend would have found it by now. I did porn, and I've had all kinds of things stuck up me. I tell you nothing. Straight up! I bet it's another thing some man invented to make certain pricks are useful. Bull shit! Stick to the magic button. You heard the song' Stairway to Heaven', well that's it for us sisters."

Black interrupted Candy at this point;

"Well sweetie I had sex with my husband and did not come. I faked it but he knew. He wouldn't let me touch myself 'cause he thought it was an insult to his masculinity. He convinced me I was frigid and I felt so bad. I got to thinkin' there was something wrong down there. One night I went out with my girlfriends. He was on a night shift and I was so down I got so drunk. I can't remember how, but I ended up in bed with one of my friends who I guess had a thing for me. Anyway, she went down on me and I just exploded. I did not know what had hit me. I got so angry with my husband and his shit that I left. I had no money and nowhere to go, so I moved in with that woman."

Candy spoke again,

"Listen, you know I feel having someone inside me is like some warm hum, and when they touch my button it's like a high pitched note. If you want to give your ladies the best you can then put the two together and you will have them screaming."

Black joined in,

"Yeah, and don't feel you have to do it all. Let them help themselves, I mean, they know, and don't get funny about it. Tell them Black told you."

Steven wanted to ask them one last question before their time was up.

"Do you prefer having sex with a woman or a man?"

Black spoke first.

"I prefer it with a woman because I think there is more tenderness between us and more orgasms because they are not hung up on penetration, and it takes longer. But sweetheart I never had a man like you, you could be different, but I always feel that men think I am a second-class bit of tail."

Candy spoke next.

"I guess I'm lucky, I found a man who I don't have to pretend with and I can open up to him, but he still likes being on top. I go down on him and he does on me, and so it's kind of equal. He wants me to stop what I do and I will soon. We need the money, and I have health bills to pay for my dad. But the way I see it is, the way I was brought up I still feel I'm expected to serve men. I still get guilty for saying no when he wants me."

Steven turned the page of his notebook and wrote down a new heading.

"Ok so what do men want?"

Black was the first to answer.

"Most men want what they can't get at home and that is B.J.'s like they see on the porn channel, someone doing it, and liking it. You know I've had women say how do you do that and I say, make sure it's clean and think of it like a lollipop or a Popsicle. Any way I tell them it's the food of life and it makes your hair shine. Hey Candy we must have some of the shiniest hair in town. Sometimes I feel sorry for my husband I told you about. I knew nothing then. He didn't get what I do for guys now and he could have had it for free."

"OK." Steven thought for a moment and then spoke. "What do you think about hair?"

Black laughed out loud. "You are one strange cookie, but yeah, it's a thing you know, because of what they see on the internet, they want it smooth, but some guys have a thing for hair, they like a jungle down there. I can say one thing though, maybe not so good, if I had a daughter

222

it could be tough for her, you know, the younger guys and the young girls they date can get the wrong idea about what is right or wrong down there. Hey Candy?"

"Yeah, ok, no I meant hairy guys?" Steven interrupted.

"Well mostly it's a tree in a bush, in some cases a twig, till I get started."

Black laughed at Candy's description.

"If they want me smooth they should do the same. Some guys do it anyway and some guys have a thing about hair. I had one guy who pulled his out with tweezers and used to look at his body in the mirror to get rid of them. Man he was a mess, I was giving him therapy. He told me I was the only one he let see him naked."

Steve unbuttoned the front of his shirt to show them his chest hair. He had no intention of dropping his trousers, but he did wonder if they would approve of what showcased his manhood, after all he was a gardener who trimmed hedges for a living.

"Do you think I should shave my chest? Or anything else?"

"Honey you look fine as you are, but I guess you can go with what most of the ladies you see like. We roll with the dice, some guys are smooth, we like smooth, some guys are gorillas, but me, I like some hair on the chest, and it kind of tickles and it's manly."

Then it was time for Candy to give her opinion on this subject.

"Sweet heart I keep mine neat and pretty, I get no complaints. I can say in my mind, most women don't take the time like we do to find out which bit of a guy's dick is the most sensitive. It's hard for a guy to pretend he's excited like we can because either you got a hard on or you ain't. We praise them erections, and tell them that it's ok, it's just the right shape and size, and they can relax. We ain't like their mama's or wives, or their daddies, gonna take nothing away from them. They don't have to be hung like a horse or no porno stud actor."

Candy was in full flow and wanted to say more, and so Steven sat back and listened.

"A lot of sisters think men are simple creatures when it comes to sex. It's true some men are real scary and you put up and shut up, or some women treat them like children dishing out sex like candy. Some just think you let them stick it in and jiggle around, they don't watch, or listen to their breathing. They are sensitive creatures like us, they like to be teased and tickled in the right places, like on their rear and between their legs. That's what they pay us for and we could teach women a few tricks that would keep their guys at home. Some just like being in a sweetshop and sampling the candy on offer. They are not a one gal guy and they should just own it and, stop giving their kids and wives grief. Some men just seem to hate women, they want to take it out on us, their mothers or some bitch hurt them in the past and they want to treat us like dirt. We try to avoid those guys. We don't do weird shit."

Black opened her handbag and pulled out a small snub-nosed revolver. Steven moved back in his seat trying not to show the fright she had given him.
"I keep this close and if anyone gets rough I will blow his fucking dick off."

"What about drugs? I've read about some celebrities use stuff to give them a kick, do any of the guys you have sex with want that kind of stuff?" Steven asked.

Candy spoke first. "We don't do drugs or that shit.... I had this old guy who was not sure if it would be hard enough so he took three of those little blue pills, but he had no water so he started choking. I said to him, man, you better spit those out pretty soon, cause if they get stuck in your throat you're gonna have a stiff neck for a week."

Black chuckled.

The ring tone on Stevens's phone burst into life, letting him know that it was the time he was expected to meet the other golfers downstairs in the casino bar and grill. His interview with the escorts must come to an end. Steven got up from his chair and the ladies got up from the bed. He shook Candy and Black's hand, thanked them for their time and honesty, and gave them each fifty dollars extra as a tip. He opened his room door and watched them make their way to the lift.

Chapter Fifteen: Tony and Selina

The number of commuters that used Russell Square tube station followed the pattern of most stations. There was a busy rush of people in the morning between seven thirty and nine thirty and then the flow of commuters settled down to a steady stream until the evening rush hour between four thirty and six in the evening. Tony and Selina had noticed that people seemed to be leaving work a lot earlier than they used to and they thought it was probably to avoid the suffocating crush of people on the tube trains during the traditional rush hours. Tony usually had two deliveries of papers in the day. One delivery was early in the morning and another at about three thirty in the afternoon to be ready for the busy commute in the evening. Selina usually arrived at the entrance to the station at about eight in the morning with her little fold out stool to sit on, her guitar, and her faithful puppy 'Chip' as a companion. Tony was amazed at the way 'Chip' the dog would sit by Selina, beg for treats or sleep for most of the day. To stop him having 'accidents', Selina regularly took him on short walks in the nearby park or gardens armed with a poop scooper and plastic bag. When she did this she left Tony in charge of her guitar and her stool, and asked him to make sure no one stole her 'pitch'. If Tony needed a toilet break she would watch over his papers, and if necessary sell them for him. Selina had grown into an attractive young woman, with her hair in a ponytail, wearing a little makeup, mostly eye shadow and pale lipstick. Sometimes she put her hair in dreadlocks and wore a woolly hat. She had a posh accent compared to Tony's, and he was pretty certain that unlike him, she didn't go to a comprehensive school, but he had avoided asking her about her past. Tony felt quite protective of Selina and he made sure that she had a good warm coat, and a woollen hat to keep out the cold. He bought the coat for her from a second hand stall in the Portobello market. It was a navy officers' great coat which she had shortened to make it fit, and the first time she wore it at the station Tony complemented her for looking good in it. He also made sure she knew he liked her music and her voice as did the passers-by and he pestered her to apply for talent shows on the television, either 'Britain's Got Talent', or 'The Voice'. Tony thought her repertoire of songs was unusual for someone of her age as it was made up of covers of tunes from the sixties and early seventies, but sometimes she would surprise Tony by secretly learning to play a song he said he liked from other eras. She surprised him by singing, 'It must have been me', by Sting, in one of the 'Lethal Weapon' movies which Tony liked because he was a fan of Mel Gibson. She also learned to play Will Young's, 'Leave Right Now', a recording she heard on the radio and which Tony confided meant a lot to him.

One day, while they were on a break together, eating a cheese roll and sharing a bottle of a lemon drink to quench their thirst he continued his campaign to get Selina to make something of her talent.

"Come on 'C'; go on the television, and when you're famous you can employ me as your body guard like Kevin Costner and Witney in the movie. I don't mean anything weird by saying that, I mean, don't get me wrong, you're lovely, and anyway it didn't work out to well for them in the movie. I'm sure no one would want to shoot you anyway. That's not my point; I think you would stand a great chance of winning."

Selina had purposely not told Tony about her experience with Mick and the singing video she made with Rosy in Brighton. As far as she knew it was still available on You Tube, but luckily Tony hated smart phones and avoided computers. She had tried to keep her past a secret from Tony as much as she could, and likewise she never enquired about his past. It was as if they had an implicit agreement, a kind of pact, to limit what they disclosed to each other. However caught up in the moment and feeling benevolent she made a decision to let Tony into a secret she had previously kept from him.

"Tony I think it's time I told you that I did go for an audition for the 'Voice' talent show."

"You what, you did? You little fibber you, I could have seen you on the Telly; I am standing next to a star. Come on tell me what happened? Did you meet Tom Jones or that 'Will' guy?" Tony asked his face looking a bit flushed with excitement.

"Come on Tony, calm down." Selina did not want to attract the attention of any passers-by.

"No it's not like that; you have to go to a mass audition first. Mine was at a big hotel near Wembley Arena, and my audition time was twelve twenty. When I got there we queued up outside in a line, about a hundred of us. When it was our turn, they took fifty of us into the foyer and then up an escalator to the first floor. We then waited to be checked in on computer by the girls at a desk. Then we were taken along a corridor to what looked like a lecture theatre where we waited. I practiced a bit on the guitar and other people were doing scales and things like that, but you could tell we were all nervous. I spoke to two contestants who had been on an audition for the programme earlier in the month but in Birmingham and Southampton and they thought they had a good chance to get through because they had been called back. I spoke to another black guy who had auditioned for 'Britain's got talent' and got through to the third round of that, but did not get on T.V. Anyway after about fifteen minutes of waiting, we were taken up one more floor to a corridor with five rooms on it and we were divided into groups of ten. The door of the room opened and we went in to be faced with two guys, one was a black guy, who was apparently a vocal coach who said he had worked with 'Jesse J' and the other one was from the show's production team. The black guy who was the singing expert, got us to do some stupid vocal exercises and make noises, then, we all sat down. I had my guitar in the case and so I had no way to get the right key to start. Some of the others had a little keyboard on their mobile and could play the note they had to start on. I had just had to sing what was in my head. They sat behind a desk while we all got up in turn to sing our songs to them without any accompaniment, and we had ninety seconds to impress them. Oh, I missed a bit. They asked if we gigged a lot, and to say something interesting about ourselves and most importantly, what we had given up for our music. I got a bit stuck at that point. All I could think of was to tell them that I liked boats and sailing, and that I would give up my education for music. So… so then it got to my turn and I sang 'Both Sides Now'. I thought it went ok, I was as good as the others and better than some, and they smiled at me when I finished. Then we all went out of the room while they deliberated and after about five minutes we were asked back into the room. I knew that if we got through this bit then we would go on to sing with our instrument. I really wanted to do that because I feel so much more in tune with the song when I feel the vibration of the music from the guitar against my body. Anyway, they said that no one in the room was going forward to the next stage. Some girls broke down and cried especially those that had been asked back by the team. We were taken along the corridor to the lift where we all got in, and everyone was silent except for those crying. There was an older grey haired man with a beard standing in the corner of the lift, I remember he sang 'Feel my Love' by Bob Dylan, but he had a cold and looked uncomfortable when he sang. When I spoke to him earlier in the day when we were queuing up outside he told me that he once met Jimmy Hendrix. He waited a while until we were all silent except for the ones who were trying to hold back their tears and then out of the blue he said;

"I think they may be giving away free razor blades in reception for those who want them."

For a minute, people were not sure how to take it, but then we all burst out laughing, and it helped to lighten the atmosphere in the lift. After all these things are not life or death, they won't save the world, and it amazes me when people are expected to say things like, 'this means everything to me', or, 'I don't know how I can live if I can't do this!' I mean what if we needed an operation and all the surgeons in the world wanted to be singers? It's like you Tony, being in the army, I don't think all of us singing would stop Sadam Husain, or the terrorists."

"Well don't be so quick to decide Selina. I guess if Sadam wanted to be a singer he might take a rest from being a dictator. He would probably set up his own talent show and make sure he'd win. If he auditioned for 'the Voice', they'd have to pick him because if not they might get tortured or shot."

"Hey, Tony, what if his stage name was, 'Dick- Tator? Something like, 'Dick –Tator, and the Fries', that's definitely got a potato ring to it!"
Tony laughed at her suggestion.

"Let me tell you Selina; he and his sons were nasty pieces of work. They were better off without him, but what he did do was stop one lot of Iraqi's fighting the other. When we pulled out it got like the wild west."

"I guess that stuff is too serious to be serious about all the time, hey?"

Tony knew now he was a casualty of war and as a surviving soldier he had tried to avoid talking about his combat experience with anyone outside of the army. He liked Selina and he was learning to trust her but he still did not want to let her in to this world. She was an outsider, hadn't known what it was like to serve her country and now was not the time to talk about such things. Tony changed the subject and asked about Selina's new revelation,

"Selina I didn't know you liked boats, and sailing. You continue to surprise me. You're a dark horse you are."

"Yes, well maybe I haven't told you before but ever since I read 'Treasure Island' and 'Swallows and Amazons' when I was little I've fancied messing about on boats. I bet you would too Tony, think how free you would feel."

Tony wasn't convinced. "Not me. I threw up on a boat, and sea sickness is one of the worst things I have experienced."

Selina had secrets, things that Tony did not know about her, things that she had not spoken to him about in the time they had been together either at the station or on their walks home together. She did not tell him that her father was a very senior serving officer in the Royal Navy. Tony also kept secrets that he was not ready to share with Selina because he was worried she might think badly of him. He had not told her of the existence of his partner and child in Brighton, or of his experience in the army. Tony wanted to tell her but all this tough painful and exciting history was locked in a box which at the moment he could only open for his therapist. Even in his these sessions he had only recently started to open up. He had still refused to share with Nigel how he felt towards Selina. If he did this, admitted his feelings for Selina, then he felt he was being unfaithful to his partner, the mother of his child, a child whom he had never held. How could Selina have any feelings for him if she knew what he had done? Deep down inside he needed to be hopeful that Selina could have affectionate feelings towards him. It seemed to him now that this previous relationship happened in another country to a different man, in a different time, even though he knew they were only a train ride away. If Selina found out he had abandoned his child he felt certain that she would hate the kind of man he was. On his better days, when his conscience was less persecutory, Tony told himself, that he was doing his partner and child a favour because they were better off without him. As far as Tony felt he had been crazy, he was a violent person who had taken lives, and memories of the horror of combat haunted him, stopped him sleeping and sent him spinning out of control. Before he left Brighton and hit the streets he was unable to show affection or let people love him. He feared that being with him was like exposing Jade and his little one to a toxic, poisonous, cloud that would harm them. He had to protect them and get away. Why did he think that he was different now and Selina would be safe with him? Tony told himself that she didn't need the trouble he would bring into her life but still he had feelings for her. She was already down on her luck singing for handouts and probably running from someone or something she had not told him about. At this time all he could do was look after her and make sure no harm came to her via him or anyone else. He decided to let her know that he was trying to work things out.

"Selina, have I told you I am seeing someone to talk to about all the rubbish in my head, my drinking, and that?"

"I'm glad for you Tony. If and when you feel ready you can tell me a bit about it, if you want. I will be interested, and I promise I won't judge, people in 'glass houses' and all that. The priest at school said we should all show compassion to others because, 'there but for the grace of God go I'."

Tony was putting his money from the sale of papers into the pouch on a belt strapped around his waist. Without looking at Selina but looking at the passers-by he said;

"God, if there is one, gave up on me a long time ago, and after what I've witnessed I definitely gave up on him."

Selina joked. "You men are all the same, what makes you think God is a man? It has got to be a woman, we make the babies, and even Jesus had a mother, and we can multi task which a God has to do.... So many people... So many countries... So many prayers! All happening at the same time, it's got to be a woman Tony, no doubt."

"Lovely to see you laugh, you have a pretty laugh, and it matches the twinkle in your eyes."

Tony stopped himself abruptly before he said too much and shifted his gaze from Selina the stack of papers he had in his hand.

"Tony, that's sweet of you. I'd better earn some money."

Selina checked that her guitar was in tune, patted Chip her dog on the head, and began to sing; "Oh my name it is nothing, my age it means less, and the country I come from is called the mid-west. I was raised and brought up there, the laws to abide; well the country was young then, with God on its side."
When she stopped singing she began to count the money collected in her guitar case on the pavement in front of her, twenty five pounds, thirty two pence.
'Not bad' she said to herself under her breath.

"C, I don't know where you go on the days when you're not here, I guess it's none of my business but I am curious."

Tony felt he was taking a risk asking this but as they were talking about things they did not know about each other, he would take a shot at it.

"Well I go to other train stations to busk. I go to Kings Cross, and sometimes St Pancras. There is a guy there who sometimes plays the piano and we play together a bit, nothing regular, just for fun. I sometimes hang out at the all night café's near Piccadilly Circus. I get food and chat with the young runaways. They worry me."

She did not tell Tony that she used the same taxi service she trusted, to take her there and back.

Tony was not amused by this revelation by Selina as he knew from people in the shelter and other street sellers that Kings Cross was potentially a dangerous place for girls or boys on their own.

"Listen Selina you could be at risk there from the street girls and male prostitutes that work there. You know that kids who run away from home get picked up there and made to work in the sex trade. The Eastern Europeans, Russians, and that lot, take you, drug you, keep you in some hellhole house and turn you out to anyone who pays. They are worse than the English gangsters or the Asians, they don't give a shit, and they are armed and more violent, even the police take backhanders to stay away. That's what I've heard. Those kids got taken for those sex parties with judges and M.P.'s; it was in the news, something to do with Saville. I don't want to be crude but one poor twelve year old boy was buggered by four men in some place near there. He had only been in London for two nights and had no food and nowhere to stay. They found him glued up, with a plastic bag stuck over his head. They put him in a car, threatened to beat the shit out of him if he told anyone who did that to him. I heard about it from a nurse I met in the pub I go to who treated him in A and E. She said he was so ripped up he had to have an operation on his bum to repair the damage that they did. Selina I don't mean to be so graphic, but please stay clear of that place, especially at night. Even if you make more money it's not worth it. Look, if you want I could go with you, just to give you some security, especially at night."

Selina was fully aware of what Tony said and knew he was annoyed about what she was doing because he cared for her safety. What Tony did not know, and what she could not tell him was the reason why she was doing what she was doing. When she returned from her voyage to the Greek Islands she decided to go to University and get a degree. She completed her B.Sc. (Hons) in Human Sciences at Oxford University and was now studying for her PHD by research at Essex University. Her motivation for choosing Essex University for her postgraduate studies was because of its history in her subject of choice. Between 1963 and 1981 it was a pioneer of Sociology in England and it had great lecturers like Peter

Townsend, Denis Marsden, and Howard Newby, who had written about poverty education and class. Her chosen research project was to study the causes of vagrancy and homelessness in London. Her aim or goal was to propose pathways and policy initiatives based on her research that if adopted by government could limit the likelihood of these things occurring, and to suggest new ways of rehabilitating those who fall through the cracks of the present system. She was not a wealthy person who was happy to sit on her fortune, and watch others in society suffer. Along with great wealth and good fortune also came a social responsibility for those less fortunate than herself. If she had learned anything good from being at her private school it was that a sense of service and duty should run in parallel with privilege. Selina felt that if more people in her position adopted this attitude there would be less animosity towards her class and economic strata. She had not made her own wealth she had inherited it from her family. Historically most of the wealth that had been accumulated by aristocrats and the wealthy classes over time had been taken from others in history and often by force. Selina knew from her studies that some had been made from slavery, either of Africans, Indians, or poor English workers who had no employment rights in law. In the past workers had little rights and little education and they were not protected from unscrupulous employers and landlords, who could fix wages make sure if they didn't work for them they would live in poverty. She could not apologise for the class she was born into but she felt that she had a responsibility to do something with her life to justify her privileged position.

Selina knew that the social welfare structure in Britain was barely seventy five years old and yet present governments were still trying to dismantle it to give back power those who felt they lost it in the Victorian times. Her time on the streets had confirmed this suspicion and she felt that if the wealthy let the gap between them and the rest of society get too big, they were sleeping their way towards a class war in which they could lose it all. They cannot live in nice houses with upmarket fashions and the trappings of wealth if they risked getting shot or their buildings invaded or burned down. They would have to spend more and more on security, prisons and the police to keep them safe. The British elite were cleverer than that. They read Marx; they saw the American and French revolutions and they avoided it happening in Britain. Democracy, the rule of law for all classes, taxation, education and social mobility, for the middle classes and then the poor, avoided revolution. The rule of law for all regardless of their wealth eased the pressure for revolution in society but sadly in the present day Selina worried that those who ignored history forgot this clear and present danger. She worried that we could evolve into a society portrayed in the film 'Elysium' where the rich and privileged, have left earth and created an alternative environment in space where they can live a privileged life separate from the workers on earth. Her father in the Navy knew the value of keeping the ranks happy because his life and those of the officers depended on their loyalty.

The philosophy of life that Selina evolved on her travels meant that she wanted to do this research but not at a distance, she wanted to get involved. She had been and inspired by Goffman's 'Asylums', and William F. Whites 'Street Corner Society', who did their research by participant observation. When she looked through some of the student research dissertations that were kept in the library at the University she came across one completed by two students in the early 1970's. They went to London for a period of time to study the politics of racial prejudice in London at that time, and to see if people had been influenced by the struggles of the Afro Americans in America. They completed interviews with some of the people involved in various political groups at that time. They found an English group in Brixton who seem to base themselves on the American Black Panthers who called themselves the Black Eagles. They went to National Front meeting and heard Martin Webster speak and at the other end of the spectrum they interviewed the English version of Malcom X who called himself Michael X. His actual name was Michael Abdul Malik, or Michael de Freitas, and he use to work for an infamous landlord in Notting hill called Peter Rackman as an enforcer. He set up Black House at the end of Portobello Road. He was given money by Sammy Davis Junior, Mohamed Ali and John Lennon of the Beatles to name but a few. They interviewed him at the height of a period of racial tension that summer and as they wrote in the dissertation, despite being white and a bit nervous, they asked to speak with him. He agreed and they went to his office in Black House to interview him. They wrote down the results of the interview independently to avoid bias any that might creep in. Their conclusions fascinated Selina. These students felt that either he was a real leader of the black movement at that time or a conman and crook, out for his own glory. They were not to know at that time that he would become a drug dealer and be the last man to be hung in Trinidad for the murder of a man and a woman whom he buried in his garden. Later it was rumoured that the woman killed was an undercover agent for the British government.

She felt inspired, this was the kind of research Selina decided she wanted to do. Let other people do surveys and issue questionnaires, she wanted to be amongst the people she studied and observed. This is what she decided to do and to this end she set a year aside to live amongst those she wanted to study on the streets of London. By blending in she could go the places where they hang out and hear from them their own stories, record what they have to say, and learn first-hand what they had to do to survive on the margins of society. She knew this was not the accepted or preferred method that the quantitative scientists at the University wanted her to adopt. They loved, questionnaires, doing experiments, and the joy of manipulating statistics. Selina was not interested in this approach, and because she was funding her own research she could do it the way she wanted to, as long as she adopted a valid methodology for her qualitative study, and had the support of her professor. She wanted her experience to be personal and humanistic. At this moment in time, she was happy, the University was happy, and her supervising professor was also happy. The only cloud on the horizon, and one that would rain on her parade would be Tony's reaction to her true identity if it was disclosed.

Tony looked at her and then at the passers-by across the road, and before she could start her next song he began speaking.

"Do you know the song 'The Streets of London'? It was out a long time ago but it is about people like us you know. There's a line in it that goes, don't worry I won't sing it;

'How can you tell me that you're lonely and say to me that the Sun don't shine? Let me take you by the hand and I'll lead you through the streets of London
I'll show you something that will make you change your mind.'

I think about that sometimes when I'm down, and I guess you know from what you have seen that we don't have it as bad as some. I mean you could change your future, you don't have to do this, you could go to college, go travelling, do something exciting, I know, work in MacDonald's?"

"No I don't know that song, but I do know Joni Mitchell songs. What about, 'Big Yellow Taxi'?" Selina replied.

Tony looked at Selina with mock disapproval on his face.

"Wasn't she the one who broke up the Hollies?"

"I don't know that about her, but I do know the she had a father who was in the air force in Canada. She got pregnant very young, had her baby in secret, and had it adopted. She kept that secret for a long time while she pursued her career and didn't see her daughter again until she was thirty two. Imagine that, I don't think I could do that, leave a child I had carried for nine months…. all that pain."

234

Tony answered immediately;

 "Maybe she thought it was for the best, she had plans, maybe she thought she would do the child more harm than good. We don't know how she felt; maybe she felt the baby would be better off without her."

"Ok, OK, sorry, didn't mean to start an argument. I just meant we don't know what life can throw at us, and we make choices."

The look on Tony's face became more relaxed and he seemed to shake off whatever thought he had been taken over by and spoke calmly to Selina.
"Sorry......I just want to see you do better for yourself than this."

Selina smiled; "...so could you Tony, you could have a different destiny mapped out for you, the fates may roll the dice in your favour, get a lottery ticket, who knows."

"Do you want to grab a burger on the way home tonight?" Tony asked.

"Yea, sure, we like burgers don't we Chip." Selina ruffled her dog's fur.

"Did they get on when they met?" Tony asked Selina.

"What, Joni, and her daughter?"

"Yes" Tony replied.

"They seemed to sort something out and are in each other's lives now."

The information that Selina gave him seemed to satisfy Tony's curiosity.

"Did I tell you I was in the police once? Well I wasn't a policeman but I was working at the end of a police radio. I thought I should tell you the truth. My therapist says truth can help to set me free."

Tony looked at Selina and smiled.

"That's one way of thinking but others might say why tell the truth when a good lie will do?" Selina replied. "A lie could make you happy when a truth would make you sad."

"I think my therapist would say that this short term gain could lead to long term pain. He says things like that." Tony's smile widened and became a grin.

"Ok, I should tell you then that this posh accent that you say I have, I got from going to a posh school but I didn't have much choice, and my dad was in the Navy."

Selina immediately regretted this sharing of information about herself because she knew Tony would want to ask her questions.

"So you had to go to school because he was at sea, I guess you and your mum had to live on the naval base, was it in Portsmouth?"

Selina wanted to close the conversation down.

"Err; yes for a bit we moved around, we were in Malta once."

"I was in Malta for a holiday once with my mates we stayed at Sliema, and we went to a great beach in Mellieha Bay. We kept clear of the navy though because they didn't take to squaddies in their bars. I didn't want to risk my guys spending time locked up and missing out their time in the sun."
"You don't talk much about your time in the army..."

Tony quickly changed the subject.

"I think you had better start entertaining your adoring public Selina, and I better get my papers ready for the rush hour, because it's going to be full on in about half hour, come on sing me 'Cecelia', you do that well, and they stop and listen when you do that. I might even join in."

Selina would not be put off, she persisted; "Tony if we are telling each other a truth, I want to ask you....is your name Tony or Anthony?"

"Is your name really Selina, you told me to call you 'C' for short but could it be..., well, Celery?" Tony responded quickly and they both giggled at the stupidity of his suggestion.

Tony looked at Selina and smiled one of his white teeth smiles.

"In answer to your question my name is Anthony as in Anthony and Cleopatra, but I must confess, and this tells you about the films my mother watched when I was younger. I hate to admit it but I did fancy

Elizabeth Taylor when I got older. I spoke to a hospital porter whom I met at some party once, who actually saw her naked when she went into hospital for an operation. She was covered only by a hospital gown and they had a peek. Apparently she had lovely skin and beautiful violet coloured eyes with a double set of eyelashes."
Selina was not happy with what she heard.

"Sounds like a bit of a pervert to me. Anyway go on."

Tony continued with his explanation.

" So, Anthony was too posh for the squaddies to cope with when I was in the Army and so mates called me Tony, or Tone, or probably 'tosser' behind my back, and it stuck. Only my mother called me Anthony, usually when I had done something to upset her."

Selina thought for a moment. "Let's play a game. I've got a puzzle for you to solve. You have twenty questions to ask me, and I can only answer yes, no, or don't know. Do you want to play? It will help pass the time. Come on, Please?"

Tony smiled at Selina. "O.K, I always wanted to be a detective, go ahead."

Selina closed her eyes for a moment, drew a deep breath and began.

"Right, Anthony, your name sake, and Cleopatra were found dead on the floor in a room. The room was locked from the outside, and the shuttered window was open. Near to their bodies was a puddle of liquid and some broken glass."

"What killed them?" Tony asked.

Selina laughed. "No, you have to say something about what happened to them and I say yes or no to that!"

"Ok, was there any one else in the room?" Tony asked Selina, staring at her face hoping she would give something away.

"No" Selina replied.

"Did they kill each other?"

Selina laughed with frustration. "No, Tony come on, you have to find out a bit more first!"

"This is stupid; it is going to take too long." Tony looked crestfallen.

"Come on stick to it, we have all the time we need, keep trying." Selina encouraged him and poked him in the ribs with her left hand.

"Were they poisoned?"

"No, but you've got the idea. I need to sing now but keep thinking."

"I've got to sell papers, the homeless depend on me."

Tony began shouting; "Big Issue, Big Issue!"
Selina picked up her guitar, checked it was still in tune, and began strumming the opening chords to the Simon and Garfunkel song, 'Cecelia'.

Chapter Sixteen: Steven and David

Steven got on with all of his golfing friends who played in the Saturday
swindle at Chapel Hill golf club, excluding Mark the publisher. Steven
had tried to like him but found him arrogant and too extroverted. He was
too concerned with status, what people earned or owned. Originally
Steven imagined that he was a business man and worked in finance, share
dealing, or some form of buying and selling. He was surprised when Mark
told him he was a literary publisher. When Mark talked of the books he
published he seemed to focus on how many 'units' he sold and in which
markets, rather than the literary merit of the work. Mark viewed his work
in a similar way to a record promoter selling his artistes to the world and
getting them air play for their records. Steven hoped at some time in his
career Mark might have actually liked reading and had been inspired by
literature. Perhaps he did once want to find and mentor a potentially great
author but some tragedy changed him. Now he seemed focused on
literature he thought would sell on the airport bookstands, or be
developed into a film. Perhaps these goals were not mutually exclusive.
When he spoke to Mark about his thoughts, Mark gave him short shrift.

"Steven I think you are a bit naïve in your understanding of publishing.
There are hundreds of books published in a year. My team and I are the
ones that get our author's noticed and stop their book from being boiled
down to make newspaper, or worse still toilet paper, within months of
its release. We need money to survive and if I didn't get my book on
Richard and Judy, or Oprah Winfrey's book lists, or whoever it is at the
time, I may as well cut my wrists. There are two sides to this business and
in the near future I am going to launch a 'vanity publishing' arm to our
company where the new authors pay us to publish their books. I get
about fifty new manuscripts across my desk each week and there is
money to be made. It is a win, win, situation. "

Steven was also aware that, unlike David, one of his other golfing
buddies, Mark was not averse to sleeping with other women on their
'boys' trips abroad to play golf. Steven had witnessed this behaviour on
golf holidays with him in South Africa, Thailand and Las Vegas. Steven
had seen in close up the impact of his duplicity on his wife. Steven had
been Marks gardener for some time and as such had grown close to

Mary. He had seen her become suspicious of and disillusioned with the man she fell in love with and married. He remembered her saying to him,

"Steven, I can still remember the pain and the pleasure of loves first kiss. In the blink of an eye how has it come to this?"

Mary had a special place in his heart and in the process of comforting her in her despair she became one of Steven's very special clients. Steven was also aware of the complicated relationship Mark had with David. It was as if Mark held something over David but he did not know what it was. Mark had given David's daughter Jodie a job at his firm and recently David had become unhappy about this situation.

"Steven, I don't know what's going on, or what has happened, but recently Jodie has not seemed happy. I caught her crying the other day, and I have asked her mother to have a word with her to see if we can help."

It was a rare occurrence for David to open up to Steven but for some reason on this occasion decided to as they walked up the fairway of the eighteenth hole at Chapel Hill. They both stood by their golf balls, which had landed on the fairway no more than three foot apart near a large tree, waiting for the game up ahead to clear the green.

"When she went there to work she enjoyed it from the beginning. Up until a couple of months ago she couldn't be happier. She went on these work trips abroad with Mark and his other directors and all seemed fine. She went from talking endlessly about her job and how great Mark was to saying virtually nothing. She's lost her sparkle. Has Mark said anything to you?"

Steven took his five-iron out of his golf bag and did a few practice swings with it.

"No, we don't talk much and when we do it tends to be about his garden or films we like, that kind of thing. He is having lessons with the golf pro here and he was telling me about that at breakfast today. He keeps other things to himself. Have you thought of asking him?

David followed suit and took a five wood out of his bag and hovered it above his golf ball.
"I want to say something but I don't want to pry, and I really wish I hadn't asked him to take Jodie on. In all honesty, I don't like that man and the ways I've seen him treat women."

David took a swing at his ball and launched it towards the left side of the green. It landed pin high to the left of the flag and rolled right towards the hole.

"That's a great shot!" Steven said enthusiastically.

Steven stood over his ball, took two practice swings and brought his club down on the back of his golf ball. His ball climbed majestically into the air, heading straight toward the pin finishing on the green, five foot past the hole.

"Oh what it is to be young!" David smiled at Steven and patted him on the back.

"Great shot Steven! Birdy chance"

"Look David, I will see what I can find out, but as you know, Mark is a bit of a mystery and tries to be all things to all men."

Later that week when Steven was at David's house tidying up the back garden Jodie happened to be sitting outside drinking tea and eating a piece of her mother's date and walnut cake. While he dug the border to get rid of some wild garlic that had spread along the path, he heard Jodie talking on her phone. She seemed to be getting upset. From what he heard of the conversation, he gathered it was her boyfriend she was talking to. She mentioned leaving something in the room of a hotel they had stayed at recently. She finished the call, leaving her iPhone on her garden chair, disappearing into the house; probably to go to the loo. Steven moved quickly from the side of the garden and picked up the phone to see her call list. The I.D. was listed on the phone as Mark Finch. Steven had a strange feeling in his stomach. The way she was talking on the phone suggested that there was more to her relationship with Mark than a caring employee. For David's peace of mind he decided that he would take on the role of private investigator. He would try to be as fair and opened minded as he could be and simply present the evidence he found. He would follow Jodie to Mark's office in London and observe their movement's throughout the day. In case he needed evidence to show David he would take a digital camera with him to record his findings.

Over the next couple of weeks he made three trips to the office of Finch and Faber near Russell Square to stake out the office. He put on his best jacket and trousers, a white shirt and a necktie as a disguise, as he rarely wore this type of clothing in the company of Jodie or Mark. To complete his outfit and to protect him from the rain he took Gordon's brolly. When he arrived at the tube station he bought a Big Issue from the man at the entrance of the tube and stood and listened to a girl with a fabulous voice singing 'Both Sides Now' which was one of his mother's favourite Joni Mitchell songs. Steven chose a bench to sit on in Russell Square garden from where he had an unobstructed view of the entrance to Faber and Finch. To try to be less conspicuous he took a paper to read and, every so often, he would get up from the bench and walk up and down the pavement, still in view of the entrance, but blending in with the passers-by. He watched as Jodie and Mark left the office at lunch time arm in arm and followed them when they went shopping together at Victoria Secrets. He saw them kiss passionately in the road outside the office entrance and he followed them to a hotel where they stayed for about two hours before returning to work. He took photographs of each of their excursions.

Steven came to enjoy his snooping role and extended his surveillance of Mark to the lessons he was taking with the lady golf pro at the golf club. This surveillance was much easier to accomplish as he was a club member and could practice with his golf clubs on the driving range while Mark had his lesson at the covered tee reserved for the use of the professional. He hid his camera in his golf bag and in between switching clubs or cleaning them in the bucket of water provided; he could take photographs of the couple. Steven could see from the familiar body language, their smiles and the discrete touching that took place between them that their relationship may be more than professional. At one point the professional, Petra, stood behind Mark, put her arms around his body, to show Mark the grip on the club and the stance he should take when addressing the ball. There was a lot of laughing while she was doing this, and finally Mark managed to chip his ball onto the practice green and landed it near the flag. Then very quickly, checking first to make sure that no one would see her, she kissed him briefly on the cheek. Later that afternoon Steven followed them to the 'Bell and Jorracks' pub, in the village of Frittenden where Mark and Petra sat on the wooden seats outside, having a beer and what looked like a fruit juice, and a packet of nuts. In between sipping their drinks and eating their snack, they kissed a number of times.

The more photographic evidence of Mark's infidelity Steven gathered, the greater his anger towards him grew. Steven knew that it would be hypocritical of him to be morally outraged by Mark's behaviour because of the service he provided for Mark's wife, however, his feelings for Mary were real and therefore he cared about the emotional hurt she would face finding out about Mark's philandering.

What should he tell David? It seemed clear to Steven from his observations of Jodie and Mark together that David's daughter was still besotted by him, but she didn't know of Mark's other interests. If David presented his findings to Jodie Steven imagined that she would be devastated and very angry. Steven couldn't predict whether she would take this anger out on herself or Mark. When David had his suspicions about Mark confirmed he would feel responsible for Jodie being used and exploited, perhaps he might decide to take revenge on Davis himself. Steven decided that discretion was the better part of valour and for the moment he would keep his findings to himself. However, Steven could not stand by and do nothing. He had to do something to scare Mark and hopefully get him to modify his behaviour. He decided to send Mark an anonymous warning. He printed off a selection of damning pictures taken on his stake outs. Then, after adding a warning message printed on yellow paper, he sent the pictures in a brown envelope to Mark. The message on the yellow paper read:

STOP WHAT YOU ARE DOING NOW YOU BASTARD BEFORE SOMEONE GETS HURT!
YOU COULD BE THAT SOMEONE! WATCH OUT!

To avoid the source of the envelope being tracked by a postmark, Steven travelled to London on the train and posted it through the letterbox of Finch and Faber himself. Perhaps it was time for him to reconsider his part in this drama before things got out of hand. After he had delivering the envelope he needed to sit and think and so he stopped and sat on a park bench near the office building. It started to rain and so he got up and walked along the road, crossed over at the traffic light and went into a shop situated opposite the entrance to the tube station. He bought a daily newspaper, and feeling hungry he decided to have breakfast at the cafe next door. He found a seat at a table by the window, ordered a full English breakfast with a pot of tea, and settled down to eat his 'cholesterol special' and read the paper. The headlines in the paper foretold of doom and gloom for Britain. Problems caused by government benefit caps, railway men, nurses and doctors on strike, fighting with Islamic State militants, the Catholic Church embroiled in sexual scandal, footballers having affairs and celebrity wives getting millions in divorce settlements. To add to this uplifting news the growth in the economy had stalled. The only good news he could find apart from film reviews, seemed to be about a dog named 'Admiral' who rescued a cat from drowning. Steven checked the date on the paper to see if it was 'April Fool's Day', it wasn't. Steven gazed out of the window in front of him. Across the street, in front of the entrance to the station, he saw a girl busker with her dog and a tall man standing next to her selling the Big Issue to passers-by. They were deep in conversation but soon stopped and the busker began playing her guitar and singing. Passers-by threw money into her open guitar case placed on the ground in front of her. An attractive, well dressed lady emerged from the entrance of the tube station, paused for a moment to listen to the busker's song and then bought a paper from the Big Issue seller. She seemed to ask him for directions because the man gestured in the direction of the University buildings and Mark's office. The woman dropped money into the guitar case then turned and walked away in the opposite direction. For a fleeting moment Steven thought he recognised this woman, and then it came to him, she reminded him of Claire, David's wife. It was unfortunate that her name reminded Steven of a girl in his past. Fortunately she bore no physical resemblance to her and so the name alone didn't have a negative affected on their relationship. Steven wondered why she was in London today. Perhaps she had arranged to meet her daughter Jodie after work? He remained suspicious because he felt certain that she would have mentioned something about her plans when he was at her house cutting the grass earlier in the week. He convinced himself he was seeing things. It was probably someone who had similar looks.

Steven turned his attention back to the singer and her dog. He wondered to himself why someone who was clearly as talented as a singer and guitarist as she was, ended up busking for a living. She reminded him of old photographs of his mother in her hippy days when her name was 'Star-shine' and lived in Italy. Steven had not intended to hang around in London after delivering his package but having time to think while he digested his breakfast he changed his mind. He would stay in Russell Square and stake out the publishers to find out if the discovery of the envelope would spur Mark into action. Steven spent his time opposite the entrance to Finch and Faber following his usual routine. He sat on the park bench reading, or stroll around listening to music on his iPhone, but at all times he made sure he stayed within sight of the office door.

It was while he was listening to Diana Ross singing 'Touch me in the morning' that he spotted his friend David, dressed in his pin striped business suit, walking along the pavement on the other side of the road. It looked as if he was heading for Mark's office with a briefcase in one hand and a walking stick in the other. Steven thought this a bit odd as David did not need a walking stick… the last time he accompanied him on the golf course he was fit and healthy. The walking stick he carried looked rather thick and looked like it could be made of metal. In David's hands it seemed more like a club than a walking stick. It was definitely a sturdy implement; any passer-by accidentally hit on the leg with it would definitely be hurt and have a large bruise. Steven imagined that a hit on the head would do some serious damage. David got to about a hundred yards from the entrance to the office, stopped in his tracks and took out his mobile phone. He looked like he was having an agitated conversation with the person at the other end of the phone; put the mobile back into his inside pocket, then abruptly turned around and walked back towards the station. Steven wondered what that conversation could be about as he watched David walked away into the distance. To pass the time Steven played a game with himself of walking up and down the pavement trying to avoid the cracks between the paving stones, but ever mindful of not being distracted from his main task. He listened to, 'Papa was a Rolling Stone' by the Temptations, 'She's Gone' by Hall and Oats and then 'Nothing Compares to You' by Seanad O'Conner. He made sure he never lost sight of the office entrance. He was enjoying Hozier's 'Take me to Church' when from behind, something struck him on his shoulder. In one swift movement he pulled out his ear phones and turned to confront his assailant.

"Steven, what are you doing skulking behind this garden hedge?"

It was Claire, David's wife whom he thought he had seen earlier in the day buying a paper at the tube station. It was that very same rolled up paper she had used to strike him on the shoulder.

"Claire, what are you doing here? Do you know I thought I saw you earlier, you bought a Big Issue at the tube; is that what you hit me with? I thought I was seeing things?"

Claire would not be put off, "Steven, I asked first, what are you here for, and looking so smart?"

"Ok, I've been to a seminar at the university near here about trees and tree surgery, and I wanted to investigate some African varieties. I guess that might seem strange to you because I'm just your local gardener, but I like to keep up to date and stay informed. Now, come on, what about you?"

"Oh well, I feel so stupid, but David said he was coming to London for a business meeting at Langans. Well I phoned them to check the reservation because it is one of our favourite places, and stupid me, I thought I could surprise him. It turns out that he doesn't have a reservation there. I phoned one of the partners and they knew nothing about it." Tears welled up in Claire's eyes.

"Steven I think he is having an affair, after all these years, I suppose I should have expected it, I am not stupid, I know what happens on those golf trips with you and his other cronies. I am getting no younger and lots of women would find him attractive, I can't stand the deceit."

Claire began to sob and her tears flowed freely. Steven felt her sadness, wanted to comfort her, but she was interfering with his stakeout of the office and somehow he needed to get her to leave him alone. He put his arms around her and held her tightly to him then gently moved her round so that he could still see the office entrance over her shoulder.

"Listen Claire I am certain you have got this all wrong. David loves you and he is one of the straightest people I know. He is not like that; I can honestly tell you that on all those trips we've been on together he has been nothing but faithful to you. Believe me; he wouldn't do anything to hurt you or Jodie. I am pretty sure that if he told you a lie it's for a good reason and probably wants to surprise you with something, or has something he is doing that he can't tell you about yet."

"That's what he said to me when I phoned him earlier." Claire replied.

"Well, there you are then, nothing to worry about."

Putting two and two together, Steven realised that it must have been Claire that he saw David speak to on his mobile.

"Steven, why would I trust you? You would say that, you men stick together, you are a part of his golfing mafia, and you are sworn to secrecy. I bet you swear in blood or something and so you would defend him. That's ok; I decided I don't care about things away from home but here? No! I know what you golfers say to each other, David told me, and don't you deny it, "What happens on golf holidays stays on golf holidays." Claire looked angrily at him and watched for his reaction.

"Ok, yes! You see! David even told you that. Why would he even tell you if he had something to hide from you? Look, yes, some of us do get up to things we may not be proud of, but not David. Honestly I swear on my dear mother's life that he is not like that."

"Really, well I phoned him just now and he wasn't very happy, he was very short with me. He didn't sound happy for me to be in London. He made some excuse about the meeting being cancelled at short notice. Anyway I told him I was going to visit Jodie, and see if she wanted to come to dinner with me. She seems so emotional lately. I haven't phoned her because I want it to be a surprise, she should be leaving work soon. Then I caught a glimpse of you standing here. Would you like to come for dinner? I would imagine you don't get to come up to town that often and I'm certain Jodie and David wouldn't mind. Steven you surprise me, you do scrub up well."

Claire couldn't help herself let out a little laugh and Steven wondered if she was being just a tiny bit flirtatious.

While Claire spoke Steven had managed to keep his look out over her shoulder and watch the publisher's entrance. He saw a man with greying hair and a beard, dressed in a cord jacket and jeans carrying what looked to Steven like a folder, come out of the publisher's front door and march off in the direction of the tube station.

"Claire it is so kind of you to offer but I have to get back to Marden. I promised to meet someone in the pub tonight to talk about a job they have for me." Steven hoped this excuse would put Claire off the scent.

"Well if you're certain, I hope you get the work. If you change your mind please feel free to come for a meal with us, you're a man with hidden talents and I'm sure Jodie would like the company."

Steven wondered if Claire was trying to match make. Jodie was young, attractive, and as he has discovered, besotted with Mark. He had looked at her in Claire's garden sometimes and felt attracted to her but he thought she was the daughter of a friend, and it would be too complicated. As far as Jodie was concerned, he had no indication that she was interested in him and as the gardener he was invisible to her.

Looking over Claire's shoulder Steven could see movement at the door of Finch and Faber. Mark Finch emerged from the entrance door in what seemed like a hurry, wearing his blue raincoat. Steven watched as he turned up his coat collar to protect himself from the sprinkle of rain that started falling from the grey clouds which at this moment blotted out the sun, causing a dark shadow to drift across the park. Mark definitely seemed in a hurry, either to catch a train or perhaps follow the man who had left the office earlier. He walked quickly down the road towards Russell Square tube station.

"Steven thank you so much, you have been so kind. I know, what about a Dracaena Draco? I know they can be big but they are so interesting, what do you think?"

"Sorry... What?" Steven looked genuinely puzzled.

"It's a South African tree, you said you were interested in African plants, I thought you would know about it after your seminar. They are beautiful trees, what do you think, too big for the garden?"

Steven felt he had fallen into a trap that he had set himself. Just as he was about to answer he saw Jodie come out of the office, pull the hood of her coat up to partially cover her hair and head off down the road towards the tube station. Steven thought that perhaps it was too much of a coincidence for Jodie to leave the office so shortly after Mark had departed, and wondered if she was following him. Whatever the reason for their departures in quick succession Steven had to go after them to see where they were going and what they were up to. Fortunately, for Steven, Claire did not see either of them leave.

"Claire I'm sorry to be rude, but I have to go now or I will miss my train."
He kissed her politely on her cheek, sidestepped where Claire was standing, and began to walk as fast as he could in the direction Jodie had taken.

"I'll look for the Dracula tree, and I'll call you..." Steven shouted over his shoulder as he moved away from Claire and broke into a run.

Claire put up her umbrella to protect herself from the rain and watched as Steven made his way along the road. She thought it was time to walk over the road across from the office of Finch and Faber and surprise Jodie. Then she remembered what she had intended to tell Steven. The last time she visited the hairdressing salon she frequented she sat next to a lovely woman who introduced herself as 'Juan'. Claire thought she might be Chinese but was too polite to ask. Claire happened to mention that her relationship with her husband David was a bit distant, he seemed preoccupied lately, and that she missed his company. Later in their conversation it came out that they shared the same gardener.

"Steven is a lovely boy, and so discrete, I really hope he does for you what he has done for me."

When Juan left the salon Claire was left feeling that Steven might need to be guarded in his dealings with this lady. She missed this opportunity to tell him that her hairdressing companion, Juan, gave her the distinct impression that her interest in Steven might be more than his ability to tend to her flower beds. She may want him to 'plough another furrow' as David might say, and she felt very naughty for having that thought.

Chapter Seventeen: The Station

The commuters who used the station in the late afternoon were a mix of students from the School of Oriental Studies, day trippers, and regular punters from offices on their way home to some distant abode. Some were going out for an after work drink, a West End show, or a meal in a restaurant. Some of the regulars passers-by would say hello and ask Tony how he was, not expecting an answer. They would buy the paper or just give him the money and refuse to take the paper, so that he could sell it again. These were the kind one's who did not perceive the street venders, or musicians with dogs as the scum of the earth, scroungers, homeless tramps, drunks and wasters, who should be purged from the London streets. Some would look at Tony with his trimmed beard, short hair, upright physical appearance, clean boots, and a wardrobe from a charity shop and make a comment like; "A chap like you, fit and healthy, should be in work. I believe if you wanted it bad enough you can get it."

One regular passer-by, a lady in her fifties, with good makeup, expensive hairdo, and sparkling rings on her manicured hands, came by at lunchtime on her way to get her coffee and baguette. She would bring them both sandwiches and fruit juice. To them she was like an angel of mercy who asked for nothing and went away without giving them the chance to find out who she was. She nearly always said the same thing, "There you are my darlings, and God bless you, stay warm."
Others would not be so kind. They bought a paper, or dropped money into Selina's guitar case, and as they did, give her sage advice like; "Don't spend it on booze!" or "Don't use this for you next fix!"
Some would make even harsher comments like; "Bloody sign off and get a job!" or
"Stop sitting around expecting fucking handouts, help yourself and just clear off!"

Tony and Selina made up stories about some of the people they saw regularly, and invented names for them with hilarious backstories. One city gent they nicknamed 'braces' or what the Americans call suspenders, because he often wore wide, brightly coloured pairs of these attached to his trousers. They imagined that he wore little versions of these to keep his underpants and socks up. They wondered if he could be a superhero

250

who could use the elastic in his suspenders to leap over buildings and
bounce all the way back to his home.

After trying to analyse the different reasons for the differing ways the
regular commuters treated them, they came to the conclusion that it
probably depended on what kind of experiences they had gone through
that day. Their benevolence or their disdain depended on events outside
of the control of Selina or Tony and so they decided not to take these
reactions personally. All of life passed in front of them.

One couple who grabbed their interest and about whom they made up a
story, arrived to work on the tube in the morning separately, but at
lunchtime and most evenings they went into the station together. Tony
and Selina thought they were having a secret affair. Evidence supporting
this theory gained momentum when they saw the two of them kissing
and holding hands as they approached the station. Despite the obvious
age difference between them the young woman seemed besotted with
him. Once they had become people of interest to Tony and Selina they
soon realised that this couple were also seen together at the station in the
middle of the day, returning about three hours later. Tony and Selina
thought it obvious that they were probably going somewhere for a 'naked
lunch' and as Tony exclaimed, 'do the business!'

On rainy days the man would wear a blue raincoat over his suit which
Selina recognised as a Burberry raincoat. She knew this because her father
had a similar one hanging in the cupboard under the stairs at home. This
make of raincoat had been immortalised in a song by Leonard Cohen
called, 'Famous Blue Raincoat'. It was a song she knew well and one she
could sing and play with her guitar. For a brief moment Selina toyed with
the idea of changing the name they used for the male of the couple to
'Leonard' and his companion to 'Suzanne', another Cohen song, but this
musical reference would be lost on Tony, and so they stuck to the
familiar names of 'Chalk' and 'Cheese'. Tony imagined that the young
woman was probably an employee. She was not a waitress he'd met in a
cocktail bar, or an escort he had a financial arrangement with. She looked
too middle class and was probably well educated. He based this
assumption on the brief snippets of conversation he overheard as they
passed through the station.

He told Selina that the young woman looked like Meryl Streep as he
remembered her in the film the 'Deer Hunter'. There was a part of Tony
felt sorry for her because, she was probably being used by the older man.
Despite his feelings of disapproval, he had to ask himself if he was jealous
of what this man had. He did find her attractive. There was an instinctual

part of him that could not help but feel this older man was a 'lucky bastard!'

Observing this relationship caused Tony and Selina to begin a conversation about the possibility of a love between older men and younger women. Selina was quick to point out that to make this proposition equal, they also had to consider the possibility of one between older women and younger men as well.

"Would you ever have a relationship with an older man Selina?" Tony asked.

Selina looked at Tony. "Depends on the man and how old you mean, 70's, 80's, probably not, but then again what about Catherine Zeta Jones and Michael Douglas?"

"I find Helen Mirren and Meryl Streep attractive. They have a sparkle. If you want me to be honest, I have to admit that when I was younger and training at Colchester barracks I met an older woman in a pub. She taught me a lot, and I'm grateful to her, but her marriage was going down the tubes. While it was exciting for me and something new for her, it couldn't go anywhere."

Selina tried to show a look of mock disapproval on her face.

"Tony you dog. How could you do that….? No sorry, I didn't mean that. I can understand the place you were at."

"She gave me a lot of confidence and I treated her well. Better than her husband who was an arsehole. He'd hit her in the past. I think the attention I gave her showed she deserved a lot better."

Selina was surprised by the new information Tony shared with her, but didn't want to interrogate him about this past liaison any further. She returned to the question she asked previously.

"So are you telling me you're not one for the younger ladies then Tony, come on I know you find 'Cheese' attractive." Selina teased Tony.

"I hate to say this Selina but men can often think with their 'dicks' and not their head. Pardon the bad language, but we can be like a dog in a forest when it comes to an opportunity like that. I have been like that in the past but not now. If you act in haste, more than likely you regret at leisure. Desire is a drug like any other."

"My god, Tony, you sound so serious. Have you been drinking that sage tea I gave you? Your sounding like you swallowed a cup of wisdom." Selina put her hands together in front of her face and bowed towards Tony as a sign of respect.

"Ok, fine, I am only human after all. I admit it, I do, but if I got to know her could I trust her. I would have to be careful not to be taken for a ride. Knowing me like you do, you know I would have to be sure that she didn't just want me for my money?"

Selina and Tony stopped talking momentarily. Looking at each other with an expression of concern on their faces, and then burst into laughter.

"Tony, I think you're still a romantic at heart, there's still time for cupid's arrow to strike and who knows from which direction it will come."

Tony looked at Selina and smiled, she did not know the extent of his feelings for her because he could not bring himself to tell her. She didn't know the details of his last relationship either. What would she think of him if he told her that his ex- partner, the mother of his child, whom he had left behind in Brighton, was eight years younger than him? It was a wound he had caused in both their hearts that he was still coming to terms with.

Tony and Selina knew that there was someone else in the life of the man with the blue raincoat. Quite often, after the evening rush hour had passed, he arrived at the station with an equally attractive older lady whom they guessed was probably his wife. On these occasions, the lady looked like she was dressed to go out to the theatre or for a meal. They had seen her walk out of the exit to the station about thirty minutes earlier, then turn left and walk up the road. It did not take them too much effort to deduce from the interval of time that elapsed until she returned with the man that he did not work far away from the station.

This attractive woman was one of the nice punters, who gave them money and smiled. They imagined what might be the consequence of telling her, in no uncertain terms what a shit she had for a husband. Tony and Selina kept silent as they knew it was not their place to break her heart and spoil her illusion of happiness.

On this particular day the late afternoon brought with it intermittent showers. Selina was in good voice singing 'Big Yellow Taxi' when Tony noticed the attractive older lady come out of the tube and walk up the road in the direction from which Chalk and Cheese usually approached the station. When she passed Tony she smiled and bought a Big Issue, she gave Tony the money and did not wait to take the change she was due. Tony had the impression that for some reason she was preoccupied with her own thoughts and money was the last thing on her mind. Tony called after her but she obviously didn't hear him and continued to walk about twenty yards along the pavement on the left hand side of the road. Then she stopped abruptly, turned back, and disappeared back into the entrance of the tube station. Selina came to the end of her song and was about to start her version of the Mama's and Papa's 'Monday, Monday', when a man who looked as if he was probably in his forties, dashed across the road from the opposite side of the street and ran to the station entrance. He made his run in front of the oncoming traffic without looking to his left or right causing one cab driver to beep its horn and shout loudly at him, out of his open window; "Oi Mate! Watch where you're going! You got a fucking death wish?"

The man was quite tall wearing an old green chord jacket, Levi jeans with greying hair and designer stubble on his chin. She noticed he was carrying something in his hand. He stopped running and stood in front of Selina. She thought he looked as if he had recently been upset, because his eyes were a bit red and watery.

"You sing so beautifully, I heard you when I came past here earlier. Like all artistes we run the risk of casting our pearls before swine. You deserve to be heard, and your talent recognised. These philistines don't deserve you, they can't know, and probably don't care, what it is like to bleed for our art. Please take this, I hope you appreciate it more than the literary prick I just left, and whose soul is as black as the fucking night. Take this; it is my gift to you."

With this last statement he dropped a printed manuscript into Selina's guitar case and strode off into the station without looking back.

"Now that is not a happy man; I was ready to grab him. I thought he'd lost the plot. "C, what was that he put in the case?" Tony asked.

Selina picked the ring bound folder out of the guitar case and read the bold black writing on the cover.

"Did you hear what he said? It looks like a draft of a story entitled 'The Gardener'."

Tony nodded, "Yes poor bastard. Well I'll read it; I think we owe him that, looks like he felt he put a lot of work into it. There is that place up near the gardens, on the way to the University, I think is the office of a publisher, maybe he came from there, anyway something has upset him."

"I feel really bad for him. He looks terribly upset. Yeah we should read it. I will and maybe there's an address or e-mail inside so we could get it back to him afterwards; he needs to know that someone in this world cares about what he does. I know what it is like to put your heart on the line, only to be rejected, poor man. People who make decisions about performers or writers are often those who have never created anything themselves. What they do create is a world of pain, they have the power to build us up or knock us down. It's like they are at the door of some exclusive club and they decide who can get in or not."

Tony wasn't convinced by what Selina had said; "Yeah I see what you're saying but it's a bit different now with the internet and You Tube. Kids do become overnight internet sensations. I don't know but, he could publish online I guess, couldn't he?"

"Come on Tony, you need a publisher to make money, even if you get noticed on the internet or Amazon there are thousands of writers and singers who still won't get heard. You need someone to put some money behind them, push their work and help make the contacts."

Selina knew by the strength of her reaction to the naivety behind Tony's statement that her own feelings of rejection had been triggered. Even though she had wealth and felt she was now doing something worthwhile, she was not completely free from dream of becoming a singing celebrity even though it was fading. Selina placed the folder safely into the body of her guitar case and then rested the guitar on her thigh and got ready to play her next song.
"I don't know about that Selina. I like the idea of you doing it on your own. I remember Woody Allen said he wouldn't want to join a club that would have him as a member. Be your own person; don't trust people you don't like."

"I didn't know you liked Woody Allen. I loved 'Annie Hall'."

"I think I remember that, and to be honest that's probably the only one I liked. He's probably a bit too clever for me. I'm more a 'Bottom' man and the 'Big Yin' Billy Connelly. Don't laugh! No offence, Selina, you know what I mean."

THE GARDENER

"Yes of course I do. Billy Connelly, yes, I got my dad a couple of his
video's for Christmas. I liked his travel one's as well, where he went
places on his motorbike. He's O.K. I guess, but I prefer Ricky Gervais."

Tony made a face as if he had eaten something sour. "Oh come on, I
could never get into that office programme. Not my thing."

Selina didn't want to argue with Tony about her taste in comedy
programmes and so tried to close the conversation down. "Tony it's
like food; we all have our own taste in things. Let's just be grateful we
can laugh at something."

Tony took the hint, nodded his head and busied himself with organising
his papers.

"Selina this will cheer you up! Listen did I tell you that when I was in the
army they made us read all this stuff about infections and diseases we
could catch from having casual sex when we were on a tour of duty. I
made a decision there and then about what I had to do for the rest of my
time in the army. I know you won't believe me, knowing what you know
about men in the services, but as hard as it was I decided it was the only
safe solution. If I was at home or overseas, I knew I had to stop
reading!"
Initially Selina pretended not to be amused, and tried to keep a straight
face but quickly lost her composure and collapsed into laughter. It wasn't
often that Tony made a joke and she was attracted to this less serious side
of him. She thought he had a lovely smile.

Tony continued with his train of thought, "C, these people make us think
that what they do is important. The media make people celebrities and
fool us into wanting to do what they do but, it's not real. It sells papers
and reality T.V. shows. They won't know what's really important until
they have to survive what we've been through. It's the soldiers, the
surgeons, the doctors, the teachers and the engineers that really are the
unsung heroes of this world. It's not the popstars, the actors, and
certainly not the overpaid footballers who get obscene amounts of money
for kicking a ball about. I can't say that I didn't enjoy football once and
wanted to be a professional when I was a kid. I played for my school and
my town but what would they do if they didn't have the people to do
important things for them. When they get to feel so important, they get
all the adoration of fans, they have to be grounded, remember, they came
into this world alone and they go out the same way."

Selina could not help but think about what Tony had said and a little voice of truth within her was getting louder. She knew she should tell Tony about the real Selina and her real reason for being a busker and living as she was. She could not help but feel that perhaps now was the time to tell Tony the truth.

It was then that her dog Chip began barking and growling at the man in the blue raincoat who was standing by her guitar case looking down at the ring bound folder containing 'The Gardener' story. Without asking Selina, and with a rapid movement that obviously alarmed Chip, he bent down to pick it up. Chip bared his teeth as the dogs growling and barking increased rapidly in its intensity.

"Shut that bloody dog up, or I'll…"

The man in the blue raincoat brought his foot back as if he was going to kick Chip. The dog suddenly threw his head forward and his sharp but small teeth bit into the ankle of this stranger and as the skin of his ankle was lacerated he yelped in pain.
Breathing in short gasps, swearing under his breath and wincing in pain, the man tried to shake Chip off by quickly moving his foot back and forth.

"You little sod!" He shouted.

Managing to shake the dog free from his foot he stepped back and let fly with his other foot. This time there was a thud as he kicked Chip in the jaw. Chip yelped. The man stepped sideways and took off as quickly as his injured ankle allowed. He hopped towards the ticket barrier of the tube station. Selina, who by this time was shrieking at the man in the raincoat gradually disappearing out of sight, dropped her guitar, scooped Chip up in her arms to hold him and check he wasn't badly hurt. She could see blood dripping out of the corner of his mouth.

Tony was the next to react by shouting at the top of his voice, "Hey you, you bastard hang on a minute, hey somebody stop that man!"

He dropped his papers on the floor and set off into the tube station after the rain coated assailant who had harmed Chip. By the time Tony arrived at the ticket barrier the man had got through it and had headed towards the stairs or the lift. Tony had no ticket to get him through the turnstile entrance and so he took two steps back and vaulted over the top of it and landing on the floor the other side. He was determined to make this man pay for the shock he caused Selina and the hurt he inflicted on his friend

Chip the dog. Chip was a part of their little family. Tony set off in pursuit of the man in the blue raincoat whom he knew must use either the lift, or the stairs to get down to the platforms. Back at the entrance Selina was still trying to recover from the shock of what had happened. Looking at Chip she could see he needed his mouth bathed but she had nothing with her to do this with. Passers-by who had seen the incident came up to her and offered sympathy and one phoned the police, but her thoughts and feelings were all over the place. What was Tony going to do? Where was he? Was Chip badly injured? Did she need to leave the station to get help? She seemed frozen to the spot when suddenly a really frightening thought came into her head. What if Tony lost his temper and in a flash of anger did something to that person that was really stupid? Some action that could lead to him being arrested and punished. As bad as this incident was for her and Chip it did not warrant Tony getting into serious trouble over it.

"Would you like my handkerchief and some water?"

Selina looked up and it was a young woman in a coat with a hood bending down and offering her a bottle of water and a handkerchief to bathe Chip.

"Thank you so much it is so kind of you. Please don't miss your train."

"No I'm fine, please take these. Is there anything else I can do?"

"No, thank you, please go."

As the young woman walked into the station she realised that it was 'Cheese' of 'Chalk and Cheese', it was the girlfriend of blue raincoat man, but by the time she realised and wanted to call her back to get his real name she had gone. If Tony didn't catch the man in the station at least she could tell him that his girlfriend was kind and they could probably find the idiot who kicked Chip by asking her to identify him next time they saw her. On the one hand she hoped Tony didn't catch him because Selina was frightened of what he might do to him. The last thing he needed was to be in trouble again with the police for a violent outburst. On the other hand, she wanted retribution for the nasty man's attack on her lovely dog.

"Sorry I don't know your name but did you see her, the woman with the hood, did she go into the station?"

Selina looked up to see a younger attractive man who was well dressed, and who by the sweat on his face and the drops of perspiration dripping from his chin, had been running.

"Yes, just now, she went into the station do you know her?

"Yes, a little, I do her mum's gardening, you don't need to know that, but anyway, was she following a man, in a blue raincoat, did you see him, there was a bit of a do with him, I saw it from a distance."

Selina stood up with Chip in her arms. "That bastard kicked my dog, he tried to take that manuscript, there, in my guitar case and Chip went for him. He just ran off and Tony went after him."

"My God, I'm sorry; he can be a bit of a prick that guy. I'll see what I can do. I've got to go, sorry"

"You know him?" Selina looked surprised.

"Sorry can't stop…If I find him, I'll get back to you I promise." Steven spoke as he hesitantly walked away.

Selina watched Steven break into a run towards the ticket machines, put his ticket in the slot and in the split second while he waited for the paddles to open shouted at him; "What's the bastard's name?" But she was too late; the sweaty gardener had gone through the barrier.

Chapter Eighteen: Harvest

David decided that today would be the day of reckoning for Mark Finch.
He wanted his money back and he wanted to know from Mark exactly
when he would transfer the money into his bank account and settle his
debt. He also wanted to confront him about his secret relationship with
his lovely daughter and to warn him that if he did not stop exploiting
Jodie he could expect a thrashing. Just in case Mark got angry and
threatened him with violence, hoping to scare him off, David had
brought with him a walking stick that belonged to his mother when she
was ill. It was a sturdy weapon and one he could use efficiently. When
he was in his twenties David had attended Kendo and Jodo classes where
he learned how to fight with a big and small stick. The opponents he
faced then were much fiercer than Mark Finch could ever be. He wanted
confront Mark face to face and show him that there was another side to
his usually benign character. He had thought of calling in a favour from
one of his less savoury clients, or talk to the Milligan brothers who might
arrange an act of retribution that could be more anonymous. He knew
the Milligan's came into contact with gangsters whose 'muscle' was for
hire at a price. David knew Mark had annoyed the brothers in the past
and owed them money. He hoped they may lose patience with him and
invite someone to 'give him a slap', just enough to 'mark his card'.

Mark gambled, and when he did he was a 'chaser'. He hated losing,
particularly at roulette, and when he did he would double his bets each
time, hoping to get back the money he had previously lost. Sometimes he
was lucky and won big, but he could not walk away from the blackjack or
roulette table, even when he recouped his losses. David had witnessed
this on many occasions while on holiday with the golfers. It took a big
effort by his golfing partners to drag him away from the tables once he
had a drink inside him, especially if he had the attention of a pretty
woman. They developed a strategy of distracting him with, entertainment,
magic shows were something he particularly liked along with good food
and of course women of easy virtue. On these holidays Mark exhibited a
split personality in as much he could be the nicest, funniest person, while
getting drunk, but then he became out of control and became annoying.
They all thought he struggled with psychological demons perhaps left
over from his experience at private boarding school. He definitely had

something to prove, be it success in business or his masculinity. If you confronted him about his behaviour he became verbally abusive and sarcastic. Fortunately his golfing buddies tolerated his outbursts because none of them felt innocent enough to cast the first stone. On their last trip to Las Vegas in America David and Steven had to save him from being ejected from a Casino. Mark had won money at this blackjack table and the woman dealer encouraged him to play one more hand, obviously betting on the likelihood that he would lose his winnings.

Mark had more than enough to drink. He just managed to avoid falling down by propping himself up against the table on a stool. The very attractive dealer with her bountiful cleavage on show invited Mark to place his bet.

"Sir, are you ready to take a chance?" she asked.

"I could, if you make it worthwhile for me. Tell you what lovely lady. If I win why don't you make use of those gorgeous lips and get down under this table and give me a B.J."

"Sir, please step away from the table! We do not tolerate that kind of language here." And with that instruction she pressed the security button under her station.

David watched as within seconds two large security men grabbed Mark under his armpits, lifted him off the floor and marched across the Casino floor to the pit manager. David listened while Mark was told in no uncertain terms, that he would be banned from the tables and thrown out on his 'ass' if he did not immediately apologise to the dealer and change his attitude. David and Steven helped him walk back to the dealer and apologise, calm things down with the management, then took him upstairs to his room and locked him in.

On more than one occasion the Milligan brothers had bailed him out of a difficult situation by paying his debts on the understanding that Mark would settle what he owed once he got back to the U.K.

David estimated that Mark still owed them about five thousand pounds from their last golf excursion. Mark was a Jekyll and Hyde character who managed to keep the wild part of himself secret and separate from everyone except his golf mates. The more David thought about Mark's behaviour the angrier he became. Despite the secret Mark kept about him it was time to confront his destructive behaviour. It wouldn't surprise David if Steven's investigation discovered Mark was cheating on his lovely wife Mary by adding his own daughter to his list of conquests and broken hearts.

In order to go to Marks office David told his wife Claire he had a business lunch in London at a restaurant with his partner, solicitor and a possible investor. He hated telling lies to her but he did not want her involved in case things went wrong with his plans. To make sure he could get Mark on his own he would ask his daughter to leave the office on the pretext of getting him a coffee and a sandwich. This would give him enough time to say what he needed to say to Mark. Leaving the tube station he passed a girl busker to whom he gave money, turned left, and walked away from the station along the road towards the office of Finch and Faber. He had just crossed the road at the traffic lights on the corner of Bernard Street and Woburn Place when his mobile phone rang. He answered it hastily without bothering to look at the caller id.

"Hello David here!"

"David, hello, it's Claire, darling where are you?"

"Oh, I'm in a taxi on the way to the station, the meeting finished sooner than I thought."

"It sounds a bit loud for a taxi darling."

"Yes well I have the windows open, it is so hot in town today, so close, and I think there might be a storm coming. Anyway how are you?" David tried to shift the focus of the conversation.

"I'm not a happy bunny David, I am very worried about us and please don't lie to me anymore. I know you are not with Stuart as he is in France for the week with Elspeth, and I phoned the restaurant from the train to join you for lunch, and they told me that you did not have a reservation today. So what is going on?"

"Yes, well I was going to tell you if you had given me a chance. The meeting was cancelled at the last minute, and I met the other guys in a pub."

David took a deep breath and hoped Claire accepted his explanation.

"I don't know what you are up to, but I am in London."

"You're in London, what now?"

"Yes, I followed you up to London on the train but I lost you in the underground."

"Sweetheart, you followed me!"

"Don't get all indignant with me, you lied to me and I am not as naïve as you think!"

Claire had no intention of being bullied and letting David make out that she was persecuting him.

"I am sorry darling, I did lie to you but only to protect you, and I didn't want you to know about the problems I have been dealing with."

Claire did not like the sound of this confession from David and she felt her protective heartstrings being pulled. She breathed deeply to calm the tone of her voice.

"Why would you think I did not wish to share any problems you have, I know you think I can be a bit ditsy now, but come on David we've always been a team, and I love you. Is it the business, us, what?"

"No, no, I'll explain, let's meet, let's go to Langans, you love it there, what about in an hour, and I'll book. Where are you now?"

Claire thought quickly before answering. "I'm on my way to see Jodie, I thought she may have known why you have been acting so differently lately and I wanted to invite her out for a meal, spend some time with her, she is another one who has been a bit off colour."

David's immediate reaction was to look around to see if Claire was anywhere near him on the street, but she was nowhere in sight. It was apparent to him that he couldn't go through with his plan of confronting Mark. He would do it another day, when he had the concrete evidence that Steven was getting for him. David had an immediate problem to tackle. He didn't want to talk to Claire about his suspicions concerning Mark's behaviour if Jodie was present at the restaurant. David thought for a moment. Perhaps it was time to pay Jodie the respect of treating her as a grown woman, stop pussy footing around the issue and tell Jodie how he felt. If her mother supported him then it would be more likely for Jodie to accept his point of view and not dismiss him as an overprotective father. If he was right and Mark was upsetting her, then both he and Claire could try to make her see the affair with him was doomed.

David spoke. "Ok that's fine; you see Jodie and I will meet you both at the restaurant in about an hour. Darling I love you, and all will be explained, I promise."

David put the phone in his pocket and headed back to the tube station to get the underground to Green Park and on to Stratton Street, Mayfair.

Steven left Claire and ran as quickly as he could along the side of Russell Square towards Bernard Street. He could still see Jodie in the distance and moderated the speed of his running to a slow jog, to make sure he would not get too close, but also not lose her amongst the other pedestrians on their way to the station. Some distance away, in front of Jodie at the entrance to the station, he could see that some kind of commotion was occurring involving the busker and the Big Issue seller. From a distance he thought he saw someone in a blue raincoat step backwards, and then disappears into the entrance of the station. Moments later, he saw the tall upright man whom he had admired earlier standing next to the girl busker, leave in a hurry, also entering the station entrance.

Steven was getting very hot and sweaty running after Jodie whom he saw, pausing, and then bending down near the busker stroking her dog, before giving her something that looked like a bottle of water. By the time Steven arrived at the entrance the busker was sitting on her stool cradling her dog in her arms and Jodie was nowhere to be seen. Steven immediately asked the girl if she had seen the direction Jodie had gone.

"Sorry I don't know your name but did you see her, the woman with the hood, did she go into the station."

The busker looked up at Steven who was sweating with drops of perspiration dripping from his chin; she could probably guess he had been running.

"Yes, just now, she went into the station. Do you know her?"

"Yes, a little, I do her mum's gardening, you don't need to know that, but anyway, was she following a man, in a blue raincoat, did you see him, there was a bit of a do with him, I saw it from a distance."

The girl busker stood up, still stroking the dog cradled in her arms.

"That bastard kicked my dog, he tried to take that manuscript, there, in my guitar case and Chip went for him. He just ran off and Tony went after him."

"My God, I'm sorry; he can be a bit of a prick that guy. I'll see what I can do. I've got to go, sorry"

"You know him?"

"Sorry can't stop…"

Steven didn't want to engage in conversation as he needed to continue following Jodie and possibly Mark to their destination. He slowly walked away from her and then broke into a jog. Steven got to the ticket machine, put his ticket in the slot and waited anxiously for the paddles to open. It was then that he heard the girl shout.

"What's the bastard's name, I didn't get his name?"

Steven had no time to answer as the paddles went back and he rushed through the barrier.

Steven joined the throng of commuters flooding towards the tube train platforms but Jodie was nowhere to be seen. He made his way, as quickly as he could, to the lift that transported passengers down to the westbound Piccadilly Line. If Jodie and Mark were heading back to Marden they needed to get to Charing Cross Station. To accomplish this, they both had to take the west bound train to Leicester Square from platform two. If Steven remembered the journey correctly, they then had to change platforms and board a Northern Line tube train to their destination.

When Steven caught his first glimpse of the station lift the doors were closing. It was packed with people, all of whom were squeezed closely together, but standing near the back, in amongst the crush, he felt certain he could just see the top of Jodie's head. The hood of her coat which she had pulled up over her hair to protect her from the rain when leaving the office had slid back slightly, just enough for Steven to be able recognise her at this distance. Steven didn't think she had recognised him walking towards the lift but if she had then he would repeat the same cover story he told her mother. He could not risk wasting time waiting for the next lift and so he quickly made his way to the stairs leading down to the platforms and get to the bottom before she exited the lift. He hoped she would lead him to Mark.

Steven followed the sign directing him to the spiral staircase that wound its way down to the platforms below. If he was to catch them before they got on the train his descent of the stairs would need to be swift. This meant running and jumping down all one hundred and seventy five steps to platform two. During his rapid, reckless descent, he must also try to avoid crashing into and colliding with any poor unsuspecting commuter on the stairs. A ticket collector once told him that the sign at the entrance to the stairs was incorrect and misleading to the public because there were actually only one hundred and seventy one steps down to the platforms. This intrepid explorer had counted each step himself six times. Steven hoped that four less steps could lead to the success of his plan. With no time to lose he ran to the top of the stairs. Without an apology, or an excuse me, he pushed past a youngish grey haired man in a green jacket and jeans and launched himself down the steps of the staircase.

"Sorry! Excuse me! Sorry make way! Sorry mad person coming through, need to catch my train. Ouch! Watch out for the umbrella it has a mind of its own. Sorry must catch my escaped penguin! Make way please, life and death emergency!"

Steven hopped, stepped and slid down the steps as fast as he could, managing to avoid most people until he turned a corner and crashed into a woman coming in the opposite direction. He grabbed her coat and she grabbed his and they spun round as if they were doing a heel turn in a ballroom dance, bumping and bouncing against each other, ending up propped up against the wall facing each other. This woman was not amused.

"For heaven's sake, you fucking idiot! You could have done some serious damage. What on earth are you doing? Are you some kind of crazy lunatic?"

The woman screamed at him. She was shaking, shouting, and crying with a mixture fright and anger.

Steven recognised her voice and quickly looked at her face. Putting his arms around her he held her tightly, trying to comfort her and stop her shaking.

"Mary it's me, Steven, it's me, I'm so sorry, Steven the gardener, it's ok. Take a deep breath, try to calm down."

"Steve, what on earth are you doing? Oh Steven you…"

Mary pushed herself away from him to give herself just enough space to slap him across his face with her free hand.

Steven winced with the pain and the shock as the palm of Mary's hand smacked his left cheek.

"Ouch! That hurt, please stop, and please let me explain!" Steven grabbed her wrists to stop Mary hitting him again. "I've been up here at the University for a Lecture on oriental plants, and I am late for my train home. I thought I would get to the platform quicker if I came down the stairs as the lift was full."

"Lucky it was me you bumped into and not some other poor person."

Mary paused as she was speaking and a little grin flashed across her face. She leant towards Steven and speaking softly, so that other commuters passing them on the stairs could not hear.

"I suppose I could say we are used to 'bumping' into each other, at least, this time we have our clothes on."

Steven smiled at her and without thinking gave her a kiss on her cheek. Mary initially pulled away slightly surprised by this affectionate gesture, and then she kissed him fully on the lips.
"For Christ's sake could you two please get out of the way, get a room, do something just get out of our way!"

A large suited gentleman pushed past them.

He was followed swiftly by a young man dressed in a red anorak and carrying what looked like a travel bag and in quick succession a line of equally serious looking frustrated people filed by heading down the steps towards the Piccadilly line.

Steven and Mary separated and tried to stand on the steps one above the other, as flat against the wall of the spiral staircase as they possibly could while commuters continued their way down the stairs to the platforms.

"What are you doing in town today?" Steven asked.

"I came to surprise Mark at his office. You probably don't know, you may not have seen it as you passed by, but his office is near here. It's our anniversary, I thought I should make an effort, and so I've got tickets to 'Les Mis' tonight. I'll probably miss him now; I'd better phone his mobile. I don't know if there is a signal in here."

"Don't bother he's left." Steven replied spontaneously.

"Sorry. What? How do you know?"

"I saw him in front of me on the street, as I was running to the station, he had his raincoat on and that's how I recognised him, but he got into the station before me. He is probably on his way home by now or on the platform waiting for a train. I heard an announcement when I got here that there may be a delay with some trains."

"So much for my idea, it was a gift, a bit of an olive branch towards him." Mary looked disappointed but the frown on her face quickly disappeared.

They started to walk down the steps towards the platform. Mary held Steven's hand in hers.

"Look it's such a waste not to use the tickets. Why don't you come with me to the theatre, and afterwards we can stay in town at the hotel I have booked."

Steven was taken aback by Mary's offer, she had never shown him any real emotion or affection that was not planned and where she was in control. This was not the Mary he recognised; she was not normally a reckless person. Their relationship was purely professional and secret, if he agreed to this mad idea Mark could find out and Stevens's covert feelings for Mary would be out in the open. Steven tried to phrase his words carefully so that she would not be offended by his response. Steven stopped walking and turned to look Mary in the face.

"Mary that is a lovely offer, you are beautiful woman and in my way I love you dearly and I hate to see the way you get hurt by Mark. You really do not deserve it and he does not deserve you, but I am not what you need right now. You have to sort out things with Mark first."

"I wanted to try to get back some of what we had tonight, but I'm just playing this game, and it can only end badly for me. I need to leave him; I wish he would just be gone!"

Mary spoke these words without tears and as if; at last, she was resigned to a future that did not include Mark. She looked at Steven, hugged him, and gave him an affectionate kiss on the cheek, "I think I will go home and tell him tonight, but did you say you saw him here?"

Steven made a quick decision not to tell Mary about the incident with the dog and the busker.

"Err, yes I'm pretty sure he came into the station before I reached the entrance, he was in his raincoat, the blue one. He should be on platform two by now, he should have been on his way to Leicester Square by now, but like I said, there was some hold up at the previous station and the tube train could be delayed. He could still be waiting on the platform."

"Let's hurry then, don't put off till tomorrow what you can do today, some fucking wise person must have said. Come on, why not strike while my irons in the fire, or something like that. I've got to tell him while I have the strength to do it. Come on Steven, platform two!"

Steven had never heard Mary swear as much as she had just done in all of the time they had been together. It was true that they hardly ever spoke before or after having sex, and he did not know how he felt about this new aspect of her character, perhaps it went with her new found determination to confront Mark. Mary strode off in front of him in the direction of platform two and Steven hurried to catch up.

When they got to the platform there was a crowd of passengers standing squeezed together like sardines in a tin, breathing hot stale air. Steven and Mary inched their way forward pushing past students with rucksacks, men in suits carrying briefcases, tourists with long handled trolley cases scraping their legs as they moved forward. Other commuters were oblivious to the crowd surrounding them because they had their heads down, reading their mobile ,listening to music with earphones plugged in, their faces illuminated by the screen of their digital device.

Mary, who was shorter in height than Steven, jumped into the air to survey the waiting commuters, hoping to spot Mark. She didn't spot Mark but instead she identified the profile of Jodie, her husband's P.A. She was some distance away, slowly working her way through the crowd to the edge of the platform. Steven also spotted Jodie at roughly the same time as his companion, and because of his height advantage he could see the direction Jodie seemed to be heading. Following her line of sight he thought he caught a glimpse of the turned up collar of a blue raincoat and the back of Mark Finch's head. To his surprise, but he couldn't be certain, he thought he also caught a glimpse of David, Claire's husband whom he had seen earlier. If it was him in his pin striped suit, he didn't look comfortable as he was wedged between a large woman in a hat, and a poster of "Mama Mia" stuck on the station wall.

"He's straight ahead Mary, waiting right by the edge of the platform, but the queue behind him is about ten deep. This way, follow me!"

Steven pressed on through the tightly packed commuters towards the place where Mark was standing. Mary followed close behind holding on to the back of Stevens's jacket. There was no point in Steven shouting to try to get Mark's attention as he wouldn't be heard above the announcement playing over the speaker system telling of the imminent arrival of the train. The level of noise on the platform increased due to the sound of the train approaching the station through the tunnel and the rush of wind that preceded it. Steven would keep the element of surprise. He looked forward to seeing the shock on Mark's face when he tapped him on his shoulder.

Chapter Nineteen: The Platform

Tony vaulted the ticket barrier to follow the man in the blue raincoat who had kicked and wounded Chip. He could see him amongst a group of commuters in front of him, limping towards the lift.

"Hey you, you with the limp, just you wait a minute, I have something to say to you. Come back here! Face up to what you did!"

Tony shouted as loud as he could to get the attention of Chips assailant while at the same time running after him as quickly as he could, dodging people in his path. He was so focused on chasing his prey that he didn't see what was coming.

"Just you hang on. Slow down! Stop there Matey!"

A uniformed arm appeared from nowhere and grabbed him on his shoulder, then, before he had time to escape or resist, his right arm was forced upward behind his back in an arm lock. The weight of his captor was thrown against his right side in a downward motion and the resulting pain from the pressure on his elbow made Tony slide to the floor.

"Hold on, my friend. Just you slow down, can't have you scaring the other people now can we?"

Tony tried to struggle as he laid there with his cheek pressed against the tiled floor, but he was held in a vice like grip.

"What the fuck are you doing? Get off me; I've done nothing wrong! I'm after the bastard who kicked my friend's dog!"

His captor spoke in a calm but firm voice. From years in the army Tony could tell it was a voice of authority.

"Now, now, language like that won't make things any easier for you. Calm down."

The radio on the uniformed man's shoulder burst into life, "Are you there? Copy, over."

"Yes I'm here; cancel the assistance, all under control, over and out!"

Tony knew he needed to say something to get this uniformed officer on his side.

"Look mate, I'm no trouble, I'm trying to get the bad guy and me stuck here means he's getting away!"

Tony felt his captors grip loosen a little.

"Firstly I'm not your mate, and we had a report of some altercation, and someone jumping the barrier. That looks like you."
"I used to work on the 'Coms' for the police down south. I know this looks odd, but I am not the bad guy here; if I don't catch that bastard he's gone!"

Tony realised that the person who brought him to the ground was a transport policeman and a big one at that. He felt the weight of the officer lift off his side as the policeman shifted his position but kept him in an arm lock.

"Right, I am going to let you up, stay still until I say so, so no funny business and I may not arrest you."

The policeman at first eased his grip on Tony's arm, then he fully let go and stood up, leaving Tony lying on the floor.

"Get up now."

Tony got to his knees and then stood erect facing the policeman. By his insignia Tony could tell he was a sergeant in the force and he estimated he was nearly six foot tall with about a forty five inch waste. His other distinguishing feature was a large handlebar moustache. The policeman stared straight into Tony's eyes as if he was trying to read his mind and then he spoke.

"You look to me as if you were in the forces like me. You're wearing an ex-army coat, you have a military bearing, and your boots are as clean as mine."

"Yes sir and you are a bit of a Sherlock Holmes." Tony replied.

The police sergeant continued speaking, "We had a report of an incident at the entrance to the station and I got here to see you running like a lunatic."

"Yes, I can see how it may have looked Sergeant, but the victim here is the busker, Selina and her dog. They are still there at the entrance, she can verify my story. I am after the idiot who did it then ran into the station. I need to go after him. Come with me and we can catch him."

The policeman could see that Tony had genuine concerns and this impression went in his favour. The policeman prided himself in being a good judge of character. This ex-soldier who may have fallen on hard times did not strike him as a man who was lying. He answered Tony immediately.

"Ok son, you take the stairs and I'll take the lift. Do nothing until I arrive, do not take the law into your own hands; just keep him in your sights. Don't let me down!"

Tony turned away from the policeman and headed for the one hundred and seventy one steps that would take him down to the Piccadilly line and platform two. The Sergeant made his way to the lift, hoping he had made the right decision by trusting an ex-soldier who was down on his luck.

Tony wasted no time getting down the steps of the spiral staircase; he was a man with a mission. He got to the bottom of the steps level with the platform before the Sergeant set foot out of the lift. He felt an excitement he had not experienced since being undercover in Ireland following rebel paramilitaries. Tony made his way slowly to the back of the platform, staying behind other passengers, and making sure he could stalk his prey without being seen. It wasn't long before he spotted the man in the blue raincoat. He definitely recognised him as one of the pair he and Selina nicknamed, 'Chalk' and 'Cheese'.

The train to Leicester Square had been delayed and the platform had filled up with extra passengers waiting for the next service to arrive. Tony walked slowly along a narrow gap behind the waiting people, keeping as close as he could to the station wall, until he got to about fifteen feet away from the man he would dearly like to punch. Despite his compulsion to punish this callous idiot Tony followed the instruction he'd been given by the policeman. His job was to watch and wait until the law could arrest him. From his vantage point he could see that 'Blue' was white faced, perspiring profusely and looked in pain. Tony thought he was probably bleeding from the bite that Chip had inflicted. Looking to his left he noticed the attractive young woman who was the other half of this romantic couple, slowly threading her way through the crowd towards her lover, the man in the blue raincoat. Tony didn't think she looked happy. He wondered if they had argued and perhaps it had tipped 'lover boy' over the edge. She looked stern and determined, as if she had some unfinished business to attend to.

Tony turned his head to the left to see further along the westbound platform towards the entrances. At last he recognised the top of the police sergeant's 'custodian' helmet at the back of the crowd of commuters heading in his direction as fast as he could. Tony raised one arm, turning his hand and pointing his finger towards where their target stood. A little distance in front of the policeman there was an attractive elder woman jumping up and down looking for someone or something on the platform near where he was standing. Next to her stood a man with a shaven head and tanned skin. Tony immediately classified him as someone who worked outside for a living or perhaps had recently returned from a holiday abroad in a place with a hot climate. They both seemed interested in finding a person on the platform quite near to where he was standing.

 Suddenly, they seemed to recognise someone and set off weaving their way through the narrow gaps, around and between, the tightly packed bodies of the commuters in front of them. To their right and near the station wall an older man in a pinstriped suit, carrying a walking stick, seemed to recognise one of this pair and began to raise his hand to gain their attention, only to quickly change his mind and duck down behind the large lady standing in front of him.

Tony managed to get the attention of the police sergeant and pointed in the direction of the man in the blue raincoat standing on the edge of the platform. If he moved quickly he could apprehend him before the next train arrived. Tony wouldn't openly admit it to the policeman, but he hoped that if 'chip's' abuser struggled while he was being arrested it would give Tony a chance to get involved. If so, he might take the opportunity to stand on the perpetrators injured foot.

"This is for Chip." He would whisper in his ear.

There was a rush of air and a sudden increase in noise level in the tunnel as the tube train approached the station at speed. The young attractive woman wearing the coat with a hood was close by and nearly in front of him now. Her eyes were fixed on her blue rain coated man friend standing three rows of people away from her, dangerously close to the edge of the platform. Tony saw her mouth move as if she was shouting words in his direction but the noise on the platform made it impossible for her voice to be heard. The shaven headed younger man with the older woman holding on to the back of his jacket had managed to force their way through the closely packed commuters to within three or four rows of people behind, and just to the side, of the young woman. Behind them, catching up fast, Tony spotted the police sergeant sweating heavily from the physical exertion of the chase and amplified by the weight he carried round his waist. Despite his outer appearance Tony had no doubt that this policeman was able and ready to pounce on the dog abuser whom he now had clearly in his sight.

The train sped out of the tunnel entering the station at the end of the platform furthest away from where Mark was standing. Focused on his prey the police sergeant rushed forward, barging a commuter standing in front of him out of his way, but in his haste he did not see the pull out handle of a trolley bag, jutting out at knee level in front of him. The bag belonged to a Japanese tourist desperate to catch the train approaching the platform. It was at that exact moment in time that he decided to make a dash for a space on the platform where he thought the carriage doors might open. He knew from his previous journeys at peak times on the London underground that it was a dog eat dog world when it came to getting a seat in the carriage of a tube train. You needed to be at the front of the crowd, the moment the doors opened. This was his chance and he took it. What the Japanese tourist had not understood from the recently broadcast platform announcement was that; due to a problem further up the line, and a delay in the service, this particular train was a through train, and would not stop at this station.

The large, bulky policeman, tripped up, plunging forward with his arms outstretched in front of him in a vain attempt to break his fall. He fell forward with the force of a large sack of potatoes swinging through the air, colliding into the woman hanging onto the coat of the tanned shaven headed man, knocking her over. Tony watched this scene unfolding in front of him in what seemed like slow motion. The people toppled over like a line of dominoes falling into each other. He moved forward as quickly as he could while at the same time shouting loudly,

"Watch out!"

Tony attempted to stop the shaven headed man falling to the ground by getting in front of him hoping to cushion his fall. He was too late. The man fell forward crashing into his chest, knocking the air out of his lungs and propelling Tony backwards. A split second before this happened; the person behind Tony had stepped aside and bent down to the floor to retrieve a copy of the big issue that she had slipped from her grasp. Tony was thrown backwards colliding into the attractive young woman who now stood behind him. She was the young woman wearing a hooded coat; the person that he and Selina had called 'Cheese', the young lover of the man who had kicked 'Chip'. The sudden impact of Tony crashing into her, just as she was about to get the attention of the man in the blue raincoat, took her by surprise and shoved her forward. Instinctively, her arms reached out in front of her to break her fall.

Unaware of what was happening behind him, Mark Finch, the man in the blue raincoat, leant forward slightly, in the hope of getting a better view of the incoming train. He felt sick and was desperate to sit down. He felt light headed, almost feverish, his shirt was damp with sweat and it made him wonder if he had an infection from the dog bite. If the carriages on this train were full of passengers then he had a better chance of getting a seat on the next, at least as far as Leicester Square.

Suddenly and without warning, he felt a strong push in his back from someone or something behind him. Jolted forward, he lost his balance and fell straight into the path of the oncoming train.

Chapter Twenty: Darkness and Light

Selina sat on her bed in the bedroom of her small flat. Propped up by pillows and with a blanket over her shoulders she turned the pages of the manuscript resting in her lap.

The Gardener: Chapter Six

Inspector Bob Kane and D.C. Lavender had visited four garden centres so far but with no success. No suspicious characters and no hint of garlic found on anyone.

While he sat in the car being chauffeured by Lavender he had time to reflect on why he became a policeman and the mind set of someone like, 'The Gardener'. Bob Kane had come to understand that in the terrible things that one human could do to another that there was a line that when crossed meant that you were damned, with no hope of forgiveness or retribution. There was no going back, and in the taking of a life you had no power to give that life back, to turn back the page, or press the rewind button on the remote control of life. Once you crossed that line you were damned but in a curious twist of fate you were also set free. He knew enough about himself to realise that although he became a policeman to protect the weak and the innocent from harm and exploitation and to make society a safer and fairer place, he had a sneaking admiration for some criminals. He knew he was a conformist and adapted to societies rules on the outside but inside there was a part of him that would love to say "fuck the Law", and do what he wanted to do, take what he wanted to take and put a finger up to convention. There was a part of him that admired the kids he went to school with who were not scared of the teachers, didn't do homework, and bunked off school. He was a prefect at school who had responsibility, and the trust of the teachers, but there was a part of him that wanted to be with the bad kids hanging out near the bike sheds, smoking and messing about with the 'naughty' fifth year girls.

Bob Kane came to realise that it was this shadow side to his personality that probably led him to become a policeman in the first place. By spending his time catching criminals and therefore being in amongst the underworld, he could live his life next to crime and criminals without actually doing the crimes or becoming a criminal. In effect he could be a vicarious criminal. He had to admit to himself that he existed as a slightly deviant and shady tree in a forest of criminals. Bob Kane wondered if this was the same process that authors of crime novels went through. They had the opportunity to work through their own attraction to criminality in the novels they wrote. Do the things that they feared to do in their real life. It was this complex in his personality that probably made him less tolerant of law breakers and much tougher in his attitudes to the criminals he caught when he first joined the force. He prided himself in being mellower now and able to tolerate some grey areas amongst the black and white compass of his morality. However his strong reaction to Sophie being kidnapped surprised him. He felt hate for her attacker and at the same time, the swell of an unfamiliar emotion which he reluctantly identified as love for Sophie. He wanted to be in a room alone with this low life and smash them in the head with something hard.

Searching for Sophie in this way was like searching for a needle in a haystack, desperate and random, but Bob Kane needed to do something to feel useful and to save Sophie from a nasty fate. The Superintendent got back to him as quickly as he could and informed him that the stores would play ball, and 'The Gardener's' demands would be met if the person had not been apprehended before the deadline.

"Sir, if you don't mind me saying so, this is a waste of time. This place just sells plants and chickens eggs and not much else. It doesn't look like there is anyone here."

"Ok Lavender, park the car here out of sight and we will walk the rest of the way up this track. You are a man of little faith Lavender. Did you see the small painted sign at the entrance that said, 'Fresh garlic for sale'? Wind down your window Lavender and take a deep breath."

D.C. Lavender did as he was told, "Jesus, what is that?"

Bob Kane smiled with a smug sense of satisfaction. "That my friend is the smell of Garlic in its many forms. Have you ever been to the Isle of White? I used to rent a cottage there for a holiday near Newchurch. They grow a lot of garlic on the Isle of White and they have a garlic festival there. You should try garlic ice-cream, lovely stuff."

"Thanks Sir but I think I will pass on that one."

Inspector Kane and Lavender got out of the car and shutting the doors as quietly as they could and walked further up the tarmac track towards what looked like a small farm shop in the distance advertising the sale of flowers plants shrubs, tomatoes, garlic and free range eggs.

"Lavender, you go into the shop and see what you can find out. I'm going to wander up behind those green houses and see if I can find another building."

"Ok. Sir, be careful."

"By the way lavender, turn your radio off, don't want it to let anyone know you're coming."

"But Sir, what if…" Lavender looked concerned.

"Do what I say." Kane insisted. He then disappeared along the dirt track behind a set of glass green houses.

Bob Kane was looking for a building of some kind that was remote enough and big enough to keep and torture a captive without their screams being heard and where they were unlikely to be found by any other workers, or passing walkers. After he had looked in about ten greenhouses full of plants and vegetation, as well as a couple of large sheds that housing tools of the trade, he came to an area paved in concrete .A tractor and a Land Rover had been parked there. He stood perfectly still and listened. Behind the vehicles stood a large building made of corrugated iron with a small wooden door that looked like it had a padlock fixed to the outside. Bob Kane did not want to speak into his radio in case anyone might hear, and he felt sure that Lavender would soon come looking for him. He stayed silent and waited, listening for any tell-tale sound of another person present. Then he heard it, a muffled knocking, and a something that sounded like someone humming quite loudly. He stealthily made his way first to the cover of the tractor and then the Land Rover. Each time he got closer to the building the noise of the knocking and humming increased. Kane paused for breath and scoured the area behind him for any signs of life, and there were none. He could not believe his luck, he was alone. He needed to use something to break the lock off the door or at least prise the lock open. Leaning against the wall of the iron building was a spade but he thought that if he used it to break the lock it would make too much noise. He made his way to the four by four and tried the passenger door which to his surprise opened. On the seat was a bar of metal which he soon realised was a tyre wrench. He picked up the wrench, left the door open and returned to the door with the padlock on it. His breathing was heavy and the sweat was pouring down his face and the back of his neck, he loosened his tie and undid his collar buttons. He stayed still and listened for any sound other than the one coming from inside the large shed and the sound of his own heart beating in his chest. Nothing! Where was Lavender? He felt certain that he should have followed him here by now.

Kane could wait no longer. He slid the bar into the ring of the padlock and wedged the end against the door. Then with as much strength as he could muster he pulled back on the lever. The wood splintered, the lock was prised open and the door swung free. Without hesitation, with the tyre lever in his grasp Bob Kane ran through the door, ready to fight any attacker who was ready to pounce on him.
No one was there and the shed, which was like a small hanger, was empty. The noise he heard on the outside was coming from somewhere over to the right of the building and it seemed to be at floor level. Bob ran over to where the sound seemed loudest and found what looked like a mettle trap door in the floor secured by a sliding bolt. He knelt down and slid the bolt open then slowly lifted the door upwards to reveal metal steps going down into the darkness. The sound was much louder now and he could distinguish the sound of a voice that was probably coming from someone who had been gagged.

"Sophie is that you? It's Bob, hold on I'm coming down."

Bob Kane wished he had a torch, or could find a light switch. He lowered himself onto the second step of the metal staircase and gradually stepped downwards, his eyes adjusting to the dark. Below was a large room with concrete walls. A chair was placed in the middle of the room with a bucket nearby. Bob could just make out dark stains on the floor and when he got to the bottom of the steps he saw a coat rack in front of him with wellingtons at the bottom, rubber trousers and a coat hanging from the pegs. In the corner of the room stood a large metal cupboard, which was also locked with a padlock and it was from this cupboard that the sounds emanated. Bob Kane strode over to the cupboard put the metal bar through the gap in the padlock and twisted. The cupboard doors flew open and there, bound and gagged and kneeling in front of him, was P.C. Sophie Tennyson. Inspector Kane pulled off her gag and tried to help her to her feet but she was too weak and so let her down gently, picked up the chair from the middle of the room and brought it over so that she could sit down. He began untying her hands and feet.

"Get out Sir, please get out, don't let him find you here, please go!" Sophie cried out with what sounded like a mixture of terror and tears.

"It's ok Sophie, Lavender's here as well, now that we've found you, I'll radio for help."

Almost before Bob Kane had stopped speaking something landed with a thump on the floor at the bottom of the steps. Both Bob and Sophie turned to look in the direction of the mettle steps. There, spread-eagled on the hard concrete floor, with blood oozing from a red slice in his throat and a bloody gash in the back of his head lay the lifeless body of D.C. Lavender.

The large metal door slammed shut and the bolt slid into place, startling the both of them. They were enveloped in darkness, trapped in the blackness of a concrete tomb.

Then from above the door their captor spoke, "I would say you are both in grave danger. I should call the police, but then again you are the police. A noble but foolish gesture, coming here Mr Kane, perhaps you need time to realise the gravity of your situation. I'm afraid I must leave you with your dear dead detective colleague. I suggest you claw your way out of there before the fruit gets over ripe. The womb is a tomb if you stay too long!"
Then all went silent......

The opening chords of Beethoven's Fifth Symphony blared out from the mobile phone on the table next to Selina's bed. It played the ring tone and vibrated at the same time, doing a little sliding dance across the table's surface. Selina put the manuscript of 'The Gardener' down on the surface of the duvet next to Chip, careful not to disturb his sleep. Then, as quickly as she could, she picked up the phone and pressed the receive button.

"Selina, it's me Tony, I'm calling from the police station they let me use their phone."

"Tony, how are you? They didn't arrest you did they, I told them what happened, I gave a statement and told them how lovely you are."

"No, no. it's ok, I'm fine. I told them everything and so did the police sergeant. His name is George by the way, honourable man, but a bit embarrassed by what happened. They are letting us go now because they have watched the CCTV from the platform. It was chaos, but I know who the others are now."

"What's his name then, and hers- 'Chalk' and 'Cheese'?"

"Well the bloke that died is called Mark Finch, and the woman we saw him with, her name is Jodie. He's quite a big wig publisher and she works for him. The bloke I tried to save, well his name is Steven and he is a gardener. The sad bit is that the woman with him is the dead man's wife. They all live down in Kent some place called Marden. I spoke to Steve. Nice bloke. He asked me if I had any gardening skills and had I been to Kent. He was really shaken. Anyway, how are you and Chip?"

"We're fine; he's asleep on the bed. His mouth and jaw seem ok; he had something to eat out of his bowl."

Selina looked at the bedside clock, one thirty; she had lost her sense of time once she began to read the story. She was exhausted when she got home from the station. She fed her dog, undressed and got straight into bed, but she could not sleep adrenalin in her body caused by the events of the day kept her awake. That was when she picked up 'The Gardener' to read.

"What about you? Did they treat you ok? Was your boss ok with it? I hope you haven't lost your job, I'd hate to think it will change us?"

"Don't worry about that, we are a team and I am still your best audience. I can't let that go to waste." Tony laughed.

Selina paused and waited for Tony to speak.

"They were gold fish by the way. I was thinking about that game we played, while I was waiting to be questioned. Anthony and Cleopatra were fish and they suffocated. Selina, please tell me tell me I'm right, it drove me mad."

"Yes they were fish, the wind blew the shutters and it knocked over the glass bowl. You don't have to worry about that any more, and you are a true detective as well as a saviour."

Selina laughed quietly and gently, she wanted Tony to feel that she was laughing with him and not at him.

There was a brief silence before Tony spoke again. "I really do care about you Selina, I know we are a few years apart but I…"

Selina interrupted him, "Look, there is something about me I need to tell you, I'll see you tomorrow at the station. I couldn't get to sleep and so I've been reading the manuscript that the guy in the green jacket dropped into my case, scary!"

"Ok, I wonder if he knew the dead man... Selina I need to tell you something about me as well. See you tomorrow; they want me to get off the phone, so I've got to go now. Take care, hope you sleep well.......love you."

"Love....."

The phone line went dead; she had been cut off from speaking to Tony before she could finish what she was saying. Selina switched off the bedside lamp, leaned back, rested her head against her comfortable pillows, closed her eyes, took in a deep breath and let it out slowly, feeling the air pass over her lips.

She listened to the sound of Chip, snoring contentedly, and drifted off to sleep.

Chapter Twenty One: The Therapist

In Ladbroke Grove Nigel met his new client in the reception area of his psychotherapy practice. He led her to his consulting room where she sat down in the comfortable arm chair facing him.

"I understand that someone you met recommended me to you. I don't know if you've been in therapy before but first I need to tell you that anything we say here will be held in confidence. If I feel I need to contact anyone else regarding your safety or your treatment I will tell you. Our sessions will last for one hour at the same time each week until you decide that you no longer wish to attend. If for any reason you cancel without giving me five days' notice, you will have to pay for the missed session. I need to get that out of the way. Would you like to ask me anything about that?

The young woman, who sat upright in her chair listening, shook her head from side to side.

Nigel continued speaking," So, please begin by telling me what has brought you here today?"

"Well, I met someone who knows of you and said that you were very good with people who had suffered trauma; we met in rather unusual circumstances. I tried to cope on my own but it's become too difficult. I don't feel that it is right to burden anyone else in my immediate circle, and so here I am."
Nigel could see his client was agitated. She had crossed her legs and as she spoke, the foot that rested on the floor in a fashionable high heeled shoe was habitually moving up and down.

"….I can't stop thinking that it could have been me! He saved my life in a way. He was in front of me when he fell forward into the train instead of me. I am such a terrible person. I loved him so much, but I hated him too. I was so angry with him that day. I went after him. I wanted to have it out with him, but instead I killed him!"

As she blurted out this last phrase, she lost her composure and began to sob deeply, her chest heaving in and out with each painful sigh.

Nigel waited, he didn't intervene. He did not try to comfort her or distract her from her obvious hurt, he gave her space. Jodie was alone with her grief. She was in touch with the pain she was feeling. She reached out and grabbed some tissues from the box on the small table by her chair and wiped her nose, then dabbed her eyes and mascara stained cheeks.

"I am sorry; I tried not to do that. I imagine I am not the first to have lost control here. I guess these tissues have heard quite a few peoples' pain and sadness. You'll probably need a bigger box if I keep coming here!"

Nigel allowed himself to smile briefly; hoping that Jodie would feel reassured that he was not fazed by her show of emotion. He did not want her to feel embarrassed by her loss of composure.

"Yes, I do wonder about the tissues being so obvious, I don't want to give you the impression that everyone who comes here either cries or ends up with a cold and runny nose!"

Jodie smiled at Nigel's attempt at a joke.

"No that's fine I usually carry tissues in my bag but for some reason I forgot them today."

Nigel's curiosity was aroused by what he had heard, and so against his better judgement he decided to ask Jodie a question.

"I would like you to clarify two things from what you have said. You seem to have accepted responsibility for what happened; you said 'I killed him'. Then, almost in the same breath I heard you say that you both loved and hated this person, would you say more about that please?"

Jodie blew her nose and dropped the tissue into the small waste paper bin by her chair. She took a deep breath and fixing her eyes on a picture on the wall behind where Nigel was sitting she answered.
"You may have read about this incident in the paper. The man who fell in front of a train at Russell Square tube station? He was both my boss and my boyfriend. We were having a secret relationship. He was married, and he knew my father because he played golf with him at a club near where we live. It was my Dad who got me the job with Mark."
Jodie started to cry.

"I'm a terrible person! You must think of me as some kind of 'slut'. I had met his wife, and it was their anniversary. I loved him so much. I wanted to have his baby but he wouldn't leave his wife. I am so stupid. I let my father and my mother down."

The tears flowed down Jodie's cheeks and her makeup began to run. She picked up the box of tissues from the table and placed them on her lap, pulled two tissues from the box and wiped her cheeks.
Nigel waited a minute to gather his thoughts before speaking.

"I did read something about this in the paper. From what I remember the Police described it as a 'tragic accident', but obviously you still feel responsible. Before we go on, I must share something with you because I want to be transparent with you. I have heard a version of this incident from the person who must have recommended me to you. I assume that it was this person whom you met at the police station. I understand that you were both interviewed by the police, and then, after looking at the evidence from the CCTV cameras from the platform where the accident occurred, no charges were brought against you. I must ask you, have you spoken to this person since you left the police station?"
Nigel watched Jodie's face intently to gauge her reaction to his question. Jodie looked surprised. It was as if she hadn't considered the possibility that the person who fell into her on the platform would talk about this with his therapist.
Jodie wasted no time in replying,

"No, no, I can assure you that I have had no contact with this man since. His name is Tony, he was very kind. He worked outside the station and I had seen him and his friend, and their dog many times. His friend has a lovely voice. He apologised so much for losing his balance. It wasn't his fault. He told me how he and a policeman were chasing Mark, that's my man friend, the person I loved, because he had hurt their dog. I don't know why he would do such a thing. I'm finding out so much about him that I didn't know. I don't want to get Tony into trouble."

Nigel believed that Jodie was being truthful. Her narrative matched that given by Tony in a previous session. Nigel decided to explain his dilemma to Jodie,

"Jodie in my work I try to keep a degree of separation between the clients. Boundaries are important to keep the work safe and confidential. I appreciate the fact that he recommended me and wanted to help someone in distress, but unfortunately I didn't know that before you arrived. I don't see people who know each other, unless I see them as a couple. I need to be assured that you will have no further contact with Tony. If that is the case then we can continue. If not then this session will have to be our last."

Jodie felt as if she had been told off by a teacher at school for something she had unknowingly done wrong, and yet would be punished for. She felt too exhausted to argue her case, or be angry with Nigel.

"I'm really sorry. It is my fault again. I'm so stupid, I should have thought about this before I made the appointment with the receptionist. I'm just so desperate. I can't sleep without dreaming of him disappearing in front of the train, and I'm falling over and over again. I can't get it out of my head unless I'm drunk or take a sleeping tablet."

Nigel repeated his previous statement.

"Are you certain that you will have no further contact with Tony in any form?"

Jodie was quick to answer.

"I won't. I live in Kent and I don't know where he lives, and apart from passing him at the station, if he still stands there, I won't say anything. I promise."

Despite being annoyed that Tony had put him in this position, Nigel felt reassured that neither Jodie nor Tony would step over the boundaries he had set.

"That's settled then, and as far as I am concerned we can continue. If that is still what you want?"

Jodie sat back in her chair resting her head against its high back and felt the tension in her chest subside and tears of relief filled her eyes.

"Yes, thank you, I do."

Nigel sat silently waiting to give an appropriate space before continuing their dialogue. After what seemed like an eternity to Jodie, Nigel resumed their conversation.

"So you felt in some way responsible for this happening to ….Mark, your emotions were confused on that day, when you went to the platform, and perhaps before?"

"He could be so romantic and so charming that I felt grateful that he showed me so much attention. He was older, more sophisticated, more experienced, and he wanted me. My father, whom I adore, got me the job at his firm through his friendship at the golf club. For some reason he wasn't keen for me to go there at first, but the timing was right, and my dad gave in. I loved the job and as I said, eventually loved him. I'm such a... slut. I knew his wife Mary. I guessed she was unhappy but in my self-absorbed way I thought it was because she could no longer please him like I could. Do you know I think of myself as a feminist, but in truth the notion of sisterhood goes out of the window when there's a man involved."

Nigel wondered if Mark was having a mid-life crisis and unconsciously doing what a surprising number of his male clients seemed to do; fall for a younger woman that reminded them of their wives at the time they first met. Nigel framed his hunch in the form of a question.

"When you looked at her, Mark's wife, did you see an older version of you? Do you think that in any way, he saw you as a younger version of her? Perhaps the person he fell in love with?"

Jodie stopped talking to think for a while before answering.

"I never thought of her as young, before she had children and became his wife. I know she was bored and fragile when I met her, because she got drunk at an office party. I think she worried that he might stray, and perhaps she saw me as competition."

"How about you, did you worry about the same thing?" Nigel asked.

"Truthfully, I thought I tired him out. I was arrogant enough to think that he didn't have the energy for anyone else. I know now, my body was in his arms, but my head was in the clouds."

"How was that?" Nigel asked.

Jodie replied with tears beginning to form at the corner of her eyes.

"My feelings were so strong, so self-centred; I guess I lost touch with reality. I didn't give a thought to the other people in his life that we were hurting. He died in the week of their anniversary. I know from my father that Mary, that's his wife's name, was traumatised when she was told of his death. She was on the way to London to see a musical with him. His children will be devastated to lose their father in such a terrible way... I am such a shit person! All the time I was doing this with him I never gave them a thought. They were away at school. I only remember thinking it proved he was fertile, and that made him even more attractive to me. I must have been so delusional and crazy. My father has told me that our gardener, Steven, is being very supportive in her grief and giving her some comfort. She seems to be coping OK. Steven knows my father and Mark through the golf club and he does our garden as well. My father doesn't know about us, me and Mark. He won't understand why I'm so upset. I mean, he does because of what happened on the platform, but not the rest."

Jodie fell silent and Nigel could guess from the direction her eyes were looking that she was visualising a place, scene or interaction from her past.
Nigel interrupted her reverie.

"What you tell me it seems that there were times in your intense emotional and physical relationship with Mark that you lost touch with reality. There is a theory that this love that infects us all, this feeling we have, is quite a primitive one. It emerges from our unconscious after puberty, where it has been sitting and waiting to tap us on the shoulder since we were very young. The last time we, as babies, experienced this merged relationship with our mother. No distance between her and us, no forced separation. It's a memory of being as if we were one with another. This innocent part of us longs to go back there again. We want this so much, that when we find someone onto whom we can project this wish, and they respond appropriately, we experience this feeling we call love and from that moment we are blind to their faults. We don't see them for who they actually are but what we want them to be. They are like us, a part of us and we are the sole focus of their attention. We are prepared to do unusual, out of character things, to protect that feeling. Mark loved your attention, as you loved his, but for some people, who didn't get enough of this when they were young, their hunger to be special needs constant feeding. Their ego needs constant stroking, and they have to find new sources of food."

Nigel could see from Jodie's facial reaction and the way she turned her body away from him, sitting in her chair, that she did not like Nigel's comments.

"Are you saying that I was not enough for him? That when I no longer excited him he would find someone else? Or are you implying that he was always on the lookout for the next young woman to sleep with. To massage his ego and anything else he wanted?"

Nigel could hear the hurt in Jodie's voice. The supervisor part of his therapeutic mind was about to smack him on the wrist for being so bold in his intervention. Perhaps it was too soon, too elaborate, too challenging, and simply a mistake, to share this observation with Jodie at this time.

"I wondered if you had any intuition, any sign that Mark might be like this. It's only a hunch."

The room fell silent. Jodie avoided Nigel's gaze and took another tissue from the box and blew her nose. Her mind was racing and her stomach was turning over. She hoped Nigel could not hear it rumbling as she had not eaten since breakfast.

"Have you got a glass of water I could have please?" Jodie asked.

Nigel got out of his chair and went to the small sink in the corner of the room where he filled a glass with water from the tap and placed it on the table within her reach. Jodie picked it up and took several sips of water from the glass before placing it back on the table. Jodie did not know how it was that this therapist, who had never met Mark, could make this insight into his character when she, who had literally been glued to Mark in the heat of passion, was so blind.

"Towards the end of our relationship I became more demanding and he would make excuses to limit our liaisons. He could always go away with his golf buddies. I wanted a commitment from him."

Jodie began to pick at the skin on the corner of her forefinger on her left hand with the manicured thumbnail of the thumb on her right hand. She looked down at her hands in her lap and continued speaking.

"When the death happened, the commotion on the platform was such that the commuters left the platform very quickly. The big Policeman who was there shouted as loud as he could to get the people to stop moving, but it was no use. He managed to stop about fifteen people from leaving the platform. The police were only interested in those of us who were in close proximity to Mark when he fell in front of the train. I didn't recognise any of them except for Tony. They took us to the police station, took our statements and questioned us. Eventually they told us that they would look at the video to check our stories. We waited, and that was when Tony gave me your card because I was so distraught. He was so apologetic, because he felt that he was partly to blame for what happened. He knocked me over. I mean I was the one who collided with Mark...... I feel I should be crying now, but I feel all cried out. Is that weird? Anyway she let me stroke her dog and that calmed me down a bit. My parents turned up. I had phoned my mother as soon as I was allowed. My father was in town anyway, for some meeting. Eventually I was allowed to go home with them. I just wanted to sleep. I was so exhausted. I woke up early the next day. It hit me that I needed to go to the office and so I left a note and got the train into London. I wanted to get to the office and touch things that he had touched, breathe the air that we both shared. I know it's odd, but that's how I felt. I knew there would be e-mails and post that I had to deal with. I also wanted to speak to his partner in the firm and tell him what had happened from my side of things. When I got there, I went straight into Marks office and sat on each piece of furniture that we had been on together. Then I sat at his desk and ran my hands over its leather surface. I knew that he had touched that surface the day he died and it was if I was touching his fingertips."

Tears were streaming down Jodie's cheeks as she tried to blot them away with a tissue. Nigel could see by the look on her face that in her memory she was reliving each moment.

"Then, for some reason I felt angry and quite desperate to know more. I knew Mark kept stuff in the drawer of his desk which he kept locked. He took the key home with him. I had to see inside that drawer. I picked up the letter opener from his desk, forced open the lock and opened the drawer. Inside I found a large envelope containing some photos and a typed message on yellow paper. The message on the paper said something like, 'Stop what you are doing before too many people get hurt, and that someone could be you!' I mean it was a threatening letter!"

Jodie had stopped crying, paused to take a breath, and in that moment Nigel took the opportunity to ask a question.

"The photographs, did you look at them?"

"Yes." Jodie responded quickly as if she did not want to miss anything out.

"Some of them were of Mark and me, at a couple of hotels that we used in the lunchtime, but the others were of Mark with different women. In one he was kissing this woman sitting outside a pub... When I saw these my stomach dropped through the floor and I had to go to the loo. Before I did, I ripped them in half. That bastard, in that moment I thought that he got what he deserved. Isn't that terrible of me?"

Despite Jodie looking directly at him waiting for an answer, Nigel ignored her request and made a statement.

"Tell me what you did next."

Jodie continued speaking, "I picked up the torn photos and the bit of paper and put them back in the envelope. I closed the drawer of the desk, went into the outer office and put the envelope into my bag, put my coat on, and left work."

Nigel, was intrigued by her decision to do this and so he asked,

"I'm wondering what made you do that. Obviously someone else had been upset by Mark's behavior."

"I didn't want anyone else to find them; particularly, his wife and also the police. She has enough to deal with at the moment."

Nigel could not resist the temptation to ask.

"Have you decided what to do with them?"

Jodie allowed herself a wry smile.
"I think that is one of the things that I need to talk through here, with you. Whoever was following Mark might have been on the platform at the station. Anyway by now they know that he is dead. At this moment in time things seem to be calming down. A revelation like this would start things up again. I don't see the point. What do you think Nigel?"

Nigel made it a rule never to respond quickly to a direct question. He needed to choose his words carefully before answering Jodie's question.

"It's not for me to give advice in this instance as, whatever you do, you have to live with the consequence of your choice. I think that decision is yours to make, and like you say, it is something for us to explore when we have more time."

When he said the word 'time', Nigel glanced at the clock on the table between them. He was surprised to see that he had gone eight minutes over Jodie's allotted hour.

"Jodie we need to stop now. We've come to the end of our time today but we can continue next week at the same time."

Jodie was not happy with this abrupt ending. She was not sure if she could wait another week before seeing Nigel again.

"Nigel can I come and see you before then if I make another appointment? I really don't think I can last seven days with my head the way it is at the moment."
"OK I will see what I can do in the next four days. Let me go and check my appointment schedule with my receptionist. Wait here and I will come back."

Nigel left the room. Jodie felt this session had gone well. She liked this man and she was glad that Tony had recommended him to her. There was much she needed to get off her chest and she felt she could trust this person with most of it. Mark kept his secrets well hidden, but he was not the only one.

That evening, when she arrived at her own home, she took off her coat, poured herself a glass of white wine and sat on a chair in the kitchen near the Fridge Freezer. She opened the door to the freezer, slid open a drawer and picked up the special box of 'Walls Cornetto' ice creams kept there. She turned in her chair and put the box on the kitchen table. She opened the lid of the box to look inside and check the contents. Everything was still there. Then raising her wine glass in the air she made a toast.

"To Mark, you shit, I loved you. If you are in another life right now, I pray you don't hurt anyone else like you hurt me. Here's to our good times!"

Jodie downed her glass of wine in one gulp and put the box back in the freezer. Jodie felt comforted by the thought that, for as long as she wanted a small part of Mark Finch would remain with her.

Chapter Twenty Two: Home

Jasmine bent down to pick up the morning post that she found on the floor below letter box of their front door in the entrance hall of their house. The envelopes rested on small plastic packets with large black print asking them to donate unwanted clothing to help research into Leukaemia, or to help Shelter find accommodation for homeless people.

"Jonathan, are you getting up for breakfast? I'll do us a veggie bacon and egg sandwich if you like. I've fed Charlie."

"Ok, I'll be down in a minute; I'm just cleaning my teeth." Jonathan replied shouting to Jasmine from the upstairs bathroom.

"There's a letter here from someone at 'Simon and Collins Press', do you know who they are?" Jasmine inquired innocently.

"What?" Jonathan appeared half naked in his pyjama shorts at the top of the stairs.

"Do you want me to open it then?"

"Yes please do and read it. If its bad news, tear it up, I've had enough for this month." Jonathan stood still at the top of the stairs with his eyes closed.

It looked to Jasmine as if he was muttering a prayer under his breath, even though she knew he did not believe in any god or the possibility of divine intervention.

Jasmine tore open the envelope and in silence read the beginning of the letter to herself. Losing control she let out a shriek and jumped into the air.

Jonathan, alarmed by her reaction opened his eyes and looked at her. Jasmine had a broad smile on her face.

"Listen! Listen! Dear Mr Hope, having read your ten thousand words submission as well as the synopsis of your novel. We at 'Simon and Collins' are very interested in working with you towards its publication."

"Yes, fucking yes! Jonathan shouted out loud before leaping down the stairs, picking up Jasmine in a big hug and twirling her around.

"Oh my God, say that again, please Jasmine just read that last bit again and pinch me."

"We are very interested in working towards it's… PUBLICATION! "

Jasmine and Jonathan began jumping up and down together.

Six months later while they were shopping in their local supermarket with Charlie perched in the seat of their trolley; they turned a corner into the book aisle. Stopping by the hardback section they each picked up a hard back copy of 'The Gardener', by Jonathan Hope. Standing next to her husband Jasmine opened the front cover of her copy and looked at the picture of Jonathan on inside of the jacket.

"Charlie, look at this picture, it's Daddy"

Jasmine turned her head and looked up at Jonathan's happy face, smiled and said, "Not bad for an old guy!"

She put her arms around him, kissed him on the cheek and they both laughed out loud.

ABOUT THE AUTHOR

Ivan Arthur is an experienced psychotherapist, lecturer and is a published academic. He is a family man whose interests include singing, song-writing, music, films and of course golf!

Printed in Great Britain
by Amazon